Outstanding praise for Kasey Michaels and
MAGGIE BY THE BOOK

"Colorful characters and humorous dialogue populate this wonderful sequel to *MAGGIE NEEDS AN ALIBI* and leave the reader waiting for more."
—*Booklist*

"Nothing is lacking in this excellent book, full of great wit and superb plotting."
—*Romantic Times*

"Romance and cozy fans will welcome this cross-genre sequel to Michaels's *MAGGIE NEEDS AN ALIBI*, with its original premise, sympathetic if reluctant heroine, and lively supporting cast."
—*Publishers Weekly*

"Kasey Michaels has written a wonderful, funny, and upbeat mystery."
—*The Midwest Book review*

"Once again, we're thrown into mayhem and enjoy every moment. Kasey Michaels's unique voice has developed another song—a true joy. Oh, what fun! More please."
—*Rendezvous*

Books by Kasey Michaels

CAN'T TAKE MY EYES OFF OF YOU

TOO GOOD TO BE TRUE

LOVE TO LOVE YOU BABY

BE MY BABY TONIGHT

THIS MUST BE LOVE

THIS CAN'T BE LOVE

MAGGIE NEEDS AN ALIBI

MAGGIE BY THE BOOK

MAGGIE WITHOUT A CLUE

Published by Kensington Publishing Corporation

Kasey Michaels

Maggie By the Book

KENSINGTON BOOKS
Kensington Publishing Corp.
http://www.kensingtonbooks.com

KENSINGTON BOOKS are published by

Kensington Publishing Corp.
850 Third Avenue
New York, NY 10022

All Kensington Titles, Imprints, and Distributed Lines are available at special quantity discounts for bulk purchases for sales promotions, premiums, fund-raising, and educational or institutional use. Special book excerpts or customized printings can also be created to fit specific needs. For details, write or phone the office of the Kensington special sales manager: Kensington Publishing Corp., 850 Third Avenue, New York, NY 10022, attn: Special Sales Department, Phone: 1-800-221-2647.

First Kensington hardcover printing: August 2003
First Kensington mass market printing: June 2004

10 9 8 7 6 5 4 3 2 1

Printed in the United States of America

This is dedicated to anyone
who thinks they're in this book.
You're not.
Fiction is fiction.

If there were dreams to sell,
what would you buy?
—Thomas Lovell Beddoes

A friend in need is a pest.
—Joey Lewis

PROLOGUE

According to Saint Just, this is all perfectly logical, easily explainable, and all of that.

Let's give it a go, shall we?

Maggie Kelly—dear girl, really, if a bit muddled at times—created us. Granted, she did it within the pages of a series of rather prodigiously successful mystery novels, but as Saint Just says, she did it quite well. Well enough, in fact, that eventually we came to life, first inside Maggie's head, and then inside Maggie's Manhattan apartment.

Not that it happens every day, this sort of thing—but it is possible.

After all, we are here, aren't we?

To the world, Saint Just is no more than Maggie's very distantly related English cousin, and she took some of his name—and all of his physical attributes—to create her perfect storybook hero, Alexandre Blake, the Viscount Saint Just.

Along with Saint Just, Maggie created his good friend, Sterling Balder (that would be me. Hallo!), both of whom have now, according to Maggie, traveled across the pond to reside for a time with her.

Of course, that's all a hum, a shocking crammer as a matter of fact, because we're not real. We're characters; fictional characters.

Who at the moment just happen to be, as the current slang goes, "living large" in New York City.

In Manhattan, my good friend Saint Just is known as Alex Blakely, but as I have difficulty with such a banal name as Alex, I still call him Saint Just (you may have noticed that?). Maggie says this is easily explained away as being a "private joke," which makes no sense at all, as I refer to him as Saint Just in public as well as in private. As I said, Maggie can be a bit muddled.

All that to one side, this does seem to explain the names and physical appearances of Maggie's new housemates. At least to her friends. There is a police lieutenant, one Steve Wendell, who is still rather suspicious, but Saint Just says he's of no matter.

And that's that. Everything explained.

Well, not quite everything.

So far, nobody has explained why our dearest Maggie seems to attract . . . murder.

CHAPTER 1

I can't do this, I can't do this, I can't do this!

Maggie Kelly dropped her hands into her lap and let herself collapse forward, until her forehead hit the desktop, then she began rhythmically banging that forehead against the wood.

I can't do this, I can't do this, Icannotfreakingdothis!

Maggie was sitting at her nifty corner desk with the wings on either side of it—all that space meant to hold notes neatly and keep her life organized . . . and all of it cluttered with candy wrappers, ash trays and, most recently, a half-eaten tuna sub sandwich from Mario's Deli down the block.

Her desk lamp was faux brass with a plastic green shade that was supposed to look like glass. The whole lamp was supposed to look expensive. It looked . . . dusty. It also had a crack in the plastic, that had been there when Maggie first pulled the lamp from its box, but returning the thing would have been too much hassle for someone as busy as Maggie. It had nothing to do with fighting with some accusing salesperson about how the thing got broken in the first place. Nothing at all. Really.

Her computer, the one with the pink and blue flowers on it, was supposed to be overheating as Maggie typed verbal pearls onto the screen. It looked . . . blank. In fact, the only "writing" on the computer at all was a yellow Post-It note stuck to one side, scribbled with the words: "Yesterday, Mr. Hall wrote that the printer's proofreader was improving my punctuation for me, and I telegraphed orders to have him shot without giving him time to pray. Mark Twain."

Seated in a huge brown leather desk chair, perched rather on the edge of it, and with her head still resting on the desktop, Maggie Kelly was having a crisis.

A crisis of epic proportions.

Her goal for the day was to write Chapter Ten of her latest Saint Just mystery. The dreaded Chapter Ten. Sometimes, so reluctant was she to write Chapter Ten that Chapter Ten became, in fact, Chapter Twelve, because she kept writing around and about and trying never to get *to* Chapter Ten.

But here it was. Staring her in the face. Chapter Ten of *The Case of the Disappearing Dandy* . . . and the dreaded love scene.

"Whimper," Maggie said, lifting her head slightly and staring at the only two words on the screen: CHAPTER TEN.

She said "whimper" because she didn't know how to actually write anything that sounded like a whimper. Because she couldn't spell the sound that would normally come from her mouth at a time like this, she said "whimper." Just as, if she were a dog, she'd say "bark," because who could actually *spell* a bark? Sure, there was always *arf,* but that was so lame. Much better to say "bark." Or "whimper."

It made sense to Maggie . . . and she was digressing.

She knew she was digressing, which was writer-speak for *stalling.*

Yes, Maggie Kelly is a writer. Being a rather punctilious sort, she would say *was* a writer, because she wasn't doing anything looking even remotely like writing this morning.

And it was all Saint Just's fault, damn him.

Once, Maggie had been Alicia Tate Evans, historical romance author. That had turned out to be pretty much a midlist bust (translaton: lousy sales), so she'd reinvented herself, become Cleo Dooley, historical mystery writer. She'd tried the three-names ploy that worked so well for some romance authors, and then opted for O's, because, to Maggie, O's looked great on a book cover, and she had been looking for any edge she could find.

It's a cutthroat world, the world of romance writing. The world of writing, period.

She'd created Alexandre Blake, the Viscount Saint Just, and he'd been one hell of a creation. Her hero. Her perfect man.

Eyes: Paul Newman blue.

Winglike, expressive eyebrows: Jim Carrey.

Full, luscious, almost sneering lips: Val Kilmer in *Tombstone.*

Aristocratic nose: Peter O'Toole.

General all-over face and body: a young Clint Eastwood, he of the spaghetti westerns.

Give that man a cheroot and hear him say "Who's your huckleberry?" in—what else?—Sean Connery's *James Bond* voice.

Handsome as sin, witty, urbane, sarcastic and sensual.

Can we all say *New York Times* Bestseller List?

And this was good. This was very good . . . until the

day just three short months ago, when Maggie had turned around to see her creation standing there, smack in the middle of her living room.

She'd made him real enough to materialize, he'd said. He'd come to help her with a plot problem in her last book, he'd said, and then stayed to help solve a murder . . . and he was still here, both Saint Just and his partner in crime-solving, Sterling Balder.

And now Maggie was facing the dreaded Chapter Ten . . . with her handsome, yummy, perfect hunk living in her guest room, leaving the cap off the toothpaste, running up her charge cards, and still playing the aristocratic, autocratic, to-die-for handsome Regency hero, for crying out loud.

Writing Tab A into Slot B scenes was bad enough, without the owner of Tab A not just visible in her mind, but running tame in her living room, 24-7.

Maggie sat up straighter, rubbed her palms together, and placed her fingers on the keyboard. She was a professional. She could do this. She had a deadline. She had to do this.

She moved her right hand to the mouse, checked back a few pages, to the lead-in that ended the last chapter.

"You know, Saint Just," Lady Sarah purred, sliding her hands down over his lapels as she stepped even closer. "I sometimes dream about you."

Maggie stifled a sigh. "Oh yeah. I hear you, Sarah baby, and I understand. Believe me, I *un-der-stand.*"

"Happy dreams, my lady, I most sincerely hope," Saint Just said, placing his hands over hers, then lifting them, one after the other, to place a kiss on each of her palms. "Your husband, ma'am?"

"Oh, Saint Just, forget him. Just hold me. I ache . . ."

"Now here's a thought. Perhaps you might wish to

cast your dear husband in the role of physician? Where is he, by the way? I probably should have asked that before accepting your kind invitation this evening. I don't much fancy climbing down a drain pipe to escape the man. Perhaps I should go."

Lady Sarah winced at Saint Just's words.

He'd kissed Maggie's palm, that first day. She took hold of the collar of her T-shirt, and sort of fanned herself with it. "Oh, sweetie, I feel your pain."

"He's in Berkshire," Lady Sarah continued, then licked her top lip with the tip of her tongue. "Hunting, he says. Drinking, that's more like it. Drinking, and wenching."

"Leaving his adoring—no, adorable*—wife here in London, to pine away, all by herself? The cad."*

"The cad? And you said it with a straight face? Oh, you're enjoying yourself, aren't you, Saint Just. You rotter," Maggie told the computer screen. "Always the man with two agendas."

Cad indeed, Saint Just thought. The Earl wasn't in Berkshire. He felt certain of that. Just as he was certain that the Earl, and the man's good chums, Levitt and Sir Gregory, were with him, the trio planning yet another murder. He had been pursuing the gang of murderers for months, and all roads had eventually led to the Earl.

Now all he needed was some proof. Because Sterling was the trio's logical next target, and they had to be stopped. Stopped, yes, but first they had to be found.

Saint Just looked past Lady Sarah's head, toward the open door to the Earl's private study. Ten minutes, that's all he'd need. Just ten minutes alone, in that study.

"Saint Just?" Lady Sarah said, rubbing herself against him, like a cat begging for attention. "I've dismissed the servants for the night. We won't . . . we won't be disturbed."

"Oh, how sickeningly coy. The bitch," Maggie whispered. "Not that I'm jealous." She sat back, lifted her hair away from her nape. "Is it hot in here?"

"How . . . anticipatory of you, my dear," Saint Just drawled, with one last look toward the study, then glanced at the tall clock in the corner of the foyer. Two o'clock. With any luck, he'd be in the study by four. He smiled down at the blond-haired vixen, a woman in heat if he'd ever seen one. Yes, two hours. Perhaps three. No need to rush. "I say, are you by any chance trying to seduce me, ma'am?"

"Oh no. No, no, no. Where was my head when I wrote that? Too *The Graduate,*" Maggie said, striking out that last sentence. "Too here's-to-you-Mrs.-Robinson."

Her fingers flew over the keyboard. *"I say, my dear, would your bedchamber be on the left or the right of the stairs?"*

Maggie sat back, lit a cigarette. Better. That was better. That was also the last line of Chapter Nine, damn it. She couldn't stall anymore.

She scrolled down to the next page, placed the cursor on the line below the chapter heading. Took a deep breath, closed her eyes, and began:

She was no shy virgin. Saint Just wouldn't have been within ten miles of her, had she been a virgin.

Lady Sarah was a harlot with a title. A hot-blooded woman with appetites that had been whispered about in the clubs, hinted at, smiled over, and sworn to by at least one peer deep in his cups and too talkative for his own good.

Ask Evan Fleming, if you could find him. Except that Fleming, minus one of his ears, was now reportedly living on the continent, safely away from the Earl and his sword.

Had Fleming's sacrifice been worth it? Was an evening

spent with the adventurous Lady Sarah worth the loss of an ear, or worse?

"Stalling, stalling," Maggie nagged at herself. "Get with it now." She sighed, plunged on. Well, someone was going to be plunging . . .

Saint Just, braced against the headboard of the large four-poster, watched Lady Sarah's long blond hair shimmering in the candlelight, shimmering against the skin of his bare belly as she bent over him, wrapped her mouth around his—

"Good gracious, woman. I see I'm having an interesting morning."

"Jesus H. Christ, Alex! Get away from me!" Maggie yelled, quickly covering the screen with both hands. Her heart was pounding hard in her throat. "Damn it! Wear shoes, will you, huh? Or *stomp.* Something?"

Saint Just remained where he was, which was directly behind Maggie. He was dressed in khaki slacks and a soft black knit collarless shirt that clung to his every sleek muscle, and he was grinning at her in a way that made her want to brain him. "Am I being amorous today, Maggie? With the Lady Sarah, I'll assume," he said, as she kept one hand on the screen while she used the mouse to click the document shut.

"I thought you were still in bed," Maggie said, grabbing another cigarette, because the one she'd lit earlier had burned down to the filter, and gone out. She used her feet to push herself around in the swiveling desk chair, to face Saint Just. She breathed heavily through her nose as she watched her hands shake, and was not at all grateful when he produced his own Bic, and held the flame to the end of her cigarette.

"I agree that I do like the morning well-aired before joining it—my dear friend, Beau Brummell said that first, remember? But it's almost noon, my dear, and I promised Sterling I'd walk with him in the park. He's never happy without his daily ice, although he's promised not to indulge in the blue one more than once a week. Stains the lips terribly, you know. Man walks about the rest of the day, looking like he's been sucking from the inkwell."

Bless and curse the man, he was rambling, deliberately giving her time to compose herself. But, hey, it was working. Maggie was beginning to get her breathing back under control. "Sterling's out already, with Socks. I guess he forgot your date. Poor baby. You've been stood up, Alex. Now go away, I'm working. I need to be able to support you in the manner to which you've too easily become accustomed, remember?"

"Whatever," Saint Just said, pulling a cheroot from the pack on the coffee table, then returning to the desk. "You know what Sterling's about, don't you?"

Maggie shook her head. "About? No. He's outside with Socks, that's all. Playing Junior Doorman again, I suppose. He gets a kick out of carrying Mrs. Goldblum's groceries up for her. Why? What do you know?"

Saint Just inhaled deeply, blew out a stream of blue smoke, looking sexy as hell, sexy enough to make a lie out of the "and it's unattractive, too" message of any number of Stop Smoking public service announcements. "What I know, dear Maggie, is that Sterling has found himself a new . . . interest."

"Besides the Nick at Nite channel? Besides his scooter? Besides learning how to fetch cabs for Socks? What?"

"Rap," Saint Just said, shuddering slightly, as if the very word was distasteful on his tongue.

"Rap? Rap what? I don't—no." Maggie sat back in her chair. "Rap? As in Snoop Doggy whatever? *That* kind of rap?"

"Precisely. The poetry of the downtrodden, I believe

he calls it. Sterling, for reasons unknown to me, associates himself with the downtrodden."

"Living with you, I'm surprised he doesn't feel just downtrodden, but damn oppressed. You can be a real pain in the—rap, you said? Is he singing it?"

"Writing it," Saint Just corrected. "The Prince Regent figures largely in his first composition. He plans recitations on several subjects. Luddites. Corn Laws. Starving peasants and cruel landlords. You know, the usual oppressions."

Maggie put a hand to her mouth, giggling. "You're kidding. He's doing a *Regency* rap? Oh, I've got to hear this."

"And I'm convinced you will, once Socks believes the man is ready. In the meantime, I do believe you have mail."

Maggie swiveled her chair around to the desk once more, to see the little mailbox blinking in the right top corner of her screen. She'd signed on to America Online earlier, and then forgotten about it. "Fan mail from some flounder?" she asked under her breath, doing her best Bullwinkle the Moose impersonation as she clicked the mouse, bringing AOL to the front of the screen.

"Enlarge your penis. . . . Hot Porn with Barnyard Chicks. . . . Viagra by mail. . . . Refinance your home, cheap. Delete, delete, delete, delete. MoveOn dot com. Okay, I'll keep that one. WAR. War? Oh, no. Not them. De—hey!"

"War?" Saint Just repeated, putting his hand over Maggie's, moving the mouse just as she was aiming toward Delete, and double-clicked it over the e-mail message from one NYTORBUST:

Maggie! Long time no talk, huh? Can you believe WAR is coming back to NY? John says no, because I'm almost due, but I've just GOT to see you! You'll be there, right? I put a hotlink at the bottom. You can just click and sign up, right on line! Oh, I can't wait to SEE you, you big NYT person, you! It's been SO long! {{Hugs}} Virginia

"Oh, God," Maggie said, sighing. "She's due? *Again?* The woman's trying to repopulate the entire state of Colorado. Yeah, well, I'll just tell her no. No, I'll tell her I'll come by and we can have lunch. But WAR? Ha! Not this lady. No damn way. Hey, cut that out!"

But Saint Just, leaning uncomfortably close to her (well, not completely uncomfortably), had already clicked on the blue hotlink, and the computer immediately connected to the homepage of We Are Romance, Incorporated, a "national association of romance writers."

"War? Didn't anybody notice that when they picked the name?" he asked, then clicked on the site's link to the conference.

"You'd think someone would have, wouldn't you?" Maggie groused, folding her arms across her chest as the page listing the highlights of this year's conference came up on the screen. "Are the dates listed? Oh, there they are. September eighteenth to the twenty-first. Damn, and here I made my GYN appointment for that week. I might even be able to fit in a root canal while I'm at it. Too bad, I'm going to have to miss the conference this year."

She gave Saint Just a push. "Would you back off? No, don't print it out. Alex, I could care less about this—oh, hell, print it out."

"Thank you," Saint Just said, watching the pages begin spitting from the printer. "I can't help myself, you know. Anything that so upsets you, dearest Maggie, will doubtless please me all hollow. Ah, here we go."

He took the pages, all five of them, and carried them

over to the couch, where he sat down, neatly crossing one leg over the other. He held his chin high, a lock of his midnight black hair falling over his forehead, the cheroot neatly clamped between his lips. Maggie gritted her teeth. The man would look good if he was standing on his head in a Bozo the Clown outfit.

Picking up her cigarettes, Maggie followed after him, flouncing down on the facing couch, half burying herself in the cushions. "It's a romance writers association, okay? Published authors, still unpublished, psychopaths, you name it."

"Psychopaths?"

She shook her head. "Kidding, Alex. It's a great group. Ninety-eight percent fantastic, hardworking people. Me, I always seem to run into the other two percent. I mean, can we say Felicity Boothe Simmons? Yeech! Oh, and I'm a charter member, for my sins, although I'm surprised they haven't drummed me out of the corps."

Saint Just looked at her over the top of the papers. "Why would they do that?"

Maggie sighed. "Why? They wouldn't, not really. But there's this annual contest, see, for published authors? There's one for the unpublished, too, but we're talking published authors. The Harriet, named after the founder. Big damn deal, if you're into awards. Anyway, I won one, for my first book, before I signed with Bernie at Toland Books. It's over there," she said, pointing to the bookcase.

Saint Just followed her pointing finger. "That?" he said, nodding toward the statuette of a naked nymph, standing on tiptoe and holding an open book high in the air. He got up, walked over to the bookcase, and removed the statuette. "Best Historical Romance, Alicia Tate Evans, *This Flowering Passion.* How . . . how, well, nauseating."

"Hey, don't blame me, I didn't pick that title. I titled

it *The Surrender of the Falcon.* Great damn title. Okay, not great, but at least it actually pertained to the story—which is a novel concept these days, let me tell you. But the publisher nixed it. I figured she didn't like the surrender part. Wrong. She didn't like falcons. Maybe she was scared by one before she got her witchly powers."

Maggie leaned over toward the coffee table, stubbed out the cigarette, and grabbed a handful of M&M's out of a crystal bowl. What was it about writing love scenes for Saint Just that had her reaching for all sorts of oral gratification . . . and did she really want to investigate that question in any depth? "Anyway, I have this theory. There's this big wheel in every publishing house, see. Like on *Wheel of Fortune?"*

She laid back against the cushions and popped two red M&M's into her mouth. "But this wheel, it has three wheels, one inside the other. There're words on each wheel, and they spin the wheels, and whatever three words come up, that's the title of your book. *Love's Fiery Passions. Desire's Sweetest Splendor. Barfing Almost Nightly.* You get the idea," she said, popping two plain brown M&M's into her mouth.

"Fascinated as I am by all of this," Saint Just said, returning the statuette to its place, and returning himself to the couch, "I still fail to see why this WAR association might drum you out of their corps."

"Okay, not drum out. But I entered my first Saint Just Mystery in the contest, and they disqualified it. It wasn't a romance, they said. Twelve romance novels, that's what I had as Alicia Tate Evans. Twelve of them, Alex, an even dozen. Put a mystery in the book, and suddenly I'm not eligible? I pay my dues, I'm still a member, I still list WAR as one of my associations, still say that I've won a Harriet in my press releases. I *sup-*

port WAR, damn it. And I'm disqualified. Hey, who cares? They can just kiss off, you know?"

"I'm not romantic?"

"Huh?" Maggie said, looking at Saint Just. He didn't look happy. He looked, in fact, decidedly unhappy. The sort of unhappy that, were she describing the look in one of her books, she'd call *dangerously alert.*

"I said, I'm not romantic? Is that what these Harriets are saying? That *I,* the Viscount Saint Just, am *not* romantic?"

Maggie grinned, beginning to enjoy herself. Everything had its up side. "You got it, Ace. You're not romantic. You're a stud, you're God's gift, but you're not romantic."

"Idiot females."

Three more M&M's hit her tonsils. "Yeah, that, too. But they're right, in a way. A romance novel, Alex, has a happy ending. Two people falling in love, happily ever after. You don't have a happily ever after, Alex. You don't fall in love with one woman, you love women—plural. You're a series."

"Uh-huh," he said, obviously no longer listening as he paged through the papers. "Interesting events, aren't they? Workshops on writing, on getting published, on staying published. Ah, and what's this? A Cover Model contest?" He looked at Maggie. "Explain, please."

Maggie sat up, held out her hand. "Gimme those," she said, grabbing the papers and shuffling them, her eyes growing wide. "They're kidding. They've invited Rose? God."

"And the mystery deepens," Saint Just said, examining the page he had reserved as his own. "Who, pray tell, is Rose?"

"Rose," Maggie said, still shuffling the papers. "From the online magazine, *Rose Knows Romance.* She's got this slogan. How does it go? Oh, yeah. Who knows romance? Rose knows! Gag me. I can't believe WAR has combined with her, just because the conference is in New York this year. They do that, add extra stuff, because it costs more to hold a conference here and they think they need an extra carrot or two. Stupid. Like, hello, this is New York. When you've got New York, what else do you need?"

"Yes, yes, Maggie, you love New York, I love New York, we all love New York. Now, back to the conference if you please? This Rose woman? She's not a nice person?" Saint Just spoke from the desk area, where he had sat down, picked up a pen.

Maggie shrugged. "I don't know. I guess she's *nice.* Pushy maybe, a little wacko with the way she dresses and these contests she thinks up, but nice enough. Like I said, she has this online magazine. She reviews romances, holds contests, has a pretty big base of readers who subscribe to her e–mail list, to hear her tell it. Once a year she holds an online contest for cover models, men and women, looking for new talent. She used to have her own conference, but that stopped a few years ago . . . oh, damn, she's not only going to be there, she's bringing along all the events she usually holds online."

"Such as?" Saint Just asked, still writing. He pulled out his wallet, extracted a credit card (made out to Margaret Kelly, but that was just something to quibble about, now wasn't it?).

"The cover model contest. A dress like your favorite character contest. A parade of local winners of the Most Favored Fan contest. A costume ball. And she's got corporate sponsors, for crying out loud. It's not just a costume ball. It's the Steelton Meats Costume Ball. What does the winner get? A side of beef? Jeez. Rose knows romance? Rose knows *marketing.*"

Saint Just pushed at the keypad of the fax machine, saying, "This costume ball? What does everyone wear?"

Maggie threw the papers onto the coffee table and picked up another handful of M&M's. "You name it. Viking furs, Renaissance gowns, slave girl costumes."

"Regency dress?"

Maggie nodded. "Yeah, Regency dress. Why not." She looked at him as the fax machine began to hum. "What are you doing?"

"Why, registering all of us for the conference, of course. You as the member, Sterling and myself as your guests. You had to pay a small late fee, but I'm sure it's cheap at twice the price. Now, if you'll just ring up the Marriott in the theater district, and reserve us a suite of rooms?"

"God!" Maggie pressed her hands to her ears, grabbed two fists full of hair. "Tell me you didn't do that."

"Done and done, my dear," Saint Just said, handing her the large Manhattan telephone directory and the portable phone. "Here you go. Three bedrooms and a lovely parlor should be sufficient for our needs."

"Why?" she asked, glaring up at him. "Why do you want to do this?"

"Why?" he said, taking his quizzing glass from his pocket and dropping the riband over his head—he might dress like a modern man, but he was still very much attached to his quizzing glass. "I want to meet these women who don't think I'm romantic. That's one."

"Oy, jeez, can you believe this? The man's insulted."

"Too true, and I admit it. I'm insulted. Possibly crushed, if I were a lesser man. But I remain undaunted, and more than ready to prove that I, indeed, am above all things a romantic hero. And, of course, there is the Fragrances by Pierre Cover Model contest, which intrigues me more than a little bit."

Maggie spluttered, nearly choked on a mouthful of

candy. "You're going to enter the contest? Be a piece of meat for all the women to scream over? You've got to be kidding."

"And you've got to have overlooked the ten thousand dollar prize for the winner, my dear Maggie, along with a guaranteed placement on a romance novel cover. Why, an entire new adventure awaits me, being handsomely recompensed just for being me. You do know how I detest any hint of insolvency. And it isn't as if I don't have a fine suit of clothes at the ready, as you've always written me as having the best of tailors. I believe Weston designed the rigout I traveled in to New York. My, but it will be wonderful to dress once more as a *real* gentleman should," Saint Just said, wagging a finger at her. "Dial, my dear, if you will. And most definitely a suite. We wouldn't want to feel cramped. Then you can finish Chapter Ten."

"Only if I can turn it into a death scene," Maggie groused, pulling the thick book onto her lap.

CHAPTER 2

Saint Just stepped into the sunshine, neatly swung his cane up under his arm, and said, "A fine day for an outing, Sterling, don't you agree? Positively brilliant."

Sterling Balder, created by Maggie to be Saint Just's stalwart companion and comic foil, obediently looked up at the sky, saying, "I suppose that would depend, Saint Just. Where are we going? You have that look about you this morning, you know. The one that Maggie calls supercilious."

Saint Just turned, smiled at his good friend. Of the same five and thirty years, shorter than himself by a good half foot, definitely pudgier, and with a thinning thatch of nondescript brown hair, he had a constant look of happy anticipation mixed with a wonderfully dependable gullibility in his dark brown eyes that could not be hidden behind the thin gold frames of his glasses. Sterling was such a pleasant companion. One of Maggie's finer works. Indeed, the man had his own fan club.

Maggie had told Saint Just, in some panic, that she'd finally realized that Sterling was a sort of kinder, gentler George Costanza, from the television show, *Seinfeld*. Maggie considered this a corruption of her imagination and fretted about it. Saint Just tuned in the show, enjoyed the show, but failed to see the resemblance. But, then, that was Maggie. God forbid she could ever believe in her own talent, even when the evidence of it was now living with her in her flat.

Sterling, Saint Just knew, remained slightly bogged down in the process of muddling through their new circumstances. Until recently he had exercised in front of a video showcasing a very highly-strung man with a mop of baby curls each and every morning, convinced that he could reduce his waistline beyond the proportions given to him in Maggie's description of her fictional character. He'd also taken to rubbing something vile-smelling on his head each night, in the hopes of growing hair, unable to believe that he could not change a thing about himself—that only Maggie had that power.

But he was adapting, quite admirably, really. After two years of observing Maggie's world from inside her head, Sterling had greeted the inevitability of living *outside* of Maggie's head with some definite plans in mind. Gaining control of the television changer was one of them. Experimenting in Maggie's kitchen was another.

In his own way, Sterling was adventurous. Sort of. He longed to try new things. The ragging of the living room walls had been a success. The cajun flounder had not.

Then there was the motorized scooter, the one Saint Just had ordered from *QVC,* the same one Sterling now mounted, started, and aimed toward Mario's. Sterling really enjoyed Mario's; especially the man's supply of ready-made, cellophane-wrapped pastries. Because, Sterling had said a few days ago, in a flash of brilliance as he finally tossed the workout video in the trash, if he could not lose weight unless Maggie wrote him thinner, then it also stood to reason that he could not *gain* weight.

Ah, yes, Sterling was a happy man. He was created a happy man, a man with few shadows to his nature, a man born to follow, not lead . . . just as Saint Just was born to march at the head of any parade. Well, saunter. Saint Just did not march.

"Not Mario's, Sterling," Saint Just said now, turning right. "We have an appointment with a few of our business associates."

"Oh, splendid, Saint Just. I'm convinced Killer is an oppressed person. I want to show him my latest lyrics."

"How fortunate that man is. He must go to his knees every night, grateful for all his wonderful gifts, although a stronger bladder might be something he could consider listing in his prayers," Saint Just drawled, as the two turned the corner, heading for the park.

Let it be said here that Alexandre Blake, the Viscount Saint Just, believes himself to be a solvent man, just as Maggie had created him. A more than solvent man. A wealthy man. A man of some stature, impeccable breeding, and with the typical Regency Era disdain of the lofty to engage in—here one could imagine a faint shudder—*trade.*

But, as Saint Just had told Sterling, when a man was in Rome a man must live as the Romans live. In Manhattan, man lived by his own sweat, his own toil.

And one thing more. Neither a man of today nor a man of the Regency Era would long be content to live on the largesse of females. Not an honorable man at any rate.

So, taking this all into consideration, Saint Just had decided to become wealthy, not just in his incarnation of fictional amateur detective Viscount Saint Just, but also as Alex Blakely, currently residing in New York City.

But there was still the problem of appearing as if he

might be dabbling in trade. A man of his stature owned extensive country estates, profited from the Exchange. It wouldn't do to earn his daily bread by the sweat of his own brow, definitely not. And no man of stature could hold his head high if his blunt had ever come within sniffing distance of the smell of the shop.

What a dilemma.

Saint Just, however, being a brilliant man as well as faintly desperate, had set about observing his fellow man these past months, and he had discovered a few things.

One, there were men and women—not gentlemen and ladies—who populated many street corners in Manhattan, standing on rude boxes, shouting into megaphones . . . and collecting money simply for speaking, mostly of doom and gloom and the price of salvation, the benefits of repentance. With such a depressing message, it was no wonder the tinkle of coins hitting the cups was more common than the soft, satisfying sound of folded paper money being slipped into a side pocket.

Two, Saint Just was an educated man, a man who could quote the bard and Byron, Milton, etc, at the drop of a couplet, a man who could, when pushed, put pen to paper with rather pleasing results. No one had accused Byron of smelling of the shop for his scribblings.

Three, he had made the acquaintance of a most amusing trio of the denizens of Manhattan in the past months; one Snake (depressingly christened Vernon), one Killer (aka Georgie of the Nervous Bladder), and one delicate waif named Mare . . . the girl refused to answer to Mary Louise.

Having gifted them with his custom—or, in other words, having hired them to create false identification papers for both him and Sterling—Saint Just had further cultivated the three, seeing the beginnings of his empire in Snake's shifty eyes, Killer's large, rather handsome, but shaggy body, and Mare's native and university-schooled intelligence.

Starting small, with the purchase of a few portable bullhorns and two rather more sophisticated boxes, and armed with scripts written by Saint Just, the trio had begun emoting on street corners. In just three short months, their number had grown to twenty-five members, on twenty-four street corners.

Killer, alas, had never quite mastered the megaphone, or reading, for that matter, so that his role in the thing had become that of standing next to Snake looking both childishly handsome and pitiful. Killer, rather good at woebegone and the aforementioned oppressed, positively *excelled* at pitiful.

Sometimes Saint Just's business associates (he refused to call them employees) mouthed soliloquies from the masters of literature. Other times, as Saint Just paid very close attention to the televised and print news, they shouted out speeches meant to inflame the populace, cheer the populace—and, always, *free* the populace of their excess monies.

It was a simple plan. A simple split, with sixty percent going to Saint Just, the other forty to his associates, and with city permits, new bullhorns and sturdy boxes taken out of the gross profits before any division of funds.

One would think there could not be much of a profit in street corner speechifying. However, so far, if one were to look on Saint Just's laptop, opening his Quicken program, one would see that Saint Just's bank balance had risen from nothing to seventy-five hundred dollars in just three months. He hoped to add another twenty-five associates well in time for the Christmas rush to redemption, at which time he would have the associates reading famous sermons.

And all without coming within a mile of dirtying his hands with *trade.*

Saint Just was also dabbling in the stock market, "borrowing" his seed money from Maggie, mostly without first asking permission. He was still depressingly dependent on her, for his room, for his board, but it was early days yet, and there was really no end to the ways one might coax money out of the dear citizens of New York.

Indeed, he'd already mentally pocketed the prize money from both the cover model contest and the costume ball. It tickled him to no end, believing he could earn money simply by being himself—the Perfect Hero.

Ah, yes, life was good.

"There they are," Sterling said, pointing to the corner, where Snake was standing on his lovely mahogany-stained box with the gold studs hammered into the edges, his megaphone to his mouth. "What's the subject today, Saint Just?"

"Corporate greed," Saint Just said, lifting a hand to his opened collar, adjusting his nonexistent neck cloth. "It works a charm, every time the Exchange drops more than two hundred points. Ah, there's Mary Louise. Good. She's just the one I wanted to see."

"Hey, there, Vic," Mare called out, waving to him. He'd first introduced himself as the viscount, and she'd somehow twisted that into Vic, and it had stuck, unfortunately. "How's the Bill Gates of the beggars world?"

Saint Just smiled at the girl, who still affected him in a way he couldn't quite understand. She was young, too young, and definitely not his type at all. But he couldn't help himself; he felt protective of her, even if she carried a rather nasty knife and could probably use it with some proficiency.

Small, almost dangerously thin, Mary Louise had taken the art of self decoration to new levels, having pierced her ears at least a dozen times each, both her eyebrows, one nostril, her chin, her navel, and—he had found out the first time she'd opened her mouth—her tongue.

Her hair had been pink spikes when he'd first seen her. The spikes remained, but the color varied. Today the hair was purple. And therein lay the rub, for Mary Louise's eyes were also purple, a deep, dangerously seductive purple, set against a smooth ivory skin and framed by a face that would have made Botticelli weep as he reached for his paints.

She was a wood sprite, a pocket Venus, a street urchin who should have been a duchess, a delicate rose piercing herself with thorns.

She was the eyes of age, with a pouty mouth, a full lower lip that drew the eye, possessor of an overall look of guarded vulnerability that brought out all of Saint Just's heroic tendencies.

Saint Just sniffed. And these ladies of WAR thought he wasn't romantic? Ha!

"Hiya, Sterling, how's it hangin'?" Mare asked Sterling, giving him a playful shove in the ribs with her elbow.

"How's what hanging?" Sterling asked in confusion. "Nothing's hanging. Is it? Saint Just?" he asked, trying to look at his own backside. "Is there a string hanging somewhere? I wouldn't wish for my ensemble to be in the least shabby. You should have told me, Saint Just. Very poor-spirited of you to see something hanging, and not tell me."

"Later, Sterling," Saint Just said, suppressing a smile and doing his best to glare reprovingly at Mare. "I'll explain later."

Mare gave him a pat on the cheek. "Never mind, Sterling. Still riding that scooter? But not for long, not with Vic here and his hotshot ideas. Next thing you know, you'll be tooling up in your stretch Mercedes. Because we're going to franchise next, I'm betting. Beggars 'R Us. Right, Vic?"

Saint Just put his cane tip to the ground, resting both hands on the knob. "I believe I detect a note of sarcasm in your usually dulcet tones today, Mare."

She shrugged her thin shoulders, which hiked up her scanty cut-off top enough to display the bottoms of her small but perfect breasts. "Hey, maybe it's PMS. Or maybe I got my grades for my summer courses. They suck."

Mary Louise, when she wasn't piercing something or forging something, was a student at NYU.

"Surely any shortcoming was that of the head master's, not on your part," Saint Just said commiseratingly.

"Nope, it was my fault. Not enough money, not enough time to study because I have to earn the money." She rubbed a finger beneath her nose. "I'd've boinked the one guy, if I thought it would have helped, but I don't do that, you know?" She shrugged again. "Some do. I don't. It just isn't honest."

"Honest? But supplying people with false identification papers? That's honest?"

"Hey, I made an exception for you because my cousin asked, okay? Sterling looked like a good guy and I took you on faith. Not that I didn't always check everyone out before I did the papers when I did them, and only ever did the work for Irish kids trying to outstay their visas. But nobody does that anymore. Not since nine-eleven. So I'm hurting here, and your street corner gig may be fun sometimes, but it's not enough."

"Which, as it most happily happens, brings me to the reason for asking you to meet with me this morning. Mare? Mary Louise? How attached—other than the obvious—are you to all of that very lovely jewelry? Oh, and while we're at it, the hair and the clothes as well."

"Drinks a bit, doesn't he?" Mare said, sotto-voce, to Sterling. "Because if he thinks he's going to pimp me, he's got another—"

"Excuse me, my dear," Saint Just said, inserting the cane between Mare and a blushing Sterling. "Perhaps I should be more specific. Here you go," he said, holding out a folded paper.

Mare took it, looked at it, looked at Saint Just . . . and grinned. Enchanting eyes; straight, white teeth. Yes, Saint Just was pleased. "You're kidding, right? I mean, have you looked at me? I mean, really *looked* at me?"

Saint Just took back the paper, tucked it back into his slacks pocket. "Have you ever heard of a young woman by the name of Kate Moss?"

"The model?" Mare said, cocking her head to one side. "She's anorexic, I swear it. I'm not anorexic. And I don't do drugs either."

"And it warms the cockles of my heart to hear that, my dear. You are, however, quite more beautiful than Miss Moss."

"Bullshit," Mare said, but now she was blushing, something she did very awkwardly, as if she was experiencing the sensation for the first time. "But keep talking."

"I fully intend to, thank you. As you've seen, there will be a book cover model contest in a few short weeks, right here in Manhattan. I have already taken the liberty of entering you, as well as myself. The winners, and there will be two, one male, one female, will each receive recompense of ten thousand dollars and a contract to appear on one romance novel cover. Naturally, we won't stop with just the one, at which point I, as your manager and mentor, will act on your behalf for a token, shall we say, fifteen percent of your earnings?"

"Bite me," Mare said, turning her back and taking three steps before whirling around. "Ten percent. And you think I can be a cover model? I mean, *really?*"

"Really. Twelve and one half percent, although working with fractions is always the very devil. I will, naturally, generously absorb the overhead necessary to prepare you for the contest."

She looked at Sterling, who nodded. "He manages Socks, you know. Our doorman? Almost got him employment on Broadway, and has already secured him something called a walk-on part on *Tyger, Tyger,* that soap opera. Have you seen it? Jessica has just found out that her husband didn't really die in that hot air balloon accident over Peru, and now she's a bigamist. I don't know how she didn't know it. I knew it, I suspected all along that Godfrey had—"

"Sterling, I must ask that you control your natural, ebullient, and always wonderfully amusing enthusiasm, please," Saint Just interrupted, smiling at Mare. "So? Now that we've decided, we'd best get busy. I've already contacted a friend, who has agreed to take you under her wing, get you groomed and dressed and deloused. Whatever is necessary."

"You're about as funny as a rubber crutch, Vic," Mare said, but then she tugged down on her skimpy top, and stood up straighter. "When?"

"There is no time like the present, my dear. Sterling, you know your way home. Come along, Mary Louise," Saint Just said, swinging his cane up under his arm once more, and setting off down the street—the viscount on the strut—Mare following along behind him, arms flailing exaggeratedly, aping his walk. He knew what she was doing, but he also liked the child, enjoyed her antics.

Oh yes. A lovely day. A lovely, lovely day.

"I need a drink," Bernice Toland-James said, collapsing into a chair beside Saint Just. "Scotch, please, Alex. Make that a double."

"Feeling put upon, Bernie? I believe I saw a well-dressed young man walking about earlier, with a tray of champagne. Will that do?"

"Not really, but it's better than nothing," Bernie said, waving her hand to shoo him off on his mission.

Saint Just smiled and rose to his feet, a man perfectly at home in his own skin, which made him perfectly at home even in this bastion of feminine fripperies called a boutique.

He had commandeered Bernie at her place of business, Toland Books. Bernie, Maggie's editor and good friend, had just inherited the business from her ex-husband, who had been the victim of foul play not three months ago. She'd inherited the business, the condo, limousine, the house in the Hamptons, the yacht, the private jet . . . and a mountain of debt, thanks to the sticky fingers of someone who considered Toland Books his own personal piggy bank.

Everything but the condo and the limousine were gone now, and Bernie had celebrated her new solvency by getting royally drunk two weeks ago, at which time she had promised Saint Just "Anything you want, Alex. Anything. Name it. You saved me from the slammer."

Saint Just would like to think he had, single-handedly, saved Bernie, who had been one of the prime suspects in Kirk Toland's death for a time. But he knew that wasn't quite entirely true. Still, if Bernie wanted to be grateful, he certainly wouldn't be a cad and discourage her.

Dear Bernie. Such a beautiful woman. Such a contradiction.

A well-preserved five and forty years, Bernie was part natural beauty, part inspired cosmetic surgery creation. Tall, never as slim as she wanted to be; with white-white skin and a startling mane of frizzy red hair, Bernie was also brilliant.

Hadn't she recognized Maggie's talent, first as Alicia Tate Evans, and then as Cleo Dooley? Hadn't she slipped Maggie back in to Toland Books after she'd been "downsized," and helped boost the Saint Just Mysteries onto the bestseller's lists?

Such a good and devoted friend. Such a kind, if sometimes flamboyant and even reckless creature. Yes, she drank. Yes, she indulged in the occasional line of coke—but only to control her weight.

Maggie worried about Bernie, constantly.

Saint Just chose to enjoy her.

And now Bernie was going to perform a miracle for Mary Louise. Wasn't that above all things wonderful?

"Here you are, my dear," Saint Just said, handing Bernie a chilled flute of probably inferior champagne. "What is our protégé up to now?"

"Well, we've gotten past underwear and casual wear, so I guess she'll be coming out here at any moment in one of the gowns I've chosen. They dress to the teeth at these WAR things, you know. If I had some extra cash lying around, I'd buy up all the sequins and bugle beads in the Northeast, and make a bundle." She lifted her flute in salute. "Here's to silk purses and sow's ears, right, Alex?"

"Referring to Mary Louise, I assume? You don't see

what I see, Bernie?" Saint Just asked, walking over to a display, to finger a particularly appealing gown of the deepest green silk. Maggie would look splendid in green silk. Ravishing. He'd buy it.

"Hey, I got the stud out of her tongue, and makeup will cover the marks from the other holes. But did you see her nails? She bites them, to the knuckle. And that hair? We still have a long way to go before she's even a sow's ear."

"And I have every confidence you know just the magicians to change that sow's ear to silk. Maggie's size, Bernie, if you will?" he asked, motioning for one of the black-crow clerks to approach him.

"I don't know. A four? Why?"

"I'm going to purchase this gown for her. I believe it suits her, right down to the ground. Do you concur?"

"Got a price tag on that, bucko? I mean, we're talking Maggie of the 'there could be another Great Depression at any moment' mentality here," Bernie said, getting to her feet to come over to the mannequin and begin fishing around inside the left armhole. She pulled out a tag. "Two thousand. Oh, yeah, Maggie'll go for that. Are you nuts? I'm just glad I finally got her the hell out of the J.C. Penney catalog."

"Wrap this, please," Saint Just said to the black crow who, silly, nearsighted creature that she must be, seemed to be laboring under the misapprehension that she was a superior being and he was some slimy slug who had just crawled in off the street. "Oh, and there's a bit of something just . . . just slightly *protruding* out of your left nostril, my dear," he continued, grimacing. "You might want to attend to it?"

"You're a beast, Alex," Bernie said as the clerk clapped a hand to her face and ran toward the dressing rooms. "God, I love you."

"Love me enough to pay for all of this, Bernie? I'll repay you with the proceeds of my profits."

" 'I'll gladly pay you Tuesday for a hamburger today,' " Bernie sing-songed, raising the flute to her lips. "Okay, okay. Maggie's good for it. I should know, I'm the one who had to sign that damn seven figure contract. Thank God Tabby's her agent. If I had to deal with you, Blue Eyes, Toland Books would be bankrupt."

"Thank you, my dear. It's always comforting to be appreciated. To be feared is merely a bonus. Here," he said, taking the empty flute from her unprotesting grip, "let me freshen that for you."

He was just returning to the small sitting area when Mary Louise stepped out from behind a long velvet curtain, looking about as if waiting for someone to see her, throw her out.

She was minus her decorative hardware, which could only be considered a blessing, and her purple hair had been tamed into a sleek cap combed back straight from her forehead, accentuating her perfectly oval face.

She was dressed in black, at least the bits of material that had been sewn together and called a gown were black. Floor length, slit to mid-thigh on both sides. Cut-out midriff except for one tantalizing bit of jet beading attaching the bodice to the center of the front waistline. More jet beading holding the bodice around the neck. No back. No sides.

"How much is that?" Saint Just whispered to Bernie.

"Five hundred. I checked. Want to know the size? It's a zero, Alex. Petite zero. I could seriously hate that kid."

"Five hundred? Worth every penny," Saint Just said as Mare walked up onto a small stage and looked into the three-sided mirror. The purple eyes grew wide as saucers . . . and then the girl smiled, and Bottacelli's angel was in the room. “Oh, yes, Bernie. Worth every penny.” He lifted Bernie’s hand to his lips. “I salute your genius, my dear.”

“Yeah, yeah, yeah, now promise me I’ll be drinking that double scotch in the next hour, and I’ll be a happy woman, not just a genius. Oh, and does Maggie know about any of this? About Mare?”

Saint Just smiled. “Bernie, I also consider myself somewhat of a genius. What do you think?”

“I think I keep my mouth shut about the girl,” Bernie said, tossing back her second glass of champagne. “Good idea, Alex. Maggie doesn’t have a cow often, but when she does, I don’t want to be anywhere around.”

CHAPTER 3

Dr. Bob Chalfont prudently stood back after opening the door to his office, and Maggie barreled past him, heading straight for the chair next to the table holding a newly-opened box of tissues.

"You said this was an emergency, Margaret," Dr. Bob said, retaking his own seat—his desk chair high-backed, and rather throne-like. Dr. Bob, thanks to Maggie's introduction to her agent, Tabitha Leighton, had gotten himself a bestselling self-help book, with another in the works. He was now a celebrity, but he knew that making time for Maggie whenever she phoned was still . . . well, it was good business.

He looked at Maggie now, seeing the same young woman he'd always seen, and that was both a good thing and a bad thing.

Maggie had begun coming to his office a few years ago, ostensibly to have him help break her addiction to nicotine. That he could smell tobacco smoke on her clothes as she'd brushed past him was one of the banes of his existence. He could help the world, it seemed, but he couldn't get this one woman to put down her cigarettes for more than a few days at a time.

What he had done, and which he congratulated himself for often, was to discover that Maggie was a mass of insecurities; that the nicotine was a symptom, not the problem. Never mind how successful she was, the girl had no feelings of self worth, of confidence.

Hence the self-destructive behavior with tobacco that served as her emotional crutch as well as a pleasurable habit. She actually gave the tobacco credit for her creativity. Oh, yes, he'd devoted an entire chapter of his new book to Maggie, without naming her, of course . . . and while thankful the emotionally addicted woman had never taken up drink. Or potato chips.

If anything, Maggie's success in the publishing world had heightened her fears. An ineffectual father, a domineering mother, being the middle child in a wildly dysfunctional family—all had combined to give Maggie more problems than she could handle without her ever faithful Dr. Bob.

How fortunate for him that she now had earned enough money to pay his hourly fee and discover that she had those problems.

But such a pretty young woman. She carried herself better than when she had first come to him for help, and he believed himself responsible for that. A slender, five and one-half feet tall, Maggie had Irish green eyes, dark copper hair that had lately sprouted rather interesting blond streaks, and her smile should, by rights, have every man in the five boroughs lining up to date her.

And yet Maggie lived with her cousin and his friend. Also fairly new additions to Maggie's life, Dr. Bob had yet to meet these two gentlemen, the ones upon which Maggie had based her fictional characters, Saint Just and Balder. Balder was herself as a child, and Saint Just was her alter-ego, the Brave Maggie. Not that she liked hearing that little piece of information.

Dr. Bob had been appreciative of this cousin at first,

during the very trying time of Kirk Toland's murder and Maggie's suspected involvement, but the time had come for the two visitors to leave. If Maggie was going to be dependent on anyone, she should be dependent on *him*.

He watched now as Maggie pulled three tissues out of the box, then drew her legs up under her on the chair seat and wrapped her arms around her waist. She wasn't crying, but she was preparing. She was, figuratively, already doing her little beetle trick. The sort of beetle that, when threatened, rolls itself up into a small, protective ball, so nobody can get through the actually quite ineffectual "armor" of her shell.

"Tell me about it, Margaret," he said, soothingly.

"It's Alex," she said, crumpling the tissues in both hands. "Yesterday he signed me up for the damn WAR conference. My old friend Virginia wrote to me about the conference, wanting to see me there, and Alex saw the e-mail. I've been a nervous wreck ever since. I can't write, I can't even think."

"WAR? Oh, dear, that strikes a chord in my memory," Dr. Bob said, sitting back in his chair, steepling his fingers in front of his nose. "Not quite your favorite thing, this WAR, am I correct?"

Maggie sniffed, nodded. "I *hate* it. I mean, I want to see my friend Virginia, but does it have to be *there?*" She raised her head, looked at Dr. Bob, her eyes swimming with tears she, as usual, was determined not to shed. "You remember, don't you? The last time? There I was, sitting on that damned panel about the business of publishing. Someone asked how to deal with a publisher, and I said I just always relied on my agent to do that."

She rolled her eyes. "Oh, boy, and then all hell broke loose. I mean, it was the *Sands of Iwo Jima* all over again."

Dr. Bob tapped his pudgy index fingers together, brought her back to the topic at hand, saying, "One of the other panel members—?"

"All of the other panel members," Maggie interrupted.

"Yes, all right, *all* of the other panel members. They all jumped on you, figuratively, saying that publishers are the enemy, that only a completely gullible fool would see editors, agents and publishing houses as anything but adversaries—you being that gullible fool. Do I have that right?"

Maggie nodded, dabbing the tissues to her nose. "There are great panels, great members. But somehow I always get stuck with whatever nut job fanatics are out there. Maybe I wear an invisible sign on my forehead, that only these people can see? I mean, I just sat there, trying to disappear. But do you know something? I don't know *squat* about this business. Everybody else was quoting statistics and trends and all this crap, and I sat there with my fingers in my mouth. There are *unpublished* members who know more about this business than I do."

"Do they make as much money as you do, Margaret?"

"Well, no. There is that, I suppose." She pointed a finger at him. "And it wasn't just that one panel. About six years ago, I ended up with writer's block after a WAR conference."

"And you blame the organization?"

"No, of course not. I blame *me,* for listening to the drivel some of these people spout. You must have a writing schedule. You must write every day. You must outline extensively. You must do character descriptions that go down to the last detail. Where was the character born? What was his grandmother's maiden name? What are his favorite foods? Did he suck his thumb in-utero? Who the hell cares! You must use this computer.

You must have a quiet space in which to write. You must freaking face *east* when you're writing."

"Oh, nobody said *that,* Margaret, I'm sure."

"Okay, okay, so I'm exaggerating, but not by much."

"You didn't have to listen to any of this, Margaret. Not if you believed in yourself, in your own talent."

She shot him a dagger glance. "Why the hell am I here, if I believed in either? I'd published seven or eight books by then, and I was going nowhere. I was desperate for anything that might help."

"Logical, I suppose. But not in any good way."

"Right. And then there was 'you must have a web site, you must have a newsletter, you must have bookmarks, you must tour even if it's on your own dime, you must contact distributors yourself, you must, you must, you must.' And I fell for it. I fell for all of it. By the time I figured out that I had a pretty good system of my own—no system—I hadn't written a usable word in four months. So, hey, it was my fault. They were selling, and I was buying. I don't listen to stuff like that anymore. But why do I always feel so stupid, so tongue–tied around these people? So . . . so *unqualified?"*

"If you're asking me if you insist upon seeing very self-confident, autocratic people as your mother, Margaret, I think we both know the answer to that."

Now the tissue was lifted to her eyes. "I know, I know. Whoever talks the loudest or sounds the most sure of herself wins. Right or wrong—and I mean, even when you *know* they're wrong—they win. I remember. It's why I can't watch *Crossfire.* You know that guy who closes his eyes when he talks? Smiles, and closes his eyes, won't look at anything or anyone? You know him? Drives me *crazy.* Never trust anyone who smiles when they talk—I'm not kidding. That smile just means, hey,

I'm so smart, and you're a poor, deluded idiot. And the spoiled, preppy Little Lord Fauntleroy with the bow tie? God, he—"

"You're digressing, Margaret."

She dropped her chin onto her chest. "Yeah. I've been doing a lot of that lately." She wadded the tissues into a ball, launched them at the waste can without looking up, then grabbed three more. "I can't do this. I see no reason to do this. I mean, the whole place is going to be *crawling* with these people, all of them bound to find me. And now they don't even think I write romance anymore. What do I need with this kind of aggravation?"

"Indeed, Margaret, what do you need with it? Stay home, don't go. Don't have that visit with Carolina."

"Virginia," Maggie sniffed, wiping her nose.

"Yes, of course, Virginia. But back to the point, Margaret. Don't go. Stay home and hide. Forego seeing old friends, having a good time, because maybe, just maybe, there will be a few people there who upset you. How many, Margaret? Three, five—ten? Out of—?"

She thought about that for a moment. "I don't know. It's New York, so it'll be big. Maybe about fifteen hundred? Conservatively, I suppose only about two hundred of them will be rabid. But, with my track record for attracting idiots, why should I do this to myself?"

"Again, very logical, in a self-protective way. Let them win."

Maggie, who had been looking at her hands, slowly raised her eyes to Dr. Bob, and sneered. "Oh, that's so . . . so *shrink* of you."

He smiled. "Yes. I learned it in shrink school. You like it?"

"No, I don't. You want me to believe in myself, take myself out of myself, face up to people like these WAR babes, and I can't do it. Why should I voluntarily put myself in a situation that makes me uncomfortable?"

"True again. You don't do well around confident, loud, or condescending personalities. You avoid confrontations. You use your witty and often cuttingly sarcastic fictional characters in the way of a ventriloquist, hiding behind them as they live what you *want* to be your life. But why just stay away from this one conference, this one group of people? I imagine there are caves, somewhere up in the Catskills, where you could successfully hide from *everybody.*"

"I need a cigarette," Maggie said under her breath, but he heard her.

"Yes, still no luck there, huh, Margaret? I smelled the smoke on your clothing as you came in."

"No, you didn't. I quit two weeks ago. I just found this new perfume that smells like tobacco smoke. I use it to piss people off."

Dr. Bob clapped his hands. "There you go! Brilliant, Margaret! Do you see? When you *care* enough about something—although your affection for nicotine baffles me—you can stand up, speak for yourself. Become almost fierce. Perhaps, just perhaps, the reason a few of these members of WAR intimidate you is because you simply don't *care* enough about any of them to poke out of your insecurity shell and take them on. When you do, my dear, you are formidable, very like your creation, Saint Just. Sometimes you just have to take what you put to paper with such skill, and *say* the words you're thinking. You cannot live vicariously through Saint Just. Not indefinitely."

"You want me to go, don't you?"

"I would never force you to do anything, Margaret."

"Yeah, right," she said, slumping in her chair. "I guess I'm going to have to go shopping, huh?"

"Some lovely new dresses, Margaret? Good."

"Cigarettes, Doctor," Maggie said, and then she smiled.

It was one of those here today, here tomorrow but looking entirely different restaurants. Yesterday, it had been painted a deep maroon, with hunt paintings on the walls. Today it looked like a garden. Lots of trailing plastic ivy climbing over white wooden trellis dividers, serving staff wearing grass green slacks, white shirts, and a pink carnation. New York had a way of taking tacky to a whole new level, then raising the prices.

Maggie followed one of the wait staff through the maze, and approached the table where Tabitha Leighton waited for her.

"Hi, Tabby, am I late?" Maggie asked as she pulled out a white wicker chair before the waiter could help her, and sat down.

"Not really. You look flustered. Are you all right? Nothing with the new book, I hope."

A few words of explanation here about Tabitha Leighton. Blonde, the sort of woman who looks to be in perpetual motion, even while sitting still; the kind who wears scarves, and knows how to tie them. A literary agent, Maggie's literary agent, as a matter of fact.

Tabby is currently (and yet again) separated from her Broadway producer husband, who is both a drunk and a womanizer, although she prefers to say he is in a middle life crisis that, so far, has lasted fifteen years. She tossed him out after reading a manuscript by one of her new authors, the book titled *Wake up Ladies! You Can Only Be a Doormat If You Lie Down.* Not that the separation would last, because next week she'd probably be reading a manuscript with a happy ending, and inviting David back, truly believing that this time he'd change.

If Maggie had to describe her friend and agent, she'd first mentally try to draw a picture that presented a cross between Martha Stewart and George Steinbrenner, with just a touch of Little Mary Sunshine that Tabby was smart enough to use to hide the Steinbrenner part.

"We're not talking about the book, Tabby," Maggie said, flourishing her linen napkin, that was large enough to slipcover a small chair, and stuffing it onto her lap. "We are *definitely* not talking about the book today. Chapter Ten, Tabby. Enough said?"

"Tab A into Slot B, as you so ickily call it? Definitely enough said. On to other things. So, how did it go with Dr. Bob?"

"The usual. I came, I cried, I buckled, I left wondering why the hell I even bothered," Maggie said, taking an oversize menu from another waiter who appeared beside the table with the promptness of a 1040 packet in January, or a guy on the lookout for a big tip—either way, it was going to involve money. "Thank you. Will you be our server?"

"No, Miss. Jared will be your server. I'm Collin, your attendant."

"Okay, what do you attend to? Drinks?"

"No, Miss. I tell you about the staff. Mary will be assisting you with your wine selection, and Duncan will be by shortly to tell you today's specials."

"Uh, right. Okay," Maggie said, making a face at Tabby as Collin walked off. "It's like a test, isn't it? He'll be back in ten minutes, to see if we remember all those names. High scorer gets a free French onion soup. Do you have the time, Tabby? I promised Steve I'd meet him at eight, while he's on a break."

"Ah, the dear *Left*-tenant Wendell, as Alex calls him. You're still dating?"

"If you can call it that. Homicide detectives work worse hours than writers. He's been on some stakeout for nearly a month now. Every time I see him, he's got doughnut sugar on his clothes."

"Yes, but you like him."

"I like him," Maggie said, smiling. "But nothing's going on between us, if you know what I mean. I'm writing love scenes from memory here, Tabby. And hey, I only have about an hour or so if I'm going to meet him on time. Where's Bernie?"

"She just called a few minutes ago. Something about Felicity Boothe Simmons and a Lady Twitters review that came in just as she was leaving the office."

"Nooooo." Maggie leaned forward, her troubles forgotten. "Ah, Lady T. Everyone's least favorite on-line book reviewer. Did Bernie sound happy or pissed? Give me a clue here."

Tabby pushed a lock of blond hair behind her ear, tilted her head as if replaying the phone call in her head. "Pissed, I'd say. Although I wouldn't say that. You would, but I wouldn't. Perturbed. Bernie seemed perturbed."

"Yes!" Maggie said, stabbing a fist into the air. "Felicity got slammed. Hurry up, order, so I can eat and go back to the apartment, look up the review on the web. God, Felicity Boobs Simmons, slammed. And I thought *my* day sucked?"

"There's also Felicity's selling history, which pretty much guarantees her at least six weeks in the top ten on the NYT no matter what the critics say," Tabby pointed out, running a finger down the listing of salads. "Oh, and if you do think it matters, I already know that *Rose Knows Romance* gave the book five kisses and a Big

Wave in her on-line review. And to think that you and Felicity used to be friends."

"Sure we were," Maggie said, pulling out her little plastic inhaler loaded with a nicotine fix and taking a deep drag, holding her breath a moment, then blowing it out. She made another face. "It just isn't the same. I don't care what they say, it isn't the same."

"You could stop, you know," Tabby said. "Soon there won't be anywhere in New York where you'll be allowed to smoke anyway. Restaurants, bars, you name it."

"I know," Maggie said, taking another puff. "That's why I've got these. Doctor Bob thinks I'm using them to stop smoking. The man is so naive sometimes. Still, they do keep me from running screaming into the night before dessert."

"I don't think that's healthy," Tabby said, frowning.

"Neither is living under a bridge, because I can't write without a cigarette. As my agent, you should be *buying* me these damn things."

"Or an iron lung," Tabby said, but she said it quietly.

Maggie stabbed at the open menu, said, "Springtime Salad? Do I like Springtime Salad? Okay, that's it." She snapped the menu shut. "And, getting back to Boobs, we were never friends, even back when she was plain old flat-chested Faith Simmons. I *thought* she was my friend, but the minute that first book hit, wham, she dropped me like a hot rock and moved on to bigger and better friends. I think half of WAR has tread marks on their backs, from Faith climbing over them."

"Bad-mouthing my author again, Maggie?" Bernie said, sliding into her chair, followed by Collin, or was that Duncan, who was carrying a small silver tray holding two double Scotches he then placed in front of her. "Thank you, darling. Keep 'em coming."

"See?" Maggie complained. "She can drink anywhere. But can I smoke? No."

"Drinking doesn't give anyone else cancer," Tabby pointed out, then quickly closed her mouth as Bernie shot her a look that was part *shut up* and part panic.

Too late.

"Sure. Smoking causes everything from cancer to the heartbreak of psoriasis. You name it, there's a health alert saying smoking caused it, oh, yeah, definitely smoking, and they wonder why we don't believe them anymore." Maggie said, glaring at the plastic cylinder. "But driving drunk never killed anyone. Obesity never killed anyone. Drunks have bars, high-carbs have their fast food, but nobody is allowed to own a bar or restaurant that's *just* for smokers? That's discrimination, and I may just get a T-shirt that says so. Can I rest my case now?"

"God, *yes,* please." Bernie dropped her head in her hands. "Had to bring it up, didn't you, Tabby? Never argue with a nicotine deprived addict. She actually thinks she's being logical." She looked at Maggie. "Although that heartbreak of psoriasis thing was pretty inspired, I will say that."

"Thank you, I thought so, too," Maggie said smugly, then frowned. "Now, if I might continue my rant, changing the subject, I have to go to the WAR conference. It will be good for my sense of self esteem."

Tabby and Bernie exchanged looks, both of them saying, "Dr. Bob."

"Doctor pain in my ass," Maggie said. "But it will be nice to see Virginia again."

"Who?" Tabby asked, pointing to the open menu and then holding up three fingers to Collin, or Duncan. Anyway, it wasn't Mary. Then again, who knew?

"Virginia Neuendorf. We're old friends."

"No, can't place the name."

Maggie rolled her eyes. "Oh, that's cold. She's one of your authors, Tabby."

"Ooooh, right, sorry," the agent said. "I remember now. Regency romances. It's like a license to peddle lousy advances and small print runs."

"She hasn't sold anything lately? I haven't been watching the business much these last few months," Maggie said, playing with the silverware. She started making little stabbing patterns in the tablecloth with the fork; anything to keep her hands occupied.

"I really don't know. I handed her over to Miranda a year or so ago. Breaking her in with my lesser authors."

"Poor Virginia. She keeps trying. I should have known she hasn't sold anything. She's pregnant again. This makes five, I think. If she goes more than a year without selling anything, she gets pregnant. I guess she feels she's got to give birth to *something.*"

"With the Regency market the way it is, maybe she can go for nine, and become the Osmonds." Bernie downed her second scotch, just as one of the servers appeared with a fresh one. "I wish Felicity had a kid. Why do women who never gave birth think they can write birthing scenes, then run them past editors who never had kids? Lady Twitters crucified us on the new book. Felicity gave her character a ten-pound baby, then had her riding a horse bareback across the badlands two days later."

"Ten pounds? I haven't had kids either, but I'm still surprised the woman could even *walk* two days later, especially if she was one of Felicity's standard petite, anorexic heroines, which she had to be because Felicity's only ever had one idea." Maggie shook her head. "Remember Rod Stewart's *Young Turks?* I think that's the name of the song. He has the kid in that having a ten-pound baby boy. I always thought that was overkill, but I guess it rhymed, or something. So, Lady Twit really slammed her? Goody."

"Totally. It went downhill from the ten-pound baby. She'd seen better writing on cereal boxes, at the spot where it says PRESS HERE AND LIFT, which she said was more inspired and evocotive prose than anything in any of Felicity's love scenes. On and on and on. I'll admit that the Twit has a way with words. I even laughed at some of it. And she slammed *us,* Maggie. I edited the book. But hey, now we've talked books, so this is officially a business dinner. Ladies, eat hearty, Toland Books is picking up the tab."

"I've got lots of quotes about reviewers and critics, you know," Maggie said, sucking on her nicotine pacifier. "Want to hear one? Of course you do. This one is from Samuel Coleridge. Good guy, old Samuel. Anyway, here goes."

She closed her eyes for a moment, concentrated on remembering the quote word-for-word. " 'Reviewers are usually people who would have been poets, historians, biographers, etc., if they could; they have tried their talents at one or at the other, and have failed; therefore they turn critics.' Or, them that can't, criticize. Besides, good review or slam, it's still only one person's opinion. So much for Lady Twitters, huh?"

Tabby made a production out of looking around the room, then leaned in close, motioning for her friends to do likewise. "Okay, okay, you two dragged it out of me. Remember that. I've got a secret," she said, "but you have to swear you won't tell anyone."

"Do we promise?" Maggie asked Bernie.

"Why not? As I think you had Saint Just say one time, if she'll believe me, she'll believe anyone."

"Very funny," Tabby said, motioning them even closer.

"But I mean it, you've got to promise. Cross your hearts and hope to die and stick a—"

"Tabby," Bernie warned. "Don't make me come over there and choke it out of you."

"Okay, okay, I can't keep it in anyway, I really can't. Lady Twitters submitted a manuscript to me."

"Get out," Maggie said, sitting back. "How do you know it's her?"

"Him," Tabby said, her smile, if Maggie were writing a Regency about this scene, much like the cat who has canary feathers sticking from the corners of her mouth.

"Who him?" Bernie asked—after all, she was pretty deep in her scotches. "I'm not following."

"Lady Twitters is a *man,"* Tabby said, rolling her eyes. "Pay attention, Bernie."

"How do you know?" Maggie asked, trying to take in this information. It had never occurred to her that Lady Twitters could be a man. She—he—was way too snide to be a man. A husband was even mentioned from time to time, she was sure. That, and an enduring passion for Pierce Brosnan.

"Simple. I was reading this manuscript a couple of weeks ago, from a certain published author who wants me to be his new agent, and stuck inside it, about halfway through, was the first part of a review by Lady Twitters. Her byline, or whatever, was on it. The review had gotten into the manuscript by mistake. Happens all the time, you know. Sometimes I find grocery lists. Why would anyone buy kumquats? I mean, I can't even *spell* kumquats."

"Moving right along?" Bernie interrupted, waving for Tabby to get back on topic.

"Okay, okay. I checked, and the review hadn't been posted on the Lady Twitters' City of Romance internet site yet. Same page set-up as the manuscript pages. Same paper—I checked the watermark, held the paper up to the light. I've been dying to tell *somebody* ever since. The guy is Lady Twitters."

Maggie picked up her fork and pointed it at Tabby. "Give me the name. Now, Tabby."

The agent did her check out the room for hidden microphones thing again, then whispered, "Regina Hall."

"Reggie? Regina Hall?" Maggie put down the fork. "But he's so *nice.* Not exactly a great writer, but nice. You're kidding. You have to be wrong."

"No, no," Bernie said, "it makes sense. A man working in a woman's world, and not doing as well as those women. It could piss him off."

"Enough to write those awful reviews? I mean, even his *good* reviews are full of snipes," Maggie said, trying to imagine quiet, shy Reggie Hall as Lady Twitters. This was sort of like trying to mentally cast Don Knotts as Hercules. "Man, it's the same ventriloquist thing Dr. Bob talks about. You know—the shy guy who wouldn't stomp on an ant, then turns into a snarky bastard when he talks through his dummy?"

"Yes, yes, but it's our secret," Tabby reminded them both. "You can't say anything."

"I can send Reggie flowers, for ripping Felicity. Anonymously, of course. Or maybe a new Buick," Maggie said with an unholy grin. "Oh, poor Felicity. Slammed by Reggie Hall, and she doesn't even know whose face to put on her voodoo doll before sticking in the pins."

Bernie sipped at another double. "Have your fun, kiddo, but do me a favor. Try not to look like you're ready to get up and do a jig on the table or I'll have to tell you that the print order for *Miracle Mountain* was just shy of four hundred thousand."

"Hardback?"

"Trade paper. The first of a homespun, down home, whatever sort of make 'em laugh, make 'em cry label you can put on it historical trilogy we're bringing out back to back to back, to promote her next hardcover. Discounted the hell out of it, too."

Maggie pouted. "You never did that for me. Damn, Bernie, you could sell anything, doing it like that, with the right promotion."

"True. But Kirk was still in charge when you were writing romance. This was my idea. Luckily, Felicity is fast—"

"I'll puff to that," Maggie interrupted, lifting the cylinder to her lips.

"Funny, Maggie, now shut up. As I was saying? We had two of the three books in the can last year. She finished the last one yesterday. I'm going to make minor history here, turning around that last book in three months. Hey, Toland Books needs the bucks. Don't hate me for trying to make money with one of our larger cash cows."

"Yeah, she sure did buy herself a big pair of—no, it's too easy. Even I can't do that one."

"For which the furiously blushing Miss Tabby and I will be eternally grateful. Oh, and when you see Felicity at WAR, for God's sake, smile. You write one book a year and make more than she does. And that's our little secret, okay?"

"Now I'll drink to *that,*" Tabby said, lifting her glass of sparkling water.

"Okay, okay. Color me mollified. And not that I'm a mean person. Well, not a lot. But when it's Felicity? Oh, I really don't want to go to this conference."

"Not even for the great Toland Books cocktail party? I'll even let you smoke on the balcony."

"You're going?" Maggie asked Bernie, who nodded. "And you?" she asked Tabby.

"Of course. I'm always on the lookout for new talent, you know that. I'll be giving interviews, even taking part in one of the panels. You know, the standard stuff. Question: what are you looking for? Answer: the best book you can write. Question: what's selling? Answer: Regency England and the American West. No Ancient Egypt or pre-revolutionary America. Question: what makes a bestseller? Answer: I'll know it when I see it. I've done this so many times, I could phone it in."

Tabby reached over and patted Maggie's hand. "See? You won't be alone."

"Great, because misery loves company," Maggie said as her Springtime Salad was put in front of her, immediately grabbing her horrified attention. If the bowl were just a little bit smaller, the contents could feed a third world nation. The greens were all dark, or red, or white and spikey, and looked sort of like someone went to the park and gathered up a bunch of weeds. There could be dandelions in there. But where was the meat? There wasn't any meat. Taco Bell salads had meat. Sort of.

Maggie tried to avoid looking at the bowl anymore. "Where were you earlier, Bernie? I tried calling you."

Bernie grabbed her glass. "Out," she said, waving her empty glass in the air.

"Out with Alex," Maggie corrected, following Tabby's lead and dousing the salad with salt and pepper. She hated salads, even small, normal-looking ones, but she was going to WAR in a few weeks, in more than one sense of the word, and needed to look her best. Best, in the world of romance authors, translated to "never too thin."

"Um, yes, I was. We were . . . we were discussing a compilation of his street corner speeches. He only has six so far, so I told him to get back to me in another year. I like your cousin, Maggie. He's such a gentleman."

"And Bernie's such a liar," Maggie said to Tabby, who had already made great inroads into her salad, seemingly without taking a bite.

There was this theory Maggie had about salads. Salad eaters were divided into two groups, those who could, and those who always lost a cherry tomato across the table. The former could neatly attack and demolish a salad without dropping a piece of lettuce to the floor. The latter could cut, chop, chew, organize and reorganize, chew some more, and still end up looking as if nothing had been eaten, and with the surrounding area appearing as if a small explosion had taken place in the bowl.

Maggie pushed the plate away from her, and reached for a roll. Then she reached for the butter, slathered it on the roll, followed it up with some salt, just because she liked salty butter. Gaining weight was the least of her problems at the moment.

"We *did* discuss the compilation," Bernie persisted, "among other things. Alex is quite excited about the WAR conference, Maggie. As a matter of fact, he and Socks will be hunting up some costumes later tonight, for the cover model contest and the costume ball."

"Alex is entering the contests?" Tabby asked, at last distracted enough to let a piece of lettuce drop off her fork, onto her lap. "Oh, he'd be *so* good. Wouldn't he be good, Maggie? I've been longing to ask him to say 'shaken, not stirred,' ever since I first met him. Or is that the other way around? His voice is just so Sean Connery as a young James Bond, you know."

Suddenly nervous, as Tabby was hitting a little closer to home than was comfortable, Maggie shifted her eyes to her lap. Someday maybe she'd tell Bernie and Tabby the truth about Alex and Sterling. But not today. She was already feeling too close to a rubber room to try to sell that particular story as real. "He does seem to have a certain . . . knack for the Regency Era, at least."

"That's because he's English," Tabby said, neatly pronounced. "It's the accent, the public schooling—something. An entire *attitude.*"

"Oh, he's got attitude, all right," Maggie groused, plunking knife and fork into the salad bowl, hoping one of the gaggle of servers would take the hint and get the damn thing away from her before her nose started twitching. "With Socks, you said? I guess that makes sense. Socks probably has lots of friends with costumes—for the theater, I mean, so stop laughing, Bernie. You know, in some ways, I'm looking forward to this conference. Especially the part where I tell Alex that most cover models shave their chests."

"And I'll drink to *that!"* Bernie said, grabbing a new scotch from the tray held in front of her. "That ought to be enough, *garçon, sil vous* whatever."

CHAPTER 4

All God's children have a writer's group. Groups for mystery writers. Groups for science fiction writers. Groups for literary types (their luncheons have little sandwiches with the crusts cut off).

Romance writers have a group, maybe twelve groups (the formula being, the more women in any group, the more groups per woman. It's a leftover of PTA, Girl Scouts, and possibly communal showers in gym class).

These groups are both varied and alike. Some were for published writers. Some were for aspirings, or pre-pubs, or whatever they called themselves these days—as long as it wasn't "unpublished" it was okay (and "wannabe" was strictly verboten). Some included readers and even fans, as well as writers. If you couldn't find a group for you in the gaggle of romance writers groups, you just weren't looking.

Thousands of published, pre-published, avid readers, and sometimes pathetic types have been welcomed into the largest romance writer's group in the country, We Are Romance, Inc., and they have been welcomed for a very good reason.

Hey, somebody has to run the annual conference.

This year, Bunny Wilkinson was Conference Chairperson, and Bunny was one hell of an organizer. It never occurred to her, thankfully, that the months spent planning the conference had taken her away from her family saga, *The Flaming Flower of Shannon.* Just as being Contest Chairperson last year had robbed her of three months that might have been spent actually finishing the book she'd been talking about for six long years.

Oh, no. That never occurred to Bunny. Because, being a chairperson got her up close and personal with editors. And agents. And published writers. Networking. That's what it was all about, that's what it took to get into print. Everybody knew that.

That's why Bunny made sure she was on hand in the lobby of the Manhattan Marriott Marquis, site of this year's WAR conference. She was there to meet and greet, foam and fawn, weasel and finagle.

She'd already copped invitations to cocktail parties hosted by two of the publishing houses represented at the conference, as well as a date for drinks in the lounge later with Melissa Blair, one of the top agents in the country. Half a dozen copies of the first four hundred purple, pulsing pages of Bunny's saga were up in her room, packed and ready to be delivered into the grateful hands of some of the most powerful people in the publishing industry. Because they would all agree to see her work. She was going to make sure of that.

The lobby was getting crowded on this Wednesday morning, and Bunny frowned as she realized that most of the crush was caused by her fellow WAR conference attendees. They were checking in, they were checking each other out. They were mingling, they were milling, and they were cutting into her turf.

"Ladies, ladies, please," she trilled, waving her arms

in the air so that the charms on her bracelet tinkled like miniature school bells, calling the class to order. "We have five whole days to enjoy each other's company, see all of our friends. For now, we need to clear this congestion, all right?"

She checked the fourteen-karat gold and diamond watch strapped to her left wrist (being pre-pubbed was so much easier when your husband was an executive vice president of a Fortune 500 company). "It's three o'clock, ladies, and the hospitality suite is open on the conference floor. Free snacks and sodas, ladies. Oh, and for you published writers, and those pre-pubs who have their own publicity packets—the Press Room is also open, and I do believe I saw a reporter from *People* leafing through the packets some of you enterprising ladies have already placed there."

Moses had needed God's help to part the Red Sea. But, then, Moses had been an amateur. Bunny Wilkinson was a pro. The crowd began to disburse.

Right before it turned into a mob.

"It's her, it's *her!"* somebody called out, pointing past Bunny. "Oh, God, don't you just *love* her?"

Bunny watched as the readers and fans in the group burst into bloom, roses in their cheeks, autograph books sprouting from their purses. The scattering of published writers in the group were suddenly abandoned, left with two choices. They could either announce pressing business elsewhere to an audience no longer interested in them, or they could join the crowd in greeting *her.* Most opted to gush, as it was safer, definitely prudent.

Someday, Bunny told herself as she squared her shoulders, turned to greet the new arrival. Someday this will be me. And then she pasted a wide smile on her face, held out her arms, and gushed along with everyone else. "Felicity Boothe Simmons! How wonderful to see you, Felicity!"

Bunny felt a tap on her shoulder and turned around, not happy to have been interrupted.

"Excuse me, but you look official," the woman said, pointing to Bunny's badge and the red ribbon proclaiming her a finalist in the aspiring writers contest for the third year in a row (and the blue ribbon for her local chapter, the royal purple ribbon for her five year status on the board of directors, her silver pin for volunteer work, the small gold medallion hailing her as Conference Chair—one more ribbon on her chest and she could pass as a Russian commissar). "Can you please tell us where the WAR group is meeting?"

"Aspiring or published, dear? Aspiring, I imagine," Bunny said, pasting her professional smile on her face. She'd taken a self-realization course at her local community college that touted "let a smile be your umbrella and you'll win, win, win."

"Published, actually." The woman actually winced as she said it. "I'm Maggie Kelly—I mean, Cleo Dooley. I mean, I used to be Alicia Tate Evans, at least that's still on my membership card, but now I'm Cleo Dooley. Except I'm Maggie Kelly."

"Good for you, dear, everybody has to be somebody," Bunny said, patting the woman's arm. "Registration desk is two flights down. Excuse me, but our keynote speaker just arrived. You won't mind if I desert you now, will you, dear? Felicity? Yoo-hoo, over here! It's me, Bunny!"

Maggie sighed. Two minutes. That's all, just two minutes in the hotel, and out of the hundreds of women she'd seen in the lobby area she'd immediately gravitated to her first oppressive person. And now Felicity?

What were the odds? And what next? Maybe she should just poke a sharp stick in her eye, and get it over with?

She looked across the lobby, doing her best to keep her upper lip from curling as she saw Felicity Boothe Simmons in all her glory. Just like any shark, she had a few pilot fish swimming with her as she advanced on the smiling ribbon lady, arms outstretched, not quite escaping her shield of cloying perfume that could probably stop a .357 magnum.

Seeing a clerk opening a new window at the registration desk, Maggie took off for it, wanting nothing more than to get out of the lobby before Felicity saw her . . . and before Saint Just and Sterling finished dealing with their mountain of luggage and came over, intent on making a scene. Well, Saint Just would make a scene. He always did, even when he wasn't trying.

Unfortunately, the new window was not that far from Felicity and the rabbit, and Maggie could still both see and hear them.

"Ladies, ladies, don't crowd the star," Bunny said quickly, herding the women, both hands moving in shooing motions. *"People,* ladies. On the conference floor."

Even the most casual observors seemed to sense that, once Bunny Wilkinson had Felicity in her clutches, they'd never get within twenty feet of her, and dispersed.

"Bunny, Bunny, Bunny, thank you so much for the rescue. And how *good* to finally see you after speaking with you on the telephone so many times," Felicity gushed, putting her hands on the other woman's shoulders (the better to keep her from crushing the Armani), then placing air kisses next to both Bunny's cheeks. "It took *forever* for my driver to make it all the way down here from the Hamptons, and even then I had two phoners in the limo before stopping off for yet a third radio interview. I'm *totally* depleted. Is my suite ready, dear? Please tell me my suite is ready."

"Oh, yes, yes, just the way you asked for it, and compliments of WAR, naturally, since you're our keynote. Have you checked in yet?"

"With that crowd over there?" Felicity said, rolling her eyes. "Hardly. Although it has thinned out considerably, hasn't it? Still, I'm *so* weary."

"Oh, well, let me take care of that. I'm sure no one would mind if I just sort of sneaked you in front of them."

Maggie quickly turned her back to everyone and held onto the counter with both hands, waiting for the clerk to pick up her charge card. The woman was still putting on a headphone, and tapping keys on her computer with inch long nails painted to look like American flags. Barely keeping herself from saying what she was thinking (which was, "Come on, come on, *come on!*"), Maggie pretended not to feel the polite tap on her back.

"Excuse me, but would you mind if we just sort of tippy-toed ahead of you?"

Maggie turned around, moving her eyes first, her rather slitted eyes at the moment, and glared at the rabbit. "Yes, I would." Then she looked past the woman and plastered a smile on her face. Today was a new day, and today she was her own ventriloquist, damn it (although she'd still have to work out the part where that would also make her the dummy). "Why, Faith, how are you? I don't think I've seen you since you were asked to leave Kirk's memorial service. *So* sorry about the Lady Twitters review."

Felicity, whose smile had faltered slightly when Maggie called her Faith, broadened again. "Oh, that. I found it highly amusing. As a matter of fact," she said, rummaging in her purse and coming out with a bright red button with white lettering on it, "I've made up these."

Maggie took the button and read its message. " 'I've been slammed by Lady Twitters.' Cute, I suppose."

"Lemonade from lemons, my dear. Although, alas, it's not such an exclusive club. I've sent them to everyone who has been slammed by that dreadful woman. We're actually having a luncheon later this week. The *cachet,* darling, you know. There are at least seven *NYT's* wearing the buttons this week. No," she said, as Maggie went to hand back the button, "you keep it. You have been slammed by Lady T, haven't you?"

"As a matter of fact," Maggie said, firmly handing back the button, "I haven't. Sorry."

"I would say so. You aren't *anybody* until you've been slammed by Lady T. Oh well," Felicity said, shrugging her thin shoulders (the woman was a petite 2, except for her boobs, which only used to be petite), "maybe someday, dear. Don't despair. Oh, look, a cowboy," she said, pointing to Maggie's left. "Bunny? I didn't think the cover model contest was scheduled for the first day."

"It isn't," Bunny Wilkinson said, watching the cowboy cross the lobby, holding a photograph in front of him, scanning faces, obviously looking for someone in particular. He was tall, potbellied, and wore fake cowskin chaps, a denim shirt with a leather vest, and an oversize cowboy hat that he could have used as a boat if the lobby suddenly flooded.

"He couldn't be one of the contestants," Bunny said. "He's *fat.*"

"He's also heading this way," Maggie said, quickly signing the hotel registration form and pocketing her platinum card. "One of your fans, Faith?"

"Someone ought to feed you, dear. You always were

difficult when you were hungry, as I recall. And, no, I don't know—well, hello, cowboy," she ended on a silky smile when the man stopped just in front of her.

That was Felicity. Fat, skinny, ugly, handsome, if he was male, Felicity smiled.

The cowboy looked at the photograph in his hand, then at Felicity. "You Felicity Boothe Simmons, ma'am?" he asked, tipping his enormous hat.

"I am," she answered, turning to smile triumphantly at Maggie. See, her smile seemed to say, *everybody* knows *me.*

"In that case, ma'am," the cowboy continued, drawing himself up to his full height and sucking in his belly—and quickly grabbing his gun belt, which nearly slipped off until he exhaled again, "this is for you." He jammed the photograph into one pocket, and pulled out another piece of paper, yellow, and looking much like a telegram. He rummaged under his chaps for a pitch pipe, blew on it several times before he found the right key, then cleared his throat before warbling, to the tune of "Happy Birthday to You:"

"Felicity Simmons, that's you,
Felicity Simmons, that's you.
A fair warning, Felicity Sim-mons,
Leave town or I kill you."

Before Maggie could react (other than to think that last line was a beat too long), the cowboy unholstered his very long-barreled pistol, pointed it at Felicity, and pulled the trigger.

Out popped a bright red flag with the words: "Bang, you're dead" written on it.

Then the guy grinned and held out his hand for a tip, while Maggie caught a swooning Bunny in her arms. But that didn't last long, because the cowboy, minus his tip, had turned to leave the lobby. Maggie deposited Bunny in Felicity's arms and took off after the guy.

"Hey! Hold it there, cowboy!" she yelled, grabbing the guy's arm. "Who hired you?"

"Ma'am," the guy said, tipping his hat to her. "Don't reckon I rightly know, ma'am. Oh, and shucks. Shoulda said shucks, huh?"

"Yeah, yeah, you're an actor. Aren't I surprised. Everybody in this town is an actor. And you were good, darn good, really. Now, who hired you?"

The hat came off, and the man pushed back a mop of mousy brown hair tipped with gold highlights. "Damned if I know. I work at The Busted Corral. Only until my agent works this deal we've got going. Really sweet. Off-off-Broadway, but quality, you know?"

"I'm sure it is," Maggie said, still keeping her hand on his arm. "But back to who hired you. Because that wasn't funny, bucko. You know that, don't you?"

He shrugged. "I guess not. I didn't really think about it. I just got this package at work, from one of the waitresses—cowgirls, I mean. In it was that picture of Ms. Simmons, a copy of the song, the pistol, what I was supposed to do, and a Ben Franklin. Hey, you hear what I'm saying here? A Ben Franklin. I don't turn down old Benny."

Maggie saw Saint Just and Sterling approaching from the bell desk and let go of the cowboy's arm. "Okay, you can go."

"Yeah, like I couldn't have gone before?" he asked, sniffing.

"Not with my knee stuck where your chaps split you couldn't. Adios, pardner," Maggie told him, waving him on his way just as Saint Just stopped, lifted one eyebrow, and looked at her questioningly.

"You do consort with the oddest creatures, Maggie," he said, watching the cowboy, who was now walking very quickly as he headed for the elevators. "What was that on his legs?"

"Chaps," Maggie said, smiling at Sterling, who was looking around the large lobby with his jaw at half mast, taking in the sight of the glass-sided elevators, and all the fairy lights . . . and all the overdressed, over-perfumed women. "Somebody played a practical joke on Felicity Simmons."

"And it wasn't you?" Saint Just said, feigning surprise. "But it's not to worry. That's only because you didn't think of it, I'm sure."

"Funny, Alex. I'm laughing so hard my sides hurt. Did you have any trouble with the bell person? Where's the baggage claim?"

"Our bags, my dear, are already on their way to our room, which means we might wish to follow after them, so as to open the door to accept their delivery."

"How could you do that? You don't know the room number." She held up the small packet containing three key cards. "I just got the keys."

"I'm quite sure I don't know," he told her. "I gave the man your name, he attacked the computer on his desk, and that was that." He half turned back toward the bell desk. "Would you like me to go ask him?"

"No, forget it. You probably were such a pompous pain in the guy's ass he would have done anything to get rid of you. Sterling? Was Alex a pompous ass?"

Sterling flushed slightly and averted his gaze. "He did begin giving very explicit instructions as to the care he expected to be shown in transporting our luggage, especially the portmanteaux holding his curly brimmed beaver and—yes, I suppose he was being . . . a trifle high in the instep. Sorry, Saint Just. She did ask."

"Yes, she did. And now I'm going to ask. Maggie, my dear, why is that poor pale creature being helped to a chair? It would please me greatly if you were to tell me you didn't hit her. I know you don't want to be here, but there's no necessity for violence."

Maggie looked toward Bunny, who was being supported on either side as she was led to a bench near the registration desk. "Oh, her. She fainted when the cowboy shot Felicity."

"Of course she did," Saint Just said smoothly. He pointed his ebony cane in the direction of Felicity Boothe Simmons and a small gaggle of fussing hens who surrounded her. "He missed, I take it."

"I'm not so sure of that," Maggie said, looking at Felicity. The woman was smiling, holding court, but she had a thin white line around her mouth, and she kept patting her chest (what she could feel of it beneath the silicone). She didn't like Felicity, but she had liked Faith, and that's who she felt sorry for now, the woman who used to be her friend. The woman who used to be. "I hate practical jokes."

"I'll remember that the next time I'm tempted to put sugar in the salt cellar," Saint Just said, holding out his arm to her. "Shall we be off? I'd like to register us for the contests as soon as possible. Mare? Are you coming?"

Maggie stopped dead, took her hand off his arm. "Mare? No, you don't mean that. You couldn't mean that. Where?" She looked around, knowing how easy it would be to spot the girl who dressed like a junkie rummage sale and had more body piercings than she probably had second teeth.

"Why, right over there, sitting on the last bench. She arrived just minutes ago," Saint Just told her, inclining his head to the right.

"No. I don't see her. All I see is—no way."

"Much as it pains me to dip into such obvious vernacular, and only because dear Mare herself has said it so often—yes, *way.* You approve?"

Maggie watched as Mare rose from the bench and smoothed down the skirt of her pastel pink suit. The skirt was short, the jacket was short, and Mare's legs were incredibly long, considering she barely stood five feet tall. Her hair was short and nearly black, loosely curling around her gamine face. She wore three-inch heels, and only stumbled once as she approached Saint Just and smiled up at him, her lips full and deeply pink, her purple eyes made up so expertly that it looked as if she wore no makeup at all.

Sure. Like everybody had eyelashes like that.

"Mare?" Maggie said, recognizing the herringbone gold necklace the girl wore, because she'd gotten it as a gift from her parents for her last birthday. "What are—cancel that. Just *what?"*

"Mare, as Mary Louise—don't you think that sounds professional?—is to be entered in the cover model contest, and as long as she's here, the costume contest as well. Socks procured the most splendid costume for her. Her winnings, for she will win, will cover her last year of schooling quite nicely. Isn't that splendid?"

"Just ducky," Maggie said, recognizing her new Coach purse as it hung from Mare's shoulder. "And let me guess. Your little *protégé* is bunking with us?"

"Ah, never slow to understand, are you, Maggie? Shall we be off? The baggage, remember?"

"Oh, yeah, speaking of the baggage," Maggie said, turning to look at Felicity once more. "Do you think she staged that herself?" she asked, speaking mostly to herself.

"Although my knowledge of the details remains lamentably scant, if you're asking me if Miss Simmons would hire someone to shoot her, I'd have to respond—why?"

Maggie nodded. "Good point. Why? You could almost think Felicity has an enemy."

"More than just you, you mean?" Saint Just quipped, depressing the elevator call button with the tip of his cane.

Saint Just strolled about the suite, idly running a hand over the keys of the shiny black grand piano in one corner, doing his best to look nonchalant, and not overly impressed with the size of their accommodations, or the magnificent view from its windows.

He and Sterling had been forced to share a bedroom, as Maggie had steadfastly refused to share with Mary Louise. The woman could be most headstrong and uncooperative. Not that it mattered, as he and Sterling had been sharing Maggie's guest room for three months now—but not for much longer.

Which reminded him . . .

He knocked on the open door to Maggie's room, and stepped inside to see her unpacking her clothing into the large closet. "There's something I probably should tell you," he said as she quickly closed the lid on the lingerie still in her smaller suitcase.

"First apologize," she said, blowing an errant lock of hair out of her face.

"Whatever for?"

"For inviting Mare here without my permission. For using my closet as some sort of private rummage sale.

For signing me up for this damn conference in the first place. I've been here twenty minutes, and I already hate it."

"In that case," Saint Just said, bowing, "my most humble and heartfelt apologies, my dear. Now, would you care to hear my news? It should cheer you mightily."

"Finding an ashtray in this place would cheer me mightily. This is a smoking room, right?"

"I have no idea. Is it?"

"It is now," Maggie said, lighting up, then taking the top off one of the complimentary glasses and carrying the glass into the bathroom to put about an inch of water in it. Very inventive, his Maggie. She returned to the room, looking considerably calmer. "So? What's the news?"

"Well," Saint Just said, sitting himself down in a rather uncomfortable chair and crossing one leg over the other, "you do remember Mrs. Goldblum, don't you?"

"Irene Goldblum. My neighbor across the hall, sure. Why?"

Saint Just folded his hands in his lap and looked at her. "Sterling speaks with her often, and she gives him tea and coconut macaroons. They've become quite fast friends, as a matter of fact. This morning, it would seem Sterling learned that Mrs. Goldblum has been called to her heavenly reward."

Maggie sat down on the edge of the bed. "Mrs. Goldblum's dead?"

"So I thought as well, until Sterling told me that, to Mrs. Goldblum, being called to her heavenly reward means that her widowed sister has invited her to come stay with her for an indefinite period, in a place called Boca."

"She's moving to Florida? Oh, well, that's okay. You scared me for a minute there, Alex."

"Not yet, my dear, but we've still time, as I'm not yet done," he said, getting to his feet and beginning to pace the floor. "You see, while you were visiting your hair dresser this morning, I went across the hall to wish Mrs. Goldblum a happy trip, and one thing led to another, and . . ." He stopped, turned to face Maggie. "Exactly what is rent control?"

Maggie's eyes went wide. "She's got rent control? Oh, wow."

"Yes. Your reaction is much like that of Socks, when I told him about it. In any case, the rental is little more than a pittance, and since she won't be taking any of her furniture with her—lovely antiques, I must say—it seemed like a most satisfying arrangement all round."

He watched as Maggie's brain worked its way through the information he'd supplied.

"You sublet Mrs. Goldblum's apartment?"

"Actually, we're housesitting for her. Is that it? Yes, I believe that is the term. It is an informal arrangement, sealed with a handshake, as a matter of fact. It would seem that the late Harry Goldblum always warned Mrs. Goldblum to avoid putting anything in writing that might interest someone other than herself."

"He was a lawyer for the mob, Socks says, so I guess he knew," Maggie said.

"In any case, Mrs. Goldblum will feed and water Napoleon and Wellington while we're here, and Sterling and I will be adjourning to her apartment within two weeks of our return from this conference. We will pay her rent, to her, and no one will think anything except that she is temporarily away from her rent controlled apartment. She seemed most pleased. Do you mind?"

"That she's taking care of the cats? I figured Socks

would do it, but this is better. She has so little to occupy her. So no, I don't mind."

"No, Maggie. Do you mind about the apartment?"

"That depends, I guess. How much?"

He quoted her a figure.

"Who's paying?"

"Now I'm crushed. Naturally, I am."

"How?"

"With my winnings from the cover model contest, of course."

"In other words, *me.*"

"That's insulting."

"That's life," Maggie said, dropping her cigarette into the water glass. "But it's a good idea, really. Low rent, you're close enough that you shouldn't get into too much trouble. And I get my privacy back."

"Meaning, if I may be so bold, that you can feel free to entertain *Left*-tenant Wendell at all hours. Or have you finally depressed his pretensions?"

"Steve and me . . . I . . . the two of us are no business of yours. I'm a grown woman, Alex, and I want my privacy back."

"Of course you do, my dear. It was never my intention to oppress you. Sterling and I merely wished to see more of this world of yours, have a few adventures. Nothing more. Why, you'll scarcely know we're still in the same universe," Saint Just said, crossing his fingers behind him and smiling at her back as she stomped out of the bedroom.

CHAPTER 5

Saint Just patted the name tag pinned to his suit jacket, feeling the orange ribbon that proclaimed him a cover model contestant, the thinner pink ribbon that told of his entry in the costume ball competition.

Normally, he would shun such nonsense, but he considered this in the way of unpaid advertising.

He'd worn his new black suit. Well, not totally black. Near black. Almost black. Definitely not gray. He'd located it in a shop just a few blocks from Maggie's condo, and had been pleasantly surprised to find that some inventive haberdasher had actually seen the benefit of longer jackets; much more flattering to the male than having half his posterior covered only by sadly loose or ridiculously over-tight slacks. This particular jacket was not quite wasp-waisted, but sufficiently fitted for all of that, and nearly knee-long, so as to put him in mind of his favored Regency hacking jackets.

His shirt was the finest cotton and white as snow, pristine in the extreme, and worn open at the collar, with no tie, as he felt a modern tie would be not enough, and his usual neck cloth (draped, naturally, in his favored Waterfall) perhaps too much for an informal evening. So he'd added only a vest, fashioned of silver and black, a creation that Socks, who had taken him to the establishment, had termed 'bitchin'."

He wore his favored boots, skin tight, so that they fitted very nicely beneath his slacks, shined within an inch of their lives, and sporting two-inch heels.

His coal black hair that, along with his perpetually tanned skin, so nicely set off his startling blue eyes, was carefully combed in Beau Brummell's favored windswept style. He carried his cane (the one with the cleverly concealed sword stick), and his quizzing glass hung from its black riband around his neck.

He was long, lean, a little bit dangerous, definitely gorgeous and, not being a stupid man, he knew it.

There were perhaps more well-dressed men in the universe, more urbane, more compelling to the female eye, even perhaps more witty. But, he was certain, none of them inhabited the ballroom at the Marriott Marquis that evening.

"Okay, okay, you're kickass terrific. Just don't strut," Maggie whispered as they showed their entrance tickets to one of the women at the door (the woman was goggling, open-mouthed, at Saint Just), then were handed different tickets, that provided them each with one complimentary cocktail. After that, the boozing was on the conference-goers.

"I beg your pardon. I do not strut," Saint Just answered in what she always wrote as his "too polite, cuts straight to the bone" tone of voice. "Saunter, from time to time, granted, but I do not strut. Peacocks strut. Are you insinuating that I am a peacock? I am crushed, madam, crushed, that you should be so cruel. Why, if I were not so confident that my toilette is impeccable as well as meticulously understated, I should think I might go into a sad decline."

"Oy, jeez. I should have made you more humble," Maggie muttered, and walked ahead of him, into the ballroom.

Sterling and Mare (another expense, as Maggie had to sign her up for the conference as well) entered behind them. Sterling wore a yellow-on-yellow striped waistcoat that Saint Just had asked, without success, he leave in the closet.

He'd stuck himself, twice, before Maggie took over pinning his name tag on him, and he was nervous in the extreme. "Don't much care for crushes," he'd said at least a dozen times as they waited for the elevator, thankfully forgetting his apprehensions as he entered the glass-sided affair, so that he spent the entire ride staring down at the lobby as it rushed up to meet them, simply enthralled. The cleaning staff would be wiping Sterling's palm prints off the glass in every elevator for the full five days.

Hanging on Sterling's arm, Mare was unnaturally quiet, surveying her surroundings with huge purple eyes. Saint Just had gone for the ingenue look this evening, a decidedly Regency style fit for young ladies just Out. She wore virginal white, a soft, flowing, high-waisted gown with irises around the hemline, to match her eyes, her only further color being a thin purple satin ribbon tied tightly around her long, swanlike neck. Her badge was pinned to a small, shoulder-type silk reticule he'd located in a plastic bag at the back of Maggie's closet.

Dear Mary Louise. She looked a cross between a young Audrey Hepburn and an even younger Elizabeth Taylor (he did so enjoy watching old movies on DVD), and earlier Saint Just had wondered, just for a moment, if she had yet attained the legal drinking age, only to be told she was "damn well old enough to drink, Vic, so mind your own beeswax, okay?"

Ah, well. She was to be a photographic model. Nobody said she had to *talk.*

Maggie also wore black, a slim sheath adorned only by an inch thick, waist length silver chain Saint Just hadn't appropriated for Mare. Her streaked hair looked wonderful, her new red lipstick—especially chosen by Saint Just and surreptitiously slipped into her makeup case—worked very well, and if she'd for pity's sake *smile,* she'd outshine every other woman in the ballroom.

"I hate this," she gritted out between clenched teeth as they walked around the perimeter of the crowded ballroom, looking for an empty table. There had to be more than one thousand people in attendance, and the noise level approached Hearing Damage Imminent levels. "Cocktail parties make no sense. Not enough chairs, not enough tables, definitely never enough food. And one complimentary drink? I paid over five hundred bucks a pop for you guys to come here, and I get one complimentary drink? I mean, why bother? It just looks cheap, you know?"

"Do you know, my dear, how crushingly boring you are when you constantly harp on how much you don't want to be where you so obviously are?"

"Oh, stuff it, Alex," Maggie said, then turned her head as she heard her name called. "Virginia!" she shouted, opening her arms as a short, red-haired, and very definitely increasing woman barreled into her, so that Saint Just had to put out his arms to steady the two of them before they both went crashing to the floor.

He watched, one eyebrow raised, as the two women hugged, then put each other at arms' length, then hugged again. Clearly Maggie liked *somebody* in this WAR group.

"Oh, Maggie, it's been so long! I can't believe you're

actually here. I thought you'd never go to a WAR conference again."

"Yeah, well, I got talked into it," Maggie said, throwing a dagger glance over her shoulder at Saint Just. "It's great to see you again, too, Virginia. Oh, we're going to have fun! Um, don't you think you should be sitting down?"

Virginia put both hands on her bulging belly. "Look ready to pop, don't I? Relax, Maggie, I've got another month. Well, three weeks."

"I can't believe John let you come here," Maggie said as Sterling, ever helpful, produced a chair he'd found somewhere.

"He can't either, considering I've left him with the other four screaming meemies. But I told him, this is my last shot." She reached up and took both of Maggie's hands in hers. "I've got to sell something, Maggie. I've just got to. You'll help me, won't you? I brought my manuscript. Three of them, actually. I've been wanting to ask you for ages, but I figured now's the perfect chance. I mean, who'd turn down a pregnant lady? You'll read them? Give me some ideas?"

"Three . . . you said *three* manuscripts?"

Saint Just bit at the insides of his cheeks as Maggie seemed to sag. He looked at Virginia Neuendorf. If there could be a universal sign for needy, she'd qualify, hands down, with an Honorable Mention for pathetic. She could give Killer lessons.

He wondered, just for a moment: if he had Mare put a pillow beneath her shirt before she mounted the box to give her speeches . . . ? No. Shame on him for even entertaining the idea for a second.

"Maggie, I do believe your manners have gone a-begging, or don't you plan to introduce me to your friend?" he said before Maggie could open her mouth again and say, "Of course I'll help you, Virginia." Maggie was like that. She could fly straight up to the boughs, rant and rave in private, but she could no more turn away from Mrs. Pathetic and Needy than she could tell Sterling that, no, he didn't cut quite the dash he thought he did in his yellow waistcoat.

"Oh, my," Virginia said, releasing her grip on Maggie as she took her first look at Saint Just. "I mean . . . *oh, my.*"

Taking hold of Virginia's plump little hand, he bent over it and kissed her fingertips, then introduced himself as Alexander Blakely, Maggie's cousin.

"Alexander Blakely?" Virginia echoed, blinking furiously. "But Maggie's hero is Alexander Blakely."

"Alexandre Blake, the Viscount Saint Just," he corrected smoothly. "Similar, I agree, but not quite the same. And this, dear lady, is my good friend, Sterling Balder. Ah, struck another chord, I see," he ended as Virginia looked at Sterling, stared at Sterling.

"My deepest pleasure, ma'am, and all of that," Sterling said, bowing from the waist. "You're not going to explode or anything, are you, ma'am?"

"Sterling, behave," Saint Just whispered as Mare, who had taken Sterling's ticket and now held two complimentary drinks, one of them already empty, snickered behind his back.

"Maggie?" Virginia asked, looking up at her friend. "I don't understand."

"That makes two of us," Saint Just heard Maggie mutter, before she answered her friend. "I patterned Saint Just and Sterling after my cousin and his friend. Names, looks, the whole nine yards. I mean, I wrote the first Saint Just on spec, right? Almost as a lark. Who knew it would sell? But I will admit that it must seem a little strange to see both of them in the flesh after reading about them."

"You could say that," Virginia said, still staring up at

Saint Just. "Gosh, he looks even better than you wrote him. First cousins? I hope not. Kissing cousins would be a lot more fun."

"You'd think so, wouldn't you," Maggie said, jabbing Saint Just in the ribs as he chuckled. "Have you seen anybody else from the old days, Virginia? I saw Faith earlier, but that's about it. It's like there's a whole new batch here now."

Virginia accepted the bottle of water Sterling had produced somehow. "Let's see. I've been here since late yesterday, so I met up with a few. Julianna Love—you might remember her as Julie Carp? She's writing single title contemporaries now. Merilee Johns. Regina Hall, of course. Reggie's a real fixture, isn't he?"

"He's something, that's for sure," Maggie said, and Saint Just looked at her, hearing a tone in her voice that made him wonder about this Reggie person, and just what Maggie knew about the man. He'd have to make inquiries.

"I haven't seen Felicity yet. I heard she had a butt lift," Virginia whispered, leaning toward Maggie. "It probably isn't true, because she's always been skinny as a rail, unlike some people I could mention," she ended, rubbing her enormous stomach once more.

"Not a butt lift, Virginia. A boob job. Major damn boob job," Maggie told her, and Saint Just decided to leave the two ladies there to natter about female things, as at last Maggie seemed to be enjoying herself. He took hold of Sterling's arm, then Mare's, and told them it was time to take a stroll.

What he meant, and did not say, was that it was time to check out the competition. All he had to do would be to look for green and pink ribbons on badges, and he'd be able to recognize the other contestants vying against both him and Mary Louise.

The first green ribbon he saw was on a name tag clipped to a waist the size of a young boy's, but the bare chest that rose above it rippled and bulged with muscles that, yes, seemed to have been oiled.

Saint Just stopped dead, and watched as the enormously tall man passed by him (closely followed by five giggling women with cameras), long legs encased in green and white striped tights that ended at the knee, a long scarlet silk scarf tied around his waist, his lower legs and feet bare. The man moved his arms as he walked, but they seemed to have been stuck on the ends of his shoulders, and were so muscular they sort of stood out from them, rather than hung at his sides. His hair was blue-black and flowed down past his shoulders. His eyes were blue, his cheekbones prominent.

"My stars," Sterling said from beside Saint Just. "Strips to advantage, don't he, Saint Just? A fit adversary for a few rounds at Gentleman Jackson's, and all of that."

"That's the competition, Vic," Mare said, still looking at the large man—who was most definitely *strutting*. "Nice tight buns," she added, most unnecessarily in Saint Just's viewpoint.

"He is wearing both ribbons, yes." Saint Just sighed. "A little *obvious,* don't you agree?"

"I will if you're going to go all bummed out on me," Mare said. "But I gotta tell you, Vic, that's some competition. I was looking a little lower, and missed seeing his name on his tag. Did you get it?"

"Giancarlo," Sterling supplied helpfully. "I read about him in our convention packet. Giancarlo means 'God's greatest gift.' "

"Pretty close," Mare said. "Although, with all that oil all over him, I'd be afraid to jump him. I might just slide off."

"You are a lady, Mary Louise. Do please be aware of your mentor's delicate sensibilites and attempt to remember that," Saint Just warned.

"Yeah, yeah, yeah, but you'd better remember that muscles and hair *sell,* Vic, baby. You just look like some slick riverboat gambler."

"I beg your pardon?" Saint Just said, lifting his quizzing glass and sticking it to one blue eye.

"Never mind. I just wouldn't go counting your prize money yet, if I were you."

"Nor you," Saint Just said as, his gaze drifting around the ballroom, his eye was naturally drawn to yet another very tall creature. This one was female, and her flowing mane of ebony hair rivaled that of Giancarlo. She wore a scarlet dress that began in the middle of her breasts and ended in the middle of her thighs, and clung to everything in-between. Her breasts were high and fairly magnificent, and her legs were a marvel, a total marvel. He inclined his head slightly to the right. "Take a look at *your* competition, Mare."

She turned to look in the direction Saint Just indicated. "Holy *shit.* Where do I go to sign up for the hormone shots these people are taking?"

Sterling frowned. "I don't remember her name," he said, looking at Saint Just. "But I know more about Giancarlo, if you want to hear about it."

"I might as well," Saint Just answered, just as a rather nervous looking woman approached, holding out a pen and a small book.

"Would you sign my book?" she asked, a quaver in her voice.

"Sign your . . . ?"

"She wants your autograph, Vic, your John Hancock," Mare told him. "Sign your name."

"Very well," Saint Just said, taking the book and

pen. He hesitated for only a moment, then asked the woman her name.

"Irene," the woman said, breathing heavily. "And then can I have a picture with you?"

"Certainly, my dear Irene," Saint Just said, scribbling a short message, and then signing his own name, Alex Blakely. "Sterling? If you would be so kind?" he then said, gesturing to the camera Irene pulled from her purse.

Irene walked into Saint Just's outstretched arm and he turned her to face the camera. "You smell divine, my dear," he said as Sterling snapped the shot, then kissed the woman's hand and sent her on her way.

"Somebody should go with her," Mare commented. "She's gonna walk straight into a wall, reading your autograph over and over like that. What did you write?"

"Nothing earth shattering," Saint Just said as another woman approached, also carrying a pen and autograph book. "Just a small snippet of Byron. 'My Irene. She walks in beauty, like the night.' Muscles are merely muscles, Mary Louise. It is *charm* that wins the ladies—and their votes. Now, if you'll excuse me? I do believe, fatiguing as it is, that my public calls."

"Where's Alex?" Maggie asked as Sterling wandered toward her, looking just a little bit lost. "And Mare?"

Sterling gave a vague wave of his hand. "Over there . . . somewhere in that crush. Holding court. Oh, I shouldn't say that, really I shouldn't. It's embarrassing. Truly. People gushing, people taking photographs, people asking for kisses. Women, that is. I watched, and the other contestants kiss the ladies full on the mouth. Saint Just merely kisses their hands, then quietly quotes them some drivel or another from the Bard, or Byron."

"Hand kissing? On the palm, I'm sure," Maggie said, remembering the tingle she'd felt all the way up her arm when Saint Just had kissed her palm the day he'd arrived in her life. The way he'd held her hand as he bent over her, the way his clear blue eyes had met hers as he lifted it to his lips. The intimacy she'd felt, still felt every time she remembered that kiss, which was way too often for her own peace of mind. "When was the last time any man kissed a woman's palm? They must be going nuts."

"They're doing a lot of silly giggling and simpering, if that means anything. But if they knew that Saint Just sees them all as just a means to an end? Sometimes, much as it pains me, the man can be cruel. Very cruel."

"He's only being Saint Just, Sterling," Maggie whispered, patting the empty chair beside her. "It's not that he doesn't care about other people." She wrinkled her nose. "Okay, maybe that's part of it. People have to *prove* themselves to him, I suppose, before he can care. Or trust," she ended under her breath.

How much of Alex was her, and how much of her could be seen in Saint Just? Man, talk about another session for Dr. Bob.

Suddenly she felt very guilty. She turned to Virginia, who was monitoring the progress of a hand or a foot or something across her pretty much "alive" stomach, and smiling. "Virginia, I'd like to see those manuscripts. Should we go get them and take them up to my room? I can order you something from room service. A sandwich? Milk?"

Virginia smiled, her full cheeks blossoming. Face it. All of her was blossoming. In her very unflattering and too-tight white dress, she was sort of like the Michelin

Madonna. "My briefcase is right over there, against the wall. But first, why does Sterling call Alex Saint Just?"

"Oh, that." Maggie tried to smile. "It's because of the books. You know. Sort of a private joke. Understand?"

"Not really, no."

"See, Maggie. I told you so," Sterling said, frowning.

"A private joke, Virginia. Like the way I call Faith Boobs. Except Sterling does it as a term of affection. Understand now?"

"Okay, I get it. And I guess we could go upstairs now. I should really put my feet up, I suppose," she said, pointing to her feet.

Maggie swallowed down hard. Someone had buried Virginia's feet and ankles under a layer of puffed and swollen flesh. "Yeah," she said, mentally figuring out how to get Virginia vertical. Another couple of weeks, and she'd need a crane to do the job. "Let's go upstairs. Sterling, do you want to come along? I think we can leave Alex and Mare to their adoring fans."

"No, that's all right," Sterling said, hopping to his feet, as the gentleman he was, and bowing from the waist. "Saint Just promised to take me all the way to the top in one of those glass elevators later, so I'll wait for him. Ladies, my pleasure."

Maggie leaned over and gave the man a kiss on the cheek. "I love you, Sterling," she whispered into his ear. "I just thought I should tell you that."

Sterling turned an immediate red, as if someone had slipped a transparent red screen in front of his face. "I . . . well, I . . . flattered, and all of that, Maggie. Yes . . . yes, indeed. Flattered. But, um, you know I'm not much in the petticoat line."

"Like a sister, Sterling," she assured him. "I love you like a sister."

He visibly relaxed. "Oh . . . well, that's all right then. No problems if it's sisterly. Saint Just understands that. Wouldn't want to find myself on the man's shady side, now would I?"

"He'd get mad? Don't be silly, Sterling. Saint Just could care less who I love."

"He'd like to think so, yes. Well, toddle off now, to have your coze with your old chum," he said, bowing to each woman once again. "Bye-bye."

"Yeah, okay. Bye," Maggie said, giving Sterling a rather weak wave. She'd created Sterling to be the obligatory comic sidekick, the comic foil; a sympathetic contrast with her perfect hero. But, because it made it more interesting to her, she'd also given Sterling occasional bits of startling insight and common sense, that never failed to surprise everyone when the man opened his mouth and, instead of something silly, pearls of wisdom tumbled out.

Still thinking over Sterling's last words, Maggie walked over and grabbed the heavy briefcase, then took Virginia's elbow and led her out of the ballroom. "Are they your usual strict Regencies, Virginia? These manuscripts?"

"Oh, no, no. I gave those up three years ago, when I finally figured out that if they sold all fifteen thousand copies of the books they'd printed, I still wouldn't even earn back my advance. Fifteen thousand copies? Divide that by fifty states, Maggie, and I end up with about three hundred books per *state,* that's all. And that's not counting the District of Columbia. I'm not going to get anywhere like that. So I'm writing Regency historicals now, after twenty little books that might stay in print forever, but that earn me about ten dollars a year in royalties. I've finished three of them, so far. But they aren't selling."

They strolled through the hallways toward the central bank of elevators, taking their time, not that Maggie believed Virginia could break into a run if Tom Cruise was waiting for her in the lobby. "And what's the difference between a strict, genre Regency and a Regency historical, Virginia?"

Virginia stopped, pressed both hands to her aching back. "Length, for one. More love scenes. That's about it. You wrote about a dozen of them, you should know. What? Why are you shaking your head?"

"Here, let's sit down," Maggie said, leading her friend to a small couch pushed against the wall. "Okay, here's the thing. A single title Regency is longer, yes. Sexier, yes. Has more subplots, sometimes. Hopefully, at least. Those are some differences, in both historical and contemporary single titles, as opposed to strictly category books. But they aren't the real difference. That's what I had to figure out, and what you have to figure out."

Virginia rolled her eyes. "Is this the part where you tell me you know the Big Secret, but as a member of some inner sanctum, you're not allowed to tell me?"

Maggie laughed. "No, I'm going to tell you." She thought for a moment, then said, "Okay, pick a scene from one of your manuscripts. Tell it to me."

"All right." Virginia thought for a few moments. "In the one I like best, I've got a great scene in the main saloon, with the ladies having tea."

"Okay, perfect. That's perfect. Now, here's the Big Secret, Virginia. In a strict Regency, you'll gather the ladies and they'll sit on Sheraton sofas, beneath intricate crystal chandeliers, and wear gowns you'll describe in some detail. They'll gather around a teapot made by so-and-so in Something-something-shire, and nibble on marvelous little pastries especially prepared by my lady's imported chef, Gustaf, who her husband the earl picked up on his last trip to the continent. Detail, lots of detail, right? All that painstaking research we've both done for years."

Virginia tipped her head to one side, then nodded. "Right. So?"

"So, Virginia, that's what's in a strict Regency, and God help you if you get any of it wrong, because your fifteen thousand readers will let you know it. But in a single title Regency historical . . . ?"

"The fans don't know the research?"

"Wrong. The fans know, readers always know, but they don't care all that much. Frankly, single title readers don't care about your scene. Because, in your scene, the teapot takes center stage. Teapot, clothes, sofas, chefs. In a Regency historical, in *any* single title book, it's not where they *are,* or what they're *wearing,* or any of that, but what they're *saying* that carries the book. You sketch the background, you give the flavor, but you don't hit them over the head with all that you've learned. Instead, you concentrate much more closely on the people, what they say, what they feel, what they think. Screw the silver teapot, Virginia. Who is Lady Such-and-such screwing, and why, and does the lady across the table know?"

"That's funny, Maggie. But, then, you always were funny."

"That's me, a laugh a minute. Now listen, Virginia. That scene you've written is probably great, but now you have to expand it, *massage* it, paint with a broader brush, on a larger canvas. But remember as you're painting on that larger canvas—you're painting emotion, plot, *people.* Not teapots. Understand?"

Virginia was quiet for a few moments, then sighed. "Let's go back to the cocktail party. You don't want to see my manuscripts. At least not until I redo them. No wonder I keep getting rejected. I'm just writing a longer little Regency, with the bedroom door open. I mean, *lots* of open bedroom door. How do you think I got this way again? Why didn't I ask you sooner? It's so simple, now that you've said it."

"Sorry," Maggie said, helping her friend to her feet. "I'd still like to see what you've got. The one with the tea party scene would be good since you like that one best. If you don't mind me going ape-shit with a red pen? I mean, I could be kind, and just tell you it's good, but what would that help? You just have to promise to not get mad, and to remember that it's only my opinion. I write books, I can't buy them."

"I like you brutally honest, Maggie, always have. You're a breath of fresh air," Virginia said, watching as Maggie retrieved the heavy briefcase yet again. "Let's go keep Sterling company, eat pretzels after I pick all the salt off them. I can bore you both silly with pictures of my hellions and—wow! Would you look at *that!*"

Maggie turned to her right, just in time to see Felicity Boothe Simmons half running, half stumbling down the hallway. She wore only one shoe, her blond hair was mussed, her face unnaturally pale, and her eyes were wide as the proverbial saucers.

Maggie stepped out and grabbed at her as she went by. "Faith? Whoa. What's wrong?"

Felicity looked at Maggie, looked through Maggie for a moment with slightly unfocused eyes, then gave a small cry and grabbed on for dear life. "My . . . in my . . . they were *everywhere!* Running across my feet, trying to climb my—oh, God, Maggie, it was *awful!*"

"Water," Virginia said. "I'll go get her some water. We can't let her in the ballroom, not looking so upset."

"Wine," Felicity whimpered, still clinging to Maggie. "White zinfandel, please. Up."

"Okay, recovering a little here, aren't we?" Maggie said, sort of half stepping, half shuffling the two of them toward the sofa. "Let go, Faith, and sit down. Virginia will be right back with the wine."

"White zinfandel," Felicity said again, sniffling. Then she held her hands in front of her and began shaking them, as if trying to rid herself of some invisible something stuck to her. "Oh, God, oh God, oh God, I want a bath. I want *ten* baths!"

"Okay, you're doing fine, Faith. But how about you try to drop it down another notch, huh? Tell me what happened. Should I be calling the police?"

"The police?" Felicity blinked at her. "Yes, call the police. Call the National Guard. Call the President. I've been violated."

Now Maggie's eyes nearly popped out of her head. "You were assaulted?" she asked quietly. "Faith, answer me. Were you raped?"

"No," she said, sort of sobbed. "Oh, I guess I am overreacting. But it was such a surprise, and so *horrible.*"

Maggie relaxed, but only slightly. She'd known Faith for years. Once she'd been a buddy. Then she'd become Felicity, and turned into an idiot shrew with an ego the size of Oxford's Unabridged. But Maggie had never seen her this upset.

Felicity took a deep breath, smoothed back her hair. "I went upstairs to freshen up before my *People* interview. I wasn't paying much attention. I just wanted to—well, you know. I hate public bathrooms. So I slipped my key card in the door, and just walked into the room. There's this lovely little foyer, and there was still some light coming in the windows, so I was in the living room of the suite before I noticed. Before I *felt* anything." She put her head in her hands, shivered.

"Felt what? Someone was in the suite with you?"

She nodded fiercely. "You could say that. *Lots* of somebodies. There had to be a million of them. Their little noses twitching, their beady little eyes glinting in the light from the window . . . their little claws clinging to my pantyhose. Oh, *bleech!*"

"Faith, what in hell are you talking about?" Maggie asked as Virginia returned with a glass of wine, then sat down beside them.

"Mice, Maggie," Felicity said on a shudder. "Millions of squeaking, running, climbing, twitching *mice.* White ones, gray ones. Everywhere. Do you think they were rabid?"

"What's she talking about?"

"In a minute, Virginia," Maggie said, waving her off. "Faith, are you telling me there were mice in your suite? *Millions* of mice? Or maybe it was only one?"

Felicity glared at her. "Don't you patronize me, Maggie Kelly. All right, it wasn't a million. But it wasn't one, either. There had to be at least two hundred of them. Three hundred. Not that I stayed to count. I just screamed and ran out. My shoe came off and I think . . . I think I *stepped* on one of them. The elevator came right away and I pressed the button that brought me back down here."

She reached across Maggie and took the wine glass from Virginia. "Thank you, Ginny."

"Virginia," the other woman corrected, looking at Maggie, who remembered that Faith had always called Virginia Ginny, even knowing she hated it. Maybe *because* she knew Virginia hated it. Faith was a hard character to figure out, frankly.

"Faith," Maggie asked after a moment—deciding she might also be a hard character to figure out, because she knew darn full well Faith wanted to be called Felicity—"What floor are you on?"

"I don't see where that has anything to—oh, all right. Same floor as you. I asked."

"You asked? Now why would you . . . no never mind. And, Faith, I know you were upset, but think about this a moment, please. Think hard. Did you shut the door of the suite on your way out?"

Felicity's head came up and she sort of scrunched her eyelids together, trying to think. Her eyes and her hands slipped right, then left, then right again, as if mentally re-enacting her steps. Then she looked at Maggie and Virginia, and emitted a slightly hysterical giggle. "Oops."

CHAPTER 6

Maggie's suite had a spacious living room, showcasing enormous white couches that faced each other with a large, free–form coffee table between them, but still with plenty of pacing space for Maggie. She was pacing now. Prowling.

"Someone's after her. Somebody wants her to go wiggy, break down, or just plain leave town. It's obvious," she said, and not for the first time since they'd all come back to the suite. "Somebody most definitely doesn't like her."

"Other than you, my dear?" Saint Just asked. He'd attempted to be good, he really had, but Maggie was beginning to wear on his nerves, which weren't doing all that well at the moment, thank you, due to a rather forward woman in the ballroom who had not just grabbed him and kissed him—she'd *grabbed* him and kissed him.

"I think she's right, Alex," Virginia said from her reclining position on one of the couches. She'd pulled a crochet hook and some yarn out of her briefcase and was constructing something she called Granny Squares that she assured everyone soon would be joined together and become a blanket. The squares were alternating blue and white for, as Virginia told them all, the doctor had declared this one to be a boy, after four girls, and her husband was demanding nothing pink be included in the child's layette.

Sterling sat on the facing couch, throwing constant, worried looks at the woman, as if she might give birth at any moment, and he wanted to be sure to miss it. Poor fellow. Virginia's explanation of something called a sonogram, and stating that the physician had seen "a stem on the apple," had stunned him to the point where he didn't realize he was staring.

Maggie was at it again: "I know I'm right, Virginia. First the cowboy, and now these mice? I wish Faith could have come up here with us, but that Bunny Wilkinson woman just *swooped* down on her and carried her off to her own suite."

"Which is on a completely separate floor from this one," Saint Just reminded her, slanting a look toward the double doors to their suite, and the thick terry bath towels Maggie had rolled up and stuffed under the doors as far as she could. "Do you think mice know how to operate an elevator?"

"Sure they do," Maggie groused from the piano bench, where she had finally (thankfully!) settled. "It's like a circus trick. The biggest one stands on the floor, raises his little arms, and another one jumps on his shoulders. Repeat, repeat, repeat, until the top mouse pushes the button. The top one's a female, and wears a pink tutu and a bow on her head. They're here all week, appearing nightly in elevator five, shows at nine and eleven. There, happy now?"

"Deliriously happy that you've finally landed, at least." Saint Just took out a cheroot and stuck it, unlit, between his teeth. "I was attempting some lighthearted diversion, my dear. You, however, are fast moving past your favored *snarky,* and heading straight to beyond the pale."

Mare, who had changed into very short shorts and one of her brief, midriff-exposing tops, giggled as she sat cross-legged on the floor and raided the mini-bar. So far, she'd downed a Snickers, a Kit Kat, two Sprites, and she was now making definite inroads on something called Macadamia nuts—the last of which had earned her a short, pithy lecture from Maggie entitled "Do You Know What Those Things *Cost?"*

"Can we get back to this, please?" Maggie asked, picking out "Heart and Soul" on the piano keys with one finger until Saint Just walked over and shut the cover, narrowly missing her fingers. "Hey. Just say so if you don't want me playing the piano, all right? I can't smoke with Virginia in here. I've got to do something."

"I hear meditation is rapidly gaining an audience. *Silent* meditation."

"Go to hell, Alex," Maggie said, standing up. "I'll be right back. I can't think about any of this anymore until I've had a cigarette."

Saint Just watched as she picked up her purse and slammed out onto the small balcony, shutting the door behind her. She rummaged in her purse for her cigarettes and lighter, and seconds later had her head thrown back, her eyes closed in ecstasy as she emitted a thin stream of exhaled smoke. Her shoulders relaxed, she smiled, and took another drag. He would gladly wager that her mind was already percolating with insights on the meaning of the cowboy, the mice, and possibly her next Saint Just book plot.

Byron and Shelley and so many others smoked opium. Many more drank, definitely to excess. Maggie called upon the gods of nicotine to wake her imagination, her muse. Plus, the woman liked it. She enjoyed smoking. How Dr. Bob thought he'd ever be able to talk her out of that particular combination of emotional crutch and physical pleasure certainly baffled Saint Just. Still, he knew he should encourage her to turn her back on Dame Nicotine. Of course, other than locking her in a dark, padded room for at least a month (or everyone else in the world except her), he had no idea how.

He watched as Maggie leaned forward over the waist high rail, one leg bent behind her, then quickly stepped on what was left of her cigarette and returned to the living room. "Three white panel trucks just arrived, with huge plastic bugs on their roofs. I wonder if they'll move us off this floor while they exterminate the mice?"

"Exterminate?" Sterling croaked, suddenly all attention. "Do you mean *kill* them? Aren't they just going to catch them up and carry them away to some nice . . . some nice . . . well, to somewhere. A farm, perhaps?"

Maggie and Saint Just exchanged knowing glances, and Maggie quickly said, "Right, Sterling. They're going to set out little bitty cages with cheese in them, catch up the mice, and take them to the country." She looked at Saint Just again. "To a mouse farm."

"Oh, good," Sterling said, relaxing once more. "For a moment there I thought—well, I wouldn't want to be a party to murder."

Maggie and Saint Just exchanged yet another look. Sometimes, Saint Just thought, looking at Maggie was like looking into a mirror inside his own mind. Moments like this always gave him pause.

Still, this time it was Saint Just who spoke. "Sterling? How would *you* be a party to murder? Is there perhaps something you want to tell us?"

Sterling hung his head a moment, then looked to Virginia, perhaps in the notion that a soon to breed woman would understand his emotions about little creatures. "I, um, well. I went to my room earlier, to—well, no matter why." He sighed. "And there he was."

"There who was?" Maggie asked, looking around the floor as she quickly sat down next to Virginia, drawing her legs up onto the cushions.

"I haven't named him yet, Maggie," Sterling said, reaching into the right front pocket of his jacket and pulling out a tiny white mouse with black beady eyes and a twitching pink nose. "He was nibbling on the plate of cheese and fruit Bernie sent up earlier."

He held his face close to the mouse and said, "You like grapes, don't you? I think I'll call you Henry."

Virginia, Saint Just saw, was smiling at Sterling, and possibly at Henry. Maggie was just sitting there, watching the mouse. Mare headed for Sterling and Saint Just's bedroom and returned moments later with three light green grapes that she then held out to Henry.

"That's it," Maggie said, uncurling her legs from the cushions and getting to her feet. "We're outta here. Alex, call down to the front desk and demand another suite. Be arrogant, be snarky, but be *fast.* I'm going to go pack."

"Maggie?" Sterling called after her as she aimed herself toward the doorway to her bedroom. "You're angry?"

She stopped, turned around. "No, Sterling, I'm not angry. You didn't set those mice loose in Faith's room, did you?"

"No," he said, looking surprised that she'd even ask. "Then I can keep him?"

"Where, Sterling? We go home in five days, remember? Napoleon. Wellington. They're *cats,* Sterling. Cat. Mouse. Can we all say *bon appetit?"*

"But . . . but if I had a cage? And we'll be moving into Mrs. Goldblum's apartment shortly. Perhaps she'll keep him for me for now?" he ended, looking up at Saint Just in appeal.

"As long as you only adopt Henry, I suppose I don't mind. But if you find any other mice, Sterling, they are to be turned over to the kind gentlemen from the exterminator, all right? Mice breed like rabbits, remember?"

"Oh. Right," Sterling said, stuffing Henry back into his pocket. "Thank you, Maggie."

"My Rosemarie has gerbils," Virginia said to anybody who might be listening, and many weren't. "I suppose they make nice pets, as long as you aren't the one cleaning out the bottom of the cage."

Saint Just smiled in answer—what could be said to that statement?—and picked up the telephone.

One hour later, they were all settled once more in another suite a floor higher, in time to see Felicity just about to enter her new suite across the hall.

"Faith, hold up a sec, okay? Let's go talk in my suite. I'm worried about you," Maggie called out before Faith could disappear.

"Worried about me? Really?"

At the sound of Maggie's voice, Bunny Wilkinson had appeared in the doorway. "So sorry," she said with a smile, "no autographs now, Miss Simmons has had a trying evening. But there will be plenty of time to have her sign your books at tomorrow afternoon's autographing."

Faith looked at Maggie, sort of waggled her eyebrows, and grinned. Evilly. "Yes, dear. I'd love to autograph a book for you. Perhaps my latest? It just came out last week, so you might not have bought it yet."

"I haven't bought anything of yours in years, Faith.

You're very cost effective for me. You know, read your plot once, and you've read all your books."

"Who *are* you?" Bunny Wilkinson asked, stepping protectively in front of Felicity. "And what are you doing on this floor? I'm going to call Security, have you tossed out of the hotel."

"Hey, there you are. You could have left a trail of bread crumbs, but then the little mee-cees would have followed you up here. Maggie? Felicity?" Bernie stopped dead, looking as if she might be planning a prudent retreat. "Oh, shit, Felicity. What idiot put the two of you within spitting distance?"

"Hi, Bernie, nice to see you, too," Maggie said, not turning around. She was too busy glaring at her nemesis. "I was just about to tell Faith here that it sure looks like somebody wants her to check out. Of the hotel, maybe more than the hotel. But then I realized, who the hell cares?"

She turned her back on Felicity, and a sputtering Bunny, and smiled at Bernie. "Come on in. I've already ordered up your favorite scotch."

"Ordered it?" Felicity said, and sniffed. "I brought some with me, Bernie, just for you. Twelve years old. Please, join *us*. I've had a dreadful day."

Saint Just watched, amused, as Bernie looked to Felicity, to Maggie, and then at her shoes. King Solomon had it easier. "I . . . I guess I really should see how Felicity's holding up, Magster, okay?"

"Sure," Maggie said, the word dropping through the air in the hallway and hitting the floor like a five hundred pound block of ice. "I'll see you later. C'mon, guys."

Saint Just stood back as Sterling, Virginia, and Mare followed after Maggie, then turned and bowed to the three ladies still in the hallway. "Ladies," he said. "To quote a certain Mr. Emerson, 'The only way to have a friend is to *be* one.' Good evening . . . or would you now care to join us, Bernie? Ms. Simmons?"

"How dare you speak to us that way!" Bunny all but shouted, pushing out her bosom like a puffed-up pigeon.

"Madam, you would be both appalled and amazed at what I dare," Saint Just drawled sweetly, staring down his nose at the insufferable woman.

Bunny backed up two steps, partly in newfound respect, partly in admiration of this well set-up gentleman . . . but, then, it was Saint Just who believed that. It was also possible the woman was dumb as a red brick.

"Felicity?" Bernie asked. "What do you say? Maybe it's time to bury the hatchet?"

"In her skull, fine," Felicity muttered, then shrugged. "Okay, okay. Maggie may have a point." Then she giggled. "Tell her to wear a hat, okay, and maybe nobody will notice?"

"I know you've had a rough day, Felicity, but don't push, okay?"

"Push, Bernie? Me?" Felicity asked, pressing both hands against her ample, and quite springy chest. "You haven't begun to see me push. Bunny, how would you like to meet Bernice Toland–James, publisher of Toland Books?" she all but chirped, turning to take the woman's hand in hers. "Bernie," she said, taking her editor's hand with her free one (rather like a minister preparing to say, "We have come here today, to join these two people . . . "), "this is Bunny Wilkinson, chairperson of this lovely, lovely convention. She's told me all about her marvelous saga that she's hoping to have published soon. Set in Ireland, correct, Bunny? Yes, I'm sure it is. Tell Bernie *all* about it."

"Oh, yes, yes," Bunny began, smiling at Bernie. "It's *The Flaming Flower of Shannon.* Set in Shannon, of course. My heroine's name is Shannon, and she was exchanged as an infant for a boy gypsy because her father needed a male heir, and they grow up and one night he sees her, dancing naked in the moonlight, as everyone knows gypsies do, and he takes her by force, several times, actually, then deeply regrets violating this sweet virgin and—"

"Not even for you, Felicity," Bernie said, and turned on her heels. "Alex? Help me crawl over broken glass to apologize to Maggie, okay? Good night, ladies."

Maggie looked up from her unpacking—more closely resembling yanking clothing out of suitcases and flinging it on the bed. "What happened to Faith?"

"I didn't kill her, if that's what you were hoping," Bernie said, sliding her hip onto the end of the king-size bed, careful not to spill her freshly poured glass of neat Scotch. "I'm sorry, sweetheart. She's a selfish, controlling bitch. Why do I keep forgetting that?"

"Probably because visions of your bottom line keep dancing in your head," Maggie said, abandoning the unpacking to sit down next to Bernie. "I shouldn't have reacted that way. Felicity's your author too, and she's had a scare. A couple of them. You probably should be coddling her about now."

"No reason to," Bernie said, sipping the scotch. "She's got that Bunny idiot, and some other woman—Martha Somebody—who showed up a couple of seconds ago, carrying a tray of fruit."

"Martha Kolowsky?" Virginia asked, waddling into

the room, waving off Maggie's offer that she sit down on the bed with them. "Thanks, honey, but I'll be leaving now. I'd never get up again anyway, and I really have to get to bed. But if you said Martha, then it has to be Martha Kolowsky. If Bunny's there, Martha can't be far behind, sucking up, sweeping up. It's pitiful, really."

"Pitiful, Virginia? Why?"

"I don't know," Virginia said, pressing both hands against her back. "Oooh, long, long day. Okay, back to pitiful. Bunny and Martha are both from my Boulder Chapter of WAR, so I'm not just saying this, I *know*. See, Bunny is conference chair, Martha is her assistant. Bunny is chapter president, Martha is her vice-president. Bunny headed up a bunch of Harriet contests over the years, Martha was always her assistant. Bunny organized the literacy signing two years ago, but it was Martha who—well, I could go on, but it's boring, and I have to go to the bathroom again. Except to say—and this is the pitiful part—mousy little Martha does *all* the real work, while Miss Ain't I Grand Bunny takes the bows, the awards, etc. See? Pitiful."

"And I care about all of this how?" Bernie asked, making a face. "All I know is Felicity pulled my chain tonight and I'm really pissed at her, *NYT* or no *NYT*."

"She made the list with this new one?" Maggie asked, grabbing a pile of underwear from the closest suitcase and heading for the dresser.

"Just heard before I came up here. Debuted at number three, trade paper. She's never done trade paper before, so this is really big. But I didn't tell her."

Maggie dropped the underwear in the top drawer and turned to look at Bernie. "You didn't *tell* her?"

"No. She tried to show how powerful she is by siccing that Bunny bitch on me to tell me about her crappy manuscript."

"And she's still alive?" Maggie grinned. "Man, we've been best friends for years, and I'd *never* try that one on you."

"Um, Maggie?" Virginia piped up, raising one hand. "If you ever do, here I am, okay?"

"Who is this anyway?" Bernie asked, hooking a thumb at Virginia—mostly at her stomach.

"Oh, God, I'm sorry. I didn't introduce you. Bernie, this is Virginia, my writer friend from Colorado. Virginia, Bernie, my editor."

"I knew that," Bernie said, smiling at Virginia. "She told me about you at dinner one night a few weeks ago. I don't forget these things, especially when you were the one who talked her into coming to the conference. I've been trying for the last five years, with no success. How did you do it?"

Maggie bit her lip so that she wouldn't say that Virginia had nothing to do with it, that it was Alex who'd forced her into attending, but Virginia just said, "I don't think I did anything, really. But I'm so glad she's here."

"That's it," Bernie said, getting to her feet. "Virginia, send me your manuscript."

"Bernie?" Maggie said, not sure she could have heard correctly.

"No, I'm not kidding. Send it, Virginia. You didn't ask, Maggie didn't ask, so I get to be magnanimous. I can be magnanimous, you know, Maggie, so stop looking like your eyeballs are going to pop out of your head. Besides, I just said no to Felicity and Bunny. Saying yes now is kind of fun. Excuse me, need a refill here," she called out as she brushed past Virginia and back into the living room of the suite.

"Maggie?" Virginia looked petrified. "What do I do now? It's not ready. I can't send it. I mean, it's really not ready. And then this kid is coming, and I'll be up to my eyeballs in formula and two o'clock feedings and little Nancy doesn't start nursery school for another year. To top it all off, your editor scares me spitless. She's so—so New York. And—oh, why does this always happen to *me?"*

Maggie put her arm around her friend. "Don't get all worked up, Virginia. I'm not sure, but I'm betting it isn't good to get yourself all worked up, not in your condition. Look, the offer still stands. Give me the manuscript—the teapot one—and I'll go over it tonight, mark it up, get it back to you in the morning. Skip the events, skip the workshops, just hole up with your laptop here in the suite and rework the thing, okay? I know you have a laptop, because I've been lugging the damn thing in that briefcase, right? Once you're done, we can have it printed out, no problem. You've got five days, Virginia. You've got the characters, you've got the plot, you've got the tea pot. Now you need to massage the book, paint the scenes with that bigger brush, get rid of the boring details. You can do this."

"I can do this. I can. I can do this!" Virginia said, nodding her head. "Oh, wow, I've really gotta go pee."

Saint Just stepped into the hallway behind Maggie the next morning, just in time to see Felicity step out of her suite across the hall. The woman was attractive, in a coldblooded sort of way, but she did not look quite fresh this morning. Not haggard, but definitely not as bright and shiny as a new penny. Clearly the mice, or perhaps Bernie's defection, had taken a toll on her.

"She appears anxious. Don't say anything," he whispered at Maggie's back.

"I wouldn't think of it," Maggie whispered right back at him. "Good morning, Faith. Sleep well?"

"No, I didn't, if you must know," Felicity said, slipping her purse onto one slim shoulder. "Bunny stayed with me for a while, but then she got called down to the desk because some flowers had arrived."

"And they weren't for you? Imagine that," Maggie said, and Saint Just gave her a slight nudge in the back of her waist.

"Actually, they were for me. A dozen dead red roses. But I'm not the only one. There were six other dead bouquets, all for top authors. None of them you, naturally."

"The cast of characters grows, and the plot thickens," Saint Just said quietly, and Maggie stepped back, just a step, to plant the heel of her shoe neatly on his instep.

"You'll pay for that later, my dear," he said smoothly, stepping around her to reintroduce himself to Felicity, who seemed completely immune to his charms. But then, the woman was so self-absorbed, she probably didn't notice much beyond her own mirror. "Have you or any of the other ladies considered departing the conference, madam?" he asked her.

"Leave? What, are you nuts? I'm Keynote. I've waited *years* for this. I'm not going anywhere. This is just a bunch of practical jokes, that's all. Maybe even a publicity stunt. Besides, this is *my* organization. I'm a charter member. I *love* WAR. I couldn't abandon her in her hour of need."

"Oh, give me a break, I just had breakfast," Maggie groused, leaning against the wall.

"That's so like you, Maggie," Felicity said accusingly. "You're so ungrateful. You got your start with WAR, remember?"

"You're right," Maggie agreed. "I did get my start here. I am a charter member. But cover model contests? Costume balls? When did WAR go nuts?"

"WAR went nuts, as you call it, when we figured out that New York is too expensive for most of our members, for a five-day conference. Rose has been most helpful, bringing in corporate sponsors for the competitions, contributing to the literacy campaign, even arranging for different authors to sponsor some of the meals. I'm sponsoring lunch tomorrow, as a matter of fact. Bernie arranged it so that a copy of my new book is at every seat. Rose is a genius, Maggie. Why shouldn't WAR take a page from her book? We're actually going to make a profit from the conference this year. In *New York.*"

"Okay," Maggie said, her voice rather small. "I guess I get the point. But there's something about the purity of our product, the coming together and networking and making friends and *learning* . . ."

Felicity made what was pretty much a rude noise with her mouth, then laughed. "You *hated* that part of it, Maggie. You hid behind me half the time, remember? We spent more hours in the cocktail lounge, or sitting around in our pajamas, just yakking, than we ever did in any workshop. You're just mad because they wouldn't let your Saint Just books in the contest."

Maggie, who had been doing her "sink into herself" trick that never failed to rouse Saint Just's protective instincts, lifted her head and said, "How would you know that? Entries are private."

"Ah-ha, right. Ha . . . um . . ." Felicity said, backing up a step or two. She looked at her watch. "Oh, my, would you look at the time? I really have to—"

"Faith? Spill it. How did you know I was disqualified?"

"One of my friends was contest chair that year?" she offered, lifting her shoulders in a nervous shrug.

"Really?" Maggie had taken a step forward. "And she told you about my entry? Maybe even asked you what she should *do* about my entry?"

Felicity rolled her eyes. "Well, I *was* contest chair for several years. Naturally, when she had a question, she—oh, I really have to run! I promised Rose I'd meet her downstairs, for Giancarlo's publicity photo shoot. He was on my first *USA Today* cover, remember? See ya!"

Saint Just grabbed at Maggie's arm as she started to follow Felicity. "Spilled milk, Maggie, spilled milk," he told her. "And you don't care, remember?"

She broke free of his hold and took a few steps toward the elevators, then turned around, headed back, shoved her hands through her hair. "Why, Alex? Why is she like that? I don't get it. We were *friends.*"

"I thought it would be obvious to you, my dear. Felicity discarded you as being superfluous to her needs when she began her climb. She left you low, with every expectation you'd stay there. Now she can't forgive you for daring to have your own success, which is even greater than hers. Understand?"

Maggie shook her head. "No. I was happy for her when she got that big contract. I sent her flowers, and believe me, I couldn't afford the gesture. I never heard from her again. And then to be the one who disqualified my book?" She looked at him. "Why aren't *you* pitching a fit, Alex. You said you wanted to find out who thought you weren't a romantic hero. Now you know. Quick, the elevator hasn't come yet, I can still see her standing down there. Go boy, sic her!"

"I think not," Saint Just said, taking her arm once more, and lacing it through his as he began slowly walking down the hallway. "Now I know why I was turned aside, and it wasn't because I'm not romantic. It's because you made the wrong friend. How above everything pleasing it is when I can finally trace all the blame back to you, as usual. Now, shall we go to see where the cover model contest is going to take place?"

"I hate you, Alex," Maggie said with some feeling.

"No, you don't," he answered, patting her hand as it lay on his forearm. "And that, my dear, is both the blessing and the bane of our mutual existence."

CHAPTER 7

Maggie asked one of the many be-ribboned women standing at strategic spots along the conference floor if she knew the location where the cover model contest would be held on Saturday night, and was wordlessly pointed in the proper direction while the woman blinked at Saint Just.

"Sterling," Saint Just said as they walked along, "has become a true fount of information about this convention, my dear, reading everything in his packet as if it had been assigned to him for memorization, with the distinct possibility of an examination to follow. The cover model contest, he tells me, consists of several tableaus set up in one of the rooms."

"Tableaus?"

"Hmmm . . . yes. Small, individual stages, each sponsored by some corporation or the other, and each depicting a different scene. Modern day, Victorian, Regency, Scottish highlands, American badlands, etcetera, etcetera. I am, of course, set for the Regency Era tableau, at precisely eight o'clock Saturday evening. Mary Louise, dear thing, will be posing with me, as she is the epitome of the ingenue. When she keeps her mouth firmly sealed, that is."

"You're really going to do this, aren't you?" Maggie asked, shaking her head as they had their badges inspected by another Door Dragon, then walked into yet another large ballroom next door to the one where the cocktail party had been. "Wow," she said, looking around. "Curtains on each stage and everything. And would you look at all those cameras? Somebody did a great job with publicity."

"Perhaps that woman over there?" Saint Just said with a slight inclination of his head, and Maggie quickly spotted Rose, of *Rose Knows Romance.*

It would be difficult not to spot her. She was a tall woman, built along Junoesque lines, with a hatchet face. She was, of course, wearing her trademark rose color, this morning's outfit a pantsuit that had all the style of Sterling's new waistcoat. She wore lizard skin cowboy boots, and a huge rhinestone tiara nestled among the bright blond bangs-and-pageboy wig slapped on top of her heavily made-up face.

She was talking rapidly, as she always did, pointing here, gesturing there, and definitely in charge of the chaos going on all around her.

Beside her stood a much younger woman holding a clipboard, and nodding a lot.

"She's a good egg, actually," Maggie told Saint Just. "She's pretty fair with her reviews, never slams somebody just for the fun of it. But, wow, she must be close to eighty now. I wonder if she's going to retire soon. I know I make fun of what she does, but I'd miss her. All we'd be left with would be Lady Twitters, and who the hell needs that?"

"I would, as you must suppose I might, inquire as to who exactly is Lady Twitters, but I'm prodigiously certain I don't care. Look, there's the Regency tableau. See? I recognize the furniture."

"The bed, you mean," Maggie said in some disgust, then grinned as they walked closer and she saw the small sign placed on a tripod beside the stage: Regency Scene, Sponsored By Brooklyn Blacktop and Paving, Parking Lots a Specialty.

"It's quite a lovely bed," Saint Just said, and Maggie noticed that he'd stepped in front of the sign, to block it from her sight, or his. Poor man. He couldn't really want to do this. But he wanted to be solvent, self-sufficient, just the way she had during those early years spent writing historical romance, when she'd had to live with her parents, depend on them for her room and board.

And, hey, he didn't have it so bad. At least she didn't complain to him about the outrageous price of meat every time he bit into a pork chop at the dinner table, wasn't made to feel guilty and worthless.

So Maggie nodded, agreed. "If memory serves, it's really a Tudor bed. But lovely."

"My Sussex estate is mostly Tudor in design," Saint Just said, earning himself a sharp look from Maggie, who still had trouble believing that, to him, that fictional estate was very real. "But the dressing table is most definitely Shearer, which puts it closer to the Regency."

Maggie, who kept a stack of reference books that would rival a small library, and who used those books often instead of committing any of this sort of information to memory, just shook her head at him. "You're guessing, right?"

"You'd be correct. I'm guessing. But I have learned to sound confident, even when guessing. It's an acquired talent, and one you might wish to cultivate. Ah, look who it is," he said, turning toward the door, as Bunny Wilkinson came rushing in, all aflutter. "Who do you suppose winds up her spring every morning? Shall we toddle over and see what's amiss in Mrs. Wilkinson's world?"

". . . and when he didn't arrive for his publicity shots, I went upstairs . . . and knocked . . . and the door wouldn't open . . . and I . . . I . . . oh, my God."

"Allow me," Saint Just said smoothly, taking the woman's arm and leading her onto the Badlands stage, where he sat her down on what could have been a camp stool. "Now, madam, as you were saying . . . ?"

"It . . . it's under control now," Bunny said, taking deep breaths as she spoke. "I thought I heard something inside, so I asked one of the maids to please open the door . . . and there he was."

"There who was, madam? Do attempt to concentrate your mind."

"Giancarlo," Bunny said, looking up at Saint Just, seeming to take strength from his steady hand, his reassuring voice.

Oh, he was *good* at what he did. Unfortunately, as Maggie knew, what Saint Just did in her books was to snoop around as a sort of amateur sleuth, solving murders, and he had carried the belief with him into her life that he was as good at solving mysteries as he was at dazzling the ladies.

"What about Giancarlo?" Maggie asked as Felicity joined them on the small stage, and then dropped the curtain, hiding the four of them from onlookers, which included quite a few from the local media. "Good move, Faith."

"Don't thank me, Maggie, it's only common sense. This sort of publicity WAR does *not* need. Bunny? What about Giancarlo?"

In fits and starts, and with several interruptions to

wait for Bunny to regain her composure, the story was at last told:

Giancarlo had his publicity shots scheduled for today at ten. At nine-thirty, Bunny sent Martha Kolowsky to his suite, to move him along, because everyone knew that Giancarlo would be late for his own funeral. Martha returned without him. Bunny, with her chairperson's hat firmly on her head, went to the suite. Knocked. Banged. Heard a sound. Possibly a moan. Got the maid. Talked her way into the room . . . and saw Giancarlo lying half on and half off a couch, semi-conscious.

The male model didn't remember much. He was flossing his teeth one more time after succumbing to a poppy seed bagel and some diet cream cheese when there was a knock on his door. He opened it, and then next thing he knew, Bunny was leaning over him, and someone was screeching in a high, Spanish voice that "The Senor is killed-ded, the Senor is killed-ded."

Maggie had to hand it to the woman; Bunny sure knew her way around description. Maggie could practically *see* the scene. Maybe there was a future for the woman in publishing, if she'd just shut up and write the damn book.

"Where is he now, Bunny?" Maggie asked as the story finally ran down.

"In his suite. He's being seen to."

"Doctor's there, huh?" Maggie said, nodding.

"Oh, no. His makeup artist," Bunny said. "He's got a real beaut of a shiner, and wants it covered up for the photo shoot. He'll be downstairs any minute now." She closed her eyes, sighed. "What a trooper. The show must go on."

Maggie peeked out through the curtains and, sure enough, there was Giancarlo, making his way into the ballroom dressed in nothing but low-slung jeans and an unbuttoned white shirt, one dinner plate of a hand raised in the air, his dark locks flowing, his bare feet slapping the floor. The guy looked like a hairy Yul Brynner on steroids, doing *The King and I.*

"He's out there," she said, turning to Saint Just, who had somehow gotten Bunny to tell him the number of Giancarlo's suite, which was also on their same floor. Figured. The suites would be pretty much concentrated on the top floors.

Saint Just took Maggie's arm and helped her down from the portable stage as Rose grabbed Bunny, demanding an explanation. "More mischief, my dear," he said with his usual maddening conviction. "Anyone would think someone wishes to sabotage this charming gathering, scare away the participants, even the contestants in the contests. Do you agree?"

"Oh, yeah," Maggie said, watching as Giancarlo walked by, close enough to smell his cologne, then hopped up on the stage. "But I don't think *he* does. I wonder what happened to him."

"Simple enough to explain," Saint Just said as they walked out of the ballroom, leaving Giancarlo and the rest to the mercies of popping flashbulbs and shouted questions from the media. "Someone filled something—I'd employ a sock, myself, for pure ease of maneuver—with coins, and smacked our Mr. Giancarlo in the face as he opened the door. The man then either reeled backwards, passing out on his couch, or he was placed there, and we both already know that the doors to our suites lock when they close. End of story."

"You're such a royal pain in my—how do you know all that?"

"I am observant, my dear, that's how. Having learned your coinage by necessity, I immediately recognized a faint tracing of President George Washington's profile still indented on Mr. Giancarlo's right cheek bone. I'm surprised the man can stand, if they were all quarters. Still, it broadens our scope, as even a woman, or a very slight man could wield a sock full of quarters to great effect."

"Maggie? Maggie, wait up!"

Felicity caught up with them, just a little breathless, taking a moment to smooth her hair as she smiled at Saint Just. Maggie had thought the woman immune, or too self-absorbed to notice him, as she'd seen him before, at Kirk's memorial service, but maybe she'd just been playing it cool, or she hadn't liked him. Not that the latter would ever occur to Saint Just, who believed himself to be, in a word, irresistible.

"What do you want, Faith? You've already made it clear that you'd like it if I got run down by a FedEx truck."

"I still would, darling, so if you've made plans, don't change them on my account," Felicity purred. "But I can't just daydream for my own pleasure, not with what's going on here. I thought the cowboy was an isolated thing. But then the mice? The dead flowers to so many of us? Maureen Bates Oakley was supposed to give the welcome speech at the continental breakfast this morning, but she got so many hang-up calls last night that she took her phone off the hook around four this morning, and missed her wakeup call—and the breakfast. My books for my luncheon are missing, as well as Patti Berken's books for her luncheon. Martha found the videotape with all the Harriet judges and their bios that we show at the award ceremonies stuck in an ice bucket full of melted ice. It's ruined. Five attendees have already checked out. We've got over sixteen hundred, but still . . . we could soon have a panic."

"How do you know all of this? I haven't heard any of this?"

Felicity rolled her eyes. "And why should you?"

"I'm a charter member," Maggie reminded her, "just like you."

"Oh, really. A charter member. That means you still pay the original low dues, as if that's something to be proud of, when WAR is always so strapped for cash. Quick, Maggie, tell me all the committees you've volunteered for, how many times you've offered to help judge the Harriet. You won one, and accepted it, but did you ever help? Tell me about how active you are in your local chapter. Oh, wait, you quit that, years ago. You *take,* Maggie, you never give back."

Maggie opened her mouth to protest, then shut it. "Okay. When you're right, you're right. So, since I'm such a slug, why are you here now?"

"I don't really know, except that you said something last night that makes me think you might want to help. Someone is out to sabotage this conference, Maggie." Felicity smiled at Saint Just. "Now, I suppose, she'll probably go upstairs and pack, and pretend this has nothing to do with her."

"Bite me, Faith," Maggie said, feeling guilty, because that was pretty much what she had been thinking. It was like—hey, who needs the aggravation? Chapter Ten was still only half done. It wasn't like she didn't have more important things to do.

Saint Just bowed elegantly to Felicity, even as his gaze was riveted to Maggie. "We would be delighted to offer our assistance, Miss Simmons. I already have a few ideas."

"Oh no. Oh, no, no, no. No freaking way, Alex. *You* are not getting involved in this."

"Pay her no nevermind, Miss Simmons. I've found

that Maggie is never quite at her best before noon," Saint Just said, taking Felicity's arm and walking her down the hallway toward the elevators, Felicity telling him to please call her Felicity, and she would call him Alex.

It was to vomit.

"And just where do you two think you're going?" Maggie asked, charging after them.

Alex's smile was dazzling, and maddening. "Why, to the escalators and then to the Lobby Lounge, of course, to discuss the problem. Would you care to join us? There might be some little thing you could contribute."

"I could write you a wart on the end of your nose, you know, Romeo, so don't push," Maggie muttered. But she followed him toward the escalator.

What Sterling had told Saint Just were workshops for the conference attendees had begun in earnest after luncheon, so that the hallways on the conference floor were alternately deserted or crowded with women going here, coming from there. All of them talking, none of them seeming to be talking about anything other than Giancarlo, and the roses, and the mice.

"This isn't good, Saint Just," Sterling said, as they both overheard a woman telling her companion that she'd already rebooked her flight to Fort Worth and was leaving that night before the whole place goes nuts. "Did you hear about Martha Kolowsky? She had to stay up all night last night, poor thing, writing out new place cards for the banquet after somebody walked off with the originals from the boardroom. She looked dead tired this morning, and that's what she told me when I asked her."

"Sabotage," Saint Just said firmly. "If I didn't know Maggie so well, I'd think she was the culprit, disenchanted as she is with WAR. Somebody, Sterling, wants this conference to be a fiasco. Leaving us with two questions, my friend. Who, and why."

"You're going to investigate, aren't you, Saint Just? Does Maggie know?"

"Maggie is aware of my interest, yes. I'd say it was a purely academic interest, but I would not lie to you, Sterling. If this conference is canceled, the cover model contest and the costume ball will likewise disappear. We can't have that, now can we?"

"Probably not, if we want to purchase that very large television machine you've had your eyes on for our new apartment. I still cannot comprehend why Mrs. Goldblum doesn't own a television machine. Or a VCR, or a DVD, and all of that."

"Ours is not to reason why, Sterling," Saint Just said, bowing to a trio of ladies who were giving him the eye. They walked some more, Saint Just bowed some more, and then Sterling stopped dead, grabbed Saint Just's arm.

"Yes, yes, I see," Saint Just said, gently prying Sterling's fingers from his forearm. "It's not a real ape, Sterling. Just as it wasn't a real cowboy yesterday. However, I do believe we'll want to be witnesses to whatever transpires next."

They quickly made their way through a growing crowd of ladies (obviously it was once more between workshops), and arrived on the scene just as a rather large, somewhat shaggy black-faced gorilla holding a photograph tapped on the shoulder of one of the few other gentlemen in the hallway.

"Reggie Hall? Regina Hall?" The words were rather slurred, probably due to the mask, but Saint Just understood them.

"Y-yes?" asked the short, somewhat pudgy man with apple-red cheeks and an embarrassing comb-over that did little to hide his shiny pate. "What—what is it?"

"Which is he, Saint Just? Reggie or Regina? I don't understand."

"Shhh, we'll learn all we need to know soon enough, I would imagine."

"A poem," the gorilla said importantly, unfolding a single sheet of typing paper, then clearing his throat. "Who is Regina? *What* is she, we await the daring decision," he began.

"What? What?"

"Sterling, hush."

The gorilla shot Sterling a look, bright green eyes visible behind the eye holes of the mask, and Sterling prudently stepped behind Saint Just.

"Again," the gorilla said sternly, shaking the paper so that it snapped, obviously a man who wished his hour upon the stage. "From the top: 'Who is Regina? *What* is she, we await the daring decision. Man, or Lady, or both is he . . .' " The gorilla paused a few seconds, obviously waiting for his audience to settle, and finished in a rush. " 'We'll know when the surgeon makes his last incision.' "

Saint Just stepped back and allowed Sterling to catch the swooning Reggie Hall, then jogged off after the departing gorilla.

"Hold on a moment, my good man," Saint Just said, stepping in front of the gorilla and pressing the tip of his ever-present cane against the plastic belly of the beast. "Who hired your services?"

"Go screw yourself," the gorilla said, pushing the cane away, which did not rank near the top of the man's best decisions, for a moment later Saint Just's sword was free from its hiding place, and aimed directly at the space between the head and body of the gorilla costume. "Don't be so hasty to depart, I beg you," Saint

Just drawled, pressing the tip just slightly against the man's throat.

"Look! He's got a sword! Omigod, he's got a sword!"

Major troop movements have probably been managed in a more orderly fashion, but not nearly as quickly as the ladies of WAR got themselves from where they had been to where they suddenly were now, which was formed in a ring around Saint Just and the gorilla.

"Make him take his mask off!"

"Make him tell us who he is!"

"Make him tell us who hired him!"

"Skewer him! Run him through!"

That last one had Saint Just turning his head, just slightly, to try to identify the bloodthirsty voice in the crowd. "No need for bloodshed, ladies," he drawled, withdrawing the sword and replacing it inside the cane before somebody official could come along and have him arrested for carrying a concealed weapon. Maggie had warned him of that, early on, and he was usually much more prudent with his actions. But the gorilla had dared to challenge him.

"Damn straight there isn't," the gorilla said, pulling off his ape head to reveal a youth of about twenty or little more, with sandy hair and a woefully vacant face. "I don't know who hired me. There was a hundred smackers in my mailbox and a note telling me what I had to do. I just do this for the bucks while I'm waiting—"

"You needn't finish," Saint Just interrupted wearily, motioning the young man on his way. "Good luck with your acting career, my man."

"You guys are all nuts," the youth said, punching the button for the elevator, and escaping into the first car that appeared on the floor.

Saint Just was immediately surrounded by the women,

who advanced rather in the fashion of cannibals encircling the poor isolated missionary, hell bent on having him for dinner.

Autograph books sprouted from purses and briefcases. Cameras blinked. Someone kissed him.

A full quarter-hour later, Saint Just at last extricated himself from the crush of admirers, to find Sterling sitting in the lobby lounge with Reggie Hall, a man who was drinking wine with the dedication of a confirmed coward attempting to either build his courage or drown his sorrows—or both.

"Quite the popular fellow, Saint Just," Sterling said, frowning as his friend sat down on the far side of a small table. "I imagine you garnered a few more votes with that feat of derring–do."

"Not enough to compensate for my loss of favor in your eyes, good friend," Saint Just said, crossing one long leg over the other. "Do you wish for me to withdraw from the competition? Taking in mind, of course that large screen television machine."

"I'll go to the bar and fetch some more drinks," Sterling said, getting to his feet. "Oh, this is Reggie Hall. Reggie, this is Alex Blakely—my friend Saint Just."

"Good to meet you, Mr. Hall," Saint Just said, half-rising and leaning across the small table to shake the man's hand, which was rather flaccid, and a tad damp. "So sorry I have nothing to add about the gorilla. He was simply a hired dupe."

"That's all right, Mr. Blakely," Reggie said, taking hold of his wine glass with both hands before subsiding into his chair again. "It was bound to happen, sooner or later. I write under a female name, for females. My wife and I are used to it. I'm just glad it wasn't the other—well, never mind. Everyone else seems to have been made the object of a prank, so it was probably just my turn."

"The other? I don't understand."

"No, I'm sure you don't. We all have our secrets, don't we, Mr. Blakely?"

"Alex, please. And, yes, we all most certainly do. Will you be leaving the conference?"

Reggie downed the remainder of his wine, then nodded. "Sadly, yes. I'm no hero, the way you seem to be, Alex. I fainted, for crying out loud. So I'm going home before someone finds another way to attack me. Whatever's going on here can go on without me."

"Pity," Saint Just said, steepling his fingertips beneath his chin as he looked toward the reception desk, and the line of women standing there, luggage at their feet. "And it would seem you're not alone. Tell me, do you have any idea why any of this is happening?"

Reggie shook his head. "We write romance novels. Happy stories. What harm do we do to anybody?"

"None, I'm sure," Saint Just answered, frowning. "However, it's possible that someone means harm to this group. Pranks like those we've seen usually escalate into more dangerous mischief if allowed to continue. I only wonder what might happen next. Ah, Sterling, there you are," he said, taking his drink from his friend. "By the bye, Sterling, where is our dear Maggie?"

"In the suite, helping Virginia," Sterling said, taking a sip of his diet soda. He now knew he couldn't really gain or lose weight, but he'd come to like the taste, which Maggie told him was as close to insanity as she was sure the sweet Sterling had ever come. "We're not allowed in there until three. She put a sign on the door."

"In that case," Saint Just said, raising his glass of burgundy, "good wine, good company, what else could a man want? To your safe trip home, Reggie," he said, and drank deep, then quickly waved down a server and ordered another round for everyone.

Reggie still hadn't told him everything, but with enough fine wine, enough friendly talk, Saint Just knew he'd have all the answers he wanted. He didn't suspect the mild-mannered Reggie of anything in the least nefarious, but secrets were an anathema to Saint Just unless they were his own. Most especially when Maggie had earlier hinted that she had information about the man that she was not about to share with him.

Silly girl.

CHAPTER 8

Maggie quickly tiptoed to the double doors of the suite as she heard Saint Just's voice, and put her finger to her lips as the door opened. "Shhh, Virginia fell asleep on the couch. Stay here. I'll get my shoes and we'll go down to the lounge. I already wrote her a note telling her we'll save her a seat for Faith's Keynote speech."

"Must I go, too?" Sterling asked as Maggie slipped into her heels and grabbed her purse. "I'd really hoped for a small lie down, besides needing to feed Henry and all of that. Look," he said, holding up a wrinkled napkin, "cheese and lettuce, from lunch."

"Yummy. Okay, Sterling, you stay here with Virginia. Do you know where they're holding the Keynote?"

He nodded. "Same place we had lunch. Virginia and I will be there at five o'clock, sharp."

"If we're quite done arranging everyone to your satisfaction, ma'am?" Saint Just asked, gesturing toward the still opened door. "You cannot smoke in the lounge, my dear."

"Yes I can, I checked. But it doesn't matter. I can't smoke at dinner, I can't smoke in the halls or conference rooms, I can't smoke around Virginia, and she's always around. Seems like as good a time as any to give it up."

"And I thank you very much for the warning, my dear. If you happen to speak to *Left*-tenant Wendell, perhaps you could beg the loan of a bulletproof vest? And perhaps all that padding and hard helmets and sundry other equipment I believe is called Riot Gear? I'd be most appreciative."

"A laugh a minute, that's you, Alex," Maggie said as they entered the elevator, remaining silent on the long ride down to the lobby, because the car was filled with WAR members.

Three of them had their luggage with them.

"We've got to do something, Alex," Maggie said as they took up seats in the lounge, positioning themselves so that they had a view of the restaurant, the bar, and the registration desk.

"I believe we've already agreed to help Felicity, yes. But, first, tell me about Reggie Hall, hmm?"

"What about him?"

"He's leaving, that's what's about him."

"The gorilla spooked him," Maggie said, nodding. "Virginia told me about it. Were you there?"

"As opposed to Virginia, who obviously was not? Yes, I was. Reggie—he bade me call him Reggie, which is infinitely more agreeable than if he'd asked me to address him as Regina—was upset by the gorilla, but seemed much more worried about what *else* could happen to him. A secret revealed, I believe."

Maggie shook her head. "Don't worry about it. It has nothing to do with what's going on here. Reggie's a good egg. Tabby just took him on as a client, so maybe he'll do better with sales and not have to keep—well, maybe he could then drop some of his *extra* writing."

"That was marvelously opaque, my dear. And totally unnecessary, as it turns out. Where on earth do you suppose his mind was when he thought up that horrid name? Lady Twitters. Really, it verges on the pathetic."

Maggie looked at him, eyes wide. "You . . . but how? Did Tabby . . . ?"

"Did Tabby tell me? Oh, how above all things wonderful. Tabby knows. Bernie, I would presume, also knows. You know. But was I told? No." He shook his head. "I'm crushed, Maggie, simply crushed, that you wouldn't trust me with what could have been important information."

"Important? Reggie slams other romance writers for fun and profit. Lady Twitters is his ventriloquist's dummy, his alter–ego, his secret macho man, his private joke. So what? And why would you need to know that?"

"Oh, I don't know. Perhaps because we're having a seeming rash of mischief, and Lady Twitters could possibly be termed a bit of mischief as well."

"Reggie wouldn't have done anything like put mice in Faith's room, or hit Giancarlo with a sock full of quarters. Especially the sock of quarters thing. I mean, come on. Reggie? That's impossible."

"And I agree. So we will dismiss Reggie, who is departing this fair city in a few hours anyway, making the point rather moot."

Maggie narrowed her eyes. "So why did you bring it up?"

"No reason," Saint Just said, smiling.

"Yeah, right, no reason, no reason at all. You just wanted me to know that I can't keep secrets from the great Viscount Saint Just, Super Crimestopper."

"Wrong again, my dear. You see, Reggie—dear man—was already all a-twitter—ha, I've made a joke!"

"Oh, shut up."

"Not quite yet. I suppose I should tell you the whole truth, and not keep baiting you this way, enjoyable as it is. You see, having realized that he'd somehow packed up a few pages of a Lady Twitters review in a manuscript sent to our own dearest Tabby, he was already prepared to have someone challenge him here about the Lady Twitters reviews."

"But you acted as if you didn't know about Tabby." She raised her hands, scrubbing the air as if to erase her words. "Never mind, you were leading me on, being your usual devious self. I remember. And I think I get it all now. He thought Tabby would talk? Oh, that stinks. Just because she's a woman, he thought she'd blab it all over the place?"

Saint Just raised one well-defined eyebrow.

"Oh, all right, all right. But she only told Bernie and me."

"Tabby told you what she knew, yes."

Maggie narrowed her eyelids. "Meaning?"

"Meaning that dearest Reggie is just the pussycat you believe him to be. His wife, however, seems to nurse a grudge against any writer who is more successful than her beloved and obviously, to her, much more talented husband. Ah, now I have surprised you. My day is complete."

"Well bully for you," Maggie said, then leaned forward. "His wife? Not Reggie?"

"Not Reggie. The rub is that his beloved makes more money with her website sniping than he does with his books. But enough of Reggie and his rather vitriolic wife, as they serve no purpose here, other than to prove, yet again, that of the two of us, my dear, I am the superior detective."

"Yeah, yeah. Mama pin a rose on you."

"Thank you, you're most kind, but not with this ensemble. Now, have there been any other pranks? I do believe it has been at least an hour since I've heard a terrified scream."

"Not that I know of, no. Faith agreed to keep me informed before she went off to study her keynote speech. Oh, look, more of your competition."

Saint Just turned his head in time to see a seeming clone of Giancarlo, in height, in muscular structure, although this particular specimen had long blond locks, rather than long ebony locks. He was dressed in an open-collared knit shirt that would probably have to be cut off him if the seams didn't eventually part on their own, and swung his legs from the hip as he walked, with a wide-legged swagger that either meant he was very proud of himself, or he had an embarrassing rash and was trying to "air it out."

"And another one," Maggie said, leaning forward, to see around Saint Just. "Ah, a redhead. Bet he poses for the Highlands covers. Hoot, mon, and all of that, as Sterling might say. I don't know, Alex, maybe if you stuck your thumb in your mouth, and blew, you could pop out some bigger muscles?"

"You enjoy yourself entirely too much at my expense, Maggie." Saint Just watched as the two men approached each other, stopped, sized each other up, tossed back their hair, sniffed, and continued on their way. "Rather like barnyard cocks. I'm surprised they didn't claw at the dirt with their spurs and attack."

"What? And ruin their pretty faces? I don't think so."

"True. Having done my research at long last, I believe the blonde is Damien, by the way, and the redhead goes by the name Lucious. L-u-c-i-o-u-s. I don't know which he has spelled incorrectly, luscious, or Lucius, but then again, I doubt he knows, either. Do you suppose they both speak in grunts? In any event, now that I have seen all of the male competitors, Maggie, I do believe we might begin counting my winnings."

"Yeah, well don't count your—wait a minute. Are you saying there are only four contestants? That's not much of a contest."

"Four males, four females. After all, it did cost one thousand dollars to enter the lists."

Maggie just sat there, her eyes growing round. One thousand dollars? For Alex? For Mare? "I'm going to kill you," she said at last.

"And well you might, if I were to lose, which I won't. And there was no entry fee for the costume contest, so you can rest easy there."

"Gee, that makes it all better—*not.* What happens if this whole thing goes belly-up, tell me that one, Alex. Do I get a refund?"

"I have no idea," he told her, "but, as it is a business expense, I imagine it is totally deductible."

"Yeah, right. I'm going to claim two thousand bucks for entry fees for cover models. I don't think so. You'd better win, bucko."

"I agree that you might believe I have somewhat overextended myself, which is why we must make very sure this conference is not further derailed, hmm?"

"Right. First win, and *then* I'll kill you." She reached for the small bowl of upscale trail mix on the table, picked out a peanut, and popped it into her mouth. "For now, what have we got?"

"Well, modesty aside, I believe I can already count on at least five hundred votes."

A salted cashew bounced off his chest. "Not that, you idiot—what have we got on who's pulling these stupid stunts?"

Saint Just plucked the cashew from his lap and popped

it into his mouth. "Perhaps six hundred, unless all of my devotees are headed back to their happy homes. Ah-ah-ah, don't scowl. What do we have? Precious little, I'm afraid, and with a cast of over one thousand to pick suspects from, if we believe, as I most certainly do, that the prankster is a WAR member in attendance."

"Not just WAR members, Alex. Rose and her gang are here, too, remember?" She frowned. "You know, Rose used to run a pretty successful convention of her own, but most writers can't pay for two large conventions a year, and WAR won out over Rose. Could she be behind this? We have to find out if your fees, if anything at all, is refundable if the events don't come off as advertised. The corporate sponsors, everyone. If they're refundable, we can take Rose off our list. Otherwise, she stands to make a pretty penny if this whole thing goes belly-up before the contests."

"I'll leave that to you," Saint Just said, nodding. "In the meantime, I should probably introduce myself to this Rose creature, talk her round my thumb, gain her confidence. You are many things, my dear, but charming does not quite top the short list."

"Oh yeah, sure, you're going to charm Rose. She's old as dirt, Alex. It would be better if you went after the editor of the e–magazine. Liza Lang, I think her name is. You know, the one we saw with Rose this morning?"

"Good enough. What else can we do? Faith's compiling a list of everyone else who has been pranked, eliminating them as suspects—I don't quite agree with that line of reasoning—and she's asked Martha to keep her up-to-date on everyone who checks out of the hotel and scurries off home."

"Yes, I know," Maggie said. "The list isn't narrowed all that much, but it's all we have. Oh, there's Liza now.

See her? The short brunette with the clipboard, coming out of the restaurant. Do you want to go—yeah, okay, sure, just leave me sitting here, talking to myself," she said to Saint Just's departing back.

Saint Just bowed apologetically before slipping into his seat at the table already occupied by Maggie, Sterling, Virginia, Tabby, and Bernie. Mary Louise had passed on the dinner and speech, preferring to stay in the suite and give herself a pedicure. "Ladies, Sterling, do forgive my tardiness. Liza and I were having a lovely coze."

"For two damn hours, you and Liza were having a lovely coze," Maggie groused, handing him a basket with a single roll left inside the linen napkin. "Eat hearty, because I asked if we could have more and was told a table of six gets six, and that's it. It's pumpernickel. Nobody else likes pumpernickel, so you can have it."

"Thank you my dear," Saint Just said, placing the roll on his plate even as he raised his eyebrows in question to Sterling, who pantomimed smoking a cigarette, then shook his head and shrugged. "Should I ask for butter, or would that be extending my hopes too far?"

"Here," Maggie said, reaching into a small bowl and pulling out a foil wrapped rectangle, then tossing it at him. "The main course is tuna. I hate tuna unless it's chopped up with celery and onions and mixed with mayonnaise. Oh, and some ground allspice. Best tuna fish salad is made with allspice."

"Really. Allspice, you say," Saint Just said, carefully tearing his roll in half. "Since the last time you entered a kitchen to prepare a meal it ended in your being a suspect in a poisoning death, I suppose Mario told you his secret?"

"No," Maggie said, sighing. "My mother makes her tuna fish salad with allspice. I haven't had hers in a year, at least, but then I'd have to go home to have it, and I'm not that crazy. Damn, what do I want with a hunk of stupid tuna? They couldn't have something *normal,* like roast beef and mashed potatoes? I'm seriously thinking of bugging out and finding a hamburger someplace. It isn't like I haven't heard Faith's speech before, you know. Anything she does well the first time, she repeats for ten freaking years."

"Isn't she lovely, Alex? She's been a real ray of sunshine ever since she sat down," Bernie said, reaching for her short tumbler of scotch. "We're thinking seriously about voting her Miss Congeniality." She lifted the glass. "Cheers."

Saint Just consulted his pocket watch. "If I'm correct, it has been approximately six hours since our dear Maggie has last smoked a cigarette. Or hasn't she told you? She's quitting, has banished Dame Nicotine to the trash bin."

"Oh, Christ, not again," Bernie said, raising her empty glass in the air, shouting, "Scotch! Here! Now!"

"Okay, that's it. You all can stay here and be funny, but I'm outta here," Maggie said, dropping her folded napkin onto her plate. "Tabby? How about you?"

The agent looked at Bernie, then at Maggie. "All right. I don't have a dog in this fight, do I? Bernie, Felicity's your author, so you stay here. I'll go find a bucket of ice water and cool Maggie down a little. We'll meet you back in the lounge?"

"Ice water?" Bernie sighed. "Better if she found a hammer, and knocked the girl out for a couple of weeks, until the nicotine's out of her system. I have no idea why she wants to quit doing something that so obviously gives her pleasure. Oh, thank you, Charles," she said to the waiter who'd put a fresh glass of scotch in front of her. The woman already knew every waiter by name, and they knew her by hers: Johnnie Walker Red.

"No," Saint Just said, shaking his head. "I imagine you wouldn't, Bernie. Where is Felicity?"

"Up there," Virginia said, pointing to the raised dais where about twenty women sat flanked on either side of a miked podium. There were also three empty chairs. "Can you believe three board members have bailed? How's that for setting an example? Ah, here's the tuna. I'm famished. Don't tell them Maggie isn't coming back, okay, and we can have hers, too."

Saint Just ate sparingly, having discovered that he, too, did not care for tuna served in one large, fairly greasy slab, and spent most of the next hour looking around the large ballroom, noticing more empty chairs.

He'd also spotted the table, quite near the front of the room, where the three male models and trio of female models were seated with Rose Sherwood and Liza Lang. There was a lot of hair, but very little conversation. He concluded yet again that these models all considered each other in the way of adversaries, and tucked away that small piece of information.

And then Felicity was introduced, and everyone turned their chairs to face the podium.

"Maggie's right, you know," Virginia whispered to Saint Just. "Felicity gives pretty much the same speech every time. Sort of like variations on a theme, I suppose. Poor but humble beginnings, the long struggle to be published, her gratitude to WAR for all the support, her success that has delighted her, yadda, yadda. She does a little comparing of herself to a teacher and inspiration to the unpubs, guiding her faithful students, helping to shape their lives, fulfill their dreams, urging them on to higher expectations, that kind of crap. Then we cry."

"I beg your pardon?" Saint Just said, leaning closer. "You cry?"

"Oh, yeah. We cry. She cries, the people on the dais cry, the people in the audience cry. Because it's so wonderful to be able to move people, encourage them, all that stuff I said before. Watch. When she gets to that part, she sort of sniffs, grabs hold of the microphone, lets her bottom lip tremble. Thanks all of her readers, her fans, the"— she held up her hands and made quote marks in the air—" 'little people' who have made her the success she is today. Barf city. But she's got it down to a science, and there won't be a dry eye in the house."

"In other words," Saint Just said quietly as Martha Kolowsky finished the introduction, "we should probably be rejoicing that Maggie has left the room?"

"Oh yeah, definitely," Virginia said, rolling her eyes. "Okay, we're getting close now. Just watch and listen."

Felicity's voice droned on, catching slightly now and again as she quoted from fan letters she'd received, and Saint Just watched the way her hands moved, the way her eyes seemed to search out each person, individually, as she spoke. She'd be wonderful as one of his sidewalk orators.

And then it happened.

". . . it is you, my good friends, fans, and fellow WAR members, who have inspired me to achieve, and I thank you all so, so much. I am so *honored* to count you all as my friends. I"—she stopped, pressed her fingers to her mouth, not quite suppressing a small sob, then gamely gathered herself and went on—"as I said in the dedication in my newest book, *Miracle Mountain,* that just debuted on the *New York Times* Bestseller List at number three—I owe it all to you, my dear fans. I really, truly—"

Felicity reached out a hand to touch the microphone, blinking back tears.

Her hand touched the metal, and there was a sudden, horrifically loud *screech* blasting from all of the speakers as she stood there, her eyes wide, her body shaking. Her hand still holding the microphone.

And then the screeching stopped, and Felicity dropped to the floor.

"My God, she's been electrocuted!" Bernie shouted, pushing back her chair hard enough to knock it to the floor as she took off at a run toward the dais.

"Saint Just, is she dead?"

"Later, Sterling," Saint Just said as he directed his gaze around the room, noticing that everyone was either still seated in shock or running toward the dais. Except for one person, at the far end of the ballroom, who was quickly walking the other way. "Find Maggie, and stay with her. Don't let her out of your sight. Every writer here is in danger now."

He took off at a quick walk as well, not wanting to call attention to himself as the man he'd seen left through one of the many doors, and he exited into the hallway via another.

The man turned right, and began trotting toward the lighted EXIT sign at the end of the hallway, Saint Just now in hot pursuit.

"You! Halt!" he called out, making no impression on the man who slammed both hands against the exit door and disappeared into the stairwell. And then: "Damn and blast! Unhand me, you dolts."

"No way, buster," said a very large man with exceedingly foul breath as he held onto Saint Just's right arm, his compatriot grasping his left. "Hotel Security.

And just where do you think you're going in such a hurry?"

"Heaven preserve me from idiots," Saint Just said in what he thought to be a perfectly normal, non-threatening tone—which got him slammed into the wall by both burly men, the wind all but knocked out of him. "I'm in pursuit of the miscreant, you fools."

"Miscre-whats?" the second man asked, looking at the first man, who was clearly in charge. As if either man was capable of being in charge of anything more challenging than scratching their own hindquarters.

"Hey, let him go," Virginia ordered, muscling herself (or, "stomaching" herself) into the middle of the fray. "That's Alex Blakely, one of the cover model contestants. He didn't do anything. Call an ambulance."

"Oh, shit lady, you need an ambulance?"

"Not me, the Keynote speaker. She's been electrocuted. He was chasing the guy that did it. That is what you were doing, wasn't it, Alex?"

"Not at all, my dear," Saint Just said, brushing down his jacket sleeves now that the security officers had let him go. He would have dearly enjoyed planting a facer on Idiot Number One, then leveling Idiot Number Two, but he did have his priorities. One of them was keeping his own counsel rather than sharing with either man. "I thought I was, at first, but then I realized my error. Unfortunately, by that time Gog and Magog here appeared out of nowhere and attacked me."

"Gog and who?"

The author of two dozen Regency novels informed Idiot Number Two: "Oh, there are many different theories. However, historically, as far as London goes, they're two huge straw figures that once stood in the guildhall and—"

"Straw, you say?"

"Shut up, Fred," the first security officer said. "I'm sorry, sir. But we got a call to get ourselves up here right away, and you were running, and . . . well, sorry, sir. If you wish to report us, we'll understand."

"No, no, gentlemen, entirely my fault. My apologies and etcetera. But I do believe you're needed inside. Virginia," he said, offering her his arm. "Shall we adjourn to the ballroom as well, to see how Felicity is faring?"

"Huh? I mean, okay. Sure," Virginia answered as Saint Just steered her back into the room. "Sterling is with Bernie, and there was no way I was going to get stuck in that crowd, not with this belly, so I came after you. So you didn't really see anybody?"

"That would depend on who is asking that question, my dear lady. If Gog or Magog were asking the question, no. If you were to ask the question, I might say that I perceived and then followed a gentleman of rather insignificant stature, possessed of mouse brown hair, and wearing a quite unflattering one piece uniform—also brown—with the words Top Star Electric written on the back, and a light bulb sketched beneath the words. As I said . . . if you were to ask."

"And you think—"

"I think nothing at all, at the moment, Virginia. Ah, here are Bernie and Sterling, ready to report, I hope?"

"She's fine," Bernie said, pushing at her remarkable frizz of red hair. "Shaken up, but fine. She got just enough juice to shock her, and then it was turned off or shorted out, or something. But they're taking her to the hospital, to check her over."

"Another prank," Sterling said, seemingly having come to a decision on his own. "And getting more dangerous, just as you said they would, Saint Just."

"Yes, one would think so, Sterling, one would think so. And Maggie?"

"She's back up in the suite with Mare," Sterling said, "partaking of a room service hamburger and french fries. I phoned, and she said they'd meet us shortly, in the lounge."

"Thank you, Sterling," he said, walking slowly toward the disbursing crowd. All six of the models had gone, which did not surprise him. They were all show, and not much more. He saw Rose. He saw the very friendly Liza who had been so amenable this afternoon, although also very business-like, and not overcome by his charms. He saw Bunny Wilkinson and her dogsbody, Martha Kolowsky. Nothing unusual in that.

However, in a group of approximately sixteen hundred people, he seemed to keep seeing the *same* people. What were the odds?

"So she's okay," Maggie said, in much the tone of "and who cares anyway," but she knew these were her friends, and wouldn't call her on it.

They'd commandeered a section of the lounge for themselves, pushing two tables together and pulling up chairs. Things were happening, and they wanted to watch.

Mostly, they watched the exodus, the WAR members lined up to check out, the bellpersons pushing trolleys filled with luggage. Mare gave a painfully rousing cheer when the blond female model trotted to the registration desk, pulling her own bags.

"Dear, dear Mary Louise, how many more times am I to be forced to speak to you of your sad lack of polish? Now, please conserve your energy so that you'll be able to remove that hideous green paint from your toes. You look gangrenous," Saint Just admonished. "In any case, you want to win because you're the best, not because you're the only one left."

"Don't bet on it, Vic. I just want to win. Besides, I've got plenty of *polish.* It's green, and on my toes," Mare said, lifting a Four Roses and Coke. She'd earlier explained that she'd done most of her underage drinking at family parties, where her Uncle Tommy would slip Four Roses into her cola. She'd liked it.

"Alex?" Maggie leaned forward, dropping her elbows on her knees. "Could that be it? Could this all be someone wanting to *win* something?"

"Such as, my dear?" Saint Just countered, steepling his fingers beneath his lips, so that she had to answer him, damn it, or look as if she had no answers. Which she didn't.

"The cover models, eliminating each other? Giancarlo was attacked. It could have knocked him out of the competition," she offered, knowing that had to be wrong.

As Saint Just quickly pointed out: "Felicity is not involved in the cover model or costume competitions. Next theory?"

"I need a cigarette," Maggie groused, sinking deeper into her chair. "I can't believe I said something that stupid."

Tabby tentatively raised her hand. "I've got a theory."

Everyone turned to look at the literary agent. Tabby was wearing a rather full skirt, a baggy silk sweater that dropped below her boy-slim hips, and a colorful scarf that could have covered one of the tables. Her blond hair, that always gave the impression that she was standing in a fairly stiff breeze, had been piled on top of her head, half of it falling to her shoulders. "What?"

she said as everyone looked at her. "I suppose I can't have a theory?"

"Sorry, Tabby," Bernie said. "Shame on us. If it isn't a nifty trick to rid our lives of bathtub scum, or a new way to piggyback bonuses on a contract, we really don't expect to hear from you."

"Very funny, Bernie," Tabby said, arranging her skirts, that reached down to end at her crossed ankles. "I think it's Rose."

"Rose? How? Why?"

"Well, Bernie, she once had the best-attended conference, remember? Of course, she invited booksellers and fans, as well as published and wannabe writers, but she couldn't keep it up when most of the published authors stopped attending, which meant the editors stopped attending, and the agents stopped attending. WAR pretty much took over as the premier event. But if her part of the conference runs smoothly, and WAR's part is all shot to heck, then maybe she profits?"

"Shot to *heck,* Tabby? God, I needed that," Maggie said, laughing.

"A good theory, Tabby," Saint Just said. "However, once again we're forgetting something. Giancarlo. He would be part of Rose's portion of the extravaganza here this week, correct? A wise bird never soils her own nest."

"We're just going in circles here," Maggie said, pulling out her nicotine inhaler. "Again with the pained looks?" she asked as Tabby *tsk-tsked.* "I'll have you know this is an accepted way to quit smoking."

"If you'd use it correctly, sure," Tabby said. "I worry about you so much."

"You worry about your percentage, you mean," Bernie said, earning herself a pained glare from the agent. "If not, you'd be happy to leave her to her vice, as long as it makes her happy. Everybody needs a vice. Booze, food, nose candy, nicotine, the occasional shoe fetish. It's the American way."

"Next subject?" Maggie said, clamping her teeth around the plastic holder. "Oh, look, there's Faith, coming around from the elevators. Who's that with her?"

"Ms. Wilkinson, for one, and Mrs. Kolowsky for two," Saint Just said, turning in his chair. "As for the gentleman? Sterling, correct me if I'm wrong, but have you suddenly caught a whiff of *copper?"*

CHAPTER 9

Saint Just excused himself and cut across the lobby lounge, making a dead set at Felicity and group.

"My dear, dear, woman," he said, taking Felicity's hand and bowing over it. "I am so relieved to hear you came through your ordeal with no lasting harm."

"Yeah, right, me too, what he said," Maggie mumbled, coming up behind him.

"Why, thank you Alex . . . Maggie," Felicity said, leaning heavily on the arm of a rather well set-up man, if his suit wasn't quite so shiny, if his thick-soled shoes didn't scream "copper" so very loudly. "Do you know everybody?"

"Although I pride myself on having a rather wide acquaintance, no, not everyone," Saint Just said, smiling at Bunny. "Ms. Wilkinson, your devoted servant." He bowed again, then continued: "And I do believe you would be Ms. Martha Kolowsky? What a lovely suit, Ms. Kolowsky, my compliments to your modiste."

He turned to the tall cop and extended his right hand. "I'm Alex Blakely, by the way. And you'd be—?"

The detective hesitated a moment, then stuck out his own hand. Manicured nails. Interesting phenomenon on a copper. Saint Just believed Lieutenant Wendell clipped his with a hedge trimmer.

"Sergeant Willard Decker, Mr. Blakely," the cop said, gripping Saint Just's hand with enough force to imply that he was either very strong, or very stupid. Saint Just squeezed back, and Sergeant Decker pulled his hand free, flexed his fingers a time or two as he dropped his arm to his side.

Childish, Saint Just knew, but there were times when one had to play games in the gutter in order to see just what might be going on down there.

"You're here because of Ms. Simmons's near tragic jolt this afternoon, Sergeant?" he asked, ignoring Maggie's not so gentle nudge in his back.

"Yeah," Decker said, nodding his blond head. Goodness, the man really was well set up. Now to see if handsome is as handsome does.

Saint Just waited for Decker to enlarge his answer, but the man just stood there, still nodding, as if once he'd begun, he'd placed all his hopes in gravity and inertia or whatever to eventually stop him.

"I'm Maggie Kelly," Maggie said, stepping around Saint Just. "Hi, Martha," she continued, waving at Bunny's loyal assistant. "I haven't seen you in a long time. Alex is right, that's a lovely suit."

"Maggie, hi. About five years, I think. Since WAR met in Denver?" Martha responded, smiling, then quickly made her expression blank as Bunny coughed, threw her a quelling look.

"If you'll excuse us," Bunny said, lifting her chin as she glared first at Maggie, then at Saint Just. "We were just about to get ourselves a cool drink, then take the sergeant downstairs, to see the ballroom."

"Ah, yes, the scene of the crime. Very astute of you, Miss Wilkinson."

Decker seemed to rouse from his stupor. "Crime? Nobody said crime here, Blakely. Coulda been an accident. It's . . . it's an *alleged* crime."

"Of course," Saint Just agreed silkily, waiting for Maggie to erupt. If there was one thing he knew, Maggie was sure to react to the man's ignorant statement. *Three . . . two . . .*

"Alleged?" Maggie repeated. "Like the *alleged* singing telegram threats, the *alleged* mice, the *alleged* assault on Giancarlo, the *alleged* everything else that's been going on around here? Because we've got some *alleged* mayhem going on around here, Sergeant."

"I wasn't told. What else has been going on here?" Bunny asked, glaring at Maggie. It was clear to Saint Just that the woman didn't want to discuss anything but the incident at the podium.

"I don't know everything, but I heard something happened to some of Martha's stuff . . ."

"Oh, that. Simple forgetfulness, I'm sure. I'm betting that when Martha goes home she'll see that she simply forgot to pack everything. Don't go saying things that could bring bad publicity to WAR, Maggie."

All right, Saint Just decided. The woman's simply attempting to protect WAR's image. She could have done a whacking lot better by presenting a motion at the annual meeting simply to change the group's name.

Undaunted, as he knew she would be, Maggie pressed on: "And the missing books? Faith's missing books?"

"Inefficiency," Bunny declared, glaring at Maggie some more.

Saint Just wasn't sure, but he thought he just might be sniffing the odor of smoke coming out of Maggie's delicate shell ears.

"The cowboy? The gorilla?"

Decker scatched his head. "Cowboy? Gorilla?"

Bunny rolled her eyes. "Pranks, just silly pranks, Sergeant. They were all just silly practical jokes. And the shock Felicity took had to be an accident. The only reason you're here at all, Sergeant, is because the hotel wants an investigation."

"Well, let's all hear it for the hotel," Maggie said. "They probably think you're going to sue, Faith."

"Sue? Why would I do that?" Felicity gave a tinkling, yet condescending laugh. "Honey, WAR's image to one side, I can't *pay* for publicity like this."

"Okay, that's it. Obviously none of you are taking this seriously," Maggie said in disgust, turning to Saint Just. "I'm going upstairs to call Steve."

"Oh, now that's depressing," Saint Just said, striking a pose. "Sergeant? Perhaps you are acquainted with Miss Kelly's friend? *Left*-tenant Steve Wendell?"

"Left? Oh, oh, you mean Lieutenant. Nope. Don't know him. He Manhattan South?"

"Manhattan North," Maggie supplied, tight-lipped.

"Oh, then he won't come here. We're Manhattan South. See, you've got your Manhattan North, and then you've got your Manhattan South. In Manhattan North—"

"Yes, Sergeant," Saint Just broke in, "I do believe that even our feeble, uneducated minds can follow along that far, be it North or South. And what a pity, Maggie. The *Left*-tenant would appear to be out of bounds were he to come here. And I so long to see his cheerful, smiling face again."

"Put a sock in it, Alex," Maggie said, taking his arm. "Excuse us, we'll be going now. Faith, I'm glad you're all right."

"Thank you, Maggie," Felicity said. "Oh, before you go? I thought you might want to know that there will be a news conference tomorrow morning. Well, not quite a news conference. The local affiliate had already planned a short piece on the conference, probably the media's typical and quite juvenile and unimaginative purple prose take on romance writing. Bodice ripping, titter, titter, all the usual idiocy. But now the spot is being enlarged to include the alleged attempt on my life."

"Attempt on your life? Which is it, Faith? Will you guys make up your minds? If Bunny here is right, it was just an accident. You got a shock."

"Yes," Felicity preened, "and now I might get the *Today* show. As I said, you can't buy this kind of publicity. Bernie will be *so* pleased. Toodles," she ended, waving her fingers at Maggie before taking Decker's arm once more and heading for the bar.

"I'm going to kill her myself. That will get her publicity," Maggie said, glaring at Felicity's departing back.

"The woman does appear to have more hair than wit when it comes to her self preservation, I'll agree, but she's also as shrewd as she can hold together as it pertains to her career. You aren't really bringing the *Lefttenant* into this, are you, Maggie?"

"Yes—no. I don't know." She looked up at him. "Do you think I should?"

"My dearest girl, I wouldn't ask to you to summon the estimable Steve Wendell if my cravat caught fire and the man possessed the last remaining drops of water in all of Manhattan, both North and South."

"Oh yeah? Oh yeah? Well, I'm calling him. I'm going upstairs right now, and I'm calling him."

Good, Saint Just thought in satisfaction, *because it could quite possibly drop me into the very depths of despair to be forced to personally apply to the fellow for assistance.*

"I'll be up shortly, Maggie," he called after her as she stomped off. "Remember, the parade of costumes is scheduled for nine-thirty this evening."

She waved back at him as she continued on, a wave that translated could quite possibly mean in Maggie's sometimes mildly crude vernacular: "Yeah, right, big whoop. Like I'm supposed to care?"

How he adored the dear girl. . . .

"Knock, knock, and all of that," Sterling said, scratching at the door to Maggie's bedroom. "Maggie? Are you all right?"

Maggie ran into the bathroom, flushed the remainder of her cigarette, and began waving her hands through the air, to dissipate the smoke as she walked over to the bed and sat down. She shot back up, grabbed her cologne from the dresser, and sprayed two quick mists into the air, returned to the bed once again. "Sure, I'm fine. Come on in, Sterling."

"Socks has arrived, about fifteen minutes ago, actually," he said, walking into the room, his usually placid expression looking puzzled. "I must say, he's looking slap up to the echo and all of that. He's brought . . . he's brought . . . he has a friend with him."

Maggie frowned. "So?"

"Well . . . his name is Jay. Except, for this evening, his name is Jayne. I finally understood about Reggie and Regina Hall, but I don't understand this. Not even a little bit."

Maggie shifted her eyes from side-to-side, pressing her lips together for a moment as she tried not to grin. "Go on. Here, come sit down. You look nervous."

Sterling chose the far corner of the bed, away from Maggie, and sat himself down, clumsily splitting the tails of his swallowtail coat—the one Maggie had described in one of her books, and the same one Sterling had worn the first day he and Saint Just had "popped" into her apartment, into her life.

"You look very nice, Sterling," she said, trying to make him comfortable. "And I don't care what Alex says, I like that yellow waistcoat."

"Thank you, Maggie. I'm quite partial to it myself. But about Jay . . . Jayne . . ."

"What's the matter, Sterling?"

"I'm not sure. Saint Just wanted another costume for Mare, just for tonight, and he phoned Socks, and told Socks there was no problem fitting him and any friend he might choose into the parade of costumes."

"You need a ticket to get into the ballroom, Sterling. He can't just invite anybody. Not that I mind, but the Gestapo checkers at the door might."

"I know. But Saint Just said that he'd simply call them props for his own costume, something like that. You know Saint Just, Maggie. He'll find a way."

"Uh-huh," Maggie said, trying not to push too hard, because clearly Sterling had much more to say.

"Saint Just is wearing the rigout he traveled in, as I am."

"O-kay. A good suit of clothes, if I must say so myself. And I will, because I made them up, didn't I?"

"Yes, you did, and a fine job. Um, yes, fine job, and all of that. Saturday night Saint Just is wearing something Socks procured for him from a cast member of some Broadway production. Not at all what I'd supposed. I'd supposed satin, and knee breeches. But he's not going that route."

Maggie wanted another cigarette. She'd only smoked half of the last one, and it had been the only one since early in the day. Early in a very *long* day. She got up, walked over to the dresser, sort of rubbed her hands over the side of her purse.

"Go ahead, Maggie," Sterling said. "I won't cry rope on you."

She didn't wait for Sterling to offer twice. She reached into her purse, pulled out cigarettes and mini-Bic, and lit up. "I'm going to quit, Sterling. I really am. But I sure did pick a bad day to give up glue sniffing, you know?"

Sterling shook his head, looking perplexed. "I beg your pardon? Glue sniffing?"

"Never mind," Maggie said, blowing out a stream of smoke. "It's part of a running gag from an old movie. *Airplane.* But this really isn't a good time to quit. I'll try again when we get back home, all right?"

"A pity you can't be Saint Just or me, Maggie. We don't have bad habits unless you've given them to us. We don't get fat unless you write us fat. Why, we don't even grow older."

Maggie turned her back on the man. She knew that. Oh, did she know that.

It had taken a long, long time for her to fully believe that Alex and Sterling weren't impostors—that they actually were her characters, that in her already fairly wacky, mixed-up world, having two of her fictional characters come to life sounded almost sane.

Sterling had been everything she'd visualized when she created him.

Alex had also been everything she'd visualized . . . and so very much more. He maddened her; he intrigued her.

But he wouldn't age. He'd stay here—if he stayed here, if the fates let him stay here—and he wouldn't change. He wouldn't age . . . not unless she wrote him aging, which she couldn't do. Yes, he'd get a little older as the series went along, but who wants to read a series about a geriatric Regency type chasing heavily corseted little old ladies around Mayfair? So he would get older over the years, but not by much.

While she . . . no, now wasn't the time to think about that. It would *never* be time to think about that. It was enough to know that she and Alex could never . . . could never . . . *be.* It was, she thought, like, okay, so Darren got around the no-aging problem with Samantha in *Betwitched,* but she wasn't Darren. Hell, these days, Darren and Samantha were a slot machine in Atlantic City, for crying out loud.

Digressing . . . digressing . . . she had to stop digressing.

She pinned a smile on her face and looked at Sterling again. "So, tell me about Socks and Jay. Jayne."

Sterling nodded, biting his lip. "Socks explained it all to me. He's wearing a pirate costume, I believe he called it. Rather attractive rigout. Very tight striped knee pants, a flowing white shirt opened to his waist—a very nice silk—and this bright red kerchief tied about his head. Oh, and a large earring. He looks . . . quite fine. Fine as ninepence, you could say."

"He would," Maggie agreed. Socks was, in "real life," Argyle Jackson, the doorman of Maggie's building, and an aspiring Broadway performer. Half of Manhattan, figuring conservatively, was an aspiring Broadway performer.

But Socks actually did have talent, and potential. Saint Just had become his agent—still a thought that blew Maggie's mind—and he was making some small steps, picking up a few minor roles in productions so far off Broadway that the last one went belly up its opening night in Secaucus, New Jersey.

"And Jay?"

"Jayne," Sterling said, audibly blowing out his breath.

"Tonight at least, definitely Jayne. She's playing his aristocratic English captive."

Maggie bit the insides of her cheeks. Okay, so her first thought when Sterling told her about Socks's friend was right-on, the guy liked to go drag. Good for him. Her. Whatever.

"How does she look?"

"Well, and that's the thing, Maggie. He looks . . . he looks beautiful. Rather tall for a woman, but beautiful. Blond hair, blue eyes, and he—I mean, *she* is quite graceful. Certainly has a way with a fan, I'll say that."

"Well, good, sounds like fun. Then the night won't be a total loss," Maggie said, stubbing out her cigarette in the ashtray she'd taken from the lounge. "Is Alex ready yet?"

"Not quite, no. He's still working on his neck cloth, with Jayne attending him. They've already gone through four of them, but you know Saint Just. It must be perfect."

"Where'd he get four neck cloths?"

"I have no idea, Maggie," Sterling said, preceding her to the door, then opening it for her. "He's very resourceful."

"He is that," Maggie said, heading into the living room of the suite. "Whoa! Mare, you look *great.*"

"Socks called me Princess Summer-fall-winter-spring. Kind of cute, huh? He says it's from some old television show called *Howdy Doody.* You know gay guys, Maggie. They know everything. He and Jay were running lines—that's what they called it; running lines—from *Gypsy* a while ago. Cracked me up, both of them, and Jay's a doll. Think I could convert him?"

"You're asking me? How the hell would I know?"

Mary Louise rolled her eyes. "I don't know. I just figure you're trying the same thing with Vic."

Maggie stepped back two paces. "You think . . . you think Alex is gay?"

The girl rolled her eyes. "Hey, like he's Bruce Willis? I don't *think* so."

Poor Alex. She'd made him a true Regency gentleman, and such a sharp contrast to the "Hey, whassup babe?" generation.

Maggie threw up her hands. "Think what you want to think, Mare."

"Oh, don't worry, I will. Vic's in the other room, doing his toilet. Honest to God, that's what he called it. Tell me that's not gay."

"Toilette, Mare," Maggie corrected, trying not to smile. Okay, so maybe she could understand how the girl could be confused. "He's English. They use different words for things. He just meant he's getting dressed. Speaking of which, again, you really look great."

Mary Louise held out her hands and spun in a tight circle, so that the fringe at the hem of her low-slung, short, dyed white and nicely beaded deerskin skirt stood out, then settled against her knees once more. The rest of her Indian Princess costume was composed of a short white deerskin vest, also heavily beaded, and tied across her bare breasts with thin strips that damn well have better been sewn on well, or the kid was going to parade a lot more than her skimpy costume in the ballroom.

She wore dyed white deerskin moccasins, a black wig parted in the middle and ending in long, thick braids, a beaded headband with a single feather sticking up at the back, a knife in a small waist holster, and several bangle bracelets on both arms. She'd put a shiny, dangly thing in her navel.

"What tribe?" Maggie asked.

"The Ohmamas, Socks told me. He said, when people see me in this thing, they're going to say, 'Oh, Mama!' Cute, huh?"

"Cute," Maggie agreed. "Old joke, but cute. Virginia, how's it going?" she then asked her friend, who was sitting at the table, pecking away at her laptop.

"If I could read your handwriting it would go a lot faster. What's P-O-V?"

"Point of view. Are you at the part where you have point of view from the coach driver?"

Virginia nodded. "Yeah. What's wrong with that?"

"What's wrong with it, Virginia, is that the coach driver appears once in the entire book. You don't give him point of view, okay?"

"Got ya," Virginia said, then nodded toward the closed door to Saint Just's bedroom. "You're not going to believe what's in there. I wish I'd brought my camera."

"Are you sure you don't want to take a break and go to the ballroom with us?"

"No way. I'm almost done here and there's no way I'm doing anything else but finishing it so I can give it to Bernie while she still remembers who the heck I am."

"All right, but put your feet up for a while, and don't forget to eat."

"Honey, I never forget to eat."

Maggie grinned. "Okay, I'm going to go check on Alex now. We should be leaving pretty soon or we'll be waiting an hour for an elevator."

"Hey, wait a minute. Where's your costume, Maggie?" Mary Louise called after her.

Maggie looked down at her simple navy sheath, navy heels, and her same favored long silver chain. "This is my costume. I'm stepping totally out of character and going as a sane person." She knocked on the door to Sterling and Alex's room, and walked in, with Sterling tagging along behind her. "Hey, let's get—what the hell?"

Socks ran over to her, a finger pressed to his lips. "Shh, Maggie. We're doing the neck cloth. It's the last one, so we have to get it right."

Maggie stood there, goggling at first, and then slowly taking in the scene in front of her.

It was a scene from one of her novels; a man's dressing room, his attendants and friends gathered round to watch the creation of a *ton* gentleman's evening *toilette.*

Except that Saint Just's friend and his attendant were a black pirate and a drag queen. But those were little things . . . incidentals in Maggie's Mad, Mad World.

Socks—looking good, as usual—returned to stand in front of the window wall, his hands folded as if in prayer and pressed to his lips, watching the proceedings.

Saint Just sat on a wooden chair brought in from the living room, his shiny Hessians firmly on the floor, his pristine white shirt covered by his waistcoat, the points of his collar upturned, to tickle at the sides of his well-defined chin. His spine was poker straight, his hands resting on his buckskin clad knees, his eyes closed, his chin tipped up at a nearly impossible angle. Waiting.

"The eel's eyebrows, ain't he?" Sterling whispered in some awe.

Behind him stood Jay. Jayne. She was definitely tall, and definitely gorgeous. If Maggie could do her eyes half as well, maybe she'd wear makeup more often. Jayne's gown was sunshine yellow, with a really nifty drape below the waist that tied back into a bustle. She had on black lace mitts that ran halfway up her arms, black feathers in her hair, fake diamonds at her throat, and Maggie would lay odds she'd get hit on by any man in the ballroom tonight. She . . . he . . . looked that good.

Jayne was holding a length of crisply starched white cotton in both hands as she approached Saint Just from the back. She stopped, sighed deeply, and then reverently began wrapping the cloth around the man's neck, then tied the material in the front, so that the ends laid neatly on Alex's chest. "There. Try that," Jayne said, stepping back, her arms still outstretched, as if guarding the neck cloth.

Saint Just dipped his chin slightly, just touching the wound cloth. Lifted his chin, dipped it again, a little more. And a third time, slightly more than that.

"Perfect!" Socks exclaimed, pushing away from the wall. "Just perfect. Three neat creases, just the way you wanted. And your shirt points? I mean, they're bitchin'."

Saint Just, his head finally level, peered past Socks, and into the mirror. "You're right, Socks. Bitching indeed. Jayne, my compliments."

"I didn't do anything. You've got great chin action, Alex."

"Oh, for crying out loud," Maggie said as Saint Just stood up and Jayne helped him shrug into his well fitted jacket of blue superfine. A moment more for "his lordship" to drape the black riband holding his quizzing glass over his neck, and he turned to her, striking a pose.

"Ah, yes, you may stare, my dear. I have no doubt dazzled you," he said, gifting her with an elegant leg—a very formal bow that included arm flourishes and the pointing of one well-muscled leg.

He turned to the mirror once more. "Such unmitigated joy, to be dressed as a real gentleman again. It is worth the insult to my sensibilities to be part of a silly contest bound to be sadly lacking in moral tone, just to be in my buckskins again. Gentlemen? My thanks, and if you'd excuse us for a moment?"

"Hey, sure," Socks said, motioning for Jay to follow

him. "We'll be waiting in the living room. Sterling wants to run some lyrics by me. You know, his rap?"

"Ah, Sterling's rap. And aren't you the fortunate one, Socks. We'll join you shortly." He waited until they'd closed the door behind him before saying, "They were both most enthusiastic, Maggie, but I would be remiss if I didn't take this opportunity to once again beseech you to paint Clarence with a clearer brush so that the dear man might soon join us. Sterling doesn't quite have his way with boot black. And this cravat? A sad, shabby affair, but it's the best we could do."

"Would you stop talking about Clarence? You don't need a valet in Manhattan."

"A gentleman, Maggie, needs a valet anywhere. Oh, and I know you are still fretting about the ending of the story in progress, so I've been thinking. I'd truly enjoy another carriage pursuit. Only a shame I couldn't use the bull horn, because—"

"Would you just *shut up!*" Maggie went over to the door, opened it, peeked out, just to make sure nobody was within hearing distance. "Sometimes you make me *so* nuts."

"Still haven't had a cigarette, I imagine. Or mayhap you have succumbed, and that has put you even more out of sorts? Perhaps we should all be taking turns puffing on that filthy plastic contraption, just to keep ourselves from running in panic for the closest exit. Now, back to the business at hand. Have you been in contact with the esteemed *Left*-tenant?"

"He wasn't answering his page," Maggie admitted, dropping into the chair Saint Just had so recently vacated. "He's probably still all tied up with that stupid stake-out. But I left a message."

"Oh, lucky, lucky us. I'm sure he'll be here tomorrow, anxious to come to heel. Possibly even panting."

"Knock it off, Alex. I like Steve."

"Apparently there's no accounting for tastes," Saint Just said, stepping past her to peer in the mirror, pushing at his already perfectly combed black hair. "Oh, all right," he said then, turning to hold out his hands to her, so that he could help her to her feet, "I also like the man. I'm not fond of him, but I do appreciate his finer points. It will be interesting to hear his opinion on what has been transpiring here for the past two days."

"He'll probably just tell me to go home," Maggie said, trying to step back, because she was awfully close to Alex. Close enough to smell his cologne. Close enough to see the sparkle in his Paul Newman blue eyes. Close enough to want to reach out and run a finger down his cleanly shaven young Clint Eastwood cheek. Close enough to really zero in on those Val Kilmer lips. *I'm your huckleberry.*

But she couldn't move, couldn't take that step back to sanity. The damn chair was in her way.

"And would you?" Saint Just asked, stepping even closer. "Go home, that is."

Maggie looked down, avoiding his eyes, just in time to see him slip his hands onto her waist. "No. I'm going to stick it out. Faith's an idiot, but she could be in real danger. Let's . . . let's go. We're going to be late."

He bent his head closer to hers. "I hope to garner more votes this evening. A kiss for luck, Maggie, hmmm?" he said, his Sean Connery *James Bond* tone low, intimate. Just the way she always wrote it.

"I . . . I don't think that's a good idea," she said quietly, still looking down. Oh great. She was playing the shy virgin. The stupid, tongue-tied shy virgin, which was even worse. Missish, wimpy, nerdy. Pathetic. And spouting trite dialogue, which might be the worst of all.

She lifted her head, stared straight into his eyes. "Okay, why not. A kiss for luck. Let's see if you're as good as I wrote you, hot shot."

His smile was slow, and sexy, and she nearly pushed him away before anything else happened . . . but she didn't. She let him claim her lips . . . claiming was the right word, for the right moment, because he took, he laid claim, he brooked no retreat. A man sure of himself and, damn him, equally sure of her.

She cupped her hands on his shoulders, because that was the best way to keep from crumpling to the floor as he slanted his mouth slightly, opening her lips to him, teasing her with his tongue.

Her arms were boneless. Her stomach had melted about five seconds earlier. There was a lump in her throat the size of Staten Island. And her libido hit the On switch with such force that her knees nearly buckled.

"Okay, that's it," she said all in a rush as she pushed herself away from him. "Good kisser. Good. Good kisser. Yet again, Mama pin a rose on you. I wrote you right. Mama pin a rose on me. Now let's get out of here."

She closed her eyes as she turned and walked away from him, praying she could make it into the living room without making a complete jackass out of herself by turning around, launching herself at him, wrapping her legs around his back, and toppling the both of them onto the bed.

Not that she'd go that far. She liked herself too much to go that far, get in that deep, with a man who might disappear tomorrow.

But, hey, at least when she got home she was pretty sure she'd be able to finish Chapter Ten.

CHAPTER 10

(*No, sorry, not* that *Chapter Ten*)

Saint Just felt appreciative eyes on him as he strolled toward the ballroom, Maggie on one arm, his cane neatly tucked up beneath his other. Gentleman that he was, he bowed to each woman in passing, a polite inclination of his head that earned him a curtsy from one young woman dressed as a Victorian lady, a whistle from a cheeky little thing who appeared to be wearing the product of several rolls of aluminum foil, and one rather intimate pat on the hindquarters.

But that came courtesy of Jay, so it didn't really count.

"You're really enjoying yourself, eating up this stuff, aren't you?" Maggie asked as their party approached the doors to the ballroom and the aptly clad woman waiting to collect their tickets of admittance—she was, at best guess, a Valkyrie, complete with spear, blond braids, and breastplate. And her enormous bare legs reminded him of a quite descriptive saying: beef to the heels.

"Most assuredly, my dear," Saint Just agreed. "I am,

at last, the Regency gentleman once more. And even more edifying, Sterling, sent to reconnoiter, discovered that none of my competition are entered in the lists this evening."

"Why not? Their loincloths got lost at the dry cleaners?"

"Oh, never start smoking again, Maggie. I adore you cuttingly sarcastic."

"Bite me."

"I do believe I already have, my dear," Saint Just drawled, pleased to see the flush of color run into her cheeks. "But back to this evening. It would seem that Giancarlo, Damien, and the misspelled Lucious are all prior winners and thus barred from the competition. The same for all three of the other females. I have very high hopes for Mary Louise this evening, as well as for myself."

"That's because you're arrogant, toplofty, and think you're . . . you're the eel's eyebrows."

"And you made me that way, my dear, for which I am eternally grateful. I have great difficulty seeing myself as anything less than who I am," he said, then looked past her, spotting Felicity Boothe Simmons.

The woman wore low-cut China blue watered silk with a Watteau train, skirts wide enough to hide silver settings for six (and a samovar) if she decided to become light-fingered during the course of the evening, a towering powdered white wig, and beauty patches on her cheek and chin, the placement of the patches making her both a Whig and a Tory sympathizer . . . or just a woman who thought patches attractive.

"Ah, Marie Antoinette, I presume," he said, releasing Maggie's arm and sweeping into a most elegant leg (he was sure of that) as he bowed over Felicity's hand. *"Enchanté,* your royal highness. And may I add, *très magnifique.* You look top of the trees, and I say that in the full confidence that I am a true arbiter of feminine beauty."

"Why, thank you, *Monsieur,*" Felicity trilled back at him, and he manfully refrained from wincing at her pronunciation, which sounded very like *Mon-sewer,* and even beat down a second wince as Maggie, obviously more than usually cranky this evening, jabbed him in the ribs with her elbow.

"Oh, my," Saint Just said, belatedly noticing Felicity's companion. "Sergeant Decker, is that really you?" He held up his quizzing glass to one eye, struck a pose, feeling himself as himself, smack in the middle of a Regency ballroom. Maggie wanted arrogant? He'd give her arrogant, in spades. "Slap me, man," he drawled, "if you ain't a stunner."

That last remark earned him another pointed jab, but it was worth it.

The sergeant, dressed as a buccaneer—there seemed to be a lot of that going around, Saint Just had already noticed—stuck out his already rather prominent chin. "Yeah, so what?"

"Nothing, dear fellow, nothing at all. You look most . . . buccaneerish. Are you by any chance working undercover? How droll."

"No, I'm off duty," he said, shaking his head. "If you must know, Rose said I should enter the contests, so I did."

"Rose as in *Rose Knows Romance?*"

"Of course. Rose met the sergeant earlier," Felicity explained, leaning against the man's muscular forearm, "when we were reconnoitering. That's what we call it, don't we, Willie? Reconnoitering. She even waived his fee. She thinks he'd be a great cover model. Isn't that something?"

"It is that, most definitely," Saint Just agreed, at last noticing that both Sterling and Mary Louise had seemed to disappear. He'd thought he'd introduce everyone to each other, as was proper, but Socks and Jay were already causing quite a stir—and more than a few stares—and Mary Louise was nowhere to be seen. Sterling, Saint Just felt sure, had sniffed out the refreshment table and was even now making serious inroads on the little puff pastries that had so caught his fancy at the first cocktail party.

"Thank you for the flowers, Maggie," Felicity said, each word bitten out, as if she would rather be saying "Go stick your head in the nearest toilet, Maggie."

"That's okay. You had a pretty nasty shock," Maggie said, then grinned at Saint Just, who pretended he hadn't understood her small, fairly feeble joke.

"Cute, Maggie, really cute. Well," Felicity said, soldiering on, "we must be off. *Au revoir.*"

Which had come out sounding like *au reservoir.*

"Until later, Felicity," Saint Just said, bowing, then added, "and you as well, *Willie.*"

"What are you looking for?" Maggie asked Saint Just as Felicity and the sergeant took their leave, heading off to be seen by as many people as possible, Saint Just was sure. After all, it was his own plan as well. Not that the addition of the good sergeant into the lists of contestants bothered him in the least, for Saint Just was a man who had no difficulty believing in himself.

"Not what, but whom, my dear. And that whom would be Mary Louise," he said, scanning the crowded hallway once more, and finally seeing her as she stepped out from behind a grotesquely rotund Henry the Eighth. "Ah, here she is. Mare? Why did you disappear?"

"Cops," Mare told him. "Don't like cops. That's Decker, right? He used to hang out near the Port Authority. He nicked me for panhandling one time, but I beat it. Do you think he remembers me?"

"In that outfit?" Maggie said. "I don't think so. But maybe you shouldn't be holding onto the hilt of that knife as if you're ready to gut anyone who comes near you. Just a thought, you know?"

"And, may I add," Saint Just said, holding out his arm to Mare, "that you lead the most interesting life. Perhaps you might write a book?"

"Sure. Everybody can write a book. Just knock one out some weekend where there's nothing else to do," Maggie grumbled from behind him . . . which he knew she would. He smiled, and headed them toward the Valkyrie.

"What about Socks and Jay?" Maggie asked as they handed in their tickets.

"They'll be fine. If you look as if you belong, act as if you belong, you belong."

"So says the guy who wasn't watching five years ago when one of these babes with a leftover hall monitor complex from grammar school tried to keep the *founder* of WAR out of the awards banquet—where she was to hand out the damn awards—because she didn't have her ticket."

"You really must endeavor to let go of the past, Maggie," Saint Just told her, but careful to maintain his distance. "Tonight is to be enjoyed. Enjoy."

"Right after I get my one complimentary drink, you bet I'm going to *enjoy,*" Maggie said, stomping toward the bar.

"Jeez, what a grouch," Mary Louise said, hitching up the belt holding her knife. "Hey, there's Sterling. I'd thought we'd lost him. Poor schmuck, he's still trying to figure out Jay-Jayne."

"At the moment, I think he has other concerns," Saint

Just said, steering Mary Louise over to where Sterling stood, looking more than usually perplexed. "Sterling? Is there a problem?"

"I don't know," Sterling answered, not looking at Saint Just. "Precisely what *is* a penile implant?"

Mary Louise gasped, coughed, began to choke.

"I beg your pardon, Sterling?"

"A penile implant," Sterling repeated in all his most wonderful naiveté. "Giancarlo was squaring off—definitely squaring off, Saint Just—with that other entrant, Damien. Damien said that Giancarlo had plastic surgery. I'm not sure of what that is, but then Giancarlo said that Damien had had this penile implant thing, and Damien seemed to take that taunt *very* much as an insult. That Liza Lang woman had to separate them."

By this point, Mary Louise was positively *hanging* from Saint Just's sleeve, dissolved in mirth; snorting, giggling, crossing her legs for some reason, until she managed to say, "Bathroom . . . gotta . . . oh, God, Sterling, I *love* you!"

"Yes . . . well . . . um . . . thank you, I suppose," Sterling said, turning to Saint Just. "Maggie loves me, too, you know. As a sister. How do you suppose Mare loves me? As a sister as well?"

"I'm sure I have no idea, Sterling," Saint Just said, having repeated the words *penile implant* inside his head several times, until he believed he understood. After all, he did watch *The Learning Channel.*

He also had thought about something Sterling had learned earlier—how, Saint Just didn't know, but Sterling did have very open ears, bless him. He'd learned that Giancarlo, long the king of cover models, was rumored to be on the verge of losing his crown to Damien. Learning that the two men were now publicly at daggers drawn came as no surprise.

"Yes, I believe I'm right. As a sister," Sterling said, obviously still mulling the question.

"Wonderful. You must be in alt, with all these sisters. I imagine they'll both be embroidering slippers for you for Christmas. Now, did you say Liza Lang separated the two gentlemen? Liza Lang of *Rose Knows Romance?"*

"Uh-huh. She grabbed Giancarlo and pulled him away. Why?"

"No reason. I'm simply attempting to match people with people."

"Why?"

"Again, I'm sure I have no idea. Ah, here are Socks and Jayne. Did you have any difficulty entering the ballroom, gentlemen?"

"No," Socks said, "although there are two ladies still in the hallway who might find their tickets missing from their purses. Jayne's a lady of many talents, aren't you, Jayne?"

Sterling goggled at the smiling Jay-Jayne. "You picked their purses? Oh, famous! Damned if you ain't a card."

Jay-Jayne dropped into a curtsy, holding out one black-mitted hand for Sterling to kiss.

"Yes, yes, famous," Sterling repeated manfully, taking Jay-Jayne's hand and pumping it vigorously as Saint Just bit back a smile.

Jay-Jayne unfurled her fan with a snap and began batting it just beneath her chin. "I'm not attractive to you, Sterling?" she asked teasingly.

"No! I mean, yes! I mean," he turned to Saint Just, who merely waggled his eyebrows at him. "What do I do, Saint Just? I mean, this would all be the greatest good fun, if he, if she . . . oh, what a queer fish."

"Hey!" Socks said. "Watch it, buddy."

Sterling turned to Socks, frowning. "What? What did I say? I didn't mean to upset anyone."

"No, you didn't, Sterling," Socks told him, clapping the man on the shoulder as Saint Just shook his head very slightly, to show that Sterling had meant no harm. "Now, come on, join us for the parade. You are in costume, right?"

"Me? Oh, no, I'm not entering the contest. I'm just dressed this way because . . . well, because I like it, don't I, Saint Just?"

"You are inordinately fond of that waistcoat, yes, more's the pity," Saint Just said with a gentle smile that took the sting from his words.

"Maggie likes it, too," Sterling protested. "But I'm not one for contests, you know, queening it about in society . . ."

"That's two, Alex," Socks said, holding up two fingers. "Are you sure he doesn't know what he's saying?"

"What? What?" Sterling asked, looking from Socks, to Saint Just, to Jay-Jayne, who was laughing behind her fan.

"Not to worry, Sterling, you're fine. Ah, I do believe Rose has climbed the podium. It must be time to begin our little parade. An embarrassment, I'm sure, but needs must when the devil and an empty pocketbook drive. Socks? Madam? Shall we be off?"

"We've already decided to go to the end of the line," Socks told him. "Last seen, first remembered, right?"

Saint Just went off on his own, having already noticed that, although there were quite a few costumes for the parade, there were an equal number of those in attendance who had, like Maggie, forgone costumes.

Bernice Toland-James, he was surprised to see as he made his way into the hallway and joined those who were to take part in the parade, had not been one of them.

"Bernie?" Saint Just said, reaching for his quizzing glass, sticking it to his eye as he held out one finger, twirled it, so that she turned about and let him admire her. "My God, woman, you're glorious."

"Yes, I am, aren't I?" Bernie replied, openly preening. "You like?" she asked, holding out her arms and doing another slow twirl.

"I most certainly do," he told her, taking her hand and bowing over it. "Who are you?"

Bernie made a face. "You can't tell? Bummer. I'm Eve."

Manfully withholding a grin, he said, "Of course you are, my dear. After the Fall, I see, as I believe those are meant to be fig leaves?"

"Designer fig leaves, extensions in my hair. And an apple with a bite out of it—see?"

"And a tumbler of scotch in the other hand. Something for every sinner?"

"Exactly. Lust, gluttony, drunkenness, all that good stuff," Bernie said, adjusting the short fig leaf dress, a one shouldered, sleeveless affair that ended at the top of her thighs, exposing some very lovely white skin as well as quite nice, and very long legs that ended in slim ankles and bright red stiletto heels. "I couldn't resist. Maggie's going to have a cow. At least she did last year, when I wore it for the office Halloween party."

"Maggie has nothing to say about this, Bernie."

"Yeah. Right. Which doesn't mean she won't say it. She's such a prude. I keep telling her: life is short, Magster, let your hair down." She gave her head a shake, so that her waist length red hair swung about her. "Yours, or anybody's you can buy."

She motioned him closer. "Don't tell Maggie, but Tabby took off."

"Took *off?*"

"Left. Went home. Bailed. Split."

"She did? Why? Don't tell me it's because of the pranks."

"Nope. It's worse. She's let the dickhead come home."

"David? She's reconciled with him?"

"Okay, if you want to be nice. Me, I don't want to. She's wimped out, that's what she's done. Caved. She'll never divorce the shit."

Saint Just discreetly coughed into his hand.

"What? Oh, okay. Sorry. But I've got two ex-assholes of my own, remember, or I did until they both dropped dead. But at least I got rid of them. Tabby's got David The Millstone around her neck, dragging her down every time she starts to believe in herself. Sleeps with everything that will lie down for him, drinks like a fish, loses more money than Tabby can make. I don't get it, you know?"

"Not everyone is as strong as you, Bernie, has such backbone, such fortitude," Saint Just said as they joined the others pairing up, two by two, for the parade.

"Liquid courage," Bernie said, holding up the tumbler. "Maggie's got her nicotine, I've got my scotch. Maybe we should find Tabby a crutch. One besides David, that is."

"Waterpaints, perhaps? That's a perfectly suitable feminine pursuit. I'll give it some thought," Saint Just promised as the lights dimmed in the ballroom and Rose tapped on the microphones with a wooden pencil, obviously making sure she wouldn't be electrocuted.

"Ladies and gentlemen! Good evening, and welcome to the Sloppy Jim's Barbeque first annual Costume Parade, a fitting prelude to our Grande Finale, the cover model contest. Perhaps tonight's winners will repeat at the end of the week." Rose began in her rather booming, gravel-gritty voice, talking into one of the two microphones on the podium. It was dead, not that Maggie couldn't hear the woman, whose discreet whispers (if the woman ever had been discreet, which was iffy) had to be audible in Queens.

Liza Lang quickly came up and turned the second mike toward Rose, and the woman began again. "Thank you, Liza." She leaned into the mike. "Can you hear me now? Ha!" Her laugh sent off a screech of feedback. "Ooops, sorry about that. But do you get it? That television commercial with that skinny little boy? Can you hear me now! Oh, thank you, thank you," she said as everyone laughed, more polite than amused.

"Tonight we kick off the first in our events meant to entertain us as well as eventually crown the newest cover models, one male, one female, who will grace the covers of our favorite romances next year. But tonight, everyone except for former grand prize winners is eligible for the awards for best costume. All you lovely ladies—and gentlemen—who have supported me all through the years, this is your reward, my thank you for all the love."

"Okay, drivel's over. Here we go," Bernie whispered. "Wait until you hear the first category. The woman damn well knows how to cover all her bases."

"There will be three prizes in each division, for five hundred, three hundred, and one hundred dollars, as well as one female and one male grand prize, each winner receiving *ten thousand dollars*."

"And the crowd went wild," Bernie muttered, rolling her eyes as everyone clapped and cheered. "What the hell am I doing here? You know, someday, somebody really should sit me down and examine what the hell goes on inside my head. On top of everything else, I'm roasting my ass off out here. Why are hallways always so damn hot?"

"Shhh, Bernie, I want to hear the categories."

Rose complied. “There are four categories. Best Plus Size Costume, male or female.”

“Oh, Jesus, and there it is,” Bernie said, pulling one of her fig leaves free and beginning to fan herself with it. “It’s all downhill from here.”

“One for Most Original Costume, European. Most Original Costume, American. And, lastly, the category for best actual historical figure. Male and female winners for all categories.”

“That last category would be Felicity,” Bernie said with a nod of her head. “She shelled out a couple thousand for that gown. Marie Antoinette, you know? She could only get more authentic if she carried around her head in a basket. I was tempted to tell her I’d help her with that part, but I restrained myself. I mean, she does sell well. So I just told her that I just *knew,* if she won the grand prize, she’d donate the ten grand to the WAR literacy campaign. I don’t think she’d have thought of that by herself.”

“You’re such an unmitigated joy, Bernie,” Saint Just said, leaning down to kiss her cheek. He held out his arm to her as the music began and the parade commenced. “Shall we?”

Maggie stood at the edge of the crowd on the left side of the ballroom, nursing a glass of white zinfandel because more than one drink would have her rubbing her nose while her teeth went numb.

“I rather like that one,” Sterling said, pointing at a plus-size Little Bo Peep strolling by, complete with tall crook and stuffed lamb. “Much better than the vampire,” he added, shivering.

“He wasn’t really a vampire, you know.”

“I know, yes, but does *he?”* Sterling asked, with yet

another shiver. "Ah, here come Miss Simmons and the sergeant."

Maggie watched as Faith floated down the ballroom, her hand laid on Sergeant Decker's arm, her head high, her smile . . . can we all say *cocky?* "Decker walks like he's got a stick up his—never mind. Oh, damn, Liza's pulling Felicity out of the line. I admit it, I'm petty, but I really don't want her to win."

Saint Just caused his usual stir as he walked to the center of the ballroom, stopped, stuck his quizzing glass to his eye, and struck a pose before turning to his partner and performing a most elegant leg as he bowed over her hand.

"Show off," Maggie said, a half second before her eyes popped out of her head. "Good God, that's *Bernie!*"

"Where?" Sterling asked, looking about for the woman.

"There," Maggie said, pointing to the center of the ballroom. "With Alex. What the hell is she almost wearing? Oh, wait, I remember now. She's Eve." She shrugged. "Better hair this time, I'll give her that."

"Oh, look, Maggie. Saint Just is being asked to join the others in front of the podium. He must be a winner."

But Maggie wasn't looking. She was too busy watching Socks and Jay-Jayne. They were the last two contestants and they walked down the middle of the ballroom separately, Socks doing a fairly creditable imitation of a swashbuckler . . . he certainly had the swash part down pat . . . followed by Jay-Jayne, who minced along, head high, employing a large silk fan to great effect. He . . . she . . . whatever, looked every inch the beauty queen, Maggie thought, then winced at that thought.

Both were asked to move to the podium.

"And there we have it, ladies and gentlemen, the

first annual costume parade, and what a wonderful parade it was, my lovelies!" Rose yelled into the microphone.

"Why do people do that?" Maggie asked, rubbing her hands over her abused ears. "What do they think the mike is for?"

"Shh," Sterling said. "She's going to announce the winners."

"Oh gosh golly gee, I'm sorry, Sterling," Maggie groused, downing the last of her wine. "I sure wouldn't want to miss this."

"Saint Just and Mare could each win ten thousand dollars," Sterling reminded her.

"Good point," Maggie said, putting her empty glass on the serving table behind her. "Okay, let's listen."

The Plus Size first place awards went to Henry The Eighth and a female viking. Vikette?

Mary Louise took first place in the American category, which seemed to please her, as she took out her knife and flourished it a time or two before accepting her prize.

Maggie clapped and whistled when Socks walked off with second prize in the same category, while Sterling let out a rousing trio of "Huzza's."

The European category winners went by in a blur until the third prize for females, won by Felicity Boothe Simmons, a woman whose smile as she accepted her, to Maggie's mind, last place award, was positively plastic.

Now it was time for the grand prizes, with cameras at the ready, both those held by attendees and those of the remarkably large number of press that had attended, and Rose asked Felicity to present them.

"Rose is so smart," Maggie told Sterling. "She knows darn well that Faith's pissed, so she's flipping her a fish.

She'll be with the grand prize winners in all the publicity pictures this way, you understand. Kind of the Julia Roberts of the Rose Awards. Understand?"

"Understand? Not really, no," Sterling told her on a sigh. "I never understand what women do. Oh, Rose is opening the envelope."

Rose slit the envelope, pulled out the single paper inside. Then she took off her glitter encrusted reading glasses, wiped them against her ample bosom, replaced them. "And here we go!" she shouted into the microphone, her voice shaking the chandeliers. "First, the male Grand Champion, one Alexander Blakely!"

Sterling, to put it as politely as possible, went nuts. He cheered, he stamped, he yelled "Huzza!" In fact, so excited was he that he grabbed Maggie by the shoulders and kissed her full on the mouth . . . then stepped back, looking stunned. "Oh my stars, did I do that? I'm so sorry."

"It's okay, Sterling," Maggie assured him. "I'm happy, too. We haven't broken even yet, but we're getting there. It almost makes up for that supercilious smile on Alex's face. You do know we're never going to hear the end of this, don't you?"

"Probably not, but the large screen television machine will go a long way toward making his preening bearable," Sterling said with a wink and a smile.

"Having it in your own apartment does warm fuzzy things for me, too," Maggie said, snagging a glass of water from the table behind her.

"And now, for our last award of the evening, the grand prize for females," Rose yelled as Saint Just bowed, and smiled, and bowed again, then held up the huge fake check Faith had presented to him. "And the winner is—excuse me."

She motioned for Liza Lang to come to the podium

and said, as Liza covered the microphone (the wrong one, unfortunately) with one hand, "Is that it? Just the one name? Are you sure? I want to get done and the hell out of here. These people are all idiots, every last damn one of them, all dressed up like Astor's pet horse. If I told them to show up naked, they'd show up naked. My lovelies? Damn sheep, that's what they are. And I'm dying here, dying. Did you pick up my Metamucil? I ask you to do one thing, you lazy slut, and you can't even do that. What? What's wrong?"

The whole ballroom had gone quiet as Rose's adoring readers heard every word.

Liza Lang noticed, smiled at the audience (sort of sheepishly herself, the long-suffering assistant) and covered the correct microphone before whispering in Rose's ear.

Rose's face went white, then turned the color of her name. Then she shrugged, as if it didn't matter.

Maybe the rumors were true, and Rose did consider this her swan song, and was ready to retire, step down as publisher of the *Rose Knows Romance* e-magazine and the whole *Rose* empire.

Maggie considered this for a moment, considered that Rose was already dead old, and then looked at Liza curiously. The woman had handled the microphones for Rose at the beginning of the program. She knew which one was live, yet had covered the wrong one.

Was it an accident, or had Liza deliberately set out to embarrass the loquacious, and way too frank-speaking Rose by covering the wrong mike? And what was that business about Liza being a slut? It couldn't have been a term of endearment, but was it just an insult . . . or was it more?

Rose tapped the microphone yet again, smiled, and shouted, "And now my lovelies, all you wonderful people, the Female Grand Prize winner for best costume is—Jayne!"

Maggie, who had been mulling this latest incident while taking a long drink of water, sprayed a fine mist of the stuff into the air before coughing, choking, and trying to stop Sterling from beating her to death as he pounded on her back.

"Isn't it above everything wonderful, Maggie?" Sterling exclaimed, still pounding on her back as she wiped water from the front of her dress. "Jay won!"

"Yeah, Sterling. For best *female,"* Maggie managed to choke out as she wiped water from her chin, then watched as Faith handed Jay-Jayne her own large, symbolic check.

Jay-Jayne took it, tucked it under her arm, and then dropped into a curtsy before rising once more and dramatically snatching the wig from his head to reveal the stocking covering his short black hair. Faith was handed the wig as Jay-Jayne took a bow. Not much looked better than Jay-Jayne in full makeup and wig. Nothing looked more ridiculous, even scary in a teenage slasher movie sort of way, than Jay-Jayne in full makeup, ball gown, and suddenly, shockingly, male.

Women screamed. Flashbulbs popped. Rose was overheard muttering "sonofabitch," into the microphone. Faith's eyes grew wide as she held the wig in both hands, her face went pale, and she yelped as she flung the thing to the floor.

And Maggie lifted her water glass in a toast, saying, "You know, Sterling, to paraphrase that same Julia Roberts while she was upstaging Denzel Washington, 'sometimes I really, really *love* my life.' "

CHAPTER 11

"What is ten thousand dollars in pounds, Maggie?"
She didn't even look up from the pages of Virginia's manuscript. "How should I know? I don't shop in London. Now shut up, I'm reading." She lifted her eyes for a moment, glared at him. "And for God's sake, stuff that thing behind a couch or something."

Saint Just looked at the oversized check and smiled. "Bothers you to no end, doesn't it, that I was right?"

Maggie smiled evilly. "Not at all, Alex, at least not once you get the real check, and endorse it over to me. I'll even be magnanimous, and call us even. Now go away. Virginia expects me to have finished this by the time she gets up here."

"And how is it, Saint Maggie, martyr extraordainaire?" Saint Just asked, putting down the check and coming to the table, to lean over Maggie's shoulder.

"Not bad," she told him, smiling up at him. "Pretty good, actually. It was good before, Virginia always has been good, about the best Regency writer I know, but I think she's getting the hang of the massage bit."

Saint Just put his hands on Maggie's shoulders and began kneading her stiff muscles. "Like this?"

Maggie bit down hard, trying to suppress the reluctant tingle that ran through her at his touch. "No, damn it, nothing like that. Don't you have something else to do, somebody else to bother?"

"Well, Sterling does want me to listen to his rap, now that Socks gave his final approval last evening. Do you suppose these windows open? I would just as soon toss myself out onto the flagway."

"Don't let me stop you." Maggie put down her pen. "No, wait, I need a break. I've been at this since six. Sterling's rap might be just what I need. Where is he?"

"Where is who? Whom? Are you talking about me? You could, yes, could, be talking about me."

"Yes, Sterling, we were talking about you," Maggie said, smiling at the man who seemed to be walking on his tiptoes, full of a strange energy he didn't quite know how to dissipate. "Are you all right?"

Sterling bounced in place. "Fine. Never better. Top, top, top of the world and all of that—*sha-ba-sha-ba.*"

Maggie stuck her tongue out one corner of her mouth, looked up at Saint Just, then said, *"Sha-ba-sha-ba?"*

Saint Just shrugged. "Earlier, Mary Louise mentioned something about Sterling being *wired* for something, but I confess I really have no idea. He does look as if someone should be pulling a plug and suggesting he have himself a lie down."

Sterling stood in the middle of the room, his eyes closed as he tipped his head side-to-side, snapped his fingers. *"Sha-ba-sha-ba."*

"Hey, Sterling, you want to come back in here and—oh, everybody's up. That's good," Mary Louise said, tripping into the room and plopping herself down on one of the couches, little bits of cotton stuck between her freshly painted toenails. "Now I don't have to suffer alone. Hit it, Sterling."

Sterling stopped bobbing and weaving, opened his eyes, and immediately flushed a deep red, all the way to his eyebrows. "I—um, I don't know about that, Mare. I worry so about performing. It would all be the greatest good fun, except for that. Maybe some other time?"

"Oh, go ahead, Sterl-man. Sock it to 'em. God knows you've been sockin' it to me long enough."

"Please, Sterling," Maggie said encouragingly as she picked up her teacup, took a fortifying sip. "I'm sure we'll all love it. Really. Alex? Certainly you'd love to hear Sterl-man's rap?"

"It would edify me greatly if you would confine your efforts to put words into my mouth to the pages of our books, my dear," Saint Just said quietly, pouring himself a cup of coffee. "I, for one, might prefer bamboo shoots shoved up under my fingernails." He looked at Mary Louise, his expression painful. "Sterl-man?"

Mary Louise nodded. "Socks says it's a good handle. The Sterl–man wanted Do-Doggy-Do, but we talked him out of it."

"Praise heaven for small favors," Saint Just said, taking his cup and sitting down on one of the chairs at the table where Maggie had been working. "Oh, carry on, Sterling. We await your performance with bated breath."

Sterling looked to Mary Louise, who grinned, stood up, and took up position beside him, to begin tapping one cottony foot on the carpet.

"It's a duet rap?" Maggie asked, lighting a cigarette. She had to do something to occupy herself because, otherwise, she was probably going to start banging her fists against the tabletop as she laughed herself silly.

"No, no duet," Mary Louise told her. "I'm the background. You know, the way rappers rub a record? That's the *sha-ba-sha-ba* part. You just have to pretend it's the usual background. Get it?"

"Unfortunately, I believe I do," Saint Just said, earning himself a kick under the table from Maggie. "Oh, Sterling, do just get on with it."

Sterling took a deep breath, let it out slowly, then began to move his head in time to some unknown melody as Mary Louise began chanting: *"Sha-ba-sha-ba-sha-ba . . ."*

Sterling tipped his head along with the beat Mary Louise counted out with her *sha-ba's,* and then jumped in: "Here's to Prinney, Prince of Wales . . . fashioned of snakes and puppy-dog tails . . . he spends his cash and shows some flash . . . bibelots and furbelows . . . cutting a dash . . . living high . . . living large on society while we all get a rash . . . I can't take it, can't take it, can't take it, won't take it . . . *sha-ba-sha-ba-sha-ba.* Gonna throw . . . a rub in his way . . . not gonna take it . . . another day . . . gonna overthrow him, gonna undo him . . . and all of that."

Sterling stopped, looking both proud of himself and slightly abashed.

"Oh . . . my," Maggie said, blinking as she manfully flicked her Bic, held it up in the air. "Wasn't that . . . grand. Alex?"

"What?" he asked, looking at her strangely, almost blankly. "Oh. You want my comment?" He looked at Sterling, smiled. "Wonderful, my friend. Truly. Wonderful."

"That's it?" Mary Louise asked, glaring at Saint Just. "It took guts to do that, Vic. That's all you have to say? Wonderful?"

"To be truthful, Mary Louise, I'm nearly overcome. I don't believe I can trust myself to say more."

"I've got another verse, but it isn't quite ready yet. That's why I ended with the *all of that,* you see," Sterling told them all, beaming.

"Oh, do it anyway, Sterl-man," Mary Louise encouraged, giving him a shove in the arm. "I get a real kick out of what you say about Princess Caroline."

"Please, no," Saint Just said quickly. "No need to set him off again, is there? Maggie has to get back to work. Maggie? Don't you have to get back to work?"

"Now who's putting words into whose mouth?" she said, leering at him. "But, if Sterling doesn't feel the second verse is ready I suppose—oh, that must be Virginia. Sterling, will you let her in?"

Looking like a man who'd just gotten a last minute reprieve from the governor, Sterling raced for the door of the suite, pulling both doors open to allow Virginia to enter.

Which she did, at a rapid waddle, what would have been a run if she hadn't been so very pregnant. "You'll never guess. I mean, you'll *never* guess! I went down for the free complimentary Continental breakfast—no more prune Danishes for me after yesterday—God knows what I was thinking—but I snagged an apricot one and—oh, but you don't want to hear that. You want to hear about Bunny Wilkinson."

"We do?" Maggie asked, stubbing out her cigarette and waving her hands in the air to dissipate the smoke. "Color me surprised, but I didn't think I ever wanted to hear about Bunny Wilkinson."

"Trust me, you'll want to hear this," Virginia said, settling her bulk on one of the couches. "They took her off in an ambulance."

Saint Just, who had risen to his feet when Virginia entered the room, walked over to stand in front of her. "She was injured? Attacked?"

Virginia shook her head. "Moved," she said, then giggled. "Oh, I'm sorry, but it is kind of funny. From what I could learn, she went to bed in her suite, and woke up on the roof, pink fuzzy slippers, hair net, and all. Somebody from the hotel heard her pounding on the door and let her back in, but then she started going a little nutso I guess, having a meltdown, because they took her to the hospital to calm her down."

"That's not funny," Maggie said, surprising herself.

"Probably not, no," Virginia agreed. "Unless you got a glimpse of her being wheeled out in those fuzzy slippers. Anyway, Martha's taking charge, calming everyone down."

"Yes, Mrs. Kolowsky," Saint Just said, beginning to pace. "Doesn't she share the suite with Bunny?"

Virginia nodded. "That's why she knew so much, could explain everything. She said Bunny took a sedative last night because she was so upset over everything that's gone wrong, and Martha borrowed one from her and took it too, because it seemed like a good idea. Said she slept like the dead. When she woke up this morning, Bunny wasn't in her bedroom and she just thought she'd gotten up early. But then she noticed that Bunny's badge and purse were still in the suite, and went looking for her. She had *everybody* looking for her. Otherwise, poor Bunny might still be on the roof with the pigeons."

Maggie stacked the pages of Virginia's manuscript and got up, headed for her bedroom to get her shoes and badge. "Virginia? Could you go knock on the door of Faith's suite? I think we all need to put our heads together. This is getting *way* out of hand. Sterling, Mare? Stay here with Virginia. I don't want anyone else on the convention floor right now."

"Good. Can we order room service?" Virginia asked. "I never did get to eat my apricot pastry. Oh, and Felicity's already downstairs, Maggie. She's autographing books in the book room this morning from nine to ten, and then there's the news conference thingie after that. I guess Martha's going to have to step in, take over for Bunny. Gee, I hope she's up to it, poor thing. She's more used to slaving in the background."

Saint Just was waiting at the doorway when Maggie returned from her bedroom, still working her left foot into her heels. "Another escalation, my dear," he told her as he ushered her into the hallway. "Much as I'd rather go back to those bamboo shoots, or even another rap from the Sterl-man—have you heard from Wendell?"

"Not yet, no," Maggie said as she pushed the button to call the elevator. "I even hit 9-1-1 when I paged him this morning, but I guess he's still working. It must be a big case for him to—Steve!"

She stepped into the elevator, and into Lieutenant Wendell's comforting hug, while Saint Just took a moment to visually inspect his well-clipped fingernails.

"Hiya, Maggie. I saw the ambulance as I came in. You've got a real mess going on here, don't you?" Steve said, nodding to Saint Just. "Damn, it's you. Why am I not surprised to see you, Blakely?"

Saint Just bowed. "My delight equals your own, *Left*–tenant. You saw Mrs. Wilkinson being taken out?"

"Heard her is more like it." Wendell shook his head. "She was really putting on a show. What happened, Maggie?"

Maggie filled him in as the elevator slowly made its way down to the conference floor, stopping at least five times to take on more passengers. Three of them had their luggage with them, and were still wearing their WAR name tags.

"Want my advice?" Wendell said as they finally piled out of the elevator, pushing past the other passengers and those trying to shove their way onto the elevator. "Because my advice is to get the hell out of here."

"Told you so," Saint Just sing-songed as he walked

along beside her on their way to the book room. "Faint heart, that's our *Left*-tenant."

"I can't just desert everyone, Steve," Maggie explained as they walked along the hallway. "Somebody's trying to ruin this convention. I'm . . . I'm a charter member, for crying out loud."

Saint Just coughed into his hand. "It's true, Wendell. Why, if I could count the times I've heard Maggie wax poetic over her dear, dear WAR."

"Shut up, Alex," Maggie groused, turning a corner in the hallway just in time to hear the first screams . . . followed by a stampede of women running toward them, so that Saint Just quickly pulled her against the wall and protected her with his own body until the worst of the congestion had dissipated. "What . . . what the hell was *that?* They were all *wet.*"

"Let's go find out," Wendell said, heading down the hallway once more, all three of them sidestepping wet stragglers who were still going the other way.

They got to the door of the book room just as Felicity Boothe Simmons exited, dripping wet, her hair hanging to her shoulders in sodden hanks, her mascara running down her cheeks—and her fists clenched.

"Don't you *dare* say anything nasty," she gritted out from between clenched teeth, glaring at Maggie.

"What happened, Faith?" Maggie asked while Saint Just extracted a fine white linen square and handed it to Felicity. "You're sopping wet."

"No shit," Felicity said, grabbing the handkerchief from Saint Just and wiping at her face. "Somebody turned on the overhead sprinklers. Everything's ruined. My hair, my dress, all the books in there—*everything.* I'm all *wet!*"

"Yeah," Maggie said, trying not to grin, "I can sort of see that. Look, Faith, I want you to meet Lieutenant

Steve Wendell. He's a friend and he's here to help us. I really think someone's out to sabotage this whole convention."

Felicity bent down and wrung out her skirt. "And now a second right-on observation. Bam, bam, two in a row. I'm impressed. You've got a mind like a steel trap, Maggie. Someone's out to sabotage the convention? Damn, girl, nothing gets past you."

"Temper, Maggie," Saint Just said as Maggie began to growl. "After all, the woman is *wet.*"

"All right, all right," she said as she glared at Saint Just, "just forget it, Faith. I thought you'd want to help. All that charter member business, all that putting up a brave front, being an example to others." When Felicity made a face at her, she added, "And the publicity will be great."

At last, Felicity calmed down. 'That goes without saying. And I do want to help. Perhaps I was a little rash," she said, looking at Wendell. She pushed at her hair, smiled at him. "Lieutenant? Please forgive my appearance. We'll talk . . . later."

"Yes, that would be good," Wendell said, stepping back, as Felicity was dripping on his scuffed shoes.

"She's flirting? Now? Jeez, give me a break," Maggie said, looking at Saint Just, who had this *smug* look on his face.

"Oh, my God, Felicity!" Martha Kolowsky came running up, skidding to a halt beside Maggie. "The press conference is in an hour. You have to change."

"Gee, you think?" Felicity said, rolling her eyes, and Maggie suddenly remembered why she used to like Faith, back when the woman was *real.* And she had been more *real* in the past two minutes than she'd been in years.

"Please, don't be upset," Martha begged. "I know

this is terrible. Terrible. But we have to keep on going. For WAR's sake."

"Screw WAR," Felicity said, handing back the handkerchief, which Saint Just declined. "I've had enough. If somebody wants to ruin the convention, let 'em."

Martha drew herself up to her full height and stuck out her chest (complete with name tag and array of ribbons). Very impressive for a woman who usually melted into the background. "Now you see here, Felicity. We have a press conference in"— she looked down at her wristwatch—"fifty-two minutes, and you're going to be there. I'm going to be there in Bunny's place, someone from the hotel is going to be there, Sergeant Decker's going to be there, and all three major networks are going to be there. Now *move it.*"

Felicity looked at Martha, wide-eyed, then said, "All three networks?"

"And the local Fox affiliate," Martha said with a sharp nod of her head. "Do you really want me to tell them all that you're a great big scaredy cat and ran away?"

Felicity pointed at Martha, shook her finger twice, then said, "Oh, forget it. You can apologize later. Right now, I've got to go change."

"Wow, Martha, that was pretty brave," Maggie said once Felicity had stomped off, her shoes squishing.

Martha patted her chest. "Yes, it was, wasn't it. My, I've never done anything like that before. Look at me, I'm shaking. But it felt . . . it felt *good.* I'm taking this on-line assertiveness class, you know. Now, if you'll excuse me? I've got to meet with the representative from the hotel about this mess in the book room. Poor Bunny, this hasn't been her most shining moment, has it? The conference, I mean."

Saint Just put a finger to his lips as he watched

Martha march off toward the book room. "Some people are born to greatness, and others . . ." he said, then looked at Maggie. "Shall we adjourn to the lounge until the press conference? I have a list of chores for our esteemed *Left*-tenant."

"Do you now," Wendell said, putting his arm around Maggie's waist as they all made their way to the escalator that would take them up to the eighth floor. "And who died and put you in charge?"

"Nobody, Wendell," Saint Just answered, standing back to allow Maggie to step onto the escalator ahead of him. "Yet."

"One more question, if you please. I am not very well versed in such things, but I have fairly well convinced myself that whoever is behind these pranks must have some technical knowledge in the area of things electrical or mechanical. The microphone, the sprinkler system. What do you think?"

"Good point. I'll look for anyone with any electrical or mechanical background, although I doubt any of these ladies wire houses on the side."

"Yes, and if it's possible, you could run the name Top Star Electric through whatever computers you might have at your disposal."

"Any particular reason?"

"Yes. I saw a man with that name written on the back of his uniform leaving the scene in some haste when Felicity got her shock. Oh, and his uniform was brown, if that helps, and had a lightbulb design sewn on the back."

"I'll start with the five boroughs, and branch out from there. But there could be a lot of Top Star Electric companies." Steve Wendell closed his little notebook and shoved it in his back pocket. "I hate saying this,

Blakely, but you've got some good ideas here. I'll get on this list right after I speak to Sergeant Decker. I don't want to step on any toes, you understand."

Saint Just inspected his fingertips. "I doubt the man will object. He's rather occupied, now that he's vying for the cover model prize."

"Say what?" Wendell asked, looking at Maggie. "He's kidding, right?"

"You wish," Maggie said, stubbing out her cigarette. "Rose—that's the *Rose Knows Romance* one Alex told you about—told him he'd make a great cover model. The costume parade was last night, and he came as a pirate." As Wendell's mouth dropped open, she said, "No kidding. Honest."

"She's telling the truth, Wendell," Saint Just assured him. "If I had a pennysworth of confidence in the twit I wouldn't have asked that you join us."

"You asked—oh, never mind. Do you really think someone on that list you gave Steve is our culprit?"

"I have no idea, my dear, but one has to begin somewhere. Rose, Liza Lang, Bunny Wilkinson, Martha Kolowsky. And all the remaining cover model contestants, excluding both Mary Louise and myself, of course."

"That's the part I don't get," Maggie said. "Why the cover models? If the convention is canceled, there's no grande finale cover model contest."

"Agreed. It is a long shot. But there's so much animosity there, between the male contestants in particular. I'd just feel better if we included them. We've eliminated Reggie Hall as he's departed the scene, and Felicity might have been a suspect save for the crushing humiliation and very real injury she's suffered. Nobody as vain as Miss Simmons inflicts such horrors on herself for any reason, even national publicity. The cowboy, yes, but not the mice, and not a dunking."

"Darn," Maggie said, leaning back in her seat. "I have

to agree with you. And she's got Decker's ear, which is why I still want her to be a part of our team," she told the lieutenant, "once she's done with the press conference. Speaking of which," she said, getting to her feet, "it's almost time. Are you coming, Steve?"

"No, I don't think so. I'd rather go find this guy Decker, then get to work on the background checks on our suspects. Stuff like this isn't top priority, but I'll try to push it through today. There's a gal in the department who owes me a favor."

"What did you do, Wendell?" Saint Just asked. "Promise to stay away from her?"

"Funny, Blakely." He put a hand on Maggie's shoulder. "You be careful, okay? Blakely's right. These aren't just practical jokes, and sooner or later whoever is doing them is going to go a step too far, either by mistake or on purpose. I don't want you to be anywhere around when that happens. But how about we meet here for lunch, say about one?"

"I'd love to," Maggie said, and Saint Just looked on in disgust as the lieutenant kissed her.

"Come on, Maggie," Saint Just prodded as she watched Steve walk away. What did she see in the man? He looked like a rumpled bed. Shaggy brown hair always in need of a cut, baggy slacks, down at the heels shoes, that ridiculous boyish grin. Ah well, Maggie probably felt she couldn't hurt the fellow's feelings after he'd helped her when Toland was murdered.

Still, how could Maggie allow herself to tumble for a copper? She was so lucky he, the Viscount Saint Just, her Perfect Hero, was on the scene now, to guide her, to protect her from her own softhearted folly.

"Where's the press conference being held?" Maggie asked as Saint Just guided her back toward the escalator.

"In the main ballroom," he told her, for Sterling, his aide-de-camp, had ferreted out the information late last night, bless him. "Hmmm, the hallway doesn't seem quite as crowded today, does it? Perhaps the convention will have to be canceled, if too many of the participants leave."

"Some of them can't leave," Maggie told him as they entered the ballroom and took up seats at the back of the large room that was already bright with television lights. About half the chairs were filled, when the place should have been overflowing with WAR members. "They bought nonrefundable airline tickets and have to stay over a Saturday or else pay huge penalties. A lot of the attendees are here on very strict budgets, so they're stuck. The rest that are staying, I think, are hoping to see another train wreck."

"I beg your pardon?"

"Never mind, it's just human nature. Romans at the Coliseum, you know. Okay, here comes Faith. She looks good, too."

Saint Just sat back to observe. He was very good at observing.

He observed Rose (complete with rhinestone tiara) and Liza sitting beside each other in the front row, Liza holding one of those mini-tape recorders, which made sense, as she probably was capturing every word for Rose's online magazine. None of the other attendees were sitting within a dozen chairs of them in any direction, most probably a reaction to Rose's damning *faux pas* at the costume parade last night.

A pariah in a tiara. Very interesting. And very loyal of Liza Lang to remain by her side. Perhaps, like Maggie, Ms. Lang fancied herself a martyr.

He observed Damien and Giancarlo, sitting on opposite sides of the ballroom. Lucious was nowhere to be found, however, and neither were the other two remaining females in the contest.

Saint Just decided he'd have to have Sterling check into that. Perhaps the other contestants had departed the scene. Otherwise, why wouldn't they have gravitated toward any lights and cameras within five miles?

Martha entered the room, along with a gentleman wearing a black suit, a prodigiously ugly tie, and a small brass badge worn by all hotel employees, and the two of them joined Felicity at the podium.

Martha handed out prepared press releases to all of the media in attendance, then began with a separate prepared statement listing all of the mishaps of the past days, delivered in a calm, controlled voice as she made eye contact with the cameras. She reported, so sadly, that the Conference Chair, Bunny Wilkinson, "That's W-i-l-k-i-n-s-o-n, as her name isn't on the press release," had been hospitalized for an emotional collapse.

She said, and said again, that the convention was *not* going to be canceled, that *she* was in charge now, all questions should be directed to her, and that all efforts were being made to ensure that no more "mischief" interrupted the proceedings. "In fact, I'm here this morning to *guarantee* everyone that there will be no further incidents now that I'm in charge."

Maggie leaned over to whisper to Saint Just. "And Alexander Haig is in charge at the White House. Jeez, what hit Martha? It's like she's just been promoted to queen of the world."

"You noticed that, too? Good," Saint Just said. "We're going to have to compare notes soon, won't we?

Martha read a list of new security measures for the workshops and the ballroom, then introduced Sergeant Decker, whom Saint Just had not seen until the man skipped toward the front of the room and bounded onto the dais.

"Good God, the man's a twit," Saint Just grumbled as Lieutenant Wendell tapped him on the shoulder and then sat down beside him.

"He's a Grade-A jerk, that's what he is. One of New York's less than finest, and the assistant chief's wife's nephew, which explains why the idiot isn't walking a beat at Coney Island," Wendell stage-whispered, so that two women in the row in front of them turned around to shush him. "Sorry, ladies," he said, then pulled out his notebook. "Did I miss anything important?"

"Just Martha turning into Alexander Haig," Saint Just told him, not really understanding the Haig part, but knowing full well that Martha had undergone a startling metamorphosis that bore watching.

"Yeah? 'I'm in charge here at the Marriott'? That sort of thing? Interesting," Wendell said, earning himself another pair of damning looks from the ladies in the next row. He spread his hands, battered notebook in one, stub of pencil in the other. "Hey, police business, okay? Now turn around or I'll run you both in for obstruction."

"Always the epitome of politeness, Wendell," Saint Just said as, on the podium, Sergeant Decker "uh-ed" and "um-ed" . . . and generally became an embarrassment to the NYPD and the entire male species as he screamed and jumped a foot (tumbling off the podium to the floor), when a small white mouse that must have escaped the exterminators ran across the podium.

"This is going well," Saint Just commented as, beside him, Maggie snorted in a most unladylike way.

CHAPTER 12

Maggie hooked up with Bernie and Virginia for lunch in the seventh floor main ballroom. The three of them decided to spend the afternoon in Maggie's suite, getting massages, courtesy of Toland Books, as it was Bernie's idea and she'd just phoned Tabby to make a two-book offer on the basis of Maggie's thumbs-up on Virginia's manuscript.

"I'm feeling magnanimous," Bernie said as they stood waiting for an elevator, only three of the seeming hundreds on the lookout for one of the dozen or so elevators that seemed to take coffee breaks every ten minutes, because the arrival of any one of them always caused a stampede of frustrated people all trying to grab the thing before it opted to go out of service again to order another latte from the Starbucks in the lobby.

"I could cheerfully kill for a foot massage, but I don't want any favors, Bernie," Virginia said, obviously not meaning a word of that last bit.

"Honey, I don't *do* favors," Bernie said, sipping on the scotch she'd carried with her from lunch. "Felicity's going to be strictly hardback from now on. I've got a historical slot to fill in paper and Regency England is hot right now. It's that simple, and you're that lucky, so don't go all soppy on me or think you're God's gift. Half of publishing is talent, and the other half is just being in the right place at the right time. Besides, I can sell anything, at least twice. After that, it's up to you and your work. Get it?"

"I'm betting you'll be awarded some big humanitarian award any day now, Bernie," Maggie said as one of the elevators opened and the stampede was on again. "Whoa, a person could get killed around here," she said as she was spun in a circle by a man carrying two briefcases and a stack of carpet samples who had cut off everyone else and barreled into the elevator, using beige berber carpet as a weapon.

"I won't let you down, Bernie," Virginia said earnestly. "I promise."

"And I'll drink to that," Bernie said, taking a sip from her seemingly ever-present glass of scotch. Everyone had their ways of coping with the stress of a WAR convention; Johnnie Walker was Bernie's. "Oh, by the way, what's the title? I should probably know that."

"The title? Um . . . my working title is *Sarah's Savage Passion.*"

Bernie coughed and choked for a second, glaring at Maggie. "She's kidding, right?"

Maggie shrugged. "She was shooting for a single title type title."

"Well, she missed. But we'll work on it," Bernie said, then stood on her tiptoes, sort of like a hound going on point. "Thought so. Here comes that Wilkinson person, back from the nut house. Quick, hide me."

"Stand back, everyone," Martha Kolowsky ordered, guiding Bunny by the elbow. "We need the first available elevator, ladies, so that Bunny can go upstairs and lie down."

Bernice Toland-James had not clawed her way to the top of the heap by being slow to move on any opportunity. The elevator doors behind her opened, and she all but flung herself into it, motioning for Maggie and Virginia to follow her. "Over here, Martha," she called out. "We've got one for her."

"I thought you wanted to avoid Bunny," Maggie said as Martha helped a pale and shaken looking Bunny into the elevator, then stepped back as other people pushed their way in for the ride.

"I want that massage," Bernie said, shrugging as Bunny staggered to the rail of the glass sided elevator. "Besides, she doesn't seem very dangerous, does she? She's got the 'deer in headlights' stare down pat."

A little redheaded WAR badge wearer, who looked like she must have been captain of her high school pep squad, turned to face everyone, saying, "We're moving, people. Floors, please. Chop, chop."

Everyone started calling out numbers, and Maggie looked around, surprised to see that there were four other passengers. The cheerleader (Mitzi Metzger, Pre-Pubbed, Cincinnati Chapter), a tall brunette (Sally Fish, Pre-Pubbed, Cincinnati Chapter, and a definite candidate for a pen name), Brenda Peterson, ditto, ditto—it would seem they traveled in packs), and a short, pudgy businessman who looked to be about three sheets to the wind.

Everyone faced front, no one speaking to anyone else, and watched the floor lights blink.

The elevator rose quietly, then stopped at eleven with a sudden jerk. "Smooth ride," Maggie said. "I hate elevators."

"Oh, I don't mind them," Virginia said, rubbing at the small of her back. "But it would be nice if the doors opened now, because it's getting kind of stuffy in here."

She leaned toward Maggie. "And that guy back there smells like a distillery *and* like he's been playing handball all morning."

"Excuse me, my floor," the businessman said, pushing past Maggie to the door, giving her a whiff of his not so great mix of odors. "Shit. Door isn't opening. Light's at eleven. The door should open." He turned to Mitzi. "What did you do, bitch?"

"Oh, nice, nice," Bernie said, glaring down at the man, who was actually shorter than her. "You must be in town for one of those how to be polite and still succeed Dale Carnegie courses. Now back off, before I step on you. Maggie, honey, push another button."

"What do you think I've been doing?" Maggie groused, still hitting buttons. "Nothing's happening."

"You know, Red," the man said, tipping up his chin to within six inches of Bernie's face, "I just lost my biggest account this morning. I need you like I need a butt rash, so why don't you just shut the fuck up."

Bernie stared down at the man, her expression ominously blank. "Maggie, are we really stuck?"

"Definitely stuck, *Red,*" Maggie agreed, tongue-in-cheek, because she had a feeling she was about to see the Bernie Does Damage Show.

"So we're going to be here for a while?"

"I'd say so, yes. Yup. Definitely."

"In that case, and outnumbering Mr. Charming here seven to one," Bernie said, smiling broadly, "what do you say we all de–pants the twerp and make fat-ass butt rash prints all over the glass? It'd pass the time."

The twerp backed down, backed away. "Crazy bitches. Hotel's full of crazy bitches," he muttered, pushing his way back to the glass. He lifted both arms and pressed his palms against the glass as he looked down at the eighth floor foyer, that was a good three floors below them.

Either his sunny demeanor (or his strong odor) roused Bunny from her near stupor, and she moved away from him, holding a hand to her nose—okay, so it was probably the Eau'd Locker Room.

"Bernie?" Bunny questioned, blinking. "Bernice Toland–James, publisher of Toland Books? That is you, isn't it? Yes, I'm sure it is. We met the other night, with Felicity," she continued, sticking out one hand. "I'm Bunny Wilkinson."

"No speaka the Eng-lesh," Bernie said, ignoring Bunny's hand and diving back into her scotch.

"No, no. I'm upset, but that's *you,"* Bunny said, waving her hands as if to shake herself back to life. "And we're stuck here?"

"Probably another prank," Maggie said, trying to step in front of Bernie, protect her. "You must hate this, Bunny, being chairperson and all."

"Prank, schmank," Bunny said, pushing back her tangled hair, "I know opportunity when it hits me in the face."

"Oh, God, no," Bernie said, actually cowering behind Maggie. "Quick, anybody have a gun? I need to shoot myself."

"Hey," Maggie said, grinning, "you're the one who got on the elevator with her."

"Shut up, I don't like you that much. And stand still," Bernie snapped.

"Maggie?"

Maggie turned to look at Virginia. "Yeah? You okay, Virginia? I know it's getting hot in here."

"Well, to tell you the truth . . ."

"You're Bernice Toland-James?" the trio from Cincinnati trilled in unison, sort of like the lead-in to a Greek chorus, as they advanced on Bernie.

Bernie grabbed her cell phone out of her purse, extended the antenna, and held it out in front of her. "Back, all of you. The first one to move gets this in the ear. Maggie, reach in my purse. I think I've got a nail file, too."

"You're being a jerk, Bernie," Maggie said, pushing the emergency button again because it seemed like the thing to do, although a quick peek through the glass walls had shown her that *all* of the elevators had stopped.

Still, Bernie had a point, and a history. A few years ago a wannabe had followed her into a ladies room at a conference and trapped her in one of the stalls, then passed her manuscript under the door and ordered Bernie to read it before she'd let her out again. It wasn't easy, being an editor at one of these conventions, one of the reasons Bernie never wore her name tag.

"Maggie?"

"Virginia," Maggie said, wondering what her friend wanted now. "Do you want to sit down or something? I'm sure everyone will make room for you."

"That could be a plan," Virginia said, then sort of rolled her lips between her teeth as she went pale.

"What?" Maggie asked, pretty sure she was going to panic if Virginia said what she had a sinking feeling she was going to say. "You're not in labor are you? Tell me you're not in labor."

"Sorry," Virginia said, and then her eyes went very wide. "Oh-boy, stand back. There goes my water."

Now, Maggie had never given birth, but she'd written several birthing scenes in her Alicia Tate Evans romances, so she sort of knew the basics. One of the basics was that, sometimes, a woman's water broke on its own, shortly before the birth.

She'd written scenes like that, envisioned them in her head. A little "Oops, what was that?" A little "Let me get you to bed, darling" as the hero scooped his wife up into his arms, ala Clark Gable in *Gone With The Wind,* and carried her upstairs. A little "Oh, dear, it's . . . it's . . . something's *happening!"* A little trickle, that sort of thing.

Yeah. Right. So much for research.

Virginia said it, and then she did it—water, water, everywhere. A real gusher, splashing on the carpeted floor, splashing on the Cincinnati trio, who jumped back as one, yelling "Oh, *yuck!"*

Niagara put out less water in an hour than Virginia Neuendorf had done in five seconds.

Maggie quickly helped Virginia into a sitting position on the floor, sliding in the fluid and trying not to think about that part at all. "Tell me again, Virginia. How long were you in labor with your last one?"

"You don't want to know, Maggie. Just push those buttons, call somebody, *do* something, or your next line is going to be 'I don't know nuthin' 'bout birthin' no babies.' "

"Oh, shit," Maggie said, grabbing the cell phone from Bernie's hand and dialing 9-1-1.

Not that Bernie noticed. She was too busy pouring scotch into her glass from a small silver flask she'd unearthed from her purse and downing it, then drinking directly from the flask as Bunny, obviously fully recovered from her "nervous collapse," began acting out dialogue from *The Flaming Flower of Shannon* for Bernie's edification.

" *'And it's teasing me you are with that heaving bosom, isn't it, m'love?' "* Bunny was saying in a deep voice, then quickly shifting to a higher voice: " *'You're a lyin' connivin' beast of nature, Devon O'Donnell! Touch me again and die, you Irish dog!'* "

"Oh, Jesus, save me. Somebody! Anybody!" Bernie whimpered, banging on the doors with her flask.

"Careful, that's *Tiffany's,*" Maggie said, taking the flask from her. "Besides, we might need it for Virginia. Brandy's like a germ killer, right?"

"That's part of my rationale, yes," Bernie said, sobering. "She's really going to have the baby now?"

"If we can't get her out of here, yes, and 9-1-1 put me on hold, for crying out loud! I heard they did that, but I've never—yes! Hello! Hello! My name is Maggie Kelly and we're stuck in an elevator at the Marriott in Times Square and one of us is having a baby and you have to get here and get her out or—what do you mean the Marriott will handle it? *You* handle it, damn it. *I don't know nuthin' 'bout birthin' no babies!*"

She hit the End button, looked at Bernie. "They hung up."

"Let me tell you something, Maggie," Bernie said, putting an arm around her shoulders. "Everybody in stuck elevators does that 'she's having a baby' routine so they can get faster service. And that birthin' no babies bit didn't help you sound real, you know?"

"Don't panic, Maggie," Virginia said, reaching up a hand to grab the cell phone from her. "But I probably should call John, just to let him know what's happening."

"Those creeps!" Brenda Patterson yelled, looking down to the hotel foyer. "They're trying to look up everybody's skirts. Look at those men—pointing, laughing. That's disgusting!"

"Cripes, lady, you're breaking my eardrums here. Who'd want to look up your skirt?"

"And then, after he deflowers her in the stables, and

I describe how the storm is moving in, lightning flashing, rain sheeting down, thunder—*boom! boom!*—Lord Devon laughs maniacally—*ha! ha! ha!*—and hands her over to his groom, who pulls out his whip and—"

"Yes, John, in an elevator. No, John, you don't have to fly here right now, this evening is fine. John? John, stop laughing. I'm hanging up now." Virginia looked up at Maggie. "He's calling my mother to come stay with the kids and flying in on the next plane. *Oooooh,* here comes another one," she said, holding onto her belly with both hands. "What was the time?"

Mitzi the cheer leader, who had a second hand on her wristwatch (she probably also had paperclips, wet-wipes, and a complete sewing kit in her purse), sighed, then said, "Two minutes. That's awful close."

Maggie grabbed Mitzi's arm. "Are you a nurse? Please say you're a nurse."

"Sorry, I'm a dental hygienist."

"Of course you are," Maggie said in disgust.

"Yes, and I can tell you, that man over there doesn't brush well, and I doubt he's ever flossed."

"Oh, well, now I can die happy, knowing that—are you out of your mind? We're having a baby here, who cares about flossing?"

"Everyone should," Mitzi said, pouting.

"Whoosh-a, whoosh-a, whoosh-a," Virginia panted, from the floor.

"But then we have three great pages of angst, angst, angst, and Lord Devon reconsiders and comes back and saves her in the nick of time and takes her to the castle. Make love, make love, make love. About ten pages. She wakes the next morning, sore and bruised, but with a beatific smile on her lovely face as she pushes her waist length, tawny gold hair away from her naked, pouty breasts with their pert, rosy aureoles, and remembers the night, that glorious, passion–filled night spent with Lord Devon O'Donnell's turgid love member sunk deep between her—"

"Turgid love member? Cripes, would you knock it the hell off?" Maggie shouted. She was definitely shouting. Her blood pressure was probably through the roof, and she was pretty sure she was no more than five seconds from outright hysteria.

"Whoosh-a, whoosh-a, whoosh-a." Virginia was really into this panting thing.

The elevator moved, climbed a few feet, then fell a good ten as Sally Fish screamed and the non-flosser tossed his cookies down the side of the glass.

"We're going to fall!" Sally screamed. "We're going to *die!"*

"No, baby, no we're not," Mitzi the den mother soothed, pulling Sally into her embrace. "Now come on, let's be calm. I know! Let's sing! I mean it, singing is always good. Here we go! *'Michael rowed the boat ashore, hallelujah,'* come on, Brenda, join in. *'Michael rowed the boat ashore . . .' "*

"Whoosh-a, whoosh-a, whoosh-a, whoosh-a . . ."

"Hallelujah . . ."

Bernie eyed the flask in Maggie's hand. "I think that's all of them," she said, leaning one shoulder against the double doors.

"All of what?" Maggie asked as Virginia sort of arched her back and then spread her legs in front of her on the floor. Was she going to push? What would she do if Virginia started to push? And shouldn't she take off the woman's underpants? The kid could end up with a flat head, otherwise.

Maggie grabbed the flask from Bernie, and took a swig. "All of what?" she repeated, trying to focus on anything but Virginia's spread legs, or helping the woman off with her underpants.

"All the stereotypes, Maggie. The hysteric—we've got a couple of them. The pollyanna. The wimps, the cowards, the pregnant lady. All we need now is a hero."

Saint Just caught Bernie as the doors opened and she fell backwards, straight into his arms. "Hello, Bernice, my love. I believe I heard you call for me?"

"Alex!" Maggie shouted, trying to protect Virginia as the Cincinnati singers and Bunny headed for the door at a run, climbing up the few feet to the hallway. "Virginia's having the baby!"

"I open doors and execute rescues, Maggie," Saint Just said, holding up the crowbar he'd used to pry open the doors, "I don't midwife. Fortunately, there are several representatives of the medical establishment here, so if you'd just let go with that death grip you have on poor Virginia, I think we have everything well in hand. Who's that?"

Maggie looked over her shoulder, to see the businessman, who was gathering up papers that had fallen from his briefcase in the rush for the hallway. "A jerk. He's been a real pain. He even told Bernie to shut the fuck up."

"Oh he did, did he? That's a pity." Saint Just neatly hopped down, into the elevator. "Sir? I hear you've been naughty. You will be apologizing to the ladies before you crawl away, won't you?"

The man looked up, got to his feet, and gave Saint Just the one finger salute, a universal gesture understood even by Regency heroes . . . which pretty much explained why the businessman was suddenly lifted from his feet and deposited against the interior wall of the elevator, to slowly slide down said wall until he ended in a sitting position much like Virginia's.

"Thank you, Alex," Bernie said, grabbing the flask back from Maggie as paramedics stepped down into the elevator and began helping Virginia to her feet. "I said I wanted a hero, and there you were. Now if you could slap that Bunny person senseless next time you see her, I'd be your slave for life."

"I don't think so, Bernie, sorry. Besides," he said, turning to Maggie, looking at her in a very intense way, as if he might be contemplating gathering her into his arms, "we've got a very large problem. That's why I'm here, rather than waiting, as the good *Left*-tenant suggested, for outside assistance. Looking up from the lobby, I ascertained which elevator was yours, and decided you needed to be rescued, now."

"I don't understand," Maggie said as Saint Just hefted himself out onto the floor, then put down his hand, helping Bernie and Maggie up and out of the elevator after Maggie found out what hospital Virginia would be going to and promised to be there as soon as possible.

Saint Just picked up his cane and tucked it under his arm. "You will, as soon as we go down to the seventh floor," he told them, leading the way to the stairwell. "The escalator from the lobby has already been placed out of bounds, and most of the elevators are still out of commission," he explained as he opened the door to the stairwell. "I'm sorry for the inconvenience, but we're several flights from the seventh floor, which is where we want to be before it can be completely sealed off. Wendell is already there, taking charge."

Saint Just had just opened the door to the seventh floor, ushering Maggie and Bernie into the hallway, when a litter went by, pushed by a pair of paramedics. Maggie tried to see who was on the litter, but only caught a glimpse of a pair of sensible navy blue two-inch heels, and an alligator attache case stuck beside the body.

Giancarlo, white linen shirt open to the waist and billowing around him, ran to the litter, leaning over it as it went by. When he was told to step back, he took the attache case and followed after the paramedics.

"Who? What?" she asked, looking at Saint Just.

"That would be Liza Lang," Saint Just told her as a uniformed policeman approached them, his hands outstretched as if to keep them back. "We're here with *Left*-tenant Wendell," he told the man, who didn't seem impressed.

"Sergeant Decker is in charge here," he said, still motioning for them to leave the area.

"Really? Now, how do I say this politely? Sergeant Decker couldn't successfully mind mice at a crossroads," Saint Just said amicably. "Do be a good fellow and toddle off to find Wendell. He'd be the one who looks as if he's slept in his clothes. There you go."

Maggie watched the cop walk down the hallway toward the semi-circle bank of elevators. "Liza Lang, Alex. What happened to her? Will she be all right? Did the elevator drop and hurt everyone? Is that why you did your hero bit? Because you were worried our elevator would drop, too?"

"When you're quite done weaving scenarios?" Saint Just said, folding his arms across his chest. "Oh, good, here comes Wendell. I'm sure he'll explain."

Maggie looked down the hallway, to see Wendell trotting toward her. His hair was its usual mess, as if he'd been dragging his fingers through it, and his gold shield was hanging from the handkerchief pocket of his rumpled sports coat. He was so cute, so wonderfully imperfect. "Maggie, you're all right! Good work, Blakely."

"Thank you," Saint Just said as Wendell grabbed Maggie in a bear hug.

"He's nuts about her," Bernie said from beside Saint Just. "Bites you, doesn't it?"

Saint Just ignored the comment.

"You want to know what's going on, right?" Wendell asked, smiling as he ran his hand down Maggie's cheek.

"We saw Liza Lang being taken out on a litter," Maggie told him as he took her hand and began walking back toward the elevators.

The entrance to the semicircle of elevators was roped off with yellow crime scene tape, but Wendell lifted it to allow everyone to follow him.

"We've got a body, Maggie," he told her, stopping at the edge of a cluster of crime scene techs all wearing latex gloves and carrying the tools of their trade. "Rose Sherwood. She's been stabbed."

Maggie sort of reeled in place, then steadied her nerves. "No. Rose is dead?"

"Murdered," Wendell reiterated. "Lang was stabbed, too, but she'll be all right. It's just a slice. They were the only two in the elevator."

"But . . . how . . ."

"How did someone stab them in the elevator?"

"Well, yes, that too," Maggie said, shrugging. "But I was wondering how they got an elevator to themselves, to tell you the truth. Sorry. And who would want to kill Rose?"

Bernie snorted. "Just about anybody who heard her slip at the mike last night, I'd say. Nobody likes realizing they've been a sucker for a bunch of fake sweetness and a tiara, shelling out money and praise to someone who calls them sheep. I almost wanted to slug her myself."

Maggie sighed. "Can we . . . can we *see?*"

"Not really, no. We don't want to disturb anything, except that this is a public elevator and there's enough prints in it to ruin any chance we'll find anything that way. What I got from Lang before they took her away was that she and Sherwood got on the elevator on their room floor, hit the button for the convention floor—that's seven—and before the doors could close a masked figure ran in, stabbed both women, and ran out again before the doors closed."

"That's possible?" Saint Just asked. "And then the elevator got all the way down here, to seven, before it either stopped for more passengers or got stuck with the others?"

"It would seem so," Wendell said, shoving a hand through his hair. "Hard to believe it got all the way down from thirty-four without stopping anywhere else, isn't it? More likely they got on at seven, and the elevator got stuck right there. Lang's pretty upset, so we'll have to straighten that out later."

Saint Just nodded. "And the murder weapon? Gone, I'm sure?"

"We didn't find one, but Lang said it was a big knife. Of course, it probably looked big, even if it wasn't. People see a small gun pointed at them, and think it's a cannon. Fear, adrenaline. You know."

"The reliability of eye-witnesses is always in doubt, yes," Saint Just agreed. "Although it pains me to ask, where is the so-esteemed Sergeant Decker?"

Wendell rubbed at his jaw, as if he was checking for a five o'clock shadow. "Well, here's the part you aren't going to like, Blakely. Decker's gone looking for your Mary Louise. Seems he remembers her carrying a knife last night."

"Oh, for God's sake, you're *kidding,"* Maggie said, looking at Saint Just in time to see a small tic begin working in his right cheek. "Why would Mare want to kill Rose? She doesn't even *know* her."

"It's her knife he's interested in, mostly. I understand she was slinging it around last night during some contest," Wendell said. "When it tests negative for blood, he'll go looking somewhere else. With guys like Decker, starting with the obvious is Rule One. But don't worry, Maggie, I'm sticking around. As long as you're here, I'm here."

Saint Just rolled his eyes, because that was what he knew Maggie believed he would do at hearing such a fatuous statement. Inside, he was secretly gratified to have the man nearby.

CHAPTER 13

"He's adorable," Maggie said, looking through the glass at young John James Neuendorf, Junior.

"He's red and faintly creased and he can only open one eye," Saint Just pointed out as Sterling put his thumbs in his ears and wagged his fingers at the child while making silly noises that would be an embarrassment to a man who believed he possessed more consequence.

"He's only a few hours old, Alex, what did you expect? Top hat and tails?"

"I have no idea, my dear. I'm not accustomed to infants."

"No, you're not, are you?" Maggie said, frowning as she turned away from the glass. "Let's go see Virginia."

Saint Just shifted the large bouquet of flowers to his other hand and followed after Maggie and Sterling, taking a moment to look at John, Junior once more.

A baby. Would Maggie want a baby? She'd seemed enthralled. Lord knew she was getting long in the tooth, soon to be two and thirty. Positively ancient! Perhaps she should give birth to a child before she had to seek out her frilly caps and rocking chair and spend the rest of her life surrounded by fat, mewling cats.

He entered the room in time to see Maggie leaning over the bed, embracing a radiant Virginia, who looked none the worse for her hectic afternoon.

"Virginia," he said, approaching the bed, "my felicitations. He's a rare champion of a boy."

"He is, isn't he?" Virginia said, preening. "Eight pounds, two ounces, twenty-three inches long. And we actually made it to the delivery room, although only by about five minutes. John should be here by about midnight tonight." She turned to Maggie. "Want to bet he shows up with a tiny *Broncos* uniform and a football?"

"I'm not taking that bet," Maggie told her, stepping back so that Sterling could approach the bedside.

Sterling stood there gazing down at Virginia for several seconds, long enough for Virginia to look inquiringly from Maggie to Saint Just, before he leaned down and kissed the new mother's hand. "It's a miracle," he whispered in some awe, then backed up again, none too steady on his feet.

"Sterling just discovered that he's crazy about babies," Maggie explained, patting his pale cheek. "Aren't you, Uncle Sterling?"

"Uncle . . . Uncle Sterling? Oh, my stars. Do I have to do something now? Teach him to box, to fence, and all of that? Can't do the fencing, though. Too clumsy by half, I'm afraid. Pinked my tutor something awful, didn't I, Maggie? You said so, remember? Sorry."

"Don't worry about it, Sterling," Maggie told him. "Maybe you can teach him to ride a scooter. But that won't be for a few more years."

"Yes. Good. I'll have time to practice being an uncle. Uncle Sterling. That has quite a nice ring to it, don't it? Well, excuse me. I want to go look at him again. I think he knows when I'm there."

"Ah, he's such a sweetheart. I'm so glad you patterned your fictional Sterling Balder after him, Maggie.

But even you couldn't quite capture just how darling he really is," Virginia said as Sterling headed back to the nursery. "Now, tell me what happened at the hotel. The paramedics were talking about it on the way here. Somebody died?"

Maggie looked to Saint Just in mute appeal, and he stepped forward to explain. "Rose Sherwood and Liza Lang were stabbed in an elevator. Someone heard Liza's screams and somehow got the elevator doors open and discovered what had happened. Liza will be fine, it was just a wound to her arm. But, most sadly, Rose has expired."

"Ex—she's *dead?"* The new mother, all pink and white and maternal, turned to Maggie and said, *"Holy shit."*

"Bunny Wilkinson checked out and flew home about an hour ago, the wimp," Maggie said in some disgust, "but the convention goes on. Martha and Liza—Liza's wound was just a slice, only took a few stitches—say they're going to carry on. As a matter of fact, they're turning Saturday night's awards show and cover model contest finale into a tribute to Rose."

"Well, they sort of have to, don't they? I mean the convention, not the tribute, although that's very nice, I suppose. They made the commitment to the hotel, for one thing, and then there's a lot of people who have Sunday or Monday airline tickets and can't exchange them. Thank goodness I had enough flyer miles to go first class. I won't have any problems." She shook her head. "Rose, murdered. I'm still trying to wrap my mind around that one."

"Sergeant Decker questioned Mare," Maggie told her. "Made her turn over her knife to him, to have it checked for blood."

"You're kidding. Mare? She doesn't even know—didn't even know Rose. Did she?"

"No," Saint Just told her, "but Decker finally remembered seeing Mary Louise in a, shall we say, not precisely stellar moment, and he seemed to think it but a small step from begging for pennies at the Port Authority to murdering someone with whom she's not been acquainted. He's terming the murder something called a random mugging. In short, Virginia, the man has an attic crawling with maggots."

"I love the way Alex talks, Maggie. No wonder you modeled the viscount after him. A regular Renaissance man. And he talks just like a Regency hero."

"Yes," Maggie said, glaring at Saint Just, "doesn't he though. I'll have to start following him around with a pen and paper, to take down all his verbal gems."

Saint Just bowed, which probably saved his life, because Maggie couldn't see his satisfied smile.

"Okay," Virginia said, "back to Rose. What do you think, Maggie? You said those pranks would escalate into something worse. But who would have thought murder?"

"Well, Steve is trying to find out if the elevators all stopped because of another prank, or if it was just some glitch that happened at exactly the wrong time."

"Oh, sorry, Maggie," Saint Just said. "I forgot to tell you. While you were attending to your toilette, Wendell, always the eager assistant, called to inform me that there was a regular maintenance inspection going on at the time, and someone cut the wrong wire, pulled the wrong plug. Something like that. So, it was coincidence, and not a prank connected to the murder. Which leads me to believe that we may have two miscreants."

Maggie rubbed at her forehead, probably still in the throes of the headache she'd complained of, earlier. Not that this was surprising, after the day she'd had. "Jeez, Alex, don't go there. Don't you think we have enough problems with *one* bad guy?"

"True, but the pranks all seemed to be very well planned, in need of some forethought. This stabbing? More a crime of opportunity, a spur of the moment, rather slapdash sort of thing. That leads me to believe we have *two* miscreants, the second taking advantage of the first."

"And the pranks came first," Maggie said, nodding her head. "Okay, that makes sense. Let's think about this. Somebody sees all these pranks going on, knows somebody's responsible, and takes a chance to get rid of Rose for some reason or another, hoping the murder will be pinned on the prankster, the practical joker, whoever—whomever, I think. Does that work?"

"As well as anything else we have at the moment, yes," Saint Just agreed as a nurse knocked on the doorjamb and announced that the babies would be coming out in ten minutes.

"I guess we'd better get going, if we can drag Sterling away from the nursery window," Maggie said, grabbing up her purse. "Are you going to be all right?"

"Sure. John's going to come straight here, then stay in my hotel room tonight and tomorrow. We can go home then, baby and all. Get a contract, have a baby—all in all, Maggie, this has been a pretty good conference for me. Not for Rose," she added, wincing. "Keep me in the loop, okay?"

Maggie smiled in satisfaction as she finally won a game of Snood at the highest level, Evil, on her laptop, then frowned when the score came up and she saw the "Eternal Fame" list of top scores. They were supposed to be Maggie, Maggie, Maggie, etc., all the way to the bottom.

But they were Saint Just, Saint Just, Saint Just, then Maggie on the bottom of the list.

"Alex!"

"You screeched, my dear?" Saint Just said, heading toward the door of the suite, as someone had just knocked.

"Damn right, I did. Who said you could play Snood on my laptop?"

He paused, turned to her. "You say playing Snood helps you think, so I thought I'd try it. Very enjoyable. Is there a problem?"

"Yeah. How did you get thirty-four thousand on Evil? I've never gotten above twenty-eight thousand."

"I'm sure I have no idea, never having played the game until a little while ago. Now, if you don't mind . . . ?" he ended, gesturing toward the door.

"The least he could have done was leave my name on the scores, so I could pretend I got them," Maggie complained as she waved him away, staring at the scores before deleting them. As soon as she filled the top scores section she deleted it, started over. A competition with herself. Sort of. Some might call Snood yet another compulsion or obsession, like smoking, but she had trained her mind to never go there. The nicotine was enough.

Still, she'd been playing Snood daily for three years. Saint Just had played this morning for the first time and beaten her best-ever top score.

Perfect. When she'd thought up the Viscount Saint Just, she'd made him perfect. Every woman wanted a perfect hero. Boy, was every woman ever *wrong*.

"What the—?" she asked, looking toward the small commotion going on at the door.

She watched as two bellmen rolled in large, portable blackboards (okay, *white* boards, but they were pretty much the same thing), and, following Saint Just's directions, placed them behind the table where she sat, in front of the windows.

"Thank you, Ramon, Kevin. I do so appreciate your kind assistance, as does Miss Kelly, here. Miss Kelly, if you would be so kind?"

"Kind of what? Oh, right." Maggie reached for her purse and pulled out her wallet. "Here you go, guys," she said, holding up two fives.

Saint Just frowned.

She dug in her purse for a ten, gave Billy two fives, Kevin the ten. "Happy now?"

"Deliriously so, yes, as those fine fellows aided me in participating in a touch of petty larceny, appropriating these boards and bringing them up here," Saint Just told her as the bellmen left the suite.

"Good. I wouldn't want your reputation as a generous tipper to suffer. So you copped the boards?"

"Appropriated them. Temporarily. And in a worthy cause."

"Sure, I knew you could explain it all away, and even come out of it looking like the good guy. Now, tell me what the hell is going on."

"Simple, my dear. I happened to peek in on two or three of the WAR workshops, and noticed these clever boards, among other—props, would you call them props?—the ladies hosting the workshops were using. Workshops are quite involved, aren't they?"

"Are you kidding? We landed on the moon with less preparation. If you want to give a workshop, you have to submit a plan, drawings, overhead projections, the whole nine yards. I'm still trying to figure out why anyone would want to bother, considering all you're really doing according to Bernie is, bottom line, helping the competition. But that still doesn't explain these," she said, gesturing to the boards.

"Visual aids, I believe they're called. A way of organizing data so that everyone can see. I observed something similar put to use on one of those *Law and Order* television programs. Allow me to demonstrate."

He went over to the boards, picked up a marking pen—there were several, in different colors, and Maggie had the sinking feeling she'd see all of them sooner or later—and wrote in blue near the top of the first board: Miscreant Number One.

"Let me guess. Miscreant Number Two goes on the other board."

"Sharp as a tack this morning, aren't you, Maggie," Saint Just said, writing on the second board (in red), then underlining the words on each board. "And, we're ready. I've taken the liberty of ordering up some coffee, tea, and a few assorted bagels. The hotel kitchen, sadly, does not stretch to scones and clotted cream. You might want to get dressed, as everyone will be here shortly."

There was another knock at the door.

"Oh, damn, here we go again. Just what I love in the morning, turning the place into Grand Central Station. Hey, wait. Define *everybody*."

Saint Just headed to the door once more, and let in the waiter pushing a large, well equipped room service cart. "Just leave it there, my good man, and let me sign that for you. Maggie? Twenty percent compensation?"

"Why not," Maggie groused. "Add that to the per-person room service fee, and we could probably have used the money to fly to Europe, but why not."

"Parsimony is always unbecoming, my dear," Saint Just said as he pushed the cart over to the table where Maggie sat, fuming. "Remember that saying, there are no pockets in a shroud. Thank goodness you did not make me into a pinch-penny. It's so embarrassing."

"I could give you dandruff in the next book," Maggie groused, losing yet another game at the Evil level.

Screw it, she'd switch to Hard, maybe even Medium. She just wanted to win one. Win *something.* "Once again, tell me who all is showing up here, and why."

Saint Just poured her a cup of coffee, added cream and three sugars, wincing as he did so, then winced again as he added a tea bag to his own cup of hot water. "I must begin traveling with my own pot and loose sort," he said. "You Americans don't appreciate a fine pot of tea. Look at this, apricot-flavored tea. Why would anyone suppose a person would want *that* first thing in the morning, or at any time, for that matter? Would you be expected to drink apricot-flavored coffee, when all you want is some strong taste and invigorating caffeine? I think not. Tea drinkers deserve the same courtesy."

Maggie lost at Medium and all the skulls were blinking and grinning at her, mocking her. She slammed down the lid of the laptop and stood up. "Okay, don't tell me. I didn't want to know, anyway."

"Sterling and Mary Louise. The good *left*-tenant, as well as the very bad sergeant, unfortunately. Felicity and Bernie. Oh, and Tabby, who read about Rose in this morning's newspaper and is quite put out that no one phoned her. That should be about it."

Maggie shook her head. "I don't get it. In our books, you gather the suspects. What are you gathering now?"

"Our team, Maggie. Normally, I would confine my musings and calculations, even my deductions, to conversations with Sterling, with a few clever asides to the dear readers, but this is a very large hotel and this is today, not Regency England. The *left*-tenant, for one, has access to information not readily available to me, but necessary to our investigation. The same could be said for Felicity, who is close as inkleweavers with Martha, our new convention chairperson. As for the sergeant? Wendell tells me the man has been playing his cards entirely too close to his chest. In other words, he isn't sharing with Wendell. But the man's a showoff—or he wouldn't be entered in the cover model contest—so I believe having an audience will unsnap his lips."

"You're in the cover model contest. Are you saying you're a showoff?"

"I, Maggie, am an entrepreneur of sorts, and somewhat in the way of being both an example and an instructor, showing the world, at least the small bit that is romance covers, that a true gentleman, a true hero, does *not* shave his chest and bare his pectorals at the drop of a heroine."

Maggie laughed, finally finding something funny in the morning. "Good one, Alex. Now, if you could do something about the nursing mothers covers, every romance author in the country would be buying you roses. Damn, there goes the door, and I'm not dressed. Don't say *anything* until I'm back in the room, okay? I've got to hop in the shower."

Saint Just handed Bernie a cup of coffee—black, as Bernie preferred all her stimulants straight—and sat down beside her on one of the couches. "Have you been on the convention floor this morning?"

She shook her head, her halo of deep red curls settling once more on her shoulders. "Haven't had time. The Toland Books cocktail party and reception is today. Friday night is party night, be on your own night. Everyone makes the rounds of the various publishing houses' bashes, eats and drinks for free, picks up free books by the armful. The whole thing pretty much resembles a smash and grab at the local jewelry store, except the burglars wear sequins. Why?"

"Oh, nothing I won't find out later, I suppose," he said, crossing one long leg over the other and deftly balancing his own cup on the side of his bent knee. "I was only curious as to how many WAR attendees are still here, still attending functions. No matter. Felicity has promised us a detailed update she'll elicit from Martha Kolowsky."

"Narrowing the list of suspects, huh? You're good, Alex, I saw that when Kirk was murdered. But even if the sixteen hundred is narrowed down to an even thousand, or less, I can't see how you're going to find the bad guy. Why don't you just leave this one to the police."

"You've met Sergeant Decker and you can ask that?" Saint Just said, one expressive brow raised.

"Okay, you've got me there, good point," Bernie said, sipping her coffee. "But what about Maggie's Steve?"

"He is affiliated with Manhattan North. He's not allowed to poach on the territory called Manhattan South, unfortunately, although he's more than willing to help in any way he can, unofficially. However, he tells me he's wrapping up some sort of major case he's been working on for over a month, and could be called away at any time."

"So what you're saying is that we're pretty much stuck with Decker? Man, if I was going to kill somebody, this would be the place and time. Hey, good morning, Sterling," she ended as Sterling entered the suite.

"And a good morning to you, Bernie. Delighted to see you, and all of that. Hallo, Saint Just, I'm back."

"Yes, I had already assumed that, good friend," Saint Just said. "Your report, if you please?"

Sterling sighed, shrugged, then headed for the teapot. "Just as you thought, the murder seems to have caused all sort of riot and rumpus at the registration desk, as ladies volley for position in line to depart the hotel. I counted fifty-six in just the short time I was down there, observing. I could tell they were WAR attendees because they were all carrying large bags of books."

"Told ya, and the really big grabfest isn't until tonight." Bernie stood up, carried her coffee cup with her to the desk. "Excuse me for a minute, guys. I'm just going to call the catering service and halve my order, except for the candied bacon. And double the booze."

Next to arrive was Tabby, who wafted in on a wave of scent, trailing a long navy and kelly green scarf she wore over a navy blue dress that went to her ankles.

"Tell me," she demanded, flopping down on the facing couch as Saint Just poured her a cup of coffee. "Tell me everything you know. The story in the paper was more insulting than anything else, calling Rose this ancient *doyenne* of cheap, trashy novels, and making dumb jokes about the cover model contest and all of that stuff. They even found a photograph of her in a bubble bath, with her tiara. And her poodle, Captain Snuggles." She stopped, sighed. "Rose never photographed well, poor thing. The dog looked good."

While Bernie filled in Tabby on the facts, and the suppositions, Saint Just knocked on Mary Louise's bedroom door, then entered, to find that she was not there. A quick check of the closet and dresser showed that her clothing was gone as well. She had left behind Maggie's things, which would have soothed Saint Just somewhat, except that the girl had taken a damn inappropriate time to do a flit.

Stuck in with Maggie's things, he found a pithy note from the girl:

> *Vic—*
> *I don't need this*—a word was scratched

out—*mess right now. Decker, the whole scene. Sorry.*
Mare

"Damn and blast!" Saint Just exploded, throwing the note back on the bed. "Idiot child. All it needs now is for Decker to find out she's gone, and he'll have her tried and convicted and hanged before lunch. Sterling!" he called out, stomping back into the living room of the suite.

"What's wrong, Saint Just?" Sterling asked, wiping at the front of his shirt, for his friend's sharp shout had surprised him just as he was taking the first sip from his over-filled teacup.

"Mary Louise has run off," Saint Just told him, told the room in general. "She has to be found and brought back here, immediately."

"Yes," Sterling said, nodding his head. "The cover model contest is tomorrow night. Oh well, she probably went to visit her parents or something, and will be back tomorrow. Yes?"

"Her mother, Sterling, as you may recall Mary Louise telling us, is deceased, and her father is doing something called three-to-five as a guest of the state of New York. No, she's gone to Snake and Killer, I'm sure of that. Damn Decker for the fool he is! Sterling, go find the boys and charge them with returning Mary Louise to the hotel, with her luggage, by dinner time this evening. Here, take this note with you and give it either to one of the boys, or directly to her," he added, scribbling on a hotel pad, then ripping it off and handing it to his friend. "Do you have money?"

Sterling nodded as he read the note, then looked over his glasses at Saint Just. "But this is wonderful. Sergeant Decker has cleared her?"

"Sergeant Decker, Sterling, operates under a distinct handicap. He's dumb as a red brick. No, he didn't clear Mary Louise's name. But she has to think so and come back here, or she'll look even more guilty."

"Excuse me for pointing this out, but that's not quite fair, Saint Just, telling her a crammer like that," Sterling said, folding the note and sticking it in his pocket.

"Sterling," Saint Just said patiently, draping an arm over the shorter man's shoulders as he turned him about and headed him toward the door, "Mary Louise did not murder Rose Sherwood. You know that, I know that, the whole world knows that, and when Decker gets the report on the knife, even *he* will be forced to know that. I am merely anticipating a happy result, so that our young friend doesn't become the object of an all-out search for her, and to avoid her certain arrest by a man who can manage to bungle something as simple as buttering a roll. Do you understand now?"

"But they're—"

Saint Just closed his eyes, briefly, having immediately recognized his error. "Bagels, yes, I know. You have one safely stuffed in your pocket right now, don't you? Good, then you can be off, hot foot, prepared for any contingency," Saint Just said, patting Sterling's shoulder and then closing the door on him.

"Good man, Sterling," he told Bernie and Tabby as he perched on the back of one of the couches. "He'll find her, bring her back." He shook his head. "Fractious child. How could she be so bumblebrained as to be frightened off like that? Doesn't she know it only makes her appear guilty?"

"She's just a kid, Alex," Bernie said, fishing in Maggie's purse for a cigarette. "But here's something. What if our murderer also saw Mare waving that knife around at the costume parade, sneaked in here somehow, *borrowed* the knife, used it on Rose and Liza, and then wiped it off and put it back. Not that you can ever really wipe off all the blood, especially when you don't want to. Have you thought of that one?"

"The thought occurred, yes," Saint Just said, taking his quizzing glass out of his slacks pocket and dropping it over his head, in preparation for the coming meeting. "Which is why Sergeant Decker is in possession of a knife I picked out in a rather rushed visit to a shop two blocks from here."

Tabby's eyes grew wide. "Because you think she did it?"

"No, Tabby," Bernie told her. "Because the scenario I just put out there also occurred to Saint Just." She looked at him with some admiration. "How did you think of that so *fast?* And find a knife?"

"If one can't find a knife in Manhattan, my dear, and excuse me for being crude, one could not find one's own backside with both hands at midday."

"Good point," Bernie said, toasting him with her coffee cup. "You could go to jail for obstructing justice, withholding evidence, but good point."

"Au contraire, my dear worrywart. The good *left*tenant is in possession of Mary Louise's knife, and is having it tested for traces of blood. Any more questions? Ah, and here's Maggie. Don't you look fresh and alert."

"What's going on?" she asked, looking at the three of them. "Something's going on . . . and I won't like it, will I?"

"Nonsense," Saint Just said, offering her a cigarette from her own pack. "We were just discussing the Toland Books reception this evening, weren't we, ladies?"

"We're having candied bacon," Bernie put forth agreeably.

"Oh, that's my favorite," Tabby said, clapping her hands. "Maggie's, too."

Maggie looked longingly at the cigarette pack, then shook her head. "That's because it's usually the only thing at a cocktail party that isn't either fishy or smothered in cheese. Nobody serves those little hotdogs wrapped in pie crust anymore. I loved those. No, Alex, I'm not smoking today."

"Not pie crust, Maggie," Tabby corrected, smiling. "It's a form of puff pastry, and I still prepare it. Of course, I use small sausages and add some cheese."

"See, see," Maggie said, as if Tabby had proved her point. "Everybody's got to take a good thing and screw it up."

"Yes, well," Tabby said as she made a great business out of searching in her purse. "That Xanax I keep for emergencies has got to be in here somewhere," she said, then looked at Bernie. "Want one? It's either that or we're going to have to leave."

"Oh, for crying out loud, knock it off," Maggie groused, picking up an "everything" bagel and ripping it in half with some force. "You guys act like I turn into some sort of homicidal maniac when I don't smoke."

"Not at all, my dear," Saint Just said, taking a small plate from the table and handing it to her even as he gently removed one mangled bagel half from her fingers and deposited it back on the tray. "We would never say that about you. Or that you have the disposition of a curst warthog. We'd never say anything even close to that. Please allow me to freshen your coffee."

"Give me one of those," Maggie said, motioning to Bernie. "I wouldn't want you guys to have to deal with a homicidal warthog, now would I?"

"This is so bad," Tabby said, then sighed. "We should be more supportive if Maggie is seriously attempting to quit."

"Hey, she has my permission to quit any time she likes," Bernie said, "as long as it's next month, while I'm in Hamburg."

"Doctor Bob says he's going to find somebody to hypnotize me," Maggie said, taking a deep drag on her cigarette.

"Good old Doctor Bob. Don't you think you've been seeing him long enough now?" Bernie asked her.

"Yes, it has been several years, hasn't it?" Tabby chimed in. "Do you really need him anymore?"

"He seems to think so, yes. Once I stop smoking, maybe not. But I've been smoking since I hid from Mom in the bathroom at home and opened the window, blowing out the smoke. I think I was fifteen. In the meantime, I guess I'll just try to taper off, or something—cigarettes *and* Doctor Bob. Look, it's ten o'clock, and this is my first cigarette today. And I haven't killed anybody, right? So if I just—damn it!"

"Jumpy, isn't she, poor thing. I'll get it," Tabby said, reaching for the telephone on the end table beside her. "Hello? Yes, this is Maggie Kelly's suite. Whom may I say is calling?"

"Isn't she polite. You'd think she'd be wearing white gloves and a string of real pearls," Bernie said, smiling up at Maggie.

Tabby raised a hand, snapped her fingers. "Mrs. Kelly, you say? Maggie's mom?"

Maggie, who had been taking a drag on her cigarette, began to cough, and ran to the other side of the room, burying her head in a small pillow she'd grabbed from one of the couches.

Tabby made faces as she alternately talked and listened. On the whole, she did *lots* of listening. "Oh, how nice. This is Tabitha Leighton, Mrs. Kelly, Maggie's literary agent? Excuse me? Yes, yes, I give your daughter very detailed records of all monies that go through my office. No, I wouldn't call Maggie naive. Or that either," she added, her expression slightly shocked. "What's that? Bonded? Why, yes, of course I am, but—no, no, I wasn't sassing you, Mrs. Kelly. I was just—um, do you want to speak to Maggie?"

Maggie had already been making wipe-out motions with her arms, even as she silently mouthed "No! No!" Now she held her hands up in prayer, looking pitiful as she dropped to the floor and made her way toward Tabby across the carpet, on her knees.

"Well, here's the thing, Mrs. Kelly," Tabby said, trying to keep Maggie from kneeling on her full skirt, that dragged on the floor when she sat down. "Maggie's not here right now. No, ma'am, she isn't hiding in the bathroom. She's really not here, but I can—the murder? You read about that?" She made a face at Maggie. "No, ma'am, Maggie's not in any danger. What? No, ma'am, she's not a suspect, like the last time. Ma'am? All right, I'll tell her. Um-hum, I'll tell her that, too. And . . . what? You want me to tell her *that?*"

Maggie rolled her eyes.

"But how did you—oh, I see. Where there's trouble, there's Maggie, so you looked up the hotel phone number and called, asking for her? How . . . how inventive of you, Mrs. Kelly. I can see where Maggie gets her great imagination. Me? Oh. Well. I . . . I'm here . . . *sharing*. Yes, I'm sharing the suite with Maggie."

Tabby's eyelids narrowed and she was now glaring at Maggie. "Yes, ma'am, I'm paying my half, including tax. But I really must go now . . . yes, yes, I'll have her call you. No, I won't forget, I don't need to make a note." Her jaw dropped for a moment. "I don't think I *have* any string to tie around my finger, Mrs. Kelly. Yes, she'll call. I promise. Scout's honor. Good . . . goodbye."

"Thank you, Tabby, from the bottom of my chicken

heart," Maggie said, getting to her feet. "I couldn't have handled Mommie Dearest this morning."

"I couldn't handle her *any* morning," Bernie said, sliding down onto her spine on the couch. "And you just smoke? You don't drink? You're my hero, Maggie."

"You *are* going to call her later, right?" Tabby said, picking up the small notepad and beginning to fan herself with it. "She might come after me, if you don't. I think I'm afraid of her."

Maggie looked from one friend to the other, then grinned. "So, no more questions about why I'm still going to Doctor Bob?"

"None," Bernie said. "Why you haven't moved to New Zealand, yes, but no more about Doctor Bob. Okay, where were we? Alex," she asked, pushing back her head and looking up at him, "do you remember? Did you tie a string around your finger, to remember?"

"Hold that thought a second, Alex," Maggie said, looking at Tabby. "What was my mother telling you to tell me?"

"Oh, nothing," Tabby said, fiddling with her scarf.

"Tabby?"

"Oh, all right. She told me to tell you to keep your face away from the camera and your name out of the papers because *she* has a reputation to consider. She told me to tell you that she always said writing that trashy pornography would get you in trouble some day. She told me to—well, she told me to tell you that she wouldn't be the least bit surprised if you were involved in some way with Rose's murder, as you always find a way to get into trouble. And then she yelled at your father to for God's sake put his teeth back in because he looked like he was sucking lemons on the front porch of a run-down cabin in the mountains, and all he needed now was a banjo, some wood to whittle, and a forty-six Buick up on blocks in the front yard. She's—she's really something with words, isn't she?"

"That's Mom," Maggie said, with a rather painful looking grin. "Always my champion, always in my corner, rooting me on, building me up. Dad married her, so the rest is his problem, poor guy. But you gotta love her. Somebody should anyway." She reached for another cigarette.

Tabby held the mini-Bic for her.

Saint Just had stood, silent, through the whole, fairly ugly recital of Mrs. Kelly's bile, longing to take Maggie in his arms and comfort her, and knowing that she wouldn't enjoy feeling the object of pity.

So everyone either stood or sat there, silent, while Mrs. Kelly's infamous malevolence settled over the suite like a wet, gray blanket.

He had never heard the phrase "saved by the bell," but he knew he was grateful for the knock on the door, and hastened to answer it, admitting Steve Wendell and Sergeant Decker.

CHAPTER 14

"Morning, Blakely," Wendell said as he shambled past him into the suite. "How'ya doing?"

"I am enjoying my customary good health, thank you."

"Right. Good for you. You get a job yet?"

"On the contrary, I remain persistently idle, as any gentleman of means should be, and devote myself mostly to charitable endeavors meant to improve the lot of those less blessed. Ah, and the so estimable sergeant joins us as well. Huzza," Saint Just said as Decker brushed past him. "You're looking well, Sergeant. How wonderful of you to agree to join us for this little exercise."

Decker stopped dead—he had been heading for the coffee and bagels without saying a single word to anyone. "What little exercise? I'm here to question Mary Louise . . ." He reached into his sports coat and pulled out a notebook, began flipping pages. "Mary Louise—hey, I don't have a last name here. Why don't I have a last name here?"

"That is her last name, Sergeant," Maggie lied quickly, figuring that as long as Saint Just was in her life, she might as well step into trouble with him with both feet.

"Remember Tina Louise? Ginger from *Gilligan's Island?* She's a cousin. Perhaps you've noticed the family resemblance? Mary Louise is descended from the Omaha Louises."

"Yeah? No kidding. Wow," Decker said, and continued on his way to the table.

Maggie watched as he picked up a spoon, loaded it with cream cheese, then tried to spread it on an entire un-split cinnamon and raisin bagel.

Three napkins and two sucked fingers later, he finally had about a half pound of cream cheese on the bagel.

Saint Just had been right. The man couldn't be trusted to butter his own roll . . . or bagel.

"No jelly? I like grape best. See any?" Decker asked, poking through the cups and saucers and such.

"Sorry, Sergeant, it's all gone," Maggie said as Bernie laughed into her fist. "Perhaps you'd like to take a seat now? I believe Alex is about to begin."

"Begin what? Wendell? What the hell have you suckered me into? Besides, I've already got a prime suspect."

"You've got a functioning brain as well, Sergeant, hopefully," Saint Just said cooly. "We thought we might take this opportunity to prod you into employing it."

"Hey! Wendell? You told me you know him. You stand for this kind of crap from pretty boy here?"

Wendell sort of shrugged, then walked over to kiss Maggie good morning. He was such a sweetheart. She really liked him. Really. He was all cute and rumpled.

Saint Just joined them as Tabby beckoned Decker to sit beside her while she spread a napkin over his knees, probably with the thought that she might be saving the upholstery.

"Has he told you anything yet?" Saint Just asked.

"You mean like what he's going to do with his prize money?" Wendell asked, shaking his head. "Know where my page found him this morning? At a Ferrari dealership, for crying out loud, pricing a red one. He's convinced he's the next Giancarlo, whoever the hell he is. If I had the smallest hope this idiot could find his way out of a phone booth, I wouldn't be here, Blakely, playing your version of Trivial Pursuit."

"And I appreciate your sacrifice, Wendell, truly. Don't I, Maggie? As a matter of fact, I daresay we will rub along tolerably well during my investigation."

"*Your* investigation? That's it. I kind of like it when you talk rings around Decker, but now I'm outta here."

"No, don't, Steve," Maggie said, getting to her feet. "Alex helped last time, didn't he? And look, he's got everyone here. Well, except Faith, but she'll show up as soon as she trowels on her face. We've even got blackboards."

"Blackboards," Wendell repeated dully. "Oh, this is gonna be good. Is there a laugh track with this little show? Oh, okay, okay. Don't frown, Maggie, I'll stay."

"Yes, indeed, stay, please," Saint Just said, undaunted, just as Maggie wished she could shove one of the napkins in his mouth, to shut him up. "I wager we'll all be merry as crickets. Now, let us cry friends for the duration, Wendell, all right? We can pick up the cudgels again once the prankster is unmasked and after the murderer has been exposed and incarcerated."

Wendell raised his eyebrows. "Okay, I think I've waded through that last part. Practical joker *and* murderer? You think so, too? Good. I thought I was the only one who figured we've got two separate perps here, two different motives. As long as you don't start parading around, swinging that monocle thing and acting like some stuffed shirt idiot, I guess I can work with you."

"Don't worry, Steve," Maggie said, pulling out a chair in a hint that he should sit down at the table with her. "Alex only pretends to be an arrogant, overweening, know-it-all. Really, you might not know it, but he's no idiot."

Saint Just bowed. "Dearest Maggie, I'm humbled by those so flattering words. Now, shall we begin?"

He walked behind the table, to stand in front of the boards. "Ladies? Representatives of the constabulary? If I might have your kind attention?"

Steve dropped into his chair. "Constabulary? I thought you said he wasn't going to be an ass."

"Oh," Maggie said, reaching over to pat Steve's hand, "Alex is always an ass. I said he wouldn't be an idiot."

There was yet another knock at the door and the sergeant was quick to answer, first licking cream cheese off his fingers, so that Maggie made a mental note to see if Lysol was sold in the gift shop, and Felicity entered, breathless.

"Am I late? I just had a phoner with the loveliest man from Chicago."

"A phoner?" Decker sort of rolled his broad shoulders, flexed slightly, and said, "You licensed for phone sex, Ms. Simmons?"

Felicity's eyes grew wide as her mouth dropped open. "Am I . . . did you say . . . oh, for goodness sake! Willie, don't be silly. A phoner is a phone interview with a radio station. To publicize my new book?" she added when Decker still looked confused. "All right?"

"For a moment there, she was ready to take him out at the knees," Maggie told Saint Just and Steve. "Do you think her eyes look a little unfocussed? I wonder if she's on tranquilizers, or just lost a contact. Anyway, good thing she must have realized we still need the jerk."

"But not for much longer, I most sincerely hope," Saint Just said, then went to settle Felicity beside Bernie, as

Tabby had suddenly found it necessary to spread her skirts on the couch cushions. Decker, either unfazed or oblivious, commandeered the piano bench.

"Learn anything, Faith?" Maggie asked, sensing that Steve was getting antsy again. Anything she could do to get this dog and pony show on the road.

"Yes, Maggie, I did. And, if I haven't mentioned it, this is sort of fun. Detecting, you know. Why, I feel just like Jessica Fletcher. You know? From that show? *Murder She Wrote?* I mean, I'm a woman, and a writer, and—well, you probably can guess the rest, can't you. I don't have a bicycle, but Jessica did move to New York when the ratings started to fall, didn't she? I could get a bicycle, if anyone thinks that's necessary?" She looked around the room, then lowered her head. "Sorry. I just feel . . . feel so . . . wonderfully *loose.*"

"Heaven help us, she's *loose.* Tell me again why we need her," Maggie muttered out of the corner of her mouth.

Felicity opened her purse and pulled out several folded sheets of paper. "I've been a busy little Jessica Fletcher. Here's the most up-to-date list of those members who are still here." She handed it over to Saint Just, who then handed it over to Wendell. "Eight hundred and twenty-six. That's almost half of the attendees already gone, and more are leaving."

"They're checking out?" Decker's face paled. "But they can't do that. Until I get enough to arrest Louise Omaha, they're still suspects."

"Cripes, give me a break," Wendell muttered under his breath as he rubbed at his forehead. "Decker, you can't hold sixteen hundred people as suspects. Maggie already gave me a listing of all the registered attendees. Or were you planning to put all these ladies up here at city expense until you solve the crime? Which could be Christmas of next year, if we're lucky. Nobody would give Willie here a homicide on purpose, but he was on the scene, so he's primary, and nobody can change that," he ended, under his breath.

"If I might continue?" Saint Just inquired sweetly, tapping one of the markers on the board to his right. "Thank you. Now, as you all can see—you all can see, can't you? Sergeant? Perhaps you might wish to move closer?"

"Nope," Decker said, popping the last hunk of bagel into his mouth.

"As you wish, Sergeant," Saint Just said, sighing. "As *most* of you can see, I have labeled this board First Miscreant, and the second—well, I should imagine that's obvious. In point of fact, I think I'd like to change this. Maggie? How do I remove something I've written?"

Maggie sighed, then dipped one of the napkins into a water glass. "Here you go, wipe with this."

"It won't ruin the cloth?" he asked, wiping the ink away.

"Hey, after being locked in that damn elevator yesterday I was offered two lousy free cocktail coupons for the lounge. I can add one napkin to that list."

"Bunny told me she's going to sue," Felicity added. "Of course, then she flew home, the chicken. Do chickens fly? I don't think so. She flew home, like a . . . turkey?"

"Turkeys also don't fly," Maggie said, shaking her head.

"Oh, you always think you're so smart. I was just making a point. Anyway, she's going to go down in history as the worst national convention chairperson we've ever had."

" 'Turgid love member,' " Bernie grumbled, going over to the small bar and pouring some scotch into a water glass. "I had nightmares last night."

"There. We'll leave the listing of suspects until another time, so please just ignore what I will now write on this first board," Saint Just said, and Maggie turned to see that he had written Second Miscreant halfway down the first board in his perfect copperplate handwriting.

He moved to the newly clean second board. "Now we're ready to proceed. I suggest we begin with a recitation of the events that have transpired since the beginning of the convention, not in any order, but completely. We will discuss each event, then place it either here," he said, writing the word *prankster* at the top of the second board, "or here," he ended, writing *murderer* halfway down the board, as we have already concluded that there are two people at work here, with two separate agendas. "Maggie? If you'll begin, as I believe you were there for the first prank?"

"She was there? Hey, *I* was the one who got shot at, remember?"

Little Willie Decker reached into his sports coat inner pocket and pulled out his trusty notebook. "Shot at? And you didn't call us?"

"It was a toy gun, Willie," Felicity told him. "But that doesn't matter. I was assaulted. Repeatedly. But that's not the point. WAR was assaulted, right from that first day. That's why I'm here, Willie. No one, *no one,* is going to do that to my beloved WAR, not while I still draw breath! I will leave no stone undiscovered, no clue unturned. We'll do it together, won't we? Because we either stand tall or we hang alone."

"Oh, good grief, would you listen to that? She's one big mangled cliché. And she looks kind of spacey, too. Screw the missing contact, she's definitely started popping some kind of happy pill," Maggie grumbled, dropping her chin in her hands.

"Yes, yes, thank you, Felicity," Saint Just said, applauding softly. "I bow to your estimable determination. Shall we charge on, for WAR?"

Felicity smiled, stuck one tightly clenched fist in the air as a salute. "For WAR."

"What's WAR?" Decker asked, obviously still lagging behind, and Saint Just silenced him with a look.

"The first incident," Saint Just said, holding up both a red and a blue marker. "The cowboy in the lobby. Anyone?"

Feeling like an idiot, Maggie raised her hand, and Saint Just called on her. "Prankster," she said firmly, hoping to get the ball rolling before Wendell made a break for the door.

"Agreed?" Saint Just asked. When no one objected, he wrote *cowboy* beneath the heading *prankster*. "Next?"

"Oh! Me! Me!" Felicity shouted, her hand in the air as if she was that character, Horshack, on the old sitcom, *Welcome Back Kotter*. Come to think of it, Maggie decided, this whole meeting was like some TV sitcom.

Saint Just sighed, and motioned for Felicity to speak.

"The second would be the mice in my suite, and I say it was the prankster."

"The prankster, in the hotel suite, with the mice," Maggie sing–songed as Saint Just turned back to the board, and at the same time wondered if good old loopy Faith had any more happy pills in her purse she'd be willing to spread around.

"Mice in a suite? Here in the hotel?" Decker asked. He was definitely slow on the uptake, this guy, but eventually his brain seemed to register pertinent phrases.

"Just shut up and listen, Decker," Wendell said shortly. "Eat another bagel, or something."

Decker dutifully walked over to the table and rummaged on the tray, discovering the bagel half Maggie had left uneaten. He plopped the rest of the cream cheese on a saucer and went back to the piano bench, dipping the bagel into the cream cheese.

The word *mice* was written beneath *cowboy.*

The list got longer with the addition of *dead flowers, missing books and place cards, phone calls to Maureen Bates Oakley, gorilla, sprinkler system,* and ended with *Bunny Wilkinson on the roof.*

"Now, that's done," Saint Just said, "let us turn to those incidents that caused bodily harm. We begin with Giancarlo."

"Bodily—?"

"Eat," Wendell warned Decker. "Maggie told me about that one, Blakely. Are you talking about the guy who got socked in the face? Is that Giancarlo?"

"Correct, Giancarlo, the reigning cover model. It is my theory, one I will expound on later if you so wish, that the man was struck with a sock or other container filled with loose change, probably quarters, in an attempt to keep him from a publicity event he was to take part in with Miss Felicity Boothe Simmons."

"Her again?" Wendell said, looking at Felicity, who was alternately trying to look both oppressed and beautiful. To Maggie's mind, she ended up looking constipated . . . but happy about it.

"Yes, but in this case, I do believe Giancarlo was the target. So. Prank, or the work of our eventual murderer? Keeping in mind, if you please, that we had already been witness to," he used a marker to tick off the events against the board, "the cowboy, the mice, the dead flowers, the phone calls that kept Ms. Oakley from her welcome speech, etcetera."

"Okay, I'm getting your drift, Blakely," Wendell said, getting up and beginning to pace. "There were enough pranks that first day—and early the next morning—to make someone think the pranks would be a good cover for something more serious. Like murder. Or assault, at the very least."

"Exactly. Now, there are two people who could benefit from the withdrawal of Giancarlo from the lists, Damien and Lucious, the other contestants in the cover model contest. I won't count myself, naturally."

"Why naturally?" Wendell asked, grinning at Maggie, who stuck her tongue out at him. Honestly, these male egos. It was sort of flattering, but could also be a major pain in her neck. "Okay, okay, never mind. But a sock in the jaw with a sack of quarters isn't murder."

"True," Saint Just agreed. "So? Is this the work of the prankster, or the murderer?"

"The murderer," Bernie declared. "Giancarlo's the big cheese in romance covers. Knocking him out of the contest he's already won four times—he's allowed to win as often as he can—would open the doors for Damien or Lucious."

"I beg your pardon, Bernice. I believe *I* am also a contestant? And, if I might be so immodest, definitely already a favorite?"

"Oh, yeah, right. Sorry, Alex."

Saint Just acknowledged her apology with a slight inclination of his head.

Tabby timidly raised her hand, and was called on.

"Thank you, Alex. I think Bernie's suggesting that Giancarlo could be our next victim, if Rose's murder isn't solved? Because Rose and Giancarlo were close? The thing is, I've heard, several times, from several sources, that Giancarlo is on his way out. He's been overexposed, used too often, and the publishers are looking for a new chest, er, face. Why hit him, chance giving him the pity vote from the WAR members, if he's already halfway out the door? I know I felt sorry for him. If he's not a potential victim, I'd be more prone to believe that Giancarlo hit himself. As a publicity stunt, as he knew the media was in the ballroom, waiting for him. And he had a makeup man right on the spot, remember, to cover the bruise?"

"That's good, Alex, very good. The woman never fails to surprise me," Maggie said, looking up at Saint Just. "Just when you think her brain's wrapped in pretty pink rickrack, and ways to make Christmas decorations out of old toilet paper cardboards, she comes up with something like that."

Saint Just stood silent for a moment, then turned to write on the board, drawing a line and making a new category: *Giancarlo.* Beneath that, he wrote *prankster?* Below that, *murderer?* And, below that, *publicity stunt?*

"There we go, ladies. We'll get back to Giancarlo later."

"Murderer, Alex? Do you really think so? Didn't you want to write potential victim?"

"We're listing events at the moment, Maggie, placing responsibility on either the prankster or the murderer. With Giancarlo, I simply added a third alternative for the moment."

"Oh, right. Still, that list seems to make him a suspect, not a victim. Sort of a multiple-choice as to which he is, huh?"

Saint Just looked at her levelly. "Yes, it could be seen that way, couldn't it? Interesting. If nothing else, I like the way you think, my dear."

"Gee, now I feel all warm and fuzzy," Maggie said, rolling her eyes.

"Good. I am, as always, delighted to be of service. Now, back to the list of incidents. Anybody?"

"Felicity again," Decker said, and everyone turned to look at him in time to see him licking the last of the cream cheese from the rim of the saucer. "The shock from the mike, remember? And it's easy. I say the murderer did that one."

"And I must most humbly disagree," Saint Just said, dismissing the man by simply turning his back on him. "If murder had been in mind, our dear Miss Simmons would not be joining us here today, but would be at this very moment being carried to bed on six men's shoulders. No, it was another prank. Decidedly nasty, but nonetheless the work of our prankster." He held up the marker. "Discussion?"

"None from me," Felicity said, sinking into the couch cushions. "I wouldn't want to think anyone wanted to murder me."

"No, someone just doesn't much *like* you, Faith," Maggie pointed out, smiling. "You're used to that."

"You never were funny, Maggie," Felicity groused.

"You know," Bernie offered, "a lot of the pranks were against Felicity. Maybe Maggie's got a point, and someone really doesn't like her. I mean, there were over sixteen hundred people here. Why not spread the pranks around more?"

"Miss Simmons is the keynote speaker, Bernie," Saint Just reminded her. "Any mishaps involving her would be sure to get media attention. Which brings us to a very large question. Motive."

"Shouldn't you put Rose's murder under the *murderer* heading first?" Tabby, ever the neat-nik, asked. "That would make the lists complete."

Saint Just dutifully recorded Rose Sherwood's murder under *murderer,* as Bernie piped up, "Yeah, can't forget Rose. Her getting killed sure blows your theory that she was pulling all these stunts, right, Tabby?"

"It was just one theory," Tabby said bravely, arranging her skirts around her. "So I may never have liked her all that much, that's no crime. She's dead now, so let's leave it alone."

"I thought she was considered to be a nice enough old tabby," Saint Just said.

"Don't say that, it's sexist," Maggie warned him, then explained: "Rose was a businesswoman, and she wasn't always aboveboard, at least to hear a lot of people tell it. Let's face it, she tried to make or break people as she put her stamp on the romance industry. It's not the sort of thing that makes you popular."

Wendell stood up. "Okay, back to business. So far we've proved that there are two perps running around here, one pulling practical jokes, one knifing nice or not so nice old ladies in elevators. What else?"

"Suspects, *left*-tenant," Saint Just said, and Wendell sat down once more. "If you would be so kind as to take out your notebook and check your previous list with the names I'll give you now?"

"You've got more names?" Wendell asked, already flipping open his notebook. "Okay, go."

"First, let me say that Wendell already is in possession of these names. I repeat them here so that everyone knows what is going forward. Secondly, I should preface my list with the admission that I am dealing almost entirely on instinct here, and needs must beg you to come up with facts to reinforce my vague assumptions."

"He talks weird, but I figured that one out. He doesn't know shit, does he?" Decker said, closing his own notebook and putting it back in his pocket.

"Setting himself up as a wit. How droll. Now, to begin," Saint Just said, directing a long, dispassionate stare at the sergeant, "I would again ask that the name Top Star Electric be investigated, as I observed a person possibly employed with that establishment fleeing the scene of Felicity's nasty shock. To hone the search, I will tell you all that the man was wearing a very unflattering, one-piece brown uniform with those words on the back, arched overtop a crude depiction of a light bulb."

"That's withholding evidence, Blakely," Decker said, jutting out his rather remarkable jaw. "You should have told me this right away. Wendell isn't in charge. I am."

Maggie closed her eyes, wondering when the fireworks would start, but Saint Just was nothing if not a master of his emotions.

"As I recall the thing, Sergeant," he said mildly, "you weren't overly interested in anything I had to say, being much more concerned with cutting your own dash as a cover model, although we are all gratified to have finally gained your attention. Wendell? Can you still do something with this information? I know they can on that television program, *NYPD Blue.*"

"That show has a bigger budget than the *real* NYPD, Blakely," Wendell told him, "and the shock thing wasn't exactly high priority. Although, if now you think it ties in with the homicide . . . ?"

"Let us say that, at least for the moment, if it makes things easier," Saint Just agreed, nodding. "Remember, it most especially ties in, as you call it, if manipulating the overhead sprinkler system in the book room also took electrical ability."

"I haven't done much yet—I've been busy. I'll check on this Top Star Electric first, although, as I already told Blakely here, there are probably a bunch of them just in the five boroughs. Once I find them, then what?"

"Then, my good fellow, I would ask you to check on any employees whose last names match any of those on the list of WAR attendees. It recently has been brought to my attention that the writing of romance novels may include the writer's spouse, and I do not believe we can overlook that sort of connection. Also, everyone, while already the *left*-tenant is employing the resources of this same NYPD, I have already suggested background checks on the following persons."

He held up one hand, and began ticking off names. "We begin with Giancarlo himself, be he victim or opportunist, or even murderer. We carry on with Damien, then Lucious, still working on the assumption that this cover modeling business is a cutthroat affair and remembering that Rose Sherwood oversees—oversaw—the cover model contest, was possibly even capable of adjusting the vote totals to guarantee the desired outcome."

"What about Liza Lang?" Maggie asked, figuring she'd been silent long enough. "I'd sure like to know why she's stuck around all these years, taking crap from Rose, if what we heard with Rose's slip at the mike means anything. The pay couldn't be that good, and we all heard Rose call her a slut. Besides, I think she might have the hots for Giancarlo."

Felicity snorted from the depths of the couch, as she'd sort of slid down on her spine. "Yeah, right. Rots-a-ruck, Riza. The woman's a mouse. Besides, Giancarlo is in love with Giancarlo. All those models are in love with themselves."

"I'll check her out, do a background search, Maggie," Wendell said, underlining yet another name. "I wish I could have gotten this started sooner."

"And then," Saint Just said, looking at Maggie, "I have asked the good *left*-tenant to do one of those same background searches on Martha Kolowsky."

"Martha?" Felicity pushed herself back up to a reasonable sitting position. "Okay, Liza was bad enough. But Martha? She couldn't have killed Rose."

"I agree, Felicity," Saint Just told her. "But we are

working under the assumption that there are two miscreants, remember?"

"Oh," Felicity said, losing her smile. Then she frowned, and her eyelids narrowed, and her ears got a bit red. "If that woman put those mice in my suite, I'll—"

"No, you won't," Maggie said, getting to her feet. "You'll keep your mouth shut about anything we're doing here, Faith. That's part of the deal, part of being invited to be on our team. Otherwise, I'll shut it for you. We're all just going to go on doing whatever it is we're doing, and say *nothing* about what we're thinking. You got that?"

"I don't take orders from you," Felicity said, crossing her arms beneath her ample breasts.

"Maybe not," Wendell said, "but you'll take them from me, Miss Simmons. Unless you want me doing a background check on you, as well. Maybe even ask the IRS to check you out? It wouldn't be the first time somebody did some pretty weird things to get publicity for themselves. If Giancarlo could, so could you."

"That . . . that's *insulting,"* Felicity said, but she nodded. "Okay. Loose lips sink ships. I won't say anything." She went through the motions of zipping her lip shut. "There," she said, talking through her closed lips. "Happy now?"

"We are all most gratified, yes," Saint Just said smoothly. "Decker? Surely you must be rushing off to do more . . . detecting, is it?"

"Yeah, okay, because we sure aren't getting anywhere this way," Decker said, heading for the door. "You coming, Wendell?"

"You go ahead. I'll meet you in the lobby in a couple of minutes." Wendell waited until Decker had gone, then said, "You know, Blakely, that's quite a list you've got going."

"Yes, I know. I wish it could be shorter. As the Abbé

D'Allainval said, 'The more alternatives, the more difficult the choice.' But I'm afraid we have to start with the many, and then winnow as we go along. You can glean some information on each person from the convention booklet. Maggie? Could you fetch that, please? Unless this assignment is too much for you, Wendell?"

Wendell looked at Maggie, who wasn't going to "fetch" anything. Who did Alex think she was? Lassie?

"You go get it, Alex. There's one over there, on the table."

Surprisingly, he did just that, and Wendell watched him as he walked away.

"He's deliberately trying to get my goat, you know." Saint Just was back in a moment, at which time Wendell added, "No, Blakely, it isn't *too much* for me. And it's not an *assignment.* We're working together, remember? Yea, team?"

"Of course, of course," Saint Just said soothingly, swinging his quizzing glass by its riband. "Forgive me. Ah, Sterling's back. How wonderful. Sterling? And were you successful? Feel free to simply nod, as I can see you at least found a street vendor. Just finish that hot dog in your own good time."

Sterling nodded as he walked past the three of them, chewing mightily, heading for the blackboards. He adjusted his glasses as he peered at the lists. "Whaff's fis?"

"We've been detecting, Sterling," Saint Just told him, then turned to Wendell once more. "Is there a way to trace—I believe that's the word, *trace*—phone calls made from one hotel room to another?"

"Good question. I don't know. Why?"

"The phone calls to Miss Maureen Bates Oakley that caused her to oversleep and miss her breakfast speech," Saint Just explained. "It would be of all things wonderful if we knew who placed them."

Wendell nodded. "Yeah, it would, but it would probably take a court order and I don't think telling a judge you've got a hunch is going to be enough to have one sign off on a warrant. Anything else?"

"I've got something," Bernie said, leaning back on the couch, so that Maggie could see the heavy phone book in her lap. "You were right, Steve. Top Star Electric must be a chain. There are two in Manhattan alone. Maybe even a national chain? That isn't going to help us a lot, is it?"

"Not much, no," Wendell agreed. "Oh, I forgot. I cashed in a few favors at the lab and got the report on Mare's knife this morning. It was clean, so she's off the hook. I didn't think you'd want me to announce that with Decker in the room, seeing as how he's still waiting for the report on the knife you gave him."

Saint Just bowed. "Thank you, Wendell. I won't forget your kindness."

Maggie bit on the inside of one cheek as she sort of raised her chin, tried to look nonchalant. Just how concerned was Alex about Mary Louise? And in what way? The girl was only twenty-one, if that. Much too young for him. Except, for Regency gentlemen, she was actually a little old. Most debutantes had their "come out" at seventeen or eighteen, and were married soon after that, often to much older men. Why had she never realized what cradle robbers Regency heroes were? It was indecent!

"Yeah, thanks, Steve," she said, because it was the right thing for a "nice girl" like her to say. Okay, she also liked Mare; she was a good kid, with an attitude problem. Maggie could relate to that.

Felicity approached, on her way to the door. "Did I tell you that fees for the cover model contest *are* refundable? Does that mean anything?"

"It did, once," Saint Just told her, "but now that Rose is gone? I don't think so. Anything else?"

Felicity looked miffed, which did a lot to improve Maggie's mood. "You'll remember to keep your mouth shut, Faith? Don't say a word to Martha, especially now that we have her listed as a possible suspect."

"And Liza Lang, I know," Felicity said, making a face that told everyone that she thought very little of either's chances as a suspect.

"Ah, yes, Miss Liza Lang," Saint Just said, adjusting his nonexistent cravat. "You suggested her, didn't you, Maggie? A recent entry into the lists, I agree, but coming on fast. As a matter of fact, I do believe it is time I sought out the woman, to console her in her hour of sorrow."

"You're not to be grilling suspects, Blakely," Sergeant Decker said from the doorway, as Felicity had opened it, and he was standing there.

"Decker?" Saint Just said, slowly pivoting to face the man, quizzing glass raised to one eye. "Must you lurk about here? I would think you'd be . . . detecting."

"Yeah, well, that's your problem," Decker said, looking very cop-like, in a Bozo the Clown sort of way. "And what's this hour of sorrow crap? I talked to Liza Lang already. The woman's upset. Doesn't that bother you?"

"You will find, Sergeant," Saint Just drawled, allowing the quizzing glass to drop, "that I often find other people's troubles to be a bit of a bore. Now, if you'll excuse me? You might have time for lollygagging, Sergeant, but I will now sally forth to solve a murder. I'd say it had been a pleasure, but I am, for the most part, a truthful man."

Maggie smiled widely, with her mouth firmly closed and her eyebrows raised, knowing she looked silly, but she'd have a long way to go to look as silly as Little Willie Decker, who was standing there, jaw agape, watching Saint Just saunter off, swinging his cane that had been propped beside the door.

"Come on, Decker," Wendell urged, waving the man toward the open door. "I'll bet the lab is done working up that knife. Who knows, you might have an arrest within the hour if your theory pans out."

"It will, which is why all of this was just a waste of my valuable time," Decker said staunchly, then marched into the hallway, did a very smart half turn to the left, and headed for the elevator.

"That man's enough to send a fellow to the dogs directly," Sterling commented as he watched him go. "A bit of a loose noodle, Maggie, don't you think?"

"He may be a jerk, Sterling," Wendell said, "but he's primary on this case, so we have to live with him. Tell Blakely I'll have the first of his information by tonight, tomorrow morning at the latest. I should have called in the names when he first gave them to me," Wendell said, then kissed Maggie and walked down the hallway, probably to make sure Decker left the building.

Maggie headed back to the table after Bernie left to oversee the preparations for the Toland Books reception, and Tabby departed in a flurry of scarves to have brunch with another of her clients.

"Very interesting, Maggie, don't you think?" Sterling said, standing in front of the blackboards, his hands clasped behind his back. "I could put all of this together into a tolerable rap, don't you think? Maggie?" he questioned when she didn't answer. "Didn't you like my rap?"

"Now that we're alone?" Maggie asked him.

"Yes, now that we're alone. Be honest."

She sighed. "All right, Sterling, I'll be honest. Let's

see, how do I do that? Okay, I've got it. I'll do it the way Alex would do it." She stood up, looked directly at him and said, "Never, I repeat, *never* do that again."

"Oh," Sterling said, immediately crestfallen. "That bad, huh?"

"No," she said quickly. "It isn't that, Sterling. It's just that rap isn't . . . isn't *you.* Sterling Balder, the Sterling Balder I know, wouldn't . . . er . . . perform in public."

"I *was* nervous," he agreed.

"Uncomfortable."

"Yes, that as well. And . . . and . . ."

"You're more familiar with sonnets. Couplets. That sort of thing."

"That sort of thing, yes. Thank you, Maggie. Now I don't ever have to do that again. Do you think Socks and Mare will be disappointed?"

Maggie had her own thoughts on Socks and Mare, and believed they'd enjoyed themselves very much at Sterling's expense. Not maliciously, but just for fun. But Maggie didn't believe in the sort of fun that ended up with someone else looking silly. "No, Sterling, I'm sure they'll be fine with it. So, no more rap?"

"No more rap," Sterling agreed, turning back to the blackboard. "What a maddening mull this is, Maggie. Who do you suppose did the deed?"

Maggie stood up beside Sterling, and both of them looked at the boards. "I don't know," she said after a few moments. "Hey, look at this."

"What?"

"Giancarlo," Maggie said, pointing to the board. "I don't know when he did it, but Alex washed off *publicity stunt* under his name. That narrows him to prankster or murderer. Does Alex know something we don't know?"

"I don't think so," Sterling said, frowning. "I mean, he can and does know many things I don't know. But can he really know anything *you* don't know, considering how it was you who created him?"

"Yeah, right. I'll bet Professor Frankenstein reassured himself with that same logic."

Sterling frowned. "You know, Maggie, I often have as much trouble understanding you as I do Saint Just. You're so alike in so many ways, and yet still so different."

Maggie smiled weakly, then picked up the ruined napkin and went to rinse it out in her bathroom sink.

CHAPTER 15

Saint Just sat at his ease in the lobby lounge, watching the world as it toddled past his table. He had a cooling cup of tea in front of him, and Martha Kolowsky behind him at another table, her back to him as she discussed the Saturday night tribute to Rose Sherwood with three minions. They had to be minions; she spoke to them as if they were at least three slates short of a full roof, poor dears.

How true, that slaves, freed, often become tyrants in their own right.

"We'll follow the prayer with the slide show," Martha was saying, her tone brooking no discussion of the agenda she'd planned. "Thank goodness Rose's was an online magazine, because we have her entire online photo gallery available for download. Irene, you'll handle that, please. Sarah? Here's a list of appropriate songs. Get together with Irene once she's downloaded the pictures and coordinate the musical clips to fit them, and I'll do the final assembly, as I have experience in these things, having compiled the video biographies of the Harriet judges for the past five years."

"Did you ever wonder, Martha," one of the minions

put forth timidly, "why we do these big video presentations of the judges, rather than the winners?"

In any group, there's always one. One who will ask the wrong question . . . and usually follow it up with yet another one. It was some sort of unwritten law, Saint Just had decided long ago.

There was a pregnant silence anyone save Saint Just would have called damned uncomfortable. "Sarah, we don't know who the winners are until the envelopes are opened. We *know* the judges. Now, Lori, you'll—"

"Yes, but we *do* know, because the names are already engraved on the Harriets, right?"

"Yes, well, that is, um," Martha said, obviously not prepared for that question, "I'll look into it."

"I think it's because we can't get judges unless we give them perks," that same, doomed voice said, sounding small, but hopeful.

"Sarah—shut up. Now, Lori, you'll assemble the programs for each attendee. I've already gathered Rose's biographical information, thanks to Liza. All rightie, then, you're off! Go! Go!"

Saint Just waited until the minions had scurried off—he could pick out the one named Sarah, for she sort of scuttled, with her figurative tail between her legs. He then stood up, teacup in hand, and approached Martha. "Excuse me," he said, bowing, "would you mind if I joined you? I . . . well, I confess to a bit of eavesdropping, Mrs. Kolowsky, and I just knew I had to tell you how very impressed I am by your . . . shall we say, take charge attitude in this time of confusion and sorrow? Mrs. Wilkinson's abrupt departure? Rose Sherwood being snuffed like a candle? Oh, the horror. And yet you are definitely bearing up most nobly under the strain. My felicitations, madam."

Martha pushed at her hair, smiling. "Why, um, thank

you, Mr . . . I'm sorry. I seem to have forgotten your name."

"Blakely, Alexander Blakely," Saint Just said, sitting down across the table from her. "May I order something for you? It would be my pleasure."

"No, thank you. I've already had several cups of coffee. I'm over my limit, I'm afraid. Oh, I think I remember now. Aren't you with that Maggie Kelly woman?"

Saint Just's right eyebrow rose delicately. He was Alexandre Blake, the Viscount Saint Just. He did not accompany anyone—people accompanied *him.* "We're attending the convention together, yes. Maggie is my cousin, you understand. Silly girl. She refuses to have her nom de plume on her badge, but she's really Cleo Dooley, you know. *New York Times* bestselling author of the Viscount Saint Just mystery novels?"

Martha's expression remained blank. "Sorry, I don't read mysteries."

"That must be remedied, Mrs. Kolowsky. If you'd give me your home address, I'll be sure to have copies of the entire series sent to you. Personally autographed by the author, of course."

"Oh, aren't you nice?" The woman might not read mysteries, but, according to Bernie, a free book was never refused, apparently, and she quickly reached into her purse, on the hunt for one of her cards. "I know I put some in here," she said, rummaging through the large purse. "I've been collecting cards all week. Oh, this is silly," she said, and unceremoniously dumped the contents onto the tabletop.

Wallet, one of those electronic notepads, lipstick, two paperback books, cell phone, comb, tissues, several pens . . . a goodly supply of loose quarters. So many quarters that some of them rolled off the table, onto the floor.

"Let me help you with those," Saint Just offered,

bending down to retrieve the coins. "My, you've got quite a collection here."

"Yes," Martha agreed, finally locating a thick stack of rubber band held cards and pulling out one. Three or four different cards, actually, and they also hit the floor, and Saint Just picked them up again, looked at them, returned them. All but one of them. That one he surreptitiously slipped into his pocket while Martha was shoving things back into her purse.

"Your purse must be quite heavy," he prodded as Martha began scooping quarters back into her bag.

"I know. I really should sit down and clean out this mess, but when would I have the time? I'm surrounded by idiots."

"Really? I've read that all great leaders have their trials."

Martha visibly puffed up at those words. "I have had destiny thrust upon me, Mr. Blakely, with Bunny's cowardly retreat." She reached into her purse again, shaking it as she scooped out a handful of quarters. "Now, if you'll excuse me? I have some calls to make."

"You're using a public telephone? Not the one in your suite?"

Martha, who had half risen from her seat, sat down once more, looking at him strangely. "Yes, I am. Why do you ask? Did you think I'd abuse my position by charging personal phone calls home to WAR, the way some person who won't be named but who was sharing my suite might have done?"

Saint Just had already stood up politely, and looked down at her, wearing his most sympathetic face. "No, no, most assuredly not, Mrs. Kolowsky. It's just that, in this day and age of telephones sprouting from nearly every ear, I'm surprised you are forced to use public telephones."

"Oh, you saw my cell phone. The batteries died, and

I forgot the charger at home, and I never got the hang of how to use one of those calling cards," Martha explained. "I've been collecting quarters everywhere I can. Now, again, please excuse me. I have a million things to do."

Saint Just watched her rush off, her heavy purse hanging from her shoulder as she made her way to the bank of public telephones at one side of the lounge.

"Making a date for the banquet, Alex?" Maggie asked, slipping into the chair Martha had just vacated. "And where's Liza Lang? I would have thought she'd be wrapped around your pants leg by now, drooling on your shoes, a slave to her own passion."

"Liza Lang," Saint Just mused, looking up at the expansive atrium. "What was it John Bunyan said? Oh, yes. 'A young woman, her name was dull.' "

"Really?" Maggie said, waving down a server and ordering a soda and an ashtray. "Let me guess, she blew you off."

"True. Not an earthshaking experience for any other man, but I admit I am more used to fawning adoration from the gentle sex, as *I* am not other men. In my vast experience, all women adore me."

"I don't," Maggie said, taking the ashtray from the server even as she rummaged in her purse for her cigarettes.

"Yes, my dear, you do," Saint Just told her smoothly, waiting for her reaction.

"I do not." She threw her cigarettes back into her purse, without taking one. "Besides, I'm not that nuts. You could disappear at any time."

"True enough. Although that has yet to be determined, has it not? We don't know exactly how Sterling and I got here, do we? On the other hand, Wendell has chosen a most dangerous occupation, and could be shot, bludgeoned, knifed—I imagine you have a variety of dangers to choose from—at any time."

She snapped the purse shut. "Do you think I haven't thought of that? I need someone . . . someone I can depend on. Which, along with everything else in my life, is still none of your business."

"Ah, and here I was just about to ask the so-estimable Wendell the precise nature of his intentions."

"Don't bother," Maggie said, sniffing. "They're the same as yours, to get me into bed. Maybe you should both remember that the last man who got into my bed ended up dead. There, happy now, or do you want me to go on?"

"Not really, no. The nail is in, my dear, there's no real need to hammer it home. Are you quite sure you don't want a cigarette?"

"I'm *not* going to smoke, damn it," Maggie told him firmly. "I'm quitting. Cold turkey. Bernie promised to hire me a lawyer who'd plead temporary insanity if I kill somebody, and I'm betting she knows one who could make the Nicotine Withdrawal Syndrome a valid defense—so watch it, bub, okay?"

Saint Just sat back in his chair, crossing one leg over the other. "Moving right along," he said with a smile, "I did learn a few things from our Miss Dull. Would you like to hear them?"

"Are they any good?" Maggie asked as she unwrapped a mint she'd pulled from her pocket and popped it in her mouth.

"Reasonably so. You may be determined to be disagreeable, but I am likewise determined to ignore your mulishness."

"Gee, thanks."

"You're welcome, my dear. First, she's amended her story to say that she and Rose Sherwood entered the elevator on the tenth floor, site of the *Rose Knows Romance* hospitality suite, and they were descending to the conference floor. That's seven, where we found them."

"I know which is the conference floor. And I still don't buy it, Alex. You've ridden on these elevators. Tell me one time that you had one to yourself. You can't. And you can't, because those damn elevators are cattle cars, especially in the middle of the day, which it was when the murder happened. They weren't on the tenth floor because lots of hospitality suites are there and the hallways are always jammed, someone would have seen or heard something. They weren't on the seventh floor, and the elevator got stuck right after they got on it. There's got to be another answer."

"All right, let's consider this. The hallways, as you say, are constantly crowded, and the elevators arrive so seldom, even when called, that the possibility of having one arrive empty, in a likewise empty hallway, with time enough for our murderer to race into it, stab Rose and Miss Dull, run off again, bloody knife dripping—well, those would be rather daunting odds, wouldn't they?"

"Yeah, and I don't know why Steve isn't working on that angle more," Maggie said, folding the mint wrapper into a very small square.

"I have something else to offer," Saint Just told her. "Mrs. Kolowsky is carrying a purse full of loose quarters. She *says* they're to use the public telephones to call to her home. That would be Colorado, correct?"

"She's calling long distance with *quarters?* What does she have, a couple hundred of them?"

"Conservatively, yes," Saint Just concurred. "Although I must admit, it is a rather ingenious and foolproof way of disposing of evidence."

"I'll tell Steve when he calls me later."

"Do that. Back to Miss Dull—Miss Lang. Who was it that said she might be in love with Giancarlo?"

"Bernie, maybe? Tabby? Does it matter?"

"Not really, no. Do you think it's possible? Remembering that she seemed immune to my considerable charms."

"Let's see. Liza is about thirty-five, fairly plain, and a glutton for punishment if Rose was always so nasty to her. Why else would she stick around? Okay, she's got a crush on Giancarlo, who has been around *Rose Knows Romance* pretty much from the beginning, if memory serves. There. Are you happy now?"

"Maggie, I was not crushed, but merely pointing out a fact. When I make a dead set at a woman, that woman crumbles—unless she is in love with someone else."

"I didn't crumble," Maggie said, taking out a cigarette and just holding it under her nose, sniffing at the tobacco.

"As a gentleman, far be it from me to argue the point, no matter how indefensible your position. To get back to Miss Lang?"

"Please," Maggie said, passing the unlit cigarette from hand to hand, as if trying it out for the most comfortable fit.

"All right. Ms. Lang was carrying a lovely attaché case, as opposed to the clipboard she could have been seen clutching to her rather insignificant bosom these past days. I commented on it and she said it was brand new, just purchased this morning, here at the hotel, as she now needed to carry more papers with her."

"So?"

"So, oh ye of little faith, how do you explain the fact that Ms. Lang's initials were on the case? In a rather lovely gold."

Maggie broke the cigarette in half and dumped it

into the ashtray. "She ordered it a while ago, maybe even has had it for a long time and just never used it. Why would she lie?"

"Because, if Rose had seen it, she would have mocked her for flauntng herself, putting on airs? I do recall seeing Rose's tiara. I think she preferred to be the only one of them who . . . shone. And she lied because she didn't want to admit that she hadn't dared carry the case—lovely thing, really—while playing dogsbody to Rose? Because she's not the sharpest knife in the drawer? Because she, like our dear Mrs. Kolowsky, is yet another downtrodden soul suddenly freed, who has yet to know how to manage that freedom?"

Maggie pointed at him. "The downtrodden and suddenly free thing," she said, frowning. "She sure did take over in a hurry, didn't she? She and Martha both. Do you think they're in cahoots? Or maybe not. Maybe it's all innocent. I mean, they could both just be really good organizers." She rolled her eyes. "Okay, okay, scratch that. I should have realized that it's too much of a coincidence, for both of them. Lack of nicotine."

"There's more. With a little prodding, Miss Lang was quite forthcoming on her plans for *Rose Knows Romance,* as if her position running the online magazine is a foregone conclusion. Do you think she's in Rose's will?"

Maggie rubbed at her forehead with both hands. "I don't know. None of this makes any sense. We should have asked Steve to do a financial check on *Rose Knows Romance.* What else did she tell you?"

"I believe that was it," Saint Just said, remembering the card he'd slipped into his pocket. "Yes, I'd say that would be all I know, about Miss Lang and Mrs. Kolowsky."

He pulled his pocket watch out and flipped it open,

looked at the time. "Ah, it would appear we are going to be fashionably late for Bernie's reception." He stood up, held out his hand to her. "Shall we?"

She hesitated, then took his hand. "I don't know, Alex. You're looking a little too smug for someone who just got the brush off from Liza, and too happy for a man who has more suspects, clues, and questions than anyone could figure out without a roadmap. What's going on? What do you know that I don't know?"

"Entire worlds, my dear," Saint Just drawled, pulling her arm through his. "Or are you going to tell me that we're not engaged in our own private contest to see who solves the crimes first?"

Maggie looked down at the floor. "This isn't a game, Alex."

"Oh? And that would mean that you've told me everything you know? As in, what have you been doing all afternoon?"

"You wouldn't like the truth, so just forget it, all right?"

Saint Just's smile faded. "You weren't with Bernie because she was putting together her reception. You weren't with Tabby, because she told me she was to be part of a literary agent panel this afternoon from two to five. You weren't with Sterling, because he volunteered to help Bernie, probably by tasting everything for her. Virginia is otherwise occupied with young Master Neuendorf. That leaves Mary Louise of the Omaha Louises, doesn't it? I saw her earlier, buying candy in the gift shop, so I know she's back."

"What? I can't do anything on my own? I'd have to have somebody with me?"

"Yes, you would," Saint Just said flatly. *How soon she forgets that her mind is my mind, and vice versa, at least most of the time.*

"Why?"

"Because you'd need a lookout?" he offered, raising one eyebrow.

"Go to hell," Maggie groused, then stopped in front of the bank of elevators and jammed her fists on her hips. "Oh, okay, you'll find out anyway. Mare and I tossed Liza's suite. Rose's suite. Liza's and Rose's suite."

Saint Just shook his head. "Tossed? No. I don't understand. And how would you have gained access to the suite? It was my understanding the suite had been sealed by the police. Liza Lang told me she'd had to change rooms yesterday afternoon when she returned from the hospital."

"Yeah, well they took away the crime scene tape this morning, and she's back."

"Interesting. And how did you manage to get inside—to *toss the place?"*

Maggie looked around, to be sure no one was close enough to hear her. "We waited until the maid propped open the door while she was cleaning up, then Mare distracted her while I ran inside, hid in a closet. Once the maid was done and gone, I opened the door for Mare. Simple, really."

"As well as devious and rather ingenious. My congratulations. What did you find?"

"Yeah, right, like I'm going to tell *you.* Do you really think I swallowed that baloney about you having told me everything you found out today? In your dreams."

"I see. *Quid pro quo?* Is that what you're after?"

"Sounds like a plan," Maggie said, punching the Up button yet again. "You go first."

"Oh, I think not, or are you seriously laboring under the misapprehension that I came down in the last rain?"

He smiled at Maggie as she glared at him, as he waited for her curiosity to get the better of her.

"All right, all right. And I didn't find it, Mare did."

"Mare? Now the mind does boggle. That she found something the esteemed NYPD missed, and that she'd be willing to help in the first place."

"You're forgetting, Alex, Mare was a suspect. She's pissed, pissed enough to offer her help."

"Logical, now that I think of it. All right, what did she find?"

Maggie put her head down and muttered.

"I'm sorry, I missed that?"

"Condoms. She found a pack of condoms in Liza's night stand. Blue ones. Blue glow-in-the-dark ones. With ribs. Extra large. Okay, happy now?"

"No, I don't believe I am. Could you possibly expound on this discovery, because I quite fail to see the relevance."

Maggie rolled her eyes, pulled him onto the elevator that had finally arrived, and hit the Close Door button before anyone else could pile into the car.

"Ah, how enlightening," Saint Just said, raising his quizzing glass to his eye as he eyed the button Maggie had pushed. "That closes the door?"

"Yeah, that closes the door, the one with the triangles pointing toward each other. This other one,"—she pointed to it—"has the triangles pointing away from each other. That holds the door open. Why? Oh, wait a minute. You think that's how it was done?"

"Can you offer another explanation?"

"No, I can't, and that explanation isn't enough. Decker's been questioning everyone he can find, and nobody said anything about seeing Rose and Liza getting into an elevator. Of course, there could be two theories about that one. That if anyone saw them they'd remember getting bumped from the elevator and report it. Or that whoever saw them, those persons left in the rush for the airports before talking to Decker."

"Again leaving us with our suppositions, and no facts. Now, back to . . . what you were talking about earlier?"

"Like you forgot. Sure. Condoms, Alex," Maggie said as the elevator rose. "We were talking about condoms. Think, Alex. Liza was sharing the suite with Rose. And she brought in a lover, with Rose able to walk in on them at any time? That could be why Rose called her a slut, right? But now we'll have to figure out who that lover was."

"Before you suggest it, may I offer a resounding *no* to you and Mary Louise chatting up every male here in the hotel, asking if they have a preference in colors?"

"I know, it's probably another dead end. But Liza does have a lover, you're right about that. So think, Alex, what if the rumors are right? What if it's Giancarlo? He's Rose's discovery, remember. She could be very possessive of him."

"Hardly a motive for murder," Saint Just said as the elevator stopped at Bernie's floor. "And, sadly, I believe yet another of your theories has fallen into the dust. We stopped nowhere, Maggie, but were taken straight to our destination."

"Damn," Maggie said as the doors opened. She walked into the hallway, then turned around, pushed a finger into his chest. "Your turn, remember?"

"Yes, it is, isn't it. All right, as long as you promise not to yell, or squeal, or whatever it is females tend to do when they're unreasonably excited?"

"Bite me," Maggie said, holding out her hand as Saint Just reached into his pocket.

"This was in Mrs. Kolowsky's purse," he said, handing her the card. "Never mind how I procured it, for that doesn't matter. We'll just agree that I have my small talents." And he did, but he certainly wouldn't wish to mention dumb luck as one of them.

Maggie, bless her, clapped a hand over her mouth to keep her squeal to a minimum.

"Much as I abhor immodesty—I believe I win?"

She just nodded, her eyes wide as she continued to look at the card.

"And I am now in charge? You will report to me? Listen to me? Follow my lead?"

"Now you're pushing, Alex. But I have to hand it to you. This one is *big*. We're going to let Steve in on it, right?"

"Once I've decided how to handle the information, yes. Now, you won't cry rope on me, will you?"

"You want your hour on the stage," Maggie said, shaking her head. "I know you, remember. When do you plan to reveal what you've got?"

"I thought the cover model contest tomorrow evening would be a good time, don't you? Being in my most comfortable clothing and all of that, as Sterling would say."

"Okay, okay, but only because you still don't know all of it. That's really why you want to do it this way, right? To smoke out the rest of it?"

"My, anyone would think you plot books, my dear," he said, holding out his arm to her so that they could move toward the considerable noise of female voices coming from Bernie's suite.

"Thank God you're here," Bernie said, grabbing Maggie the moment she'd made it through the crush at the door and entered the suite. "Vultures, Maggie, they're vultures. Look," she said, pointing to the tables scattered around the suite. "They're gone, all gone. Every last book, in twenty minutes, tops. Two hundred fucking books! Now what do I do to entertain them? Tap dance?"

"How about you push the liquor?" Maggie suggested, her smile fading as she recognized the woman walking toward her, holding a copy of *The Case of the Pilfered Pearls.* "Hello again," she said to Mitzi Metzger (Pre-Pubbed, Cincinnati Chapter). "You want to know how Virginia is doing, I suppose? She had a boy, and they're both just fine. I want to thank you for all your help."

"Huh?" Mitzi said, looking puzzled. "Oh, the woman in the elevator. That's nice. But why didn't you tell me you're Cleo Dooley? My God, when I saw your picture on the back cover of this book I nearly peed my pants! I *love* your books!"

Maggie was never at her best with fans. Not that she didn't love them, she just never knew what to *say* to them. Especially ones who threatened to pee their pants. "Why, thank you, Mitzi, that's very nice of you."

"No, no, it's nice of *you!* I can't tell you how much I've enjoyed every one. Why, I even read them in hardback, and I never do that. From the library, of course. Will . . . will you sign this for me?"

"I'd love to," Maggie said, relaxing. She pulled out a pen and signed the front page of the book: "To Mitzi, a friend in need . . . and in elevators. Regards, Cleo Dooley."

"Oh! Oh! That's wonderful!" Mitzi gushed as she read the inscription.

And then it happened. Not that Maggie hadn't been expecting it, considering the fact that Mitzi was as yet unpublished.

"I'm writing a mystery series of my own, you know," Mitzi told her, stepping closer, into Maggie's personal space. "It's set in Regency times, with my hero a titled gentleman who solves murders with his sidekick."

"Really. That sounds almost . . . familiar."

"Oh, no, no, it's not like your series at all, Cleo. I'd

never do something like *that.* Well, maybe a little. But not much, as I truly believe in order to get my own series, or into single title at all, I have to do something different, daring. So, my hero's a dentist."

Bernie, who had been sipping on one of her ever-present scotches, sprayed some of the liquid as she coughed.

Maggie reached over and patted Bernie on the back as Mitzi went on: "Write what you know, isn't that what we're always told? Well, I work for a dentist, so I know that. It's simple, really."

"So your English peer, your earl or duke, is a dentist?"

"Oh, he doesn't actually have an office or anything like that. He just dentists for friends."

"He *dentists for friends?* Okay, that's it," Bernie said, taking Maggie's arm. "Excuse us, dear, but now that Cleo's here, she really must mingle. You understand, don't you?"

Mitzi nodded, quickly reaching in her purse and pulling out two packets of cinnamon-flavored dental floss imprinted with her name and website address. "I'd be so pleased if you'd each take one?"

"Grab 'em," Bernie muttered under her breath, and Maggie quickly took the packets before being hauled off into another room of the large suite.

"A *dentist?*" Bernie said, falling into a chair in the small, thankfully deserted room. "But, hey, now you've heard it, Maggie. This is the kind of stuff we get over the transom every day. And you wonder why I love you? Even Felicity, who at least never tried to palm off a dentist on me."

Maggie looked toward the closed door. "Someone really should tell her that—"

"No. No way, no how. Maggie the Girl Scout will

not get involved, you hear me? God, you're such a soft touch."

"You're right," Maggie said, sitting down. "So, other than the run on the books, how's the party going? And shouldn't you be out there?"

"What?" she said, patting a thick pile of typing paper, "and miss reading Bunny Wilkinson's opus? She sent a copy up here before she took off. I've actually read some of it. She uses 'he ejaculated' a lot, as sentence tags, no less. You know, 'I love you, he ejaculated.' "

"No."

"Ah, but yes, Maggie. You wouldn't believe some of the stuff that comes to me, and some of them are from WAR members. Don't they go to the workshops? 'She walked through the door.' "

"Doorway," Maggie corrected automatically.

" 'His eyes were glued to her bosom.' "

"Painful, and rather embarrassing for both of them, I'd imagine," Maggie said, laughing.

" 'She ate her roasted beef with relish.' "

"Okay, that one was mine, in my first book," Maggie told her. "Which proves my point. There are some good writers out there, making silly mistakes. Like maybe Mitzi. Not Bunny Wilkinson, I'll give you that one. I mean, I did hear some of what she was quoting to you in the elevator. She's beyond hope, because she thinks every word she writes is a perfect pearl."

"I know what you're doing, Maggie. You want me to ask Mitzi to send me her manuscript, and I'm not going to do it. I don't care if she did help out a little in the elevator. There is no way in hell anyone can make a dentist into a hero, not to anyone who's ever had a root canal."

"Hey, I tried," Maggie said, then leaned forward, her elbows on her knees. "We've learned a few things, Bernie. Want to hear?"

But what they heard was a frantic knock on the door, followed by Sterling stumbling into the room, looking positively green. "Bathroom?" he asked through his fingers.

"That way," Bernie said, pointing behind her. "What's wrong?"

"Sick. Everyone. Sick," Sterling said, and disappeared into the bathroom.

"Shit," Bernie said, getting to her feet. "We'd better go see."

Maggie opened the door into a very different room than she and Bernie had left. It had been wall-to-wall people, but now most of them were gone, or sitting on the floor, moaning. Two were throwing up into the punch bowls.

Saint Just approached them, carefully stepping around a woman sitting on the floor, looking intently into an empty potato chip bowl.

"A sudden illness, my dears," Saint Just said, leading them back into the room they'd just left, and closing the door behind him. "I suggest a phone call to the housekeeper, a few more buckets, and a cleaning crew of at least ten."

"Food poisoning?" Maggie suggested, glad she'd arrived late.

"I don't know. I'm fine. Then again, I didn't eat anything," Bernie said. "But everyone else was scarfing up anything that wasn't nailed down. What do you think it could be?"

At that moment, Sterling walked out of the bathroom, looking as white as a porcelain bowl, and collapsed into a chair. "Excuse me, all of that. Not quite in plump currant, you know."

"Sterling," Saint Just said, heading for the bathroom. "Would it be possible for you to tell us what all you ate out there?"

"Must I?" Sterling groaned, holding his stomach.

Saint Just quickly returned with a washcloth he'd wet in the sink, and placed it, folded, on Sterling's head. "Yes, I'm afraid you must."

"All right," Sterling said as Maggie sat down beside him, patted his clammy hand. "I think I ate everything."

Bernie was on the phone, calling housekeeping, and asking for a doctor to be sent to the suite.

"A tad more specific, if you please," Saint Just said.

Sterling looked at Maggie, his expression as pitiful as a puppy who'd just widdled on the new carpet and was hoping for forgiveness. "This is so hard. Just the thought of food—but all right." He closed his eyes, the better to concentrate, perhaps. "Potato chips. Pretzels. Shrimp dip. Candied bacon. Everything being passed around on trays. You know, all those lovely cheese pastries and chicken bits? Punch. Those little fish eggs. I spread them on crackers."

"Caviar?" Bernie sniffed, hanging up the phone. "Like Toland Books would spring for caviar for those scavengers. I didn't order caviar."

Maggie and Saint Just exchanged looks, and Saint Just left the room, returning with a nearly empty bowl of caviar. "The dish isn't the same pattern as the others brought here by the caterers," he pointed out, holding the dish at arms' length. "There are two others still out there."

"A plant?" Maggie suggested.

"No, Maggie. Fish eggs. They aren't plants," Sterling said, and then he sort of burped, urped, and ran for the bathroom once more.

"You know, this is getting pretty old," Bernie said, subsiding into a chair. "But it has to be the prankster again, doesn't it?"

"Not necessarily, no," Saint Just said, looking meaningfully at Maggie.

"What? You think it was the murderer?"

"I don't know, frankly. What I do know is that Sergeant Decker has a very large mouth, and that he runs it constantly. Not to mention Felicity, who seems to believe she's part of some super-sleuthing gang, and earlier seemed to be hot-foot to tell the world. Perhaps our murderer has gotten wind of our investigation, and planned to put us all out of the picture by the simple expedient of having us all take to our beds, dog-sick? We are all Bernie's friends, and could be reasonably expected to be here, at the Toland Books reception. We may be closer to learning the truth than even we know."

"But, Alex, so far, only Sterling is sick," Maggie pointed out.

"And Miss Simmons, and our dear Tabby," he corrected. "And may I say, neither woman looks at all becoming in that particular shade of green."

"Oh, God, Tabby! I'll take care of her," Maggie said, heading back into the main room of the suite, to see that it was now nearly deserted. Only Tabby and Felicity remained, the two of them lying in fetal positions on identical couches.

Their little band of sleuths had just lost three members, at least until the caviar was out of their systems . . .

CHAPTER 16

"Well, now, here's a piece of news to brighten our Saturday morning," Saint Just said as he entered the suite after a quick reconnoiter of the conference floor and lounge. "Our friend Decker also went down for the count at Bernie's fashionable soirée and food poisoning party."

Maggie looked up from the note cards she had scattered in front of her on the table. That was how she plotted her Saint Just mysteries, putting facts on file cards she'd shuffle, reshuffle, until every card was used, somewhere. So far, the method wasn't working well on figuring out the prankster and the murderer. "Decker was at Bernie's party?"

"The good sergeant, Maggie, is everywhere he can be seen. The cover model contest, remember?"

"Or investigating Rose's murder," Maggie pointed out, which made Saint Just laugh, damn him. "Oh, all right, the man's a total waste of space."

"The fellow's also revolting, let's not forget that," Saint Just said, pouring himself a cup of tea from the electric kettle he'd picked up somewhere; Maggie didn't want to know where.

"Mare's gone home for a few hours, to check her mail, she said," Maggie told him, "but I think I heard Sterling stirring a little while ago."

As if on cue, Sterling entered the room and aimed himself at one of the couches. He sat down, then tipped to one side and lay there, his hands folded between his thighs, his feet on the floor. Moaning. "Oh, gloomy hour . . ."

"Ah, Sterling, feeling more the thing now? Splendid," Saint Just teased, pouring another cup of tea, liberally lacing it with sugar and milk before taking it to his friend. "You do know you have to buck up soon. We talked about it, remember?"

Sterling pushed himself up, took the cup and saucer, both of which shook visibly in his two-handed grip. "I'm weak as an infant, and all of that. Must I really? Maggie said I shouldn't. Come to think of it, you so said, too. Quite firmly."

"I'm making an exception. Everyone loves a show, Sterling. Tonight, good fellow, you get your chance to shine. I phoned Socks, and he'll be here soon, to assist you. His friend Jay, alas, has another engagement. Something about dragging something. Mary Louise, contrary to what she told Maggie—the child lies almost automatically—is procuring everything else we'll need."

Maggie, dismissing Saint Just's obviously innocent reference to Jay's drag queen activities, raised her hand. "Excuse me. Yo. Over here. Me. I've got a question. What the *hell* are you talking about?"

"A small surprise, my dear, don't worry your head about it. Now, as to costumes for this evening. You've as yet to wear your new gown, but I understand that no one is allowed to enter unless they're in costume."

"I know, and I'm wearing the gown. It's taken care of."

"How?"

Maggie leered at him. "What are Sterling and Socks and Mare doing tonight?"

"All right, I'll allow you your little surprise as well. Satisfied now?"

"No, that didn't work out at all the way I planned it," she admitted, then went back to shuffling her cards. "Oh, Steve called while you were out. Bad news, he said. It seems Top Star Electric has over two hundred stores across the country. It's going to take some time to get the names of every employee in order to match them with the list of WAR attendees."

"Did you tell him?" Saint Just asked, sitting down at the table and picking up one of the file cards.

"No, I didn't tell him," Maggie sing-songed, making a face at him. "He's a cop, he wouldn't understand how you're going to try to use one to get the other. He'd just make the arrest he could make. I understood that when you explained it to me. But it felt . . . dishonest."

"Only because it is," Saint Just said, smiling at her. "What's this?"

She took the card from him and read aloud: "Martha. Microphone. Introduction. Didn't touch." She put it back on the table. "I think that's self-explanatory."

"True, it is. And quite unnecessary at this juncture, which begs the question—why are you doing this?"

"Because I forgot to bring my tiddlywinks," Maggie grumbled, gathering up the cards. "Go away."

"No, no, don't stop, Maggie. Just perhaps go in another direction. Toward the murderer?"

"Why should I? I know who that is," Maggie said, sifting through the cards and pulling out three. "One, no matter if we did get lucky, nobody gets to ride one of these elevators more than a few floors at a time or without other passengers, and you'd have to go some to get me to believe otherwise. Two, Liza Lang was the only one in the elevator with Rose. Three, blue condoms." She laid down the cards. "I have more. I could go on, but what's the point? Liza is our murderer . . . murderess . . . killer."

"You're convinced of that?"

"One hundred and ten percent."

"All right. Where is the murder weapon? The police haven't found it."

"Easy. It was in the attaché case Giancarlo took from the litter. Rose's case. Liza must have asked him to keep it safe for her while she was at the hospital, poor, dumb sap. Liza only carries a clipboard, remember?"

"Ah, the attaché case. Would that be the one the police confiscated approximately ten seconds after Giancarlo picked it up? Along with Liza's purse, because I asked, and Wendell told me. I'm surprised you missed that, although I can understand your rush to see the body. Care to try again?"

Maggie reached for her purse, and her cigarettes, then stopped herself. "Steve checked the attaché case? Damn."

"I agree. It is a conundrum. Unless, of course, just as Liza claims, somebody else murdered Rose, and took off with the bloody knife."

"The alleged guy with the mask," Maggie said, nodding her head. "Why can't I buy that one?"

"Probably because you're not a stupid woman. The hotel is much too crowded to go running down one of the hallways in a mask, holding a bloody knife," Saint Just told her, smiling. "I've been giving this some thought. If we could know, once and for all, the precise floor Rose and Liza were on when they entered the elevator, I believe we could locate the murder weapon."

"Unless whoever stashed it wherever they stashed it—if they stashed it and didn't take it with them in case they were searched—has already come back and recovered it."

"I would be grateful if you would not complicate things further with logical deductions, my dear. Would you care to take a small excursion with me?"

"Where to?"

"Why, elevator seven, naturally, and every floor in the hotel."

"You're kidding. I mean, you've got to be kidding. Do you know how many floors there are in this place? Plus the basement? Maybe a couple of basements?"

"You have something more pressing to occupy your time? Scribbling on more cards, for instance?"

"I hate it when you're supercilious. But wait, I'll get my purse. Sterling? Are you going to be all right here?"

Sterling, having once more listed to his side on the couch, weakly lifted a hand and gave a small wave.

"Poor baby," she said, bending to kiss his forehead. "If Steve shows up, tell him Alex and I are on a wild goose chase, okay?"

"There are wild geese in the—?"

"Just tell him we'll be back in an hour or so," Maggie added quickly, shrugging as she looked at Saint Just. "I always forget," she said as they headed for the door.

"You go ahead, Maggie," Saint Just told her. "I want to find something to bring with us, to hold the knife when we find it."

"Cocky son of a bitch, aren't you?"

"Confident, Maggie, and don't swear. You know, there are times you evince a deplorable lack of confidence in me, your own creation and, as you have suggested—often with wide and frightened eyes—a bit of your alter ego. That said, perhaps it is because of some crisis of confidence in your own life? Feel free now to say *bite me.*"

She slammed the door on him instead, and stomped off down the hallway. Alter-ego? Maybe. Conscience, definitely. Everything she was, plus everything she had always wanted to be, and wasn't. Maybe that was why she had this love-hate thing going with him?

And maybe she'd think about that another time. She had enough going on right now, thank you.

Saint Just joined her at the bank of elevators, carrying a plastic liner-type bag he must have filched out of one of the wastebaskets in the suite. "Okay, Alex, which is elevator seven? I mean, I'm supposing you want to start by checking the elevator where Rose was killed."

"This one," he told her, as the doors on the elevator next to it opened. "I can see this might take some time. Tell you what, let's just go floor to floor, in any elevator, and hopefully catch number seven at some point. Agreed?"

"Agreed. You know, we could grow old, waiting for elevators in this place."

"You could," Saint Just said, pressing his cane against the open door, to hold it while Maggie stepped inside.

"I hate when you remind me of that."

"I know. My apologies, my dear. You're simply going to have to write Sterling and me as older in forthcoming books. Otherwise, Bernie will be constantly quizzing me as to the identity of my cosmetic surgeon."

"True," Maggie said, relaxing a little, just in time to get off the elevator again, at the fortieth floor. "Why here?"

"The process of elimination, Maggie. The bank of elevators that includes number seven are all glass-sided conveyances. Now, anyone who looks can see the glass-sided conveyances from the ground floor, on any of the convention floors, again once past the eighth floor lobby, and for a good ten floors above the atrium lobby, depending upon the position of the passengers in the elevator and the placement of the person in the lobby, with whatever the angle of sight might be. If I was the killer, which I'm not, I would make sure I committed the dastardly deed on a level that does not make the interior of the elevator visible. So, we start here. Forty is a good, round number, and work our way down, as not even I could expect an elevator to go from anywhere above the fortieth floor, straight down to seven. Does that help?"

"Actually, it does. Good thinking, Alex. Now what are you doing?"

"Trying to think like our murderer, I would wish to stash—I believe that's the term—the knife almost immediately, and somewhere it would be easy to retrieve, say, at three in the morning, when few people are about? Remember, the elevators failed on a fluke. Our murderer must have supposed his crime would be immediately discovered, not locked away in a stuck elevator between floors for over an hour. Time was of the essence."

"Not if it was Liza, because all she had to do was stay in the elevator. But she could have had time to step out, ditch the knife, and step back in before the doors closed, I suppose, so my theory still works."

Maggie watched as Saint Just walked from standing ash tray to standing ash tray, lifting the top off and inspecting the drum-like interior. "You're lucky they're just ash trays and aren't the kind with a trash can attached. Those would have plastic bag inserts and be emptied at least once a day," she remarked as he finished his inspection and dusted his hands.

"Yes, I concur," he said. "Do you wish to wait for another elevator, or take the stairs to thirty-nine?"

"Stairs," Maggie said. "My ears start popping if I ride elevators too much. Let's go."

And go they did. At each floor Saint Just repeated his inspection of the cylinder-like ash trays, with no luck . . . until they got all the way to the concierge level.

Maggie had been helping Saint Just, and when she lifted the top off the ash tray to the left of elevator seven, she saw something at the bottom of the shiny, stainless steel container.

"Alex? Come here a minute," she said, then took the plastic bag from him and used it like a glove as she moved the can under a light. "I wish we'd brought a flashlight, but I think I see something interesting. Look. Could that be what I think it is?"

She waited, attempting to push down her excitement at the same time she glared at two men who were looking at them as if they'd gone crazy and might attack them at any moment. "Well?"

"Blood. Definitely blood. There's a sort of rusty smell, did you notice it? Dried, but enough of it that it had to come from the knife when it was placed in here. Splendid, Maggie. What floor is this, again?"

"Concierge floor. The one where they get free breakfast buns and stuff. But it's not Liza and Rose's floor. Remember, I tossed their suite. We'll have to get Steve to make the hotel hand over their room list, and see which WAR attendees sprang for the concierge floor. Come to think of it, it's probably all the Board. They get this stuff comped, for working at the convention."

The elevator door opened and Saint Just waved her inside, with her still holding the ash tray lid (complete with several cigarette butts), and he carried in the cylindrical base.

"Hey, you can't take that!" one of the men yelled at them.

"Ah, good sir, but I just did," Saint Just said, then saluted as the doors slid shut.

"You know, Rose is dead, and I'm sorry about that. I really am. But this is . . . well, it's sorta fun, you know? And if you tell anyone I said that, I'll have to hurt you, because I think I just sounded like Faith. God, these cigarette butts stink. Do I smell like that?"

"Of course not, my dear," Saint Just said as they exited the elevator and walked toward their suite. "Everyone else in the world who smokes, but not you. And if you believe that, Maggie, you'll believe anything."

"Why did I even ask?" Maggie put her head down and pretty much crawled into the suite, then headed straight for her room and the shower, while Saint Just punched in numbers on the telephone after asking her how he could contact Steve.

"I think he'll be pleased, don't you?" he asked as she paused at the doorway to her room.

"That would depend. *Now* are you going to tell him everything?"

"I think so, yes. After all, in eight or ten short hours, we'll have both miscreants firmly in hand. If, that is, Wendell has more information of the sort he forwarded to me this morning about the prankster."

"Whoa. He *forwarded* information to you this morning? When? How?"

"By fax, my dear, and I picked it up in the lobby, as we'd arranged. Interesting reading. Very interesting. And Wendell is most grateful to me, as it may have been his sleuthing, but it was I who told him where to sleuth."

"The list of names," Maggie said, deciding her shower could wait. After all, she'd already had one today, and had only sneaked two cigarettes after that.

"Yes, the list of names. Our suspects. My instincts. Sometimes, even my mind boggles at my brilliance."

"Now I *really* want another shower," Maggie muttered, and headed toward her room once more. "And I want to see that fax when I'm done, you got that?"

Saint Just's answer was fairly noncommittal, but she didn't notice. Bad thing, not noticing what Saint Just said . . . and what he didn't say.

"Maggie seems to be in a bit of a miff," Sterling said as he finished his bowl of chicken broth and bit into a slice of unbuttered toast in the lobby restaurant. "Did you show her everything?"

"Everything she needed to see, yes," Saint Just said, taking a sip of wine. In Regency England, water was more of an adventure than wine, as one never knew what had been swimming in it last, and so he, as a character, had never developed a taste for the stuff. Much safer to drink wine.

"But not all of it?" Sterling frowned. "She's not going to like that, when she finds out."

"True. But Wendell and I have decided between us that Maggie is to be kept blissfully ignorant as far as the murderer is concerned. To that end, I have sacrificed her good opinion of me by inciting her to riot at least three times this morning. She'll be so caught up in devising ways to boil me in oil, put me on the rack, whatever, that we should be able to complete what must be done without her interference . . . and without putting her in harm's way. Wendell was most adamant about that, and I concurred. You know, Wendell and I seem to work well in harness. I'm not sure if that pleases me, or not."

"Because you're a lot like Maggie, and Wendell likes Maggie, and if you like Wendell, that means Maggie likes Wendell? Possibly more than you do, because she's a female, and all of that?"

Saint Just looked intently at his good friend. "Sometimes, Sterling, your acuity astonishes me. But, yes, Maggie holds other reservations about me, and those can only be dealt with in the passage of time. However, in the interim, I would not much care to see her form an emotional alliance with the good *Left*–tenant. But enough of that, as the man approaches even now. And looking smug, if I might say so."

"Decker's with him," Sterling said, twisting in his chair to see the two men on the other side of the low wall that separated the restaurant from the lobby. "Oh, dear me. Do *I* look that bad?"

"You two do seem to share your complexion, yes," Saint Just said, throwing money on the table and motioning for Sterling to get up. "I'd rather we were somewhere more private for this conversation, Sterling, if you don't mind?"

"No. Not at all," Sterling said, wrapping the rest of his toast in his napkin. "May I take my tea, too?"

"As we're only going into the lounge area, I suppose no one will attempt to stop you. Lead on, Sterling," he said, waving Wendell and Decker away before they could enter the restaurant.

"Good afternoon, Sergeant Decker," Saint Just trilled as the four men commandeered a small conversation area away from others using the lounge. "You're looking . . . I'm so sorry, politeness forbids a truthful observation. But, odds fish, man, look at you."

"Why don't you and your faggy English accent just go to hell. And shut up about fish, okay," Decker said, taking a swig of something pink from a bottle he'd removed from his jacket pocket. "Now, what's up? I've got that contest tonight, you know, and I have to rest."

Saint Just sighed, just as Wendell sighed. They really did have a lot in common. "You know, Sergeant, I've been thinking. If you had one ounce of pride you'd withdraw from the contest. A flesh market, when you get right down to it. So demeaning."

Decker's rather remarkable jaw jutted out. "Why? You're in it, right?"

"Ah, but there's a difference. I, my good man, am going to win. You, on the other hand, will only be making a cake of yourself. Won't he, Sterling?"

Well, that put some of the color back in Sterling's cheeks. "Me? You want me to—? Um, Sergeant? Forgive Saint Just if you can. He can be excessively disagreeable at times."

"Disagreeable? He's a no good bas—"

"Ah, Sergeant, I know what it is. It's those ugly shoes you wear that make you so cranky," Saint Just drawled, holding his glass of wine in both hands. "It's possibly also why you wrongly accused dearest Mary Louise. As you may recall, when you first put forth Mary Louise as your suspect, I did beg you not to be such an ape. Do they pinch? The shoes, Sergeant, the shoes."

"He's a right'un at heart, really," Sterling offered quickly, but obviously not with much hope of being believed.

Decker stood up, then angrily glared down at Saint Just, who remained at his ease, one leg crossed over the other. "The girl had a knife and she's a born felon. It was a logical assumption."

"It was an astonishingly nonsensical conclusion, Willie, even for you. Again, could be the shoes."

Decker pushed back his seat, so that the chair nearly tipped over. He was a muscular man, even if the majority of that muscle, to Saint Just's way of thinking, was located between the man's ears. "Once was enough, Wendell, I'm not doing this again. You got something to tell me, you tell me later. Remember, I'm primary."

The sergeant stomped off in his "unlovely shoes,"

and Saint Just sighed in pleasure. "That didn't take as long as I thought it might. Couldn't you shake him, Wendell?"

"You heard of gumshoes? Decker's kind of like that—he's gum on the bottom of my shoes. Seems he thinks I might know something, and if he wants to take credit for the bust he has to be close by when it happens. Thanks for getting rid of him."

"You're welcome. I've gotten fairly adept at angering people today and making them go away. Now, what have you learned? I thank you for the information on our prankster, as well as the bits and pieces you forwarded me on my list of suspects, but now that we're settled on the prankster, I wish to concentrate on our murderer, as your fax intimated that you have much more information for me. Please, you have the floor."

"Not until you tell me how you plan to use the information."

"Ah, you don't entirely trust me. I must say, my hopes are quite cut up, although my estimation of your intelligence has moved up a notch of two. Very well. We'll start at the beginning, with the prankster. That's where Sterling will shine."

"And Maggie? I mean it, I want her out of this. You remember what happened last time."

"Safe as houses," Saint Just promised. "This will all be very quick, very public, and quite possibly entertaining. But our inquisitive and at times disaster prone Maggie will be in no danger."

"Okay," Wendell said, pulling several folded papers from his inside jacket pocket.

He was just about to consult the papers when Sterling said, "Oh, would you look at that. Like black crows, the two of them."

Saint Just had already seen them. Miss Liza Lang,

hanging on the arm of the very large Giancarlo, the two of them dressed in black from head to foot as they entered the lounge. That Giancarlo's black silk shirt was open to his waist detracted somewhat from his air of mourning, but Saint Just had never believed the man to be the epitome of fashion, or good sense, in any case.

Liza sat down while Giancarlo went to the small bar and procured bottles of iced water for both of them, then returned, sat down as well.

"Excuse me," Saint Just said, standing up. "I've spoken to Miss Lang before, but now I wish to give my condolences to Giancarlo."

"I don't understand. Why does he get condolences?" Sterling asked.

"I have no idea. I imagine he and Rose were friends? But a man dressed for a funeral invites condolences, and I never fail to accept an invitation."

"Hello, Alex," Liza said, looking up at him. Her eyes were red-lidded, and she held a crushed white handkerchief in one hand. "Please excuse the way I look. I . . . I think it's finally sinking in. Rose's death, I mean. Yesterday . . . yesterday I was in a sort of fog, from something someone gave me to calm my nerves. You've met Giancarlo?"

Saint Just bowed to the man. "Blakely here," he said. "My condolences. You must have loved her very much."

Giancarlo's handsome face—and the man was quite a specimen, no matter how blatantly he displayed himself—softened into an expression of sorrow. "She . . . Rose . . . was my mentor. I was nobody, until she made me a star. The world will never be the same without Rose in it."

"Ah . . . yes, well, I'm afraid I didn't get to know the woman, and that would appear to be my loss, wouldn't it?" Saint Just turned to Liza once more. "I wish to thank you for continuing with the ball and cover model finals this evening. If I might be of any service . . . ?"

"No, thank you, we've got it all in hand. Martha Kolowsky has been a godsend, helping me with everything. Please just be there early. Not that there are many people still here, although the media will be well represented. Because of poor Rose, you understand. She would have loved all of the attention."

"Yes, of course," Saint Just agreed. "Tell me, would you know if a Miss Holly Spivak, of Fox News, happens to be one of those attending? Television, you understand. Lovely woman. I met her a few months ago, on quite another matter."

"I don't know," Liza said, and she pulled her attaché case onto the table and unsnapped it. All that was revealed was her clipboard; she'd seemed to simply have found another way to carry the thing around everywhere she went. She paged through the pile of papers held by a clip. "Here's the lists. Radio, newspaper . . . television. Yes, she'll be here. I don't know what they think they're going to see. It's like they expect another murder and want to have the cameras ready. It's disgusting."

"Alas, the world can be a cruel, unfeeling place, Liza," Giancarlo soothed, and Saint Just had to force himself not to laugh out loud.

"Well, I didn't wish to intrude. I simply wanted to offer my condolences, again."

He bowed once more, and returned to his own small group. "That was relatively nauseating," he said as he sat down, picked up his wine glass once more.

"Why? What happened?" Wendell asked, sneaking a look at the black-clad couple.

"Why? Because, my good fellow, Liza has suddenly,

and probably because she has been tutored, developed a crushing grief for Rose Sherwood that I did not witness during our meeting yesterday. And, secondly, because Giancarlo—I can't imagine why I haven't had the pleasure of speaking with him until now—has all the right words, the right expressions, and he's cold and hard as nails. The smooth, oily sort who could probably successfully peddle earthquake pills to protect the gullible from tremors."

Wendell looked at his papers. "Sometimes, I wonder why I even bother. How did you know that from just talking to the guy for a couple of minutes?"

"Know what?" Saint Just asked, genuinely puzzled.

"This," Wendell said, handing over the papers. "We dusted Sherwood's suite for prints after the murder, then ran them. Interesting guy, Giancarlo. Everyone's pretty damn interesting. You know, officially, I'm off duty. I'm going to go get a beer. Sterling, you want one?"

Sterling unfolded the napkin and lifted a slice of unbuttered toast. "I don't think so. No, thank you."

"Yes. I need you sober, Sterling, and fully fit, if we're to carry off your portion of the evening. Let's see if these papers will change anything. Oh . . . oh my, yes. How very devious. And Liza is . . . now why didn't I think of that? Ah, what a tangled web. Sterling, finish your tea, we have extensive revising ahead of us."

CHAPTER 17

"How gratifying that the airline company is being so accommodating, Virginia," Saint Just said, standing at the window of the suite, looking down on Times Square. "Maggie, Sterling, and I certainly wish you all the best. You will keep in touch, won't you?" He smiled as he listened to her answer. "Yes, we will most definitely phone you with the news of the arrests, as soon as they happen. Travel safely, my dear."

He put down the phone and sighed. Sterling would be disappointed that he wouldn't get to see young Master Neuendorf again, but there really was no way to dash over to the hospital for a last peek, not with having to write everything over again and have the man commit it all to memory.

Pulling out his pocket watch, Saint Just checked the time. In truth, the evening had already begun with the annual awards ceremony in the main ballroom. That bit of falderal would drag on for nearly two hours, according to Felicity, who had popped into the suite earlier, looking quite a bit the worse for wear.

The tableaus had been set up in the adjoining ballroom, and once the awards ceremony was done with, the dividing doors would be opened and everyone would move on to the next event.

Felicity, bravely pushing on even as she suffered the aftermath of the food poisoning, had also told him something else. According to Liza's grass poll, Damien led the contestants at the moment, and by a goodly margin.

While unhappy with this news, Saint Just had pushed himself through any tug of disappointment, to consider Damien's place in all of this.

Was he simply another cover model contestant? Or was he more? Would he kill to win? What would killing Rose do to improve his chances? Or, because he was so highly favored, was he in danger himself?

Possibly. Once murder is done, it is simpler to do it again. Suddenly, it seems the obvious answer, the most definitive answer to any problem.

He walked over to the table, shuffled through some papers until he found what he wanted, then committed that small bit of information to memory.

"Sterling?" Saint Just called out after knocking at their bedroom door and stepping inside. "Would you mind horribly if I were to borrow Henry for a space?"

Sterling, nearly dressed now in his superfine jacket, buckskins, and passably shined Hessians, looked up from the paper he was studying. "Henry? Why?"

Saint Just went to the dresser and picked up Henry's boxy mesh cage. "He'll come to no harm, I promise you. Thank you, Sterling. Socks? Has he learned all the words?"

Argyle Jackson, once again dressed in his pirate costume, nodded. "He's just about got it down, yes. Is this all really true? It sounds like some sort of play."

"Ah, and the play's the thing, or some such rot," Saint Just said, bowing to Mary Louise. "My dear, you are breathtaking in that gown. Have you prepared a small speech for the moment you are crowned the female cover model of the year?"

Mare shrugged her slim shoulders. "Yeah, right, Vic. Who says I'm going to win?"

"One of us will. I'm convinced of that. All right, troops, carry on," he said, leaving with Henry, just to be stopped in his tracks by the sight of Maggie exiting her room, hands to her left ear as she attached her second earring.

She looked taller than usual in the floor length gown, and the green silk shimmered as she took each step, outlining her long legs. The bodice plunged nearly to her waist, where the material was held by a rhinestone brooch, and when she turned to frown into the mirror over the credenza, he could see the smooth sweep of her back, where the material was cut into a nearly waist deep cowl of folded silk.

"There," she said, allowing her arms to drop to her sides, and turning around, so that he could see the artful cascades of rhinestones on her ears. "So? How do I look? I *feel* naked. All I need is some flowery print in with the green, and a slit up the front of the skirt, and I could be J-Lo. Alex? Say something? After all, you're the one who picked it out."

Saint Just remained where he was, while Henry, clearly agitated by the move, raced round and round inside his cage. "I am, for the moment," he said at last, trying for a lazy drawl, "rendered nearly speechless."

"And would that be a good thing or a bad thing?" she asked him, and he snapped back to some semblance of sanity, realizing that she wasn't goading him. She really didn't know. So lovely, so intelligent, so talented. And with the self-confidence of a sea sponge.

He longed to taste her soft, almost golden lips. He

longed to run his fingers through the clean sweep of her hair . . . and elsewhere.

"It's most unbecoming for a beautiful woman to so obviously dredge for compliments," he scolded her. "And I do believe there is a bit of string, um, hanging from the back of the gown."

"Where?" Maggie asked, trying to look over her shoulder, into the mirror. "Oh, damn, you're right. I don't want to take this thing off again, it took me forever to figure out which was the front and which was the back. Alex? Could you see if you can pull it off? But don't rip the material, okay?"

Henry was deposited on a side table as Saint Just approached Maggie from the rear, got close enough to inhale the faint powdery scent emanating from her skin. He put his hands on her shoulders, then slowly ran them down her back, smiling as he watched her expression in the mirror. She seemed caught between surprise and pleasure.

"There we are," he said a moment later, plucking the bit of string from the very edge of the artfully concealed zipper.

"You're done?" Maggie asked, looking back at him over her shoulder.

"Actually, if I had my dearest wish, I've only just . . ." he drawled, then stepped back, smiled. "Ah, but not now. Tell me, lovely as you look, how does this constitute a costume?"

"Hold that thought," Maggie said, and headed back into her bedroom, returning scant moments later, a tiara on her head and a white satin sash over one shoulder, crossing to rest on her opposite hip. On the sash, picked out in silver lettering, were the words *Miss Apprehension 2003*. "Socks had Jay make it up for me. Like it?" she asked, twirling in a circle.

"Again, I am speechless. Now," he said, picking up Henry's cage once more, "if you'll excuse us?"

"Wait a minute. You're not dressed yet. Where are you going? And why take Henry?"

"I shall return in time for Socks and Sterling to help me with my toilette, I'm sure. In the meantime, I have a quick errand to run."

"Wait. What are you going to wear? You don't have time for one of those silly routines with your neck cloth. Or are you just going to keep your shirt open to the waist, like the rest of the contestants? That could be how to get the most votes, you know."

"I would not so demean myself," Saint Just said haughtily. He opened the door, then paused for a moment. "Ah, forgive me. I seem to have misplaced my brains for a moment, my dear. Virginia phoned a little while ago. She and her husband and son will be flying back to Colorado in a few hours. Perhaps you'd like to call her while she's still at the hospital?"

"Oh, damn, and we didn't get back to see her again. Yes, I'll call her. Thank you, Alex."

He closed the door, satisfied that the phone call would keep Maggie occupied while he was gone, and too busy to listen at Sterling's door, which she would think to do at some point if left alone too long.

He only had to travel three floors, so he took the stairs rather than wait for one of those infernal, slow moving elevators to arrive . . .

"All right, Virginia, be careful. Yes, I'll call, the minute I know anything. Well, tomorrow, once you're home and settled. I love you, too. Gotta go, there's someone at the door. Kiss the baby for me, and John, Senior, too. Bye."

Maggie put down the phone and hurried across the room to let in Bernie and Tabby, both of them dressed to the teeth in their costumes. Bernie had opted for her version of Lady MacBeth, complete with a jeweled dagger and bloody handkerchief, while Tabby was dressed *in scarves.* "Tabby? Scarves? I mean, I guess it's typecasting, but *scarves?"*

"I'm Salome. Bring me the head of David the Fornicator," Tabby said as she breezed past Maggie in a haze of alcohol. Maggie looked at Bernie, who just shrugged.

"David's catting around again?"

"What again?" Bernie asked, pulling a small silver flask from her jeweled girdle. "Still. Yet. Constantly. She tossed him out again. They should think about putting in a revolving door."

"And she's been drinking?" Maggie asked in a whisper, watching as Tabby sat down on one of the couches, her scarves floating around her. "That's not like Tabby."

"That's because this time the prick went after her assistant, Miranda. She found them in her office, going at it like rabbits on her own desk."

"Oh, *yick!* Why doesn't she just divorce the bastard?"

"Yeah. Now she's got to break in a new assistant, and Miranda had been one of the good ones. You know, the ones who actually knew how to take a phone message? Oh, and speaking of messages, Steve called me in my suite, since your phone was busy. He said to tell you he's sorry, but it's going down now, and he'll be late, if he gets here at all. Sorry."

Maggie closed her eyes for a moment, and sniffed. "A month. He's been working this case for a whole month, and *tonight* it's all going down? It figures. Now all we have is Alex."

"All we have is Alex for what?" Tabby asked, arranging her scarf skirt over what Maggie could see was a tan taffeta underslip.

"I don't know," Maggie admitted, wishing she could have a cigarette without the accompanying sermon she'd get from Tabby. "Nobody's talking. I mean, it isn't as if I haven't *tried* to find out what's going to happen, but both Steve and Alex say I'm supposed to be part of the audience tonight. I could seriously hate both of them. They act as if I could get into some kind of trouble."

"Now where would they get an idea like that?" Tabby asked, exchanging looks with Bernie. "Oh, wait, I know. Trouble. Like almost getting killed? Would that be it?"

"It wasn't that bad. Besides, everything worked out, didn't it?"

Again the exchanged looks.

"Well, what *do* you know?" Bernie asked her, tugging at the jeweled girdle, which kept slipping lower on her slim hips.

"I know that Liza's the murderer," Maggie said firmly.

"Liza? Really?" Tabby began fanning herself with one of the scarves. "She stabbed Rose, then stabbed herself? Wow."

"I couldn't have done that," Bernie said, pouring herself a tumbler of Scotch. "Stabbed myself."

"But you could have stabbed somebody else?" Maggie asked her, grinning.

Bernie shrugged. "I think I could, yes, if I had a good reason. Tabby? What about you?"

Tabby shivered. "Never. I'd rather die."

"Which she would," Bernie said, brushing past Maggie on her way to the windows, "if somebody attacked her. Hey, he's going to rape and kill me, but I don't want to poke him in the eyes with my inch-long nails because that would be so . . . icky. Women are such wimps."

"You're a woman," Maggie pointed out, watching her editor and friend sort of slide and sway her way to the windows.

"The body, Maggie, but not the mind. The mind is male. You know, cold and analytical and—well, sometimes. All right, so I'm a woman. But I'm a woman who damn well would use a knife, a gun, a chair, anything at all if I was threatened." She turned to look at Maggie. "Is that it? Did Liza feel threatened by Rose?"

"Threatened by a seventy-six-year-old woman?" Tabby shook her head. "No, there has to be another reason. How about greed? Greed is always a good motive."

"Yes, that's what I've always—oh, Alex, you're back. Where's Henry?"

"Auditioning," Saint Just said, bowing to the ladies, and then disappeared into his bedroom.

"Auditioning? The mouse is auditioning. Right." Maggie reached for a cigarette. "Pardon the pun, but I smell a rat. Bernie? Tabby? We're being squeezed out of our little gang, you do know that, don't you?"

"Suits me," Bernie said, sipping her Scotch. "Tabby, how about you?"

"I never was much for anything violent," Tabby said, avoiding Maggie's eyes. "It could get violent, couldn't it?"

Maggie lit her cigarette, then just as quickly put it out in the ashtray. "Only if Saint Just thinks he's going to stick me on the sidelines while . . . while this *goes down.*"

Sterling walked along beside Saint Just, huffing a little in an effort to keep up with his longer strides.

"You know, Saint Just, this would be the greatest good fun, if it were not for the worrying. Socks calls it stage fright, but I won't really be on a stage, will I? And I would be so much calmer if Lieutenant Wendell were here."

"And thank you so much, Sterling, for that rousing vote of confidence. Now, come along, we can only be fashionably late when it is fashionable to be so."

The small party, that included Maggie, Bernie, Tabby, Socks, Mary Louise, and a rather vacantly smiling Joan of Arc, better known as Felicity Boothe Simmons, entered the small lobby of the ballroom set aside for the awards ceremony and stopped, careful to keep out of sight of most of the WAR attendees.

"There you are," Liza said, rushing up to them, her clipboard once more clutched to her paltry bosom. "Is Damien with you? We can't find Damien."

"Primping, I imagine," Saint Just offered smoothly, taking hold of Liza's arm above the elbow. "Now, if you could just tell Mary Louise and me what we're to do?"

"You'd know, if you'd attended the rehearsal, so we simply slotted you second to last in line, ahead of Damien. It would have been much better if you'd attended," Liza said peevishly. "Oh, I'm sorry. It's just that it has been a very emotional evening. Rose's life in pictures, you understand. I don't think there was a dry eye in the house."

"Except for a few hoots and snickers in the back rows, from the sane people," a helmeted Valkyrie said as she marched by carrying a glass pitcher of beer she then took a sip from before moving on.

"Oh," Liza said, blinking back fresh tears, "why did she say that? People can be *so* cruel."

"There, there," Joan of Arc said, putting an arm around Liza's shoulders. "That was Janine McDonald under that pot, Liza. You know Rose never gave her books a good review. I'm sure the program was everything you said it was. I'm so sorry I missed it, but as I'm not up for any awards this year—I've so many now it's almost embarrassing to keep entering—I'm afraid I took a nap instead. Did I miss anything?"

Liza made a face. "Well, Bunny Wilkinson won again, for best unpublished novel, and everyone booed."

" 'Society, like the Roman youth at the circus, never shows mercy to the fallen gladiator.' Balzac, I believe," Saint Just said, smiling.

"But everyone cheered Martha for all her good work. I hear she's going to be nominated for president of WAR next year."

Maggie tugged on Saint Just's sleeve. "You're not the only one who can toss quotes around, you know," she said quietly, so that only he could hear her. "How about this one? Edmund Burke. 'Well is it known that ambition can creep as well as soar.' "

"Brilliant, my dear," Saint Just said, smiling down at her . . . and her cleavage. "If you're cold, Sterling wouldn't mind running back to the suite to procure you a sweater to cover you up."

"Great. Alex the prude. Remember, you picked it out."

"A moment of madness, I assure you," Saint Just said, sending up a silent prayer that the good *left*-tenant would be kept away for the entirety of the evening. Unfortunately, it would appear that Sergeant Decker had not been similarly inconvenienced. "Hallo, Sergeant. Don't you look . . . yes, well. As I said, hallo, or should that be, Hail, Caesar!"

Sergeant Decker ran his hands down his hammered breastplate, then grabbed at the hilt of his sword with one hand. His skirt—Saint Just didn't know any other name for it—was of short, broad strips of brown leather studded with metal and ended just above his knees, everything worn over a deep burgundy tunic. The man wore soft leather sandals with straps crisscrossing over his calves, and a silver helmet with a burgundy plume in it.

"I'm not Caesar; he wore sheets. I'm a Centurion," Decker said proudly.

"Of course you are," Saint Just said soothingly. "I imagine those nasty Goths would have taken one look at you, Sergeant, and run screaming back to their homes."

"Are you trying to poke fun at me?"

"Me? No, of course not, I never indulge in the obvious. Goodness, people imagine the oddest things. On the contrary, my good man. Here we are, all chockfull of good spirits, about to compete for the grand prize. By the way, that's a lovely sword. Wooden, isn't it?"

"Sure, like I'd carry a real sword. This is a *costume.* I have a gun, mister, I don't need a sword."

"A gun, is it? Keep it under the skirt, do you?"

"Go to hell, Blakely. We'll see who's laughing out of which side of his mouth when the winner is announced."

"It's just as I told Maggie. The man has an attic positively crawling with maggots," Saint Just said in an aside to Sterling, who coughed and turned away, clearly not hot to get between his friend and a man who admitted to carrying a gun.

"Oh, dear. We're running late. We can't wait any longer for Damien," Liza said as the other two remaining female contestants joined them at the back of the room, along with Giancarlo and Lucious (who was looking around him as if he expected a knife between his shoulder blades at any moment).

"Liza, it's time," Giancarlo said, showing off his straight white teeth even as he flipped back his mane of ebony hair. "I've ordered the doors opened into the adjoining ballroom."

"Yes, good, thank you, Giancarlo," Liza gushed, and Saint Just turned to Socks, who stepped up smartly, holding the rest of Saint Just's costume. "Now, if everyone will get in line the way we rehearsed, I'll get this started. I mean, I just want this over, don't you all?"

Everyone sort of backed up into the hallway, the female models pairing off with Giancarlo and Lucious. Damien, it would appear, had lost his assigned companion in the first rush to the exits when the pranks had begun to turn dangerous, and Decker's late entry had also deprived him of a companion for the march.

Saint Just allowed Socks to drape the black evening cape over his shoulders, and then positioned his curly brimmed beaver on his head at an angle. He spread his arms, deftly tossing back the sides of the cape to show its scarlet lining, and flourished his cane even as he held out his arm to Mary Louise, who was already similarly covered head-to-toe in an evening cape, hers silver, with a pink lining.

Socks lifted the large, loose hood onto her upswept curls, then stepped back, clasped his hands together and said, "Perfect. Break a leg, people."

"Well, that certainly wasn't nice," Sterling said, and Maggie pulled him aside, to whisper in his ear. "Oh. Really? It doesn't sound lucky in the least to me."

The ballroom went dark for a moment, and then the lights flashed on again, now shining in both ballrooms, and Liza was standing at the podium. "Lords and ladies, queens and princes, cowboys and frontierswomen—and I believe I can safely say, having walked through the crowd—leprechauns and fairies, it's time for the March of the Contestants."

She pointed toward the back of the ballroom as she said the last words of her introduction, and suddenly the air was filled with music blaring from every speaker.

Multi-colored strobe lights came on, and a large spotlight traveled around the room, at last locating the entrance. Lucious and his female companion (Lucious in black leather, the female contestant similarly dressed, her clothing so tight she may have been sewn into the slacks) began their strut around the first ballroom, wending in and out between the tables to the blaring sounds of "Bad to the Bone."

As they swaggered into the second ballroom, the curtains in front of the first tableau opened to show a pair of very large motorcycles, and they each straddled one, frowned imperiously at their audience, and then waved.

Next up was Sergeant Decker, and Saint Just could barely watch as the man drew his sword and leapt into the ballroom to the strains of—of all things—"Simply Irresistible."

The face was right, the body was right, but the man was an idiot. He kept leaping, and thrusting his sword, and growling in a ferocious manner, all the way through the tables. When the drapes pulled back on his tableau he jumped, two-footed, onto the low stage, lost his balance, reached out . . . and knocked over the stuffed white horse that stood in front of a small gilt chariot.

"That was embarrassing," Saint Just said, actually wincing as he watched Decker try to right the horse, only to knock the chariot completely off the stage.

"Poor fellow," Sterling said, shaking his head. "He did his possible."

"Yes, Sterling, that's true. And therein lies the rub, when you consider that he is investigating Miss Sherwood's murder."

"He just fell again. What a fool," said Giancarlo.

Saint Just narrowed his eyes as he looked at Giancarlo. "George Villiers, second Duke of Buckingham once commented, 'The world is made up for the most part of fools and knaves.' If Decker is the fool, which are you?"

"Screw you. None of you has a chance. They never do," Giancarlo said with a smirk on his handsome face. "Watch, and see how it's done."

The music died, then started up again, and again, Saint Just recognized the tune because it was one Maggie often played while working. "Radar Love" ripped and beat and screamed as Giancarlo, in hip hugging jeans, knee-high brown (and fringed) suede boots, and a full sleeved white shirt open to the waist, took his companion's hand and danced her into the ballroom.

"Flamboyant fellow," Saint Just observed mildly as Mary Louise cringed. "No, no, no. Don't worry, we're fine."

"With that crappy music you picked out? Yeah, right."

Giancarlo and the female model—wearing a very short jean skirt and a bright red halter top—leapt up onto their tableau as the curtains opened for them. There was a bed there, naturally, and Giancarlo lifted the blond woman and flung her down onto the mattress before turning to the screaming audience and running his tongue over his top lip.

"Oh, brother," Mary Louise said, shaking her head. "Not *too* obvious."

"He's won for the last four or five years in a row, maybe more," Bernie pointed out from her hiding place against the wall. "Sex sells, child. I don't know what you've got on under that cloak, but whatever it is, *sell* it."

The sweeping strobe lights that had accompanied Lucious, Decker, and Giancarlo into the ballroom were switched off, and only the spotlight remained as the first strains of "Greensleeves" floated out into the air—Socks, to whom Saint Just had given strict instructions, and enough money to grease the palms of the disk jockey—had taken care of all of these details.

Saint Just, with a barely perceptible nod to Maggie, held out one arm, and led Mary Louise into the ballroom, her hand resting on his. And then, once firmly in the spotlight, they stopped.

Saint Just inclined his head to his audience as Sterling, also in Regency dress, stepped up beside him, and also bowed. Saint Just handed his curly brimmed beaver to his friend, stripped off the gloves he'd donned in the hallway, then untied his cloak and pushed it off his shoulders with a flourish, Sterling catching it neatly.

Beneath his cloak, he wore the finest evening dress, tailored in the Beau Brummell manner. Black superfine, and whiter than white linen. Immaculate white hose and evening slippers with silver buckles. His neck cloth was a marvel. Only his pocket watch, quizzing glass, and a single fob broke up the stark black and white.

He swept into a most elegant leg, then struck a pose, one hand on his hip, the other outstretched, to indicate Mary Louise.

Once more, Sterling stepped forward, this time to catch Mary Louise's cloak as she shrugged it from her shoulders.

There was an intense, collective sigh from the audience.

Mary Louise's gown was exquisite. High-waisted, in the Regency style, it seemed to have been woven of purest ivory gossamer and then drifted with diamonds. The spotlight hit every sparkle, turning her into a petite fairy princess; all that was lacking were the wings. Her head held high, that wonderfully sculpted chin higher, she placed her hand on top of Saint Just's once more, and they moved into the ballroom, the spotlight following them.

Every few tables, Saint Just would stop, bow, as Mary Louise dropped into a faultless curtsy, until finally they approached their tableau and the curtains opened to show a miniature Regency drawing room.

Gone was the ridiculous bed, replaced by props Socks had procured for the scene. A burled chest. Candelabra. Satin chairs.

Saint Just assisted Mary Louise onto the low stage, and the two of them began an elegant waltz, Mary Louise holding up one side of her gown, Saint Just faultlessly turning her, dipping her and, at last, as the music died, lifting her hand to his mouth.

"Damn, he's good," Bernie said, fanning herself with the program she'd picked up somewhere. "Tabby? Wasn't he great?"

"All men are pigs," Tabby said, and took another drink from Bernie's flask.

"Hey, here's more music," Socks said, pointing into the air, as if the women could look up, see the notes as they came out of the speakers. "But there's nobody left."

"Damien," Maggie all but yelled as "Hit Me With Your Best Shot" blared from the speakers. "Dumb music for a guy, isn't it? Yeah, well, he's not here. But it kind of wakes you up after Saint Just's music."

The spotlight was searching the doorway, and women were turning around in their seats, waiting for Damien to appear.

"Oh, what the hell, I never could resist a spotlight," Socks said, shaking his head and throwing back his shoulders before leaping into the spotlight and spreading his arms wide.

"God, look at him," Maggie said as Socks swaggered and bounced and danced his way through the maze of tables. He didn't stop and bow to the women, he stopped and *posed,* throwing his elbows back and his hips forward, then doing a truly impressive bump and grind.

"Oh, yeah." Bernie put out her arms, her fists held together as she moved them in a circle, saying, "Go Argyle, go Ar-gyle, go Ar-gyle. Come on, Maggie, Tabby. Put your fists together, like this. Go Ar-gyle, go Ar-gyle."

Maggie rolled her eyes, then joined in, even as Tabby unscrewed the top of the flask and took another drink. "Go Ar–gyle, go Ar-gyle, go Ar-gyle."

There was laughing, and clapping, and one woman grabbed Socks, pulled him down for a kiss.

"Open bar," Felicity informed Maggie. "Martha said WAR would foot the bill, because there are only about eight hundred members still here. I think they've been hitting the booze pretty hard, don't you?"

"Free is free," Bernie said. "If they take to free booze the way they take to free books, I'd say WAR is running up one hell of a tab. Look at him grinding those hips. Wowzer. He sure is hitting them with his best shot. They're *drooling.* If they only knew, right, Maggie?"

Maggie only nodded, which left it to the usually lady-like Tabby to hoist her borrowed flask and say: "Wrong music. Should have been 'Dancing Queen.' Right, Maggie?"

Maggie confiscated the flask.

Bernie pointed. "Okay, there goes Socks to his tableau. What do you suppose it is?"

"If it's not a pirate ship, he's screwed," Maggie said,

laughing. She turned to smile at Bernie, then looked back into the ballroom just as the curtains opened.

There were a few shrieks, one of them from Socks, before Maggie could focus enough to say, "Henry? What's Henry doing there?" She closed her eyes a moment, then opened them wide. "Alex. What the hell did he do with Damien?"

"Never mind that," Felicity said, jabbing her in the ribs with her elbow. "Look at Liza. I know she didn't expect Socks, and I'm pretty sure she didn't expect that mouse, but she sure expected *something* she isn't seeing. What's going on?"

Maggie looked at Liza, who was just standing at the microphone, saying nothing. The music had been shut off, and everyone was looking toward the podium. When the silence became uncomfortable enough for some of the women to start muttering and fidgeting, Liza seemed to blink herself awake and leaned over the mike.

"And . . . and that's it, everyone. You, um, you each have a ballot on the last page of your program. Please fill it out, tear it off at the dotted line, and deposit it in one of the boxes up here in front of the podium. We'll have our announcement before the evening is over, but for now—the bar is open and the dance floor is waiting!"

"Something's wrong," Maggie said, heading toward the second ballroom and the tableaus, her companions bringing up the rear. She made her way to Saint Just's tableau, then had to wait until a line of autograph seekers was done having their programs signed before she could get close enough to yell to him.

But he wasn't listening. He was talking to someone, someone who looked familiar. "Oh, damn. Her," Maggie said, recognizing Holly Spivak from Fox News.

Months earlier, when Maggie had been a murder

suspect, Holly Spivak had led the band of reporters dogging her every step. Was she here on assignment, or had Saint Just called her? He actually *liked* the woman, which was nuts, because Holly Spivak would run over her own grandmother to get a story.

Saint Just was whispering in the reporter's ear, and pointing toward the smaller podium and microphone set up in this second ballroom. Holly called over her cameraman, who also listened to Saint Just, and then the two disappeared back into the crowd, Holly grinning like a hungry hyena that had just spotted a downed gazelle.

"What are you up to now?" Maggie asked Saint Just when she finally got close enough to him. "What did you say to that Spivak woman?"

"Do you know, Maggie, that Miss Spivak is really a very nice woman? She'd planned to film the March of the Contestants, then leave, but I persuaded her that time spent here would be to her advantage."

"Why? Don't tell me you *like* being on the ten o'clock news. Wasn't twice enough?"

"And I thought you knew me," Saint Just said, frowning in a way that made her palm itch to slap him. "This is for Wendell, our good and helpful friend. I thought it might be nice to showcase his talents."

"Why?"

Saint Just shrugged. "To thank him, I suppose. When I am being kind, I rarely like to investigate my motives. I might shock myself."

"Okay, I'll swallow that one. Now, what's Henry doing in Damien's tableau. And where is Damien?"

"Damien, I'm sorry to say, was unavoidably detained. But do hold that thought about the man, please, as I might forget, and his needs must be dealt with after tonight's scenario has played itself out. As for Henry? I merely substituted him for Damien, so that the tableau wouldn't be bare."

"Or to show that you smelled a rat . . . or should I say, a mouse?"

"You're right, my dear. You do know me so well. Tell me, did you happen to notice our flustered Miss Liza Lang when the curtains opened on Damien's tableau?"

"Faith pointed it out first, but yes, I noticed."

"And did you also notice that, after making her final announcements about the voting, she made a dead set at Giancarlo, pulling him aside as she whispered into his ear?"

"No. Missed that. Why?"

"I would say, if I were speculating, that my first inclination as to who is the leader of our coterie of murderers was incorrect. I should have remembered. The female is always deadlier than the male. Damien, my dear, was supposed to be already behind the curtains in his tableau, very dead."

Maggie felt her cheeks going cold. "No. Are you sure?"

"Postitive, my dear. Athough a stuffed ballot box and a win tonight would both be gratifying to Giancarlo, Damien would remain a threat to his status. Publishers hire whom they wish, not just the winners of contests, and the handsome young Damien is clearly a top choice to be the next premier cover model. No, Damien was to be dead, his murder blamed on the murderer of Rose Sherwood. And since Liza and Giancarlo are not suspects in that murder . . ."

"Okay, okay, I've got it. I wish you'd told me sooner, but I've got it. They figured Rose's murder would be blamed on whoever was pulling the pranks, and Damien's as well. And, with Decker in charge, that could be highly possible. And I was right—right? Liza's our murderer."

She frowned. "Wait a minute. *Both* of them? Wow. So now what?"

"Now, Maggie, you will allow Sterling and myself to play out the remainder of the game, keeping yourself firmly on the sidelines. I promised the *left*-tenant, remember?"

"But—"

"Excuse me."

Maggie turned around to see a short, fairly squat man standing behind her, grinning at Saint Just.

Saint Just eyed the man, one brow raised. "Yes, may I be of some assistance?"

"You sure could. That was great, you know. Really terrific. Classy. High-brow, even. I can see an entire ad campaign built around you and that little girl. Magazines, TV, you name it. Remember those ads with the violinist bending that woman back over his arm and laying one on her? Something like that. Sophisticated sex, you know? You'd be even better. Oh, by the way," he said, putting out his hand, "I'm Pierre. *Fragrances by Pierre?* Sponsor of this whole cover model party?"

Maggie bit the inside of her cheeks as Saint Just went all silky smooth, taking the man's hand and pumping it firmly. *"Monsieur Pierre,"* he said happily, "we would be so pleased. This is all Mary Louise could have hoped for, and more. As you French say, *vouloir, c'est pouvoir.*"

"Huh?" the little man said, looking at Maggie, who knew a Bronx accent when she heard one.

"He's just showing off," Maggie told the man. "But could we do this later? Perhaps even tomorrow?"

Saint Just, never slow on the uptake, bless him, quickly seconded Maggie's suggestion, and after exchanging room numbers, Pierre, smelling very much of his own fragrances—and they didn't seem to include perfume—took his leave.

"Well, hard as this is to say, Alex, it looks like you and Mare are going to be making some serious money. Congratulations. You and Pierre from the Bronx. What a lovely couple you'll make. Tell me, how do you say *yo, yer muther* in French?"

"You'd throw a damper on anything, wouldn't you, my dear? But I know you're happy for Mary Louise, and for me. You're simply sulking because you've been reduced to spectator. Remember. Wendell and I are only protecting you, as is our desire."

"I don't need protecting."

"So says the woman being held at gunpoint not so very long ago."

"Oh, all right, all right. Just get this show on the road, okay? I can't figure out how you're going to do it, and I'm curious, okay?"

"Thank you, my dear, and we'll be doing just that, anon. For now, how do you think it went? I'll admit to hating myself the entire time, but Mary Louise is in alt. She and Socks are at the bar, celebrating. And, speaking of Socks, what on earth did he think he was doing?"

"Taking advantage of an opportunity that presented itself. Not that you'd understand that, right? Oh, no, not you. Not the great Viscount Saint Just."

"I think you need a drink, my dear, to take that sour taste out of your mouth. Fragrances by Pierre. Yes, it seems suitable, don't you think? Not at all déclassé," he said, taking her arm and heading toward one of the portable bars. "As always, please feel free to say *bite me.*"

"I try not to be redundant. One more thing," she said, pulling him to a halt. "Who provided the costume and props for Decker? Was it Socks?"

"Provided, and set them up, at my suggestion. I am nothing if not generous, to a fault, sometimes."

"And yet Socks *forgot* to secure the horse so it wouldn't fall over?"

"By your tone, I do believe you might be insinuating that we set out to make Decker more of a fool than he is naturally."

"Naturally," Maggie said, grinning. "Well, did you?"

"Are you now my confessor?"

"You did. I thought so. Okay, get me that drink."

"Wait up."

Maggie stopped, and turned with a smile. "Steve, you made it," she said, then blinked. "Wow. Is that a real uniform?"

Wendell nodded. "My dress blues. You said I had to have a costume to be admitted, and there was no way I was going to wear the costume Socks sent over to the station house."

"What did he send?" Maggie asked, looking at Saint Just, who was diligently inspecting his fingernails.

"A big, yellow, fuzzy duck," Wendell said, now also looking at Saint Just, who was looking more than usually innocent—like he was working at it. "Okay, are we ready? Did I miss anything?"

"Not at all. We're just about to begin. Maggie, if you would be so kind as to fetch Sterling, Socks, and Mary Louise, and have them report to me at the microphone that has been set up over there to announce the winners of the cover model contest?"

"Do I bring Decker? God, Maggie, did I really ask that?"

"Yes, Wendell, you might as well bring him along," Saint Just answered. "If we can get him to understand what we're saying, then I doubt we'll have any problems with anyone else."

"Good point. Although maybe you should have

brought along the blackboards, some pictures, and maybe a hand puppet or two, so you could keep his attention."

"You guys are such cards," Maggie groused, rolling her eyes. "I feel like I'm in the middle of a *Saturday Night Live* skit. A *bad* one."

CHAPTER 18

Saint Just counted noses, and concluded that everyone was there, except for Liza, Giancarlo, and their mystery guest. But they'd all be along shortly, once he'd taken control of the microphone.

It seemed a pity to disturb everyone, as the party appeared jolly enough. In fact, with all the costumes, it reminded him of a typical Regency masked ball. Even more so, with all the mischief afoot, and one dastardly murder. All the ingredients were here: intrigue, back biting, jealousy, suspicion. The only thing missing was a romantic interlude, although there was that one couple in the corner, garbed as Romeo and Juliet, who were giving it a valiant try.

Holly Spivak, at a nod from Saint Just, signaled for her cameraman to switch on his lights, which attracted several more WAR attendees in the way a porch light attracts moths, although the crush was already considerable.

Saint Just tapped the microphone, as he'd seen others do, then spoke into it: "Ladies, our few gentlemen, members of the media, if I might have your kind attention."

Other camera lights went on, more people gathered, and a quick look at the profusely perspiring Sterling told Saint Just he'd best proceed quickly, before the poor fellow suffered a minor apoplexy.

"I am pleased to say that a few of our attendees have put their heads together and come up with a most singular piece of entertainment for you all. An original song, in point of fact. Isn't that wonderful?"

It didn't seem so. Several people turned away, their disinterest palpable, and Saint Just was almost grateful for Maggie's intrusion as she took the microphone from him.

"Hey, hey, hey, here we go!" she shouted into the microphone. "Let's give it up for . . . for Sterling 'The Sterl-man' Balder and his Rockin' Regency Rappers! Hit it, Sterl-man!"

Sterling, face white as a country washed sheet, was pushed in front of the microphone even as Mary Louise and Socks flanked him on either side, Socks waving to the disc jockey who had been brought in to provide the music for the evening.

A firm backbeat pulsed from the speakers, and Mary Louise and Socks chanted along: Ba-ba-BA, Ba-ba-BA, Ba-ba-BA.

Saint Just sighed. "There he goes, bobbing his head, tapping his foot. Lord bless the man, he's got a bit of the flamboyant in him that's been hidden for years."

"Yeah, and if we're lucky, after tonight, it will be hidden for a whole lot more," Maggie said. "Oh boy, here comes Martha, and Liza's with her. Do you think they're going to pull the plug?"

"Not once Sterling gets started, no," Saint Just said confidently.

And that's just what Sterling did. Head still bobbing, he reached up and untied his neck cloth, so that the ends hung down past his waist. He began snapping his fingers.

The Rockin' Regency Rappers kept the backbeat going: "Ba-ba-BA, Ba-ba-BA, Ba-ba-BA."

Sterling grabbed the microphone, tipped it to his left, sort of leaned into it. "They came to Manhattan, to go to WAR . . . never knowing what they were . . . in for . . . pistols at dawn . . . gorillas at three . . . here a mouse, there a mouse . . . who's the louse was in this house?"

"Ba-ba-BA, Ba-ba-BA, Ba-ba-BA."

"Phone calls ringing all through the night . . . rain comin' down inside . . . what a sight . . . place cards . . . missin' . . . shocks to the system . . . look out . . . don't blink . . . who did it all, do you think?"

"Ba-ba-BA, Ba-ba-BA, Ba-ba-BA."

Maggie began rhymthically hitting her hip against Bernie's, and they both began chanting, "Ba-ba-BA, Ba-ba-BA, Ba-ba-BA."

"Here's a theory . . . here's a plan . . . could be a woman, could be a man . . . could be ambition, crawling like a bug . . . could be . . . could be . . . her . . . her . . . or her, over there . . . looking smug."

Sterling pointed straight at Martha Kolowsky, who stepped back a pace, her complexion paling.

"Ba-ba-BA, Ba-ba-BA, Ba-ba-BA."

"Every dog has its day . . . every person has her say . . . upshot . . . a plot . . . and the Bunny . . . hops . . . hops away."

"Ba-ba-BA, Ba-ba-BA, Ba-ba-BA."

"Martha, Martha, what did you do . . . are you a rotter, through and through . . . years spent . . . light under a bushel . . . now here she comes, doin' what she'll do . . . roust the Bunny, shine like a star . . . did you think we didn't know who you are . . . all those pranks, my . . . what a thriller . . . that's our Martha . . . a real . . . killer."

"No!" Martha said as Sterling and his Regency Rappers took a bow and stepped away from the microphone. "No! It wasn't me! It wasn't me! I didn't kill anyone!"

Saint Just stepped up to the microphone once more, as Decker and Wendell handled crowd control, because it looked as if a few of the WAR members had mayhem on their minds.

"Ladies! Gentlemen! Let the woman speak! Martha? Come here," he said, then covered the microphone to add, "I'll protect you, my dear."

"I . . ." She pushed Saint Just's hand away from the microphone. "I didn't kill Rose. I didn't! It's just . . . it's just that . . ." She turned to Saint Just in mute appeal.

"It's just that tagging along behind Bunny, sweeping up after her, for no thanks at all, had begun to pale as a life's work, yes?"

Martha nodded furiously. "Yes, yes, that's all. I . . . I just wanted her to look bad, then step in and make everything right."

The low rumble of quite abused WAR members signaled the beginnings of a mob, and Wendell and Decker had their hands full, pushing everyone back, until Giancarlo and Lucious (they had the muscles for it) stepped in to help.

"Everyone, let her speak," Saint Just pleaded, holding his cane in the air. "Go on, Martha, you may as well tell the whole of it."

But Martha seemed to be beyond speech.

"All right," Saint Just said, wondering if the woman might faint, "I'll speak, and you may nod in the appropriate places?"

Martha nodded, then ducked as a fairy wand wrapped in silver foil and topped with a lopsided star came winging in her direction.

"That aids nothing, madam," Saint Just said, staring down the Tooth Fairy, who had the good grace to look away. "Now, Martha, from the beginning. You'll feel better, really. The cowboy and the gorilla. Yours?"

Martha nodded.

Felicity growled.

"The mice in Miss Simmons's suite? The shock Miss Simmons sustained during her keynote speech?"

Martha nodded. Twice.

Felicity had to be held back by Wendell, her feet actually leaving the floor as she reached out with both hands, her fingers curled into claws.

"And you weren't tired the following morning from staying up all night, re-doing the place cards, were you? You were tired because you spent the night making phone calls to the breakfast speaker in the hope she'd oversleep and miss her speech?"

Martha nodded.

A shoe flew by Martha's ear.

"Let me hazard a guess," Saint Just drawled. "Miss Maureen Bates Oakley, I presume?"

The woman in the front row of onlookers, now balancing rather precariously on one foot, said, "Damn straight, I am. I worked on that speech for *months.* Martha, I could kill you!"

"Yes, yes, how lovely. WAR seems to be such a bloodthirsty group at the bottom of it, doesn't it?" Saint Just said, putting an arm around Martha's quivering shoulders. "Let's finish this up, shall we? You, Martha, in an attempt to discredit Bunny Wilkinson, and allow your own light to shine, are responsible for all the pranks that have taken place this week. Just nod, dear."

Instead of nodding, Martha seemed to at last find her voice. "She made me so *sick.* Martha do this, Martha do that, Martha, for God's sake, can't you do anything *right?* I did it *all,* for years. And who took all the credit?

Who got all the awards? I *hate* her, and I'm glad I put her on the roof."

"Ah, yes, I believe I forgot to mention that one. Poor, poor, beleaguered Martha. How you have suffered, although I would suggest you refrain from indulging in a further orgy of expiation at the moment, as the constabulary is present. You were badly used, my dear, but what you did was not the answer. Jealousy, my dear Martha, often called the jaundice of the soul, is not a healthy emotion. This is what led to all the pranks. Everything Sterling and I have mentioned, plus the assault on Giancarlo, *and* tampering with the caviar at the Toland Books reception."

"No!"

Saint Just turned to look at the rather brown little man who had pushed his way through the crowd. Definitely brown, as he was dressed to resemble Friar Tuck. "Ah, Mr. Kolowsky, I presume? Martha's husband, and a loyal employee of Top Star Electric in Boulder, Colorado? You see, I have one of your business cards in my possession. Never mind how."

"Yeah, yeah, leave her alone, you big ape. She didn't do anything bad."

Wendell redoubled his grip on Felicity, who might just foam at the mouth at any moment.

"Placing tainted caviar at Miss Toland James's party wasn't bad?"

"We didn't do that."

Saint Just pressed on. "Hitting Giancarlo with a sack filled with quarters wasn't *bad,* Mr. Kolowsky?"

"We didn't do that, either," Martha said. "George? Did you do that?"

"No," George said, shaking his head. "But I thought you did." He looked at Saint Just. "A sack of quarters, you say? Martha, you have a lot of quarters in your purse."

"Yes, but I got them from Liza." She looked at Liza

Lang. "Liza, tell them. I was looking for quarters, and you said you had a bunch of them. Remember?"

Now Liza Lang backed up a few feet, until she hit the solid wall of Holly Spivak and her cameraman.

"Turn around, dear," Holly prodded. "We'd like to get you full-face."

Liza put up a hand to shield her face. "I didn't hit Giancarlo. I didn't even know he was hit with quarters. I found them in Rose's bedroom, in a big, knitted change purse she always carried. She saved them up to use in the vending machines in the hall. She hated paying for room service. Martha . . . Martha needed them, that's all, so I borrowed them from Rose. I mean, Rose was dead, and all."

"You killed Rose!" somebody shouted from the back of the crowd (Mary Louise, actually, who had been told to shout her accusation at what she thought to be an appropriate time). "Get her—she killed our beloved Rose!"

"Ladies, ladies, we can't prove that," Saint Just said reasonably, then smiled. "At least, not yet."

Maggie felt as if she was a spectator at a tennis match, her head snapping back and forth so that she didn't miss a single shot.

What was Saint Just up to? All right, so they knew Martha had pulled all the pranks, the practical jokes. Martha and her husband. They'd known that since yesterday. And now he was going after Liza. That also figured, especially since Maggie was convinced Liza *was* the murderer, and Saint Just had as good as said she'd been right. Or at least half right.

But how to get Liza to confess? He wasn't about to have Sterling do another rap, was he?

Martha was babbling now, as her husband held her.

"I didn't kill Rose. I didn't hit Giancarlo with any quarters. I just wanted to be convention chairperson next year, that's all." She lifted her head from her husband's shoulder and looked pleadingly at Saint Just. "I didn't hit Giancarlo. I didn't!"

"Yes, dear lady, I know," Saint Just said, and Maggie began to grind her teeth. Look at him, standing there, so cocksure of himself. Damn the man!

Sergeant Decker (holding up his wooden sword . . . he must have left his badge in his other tunic) pushed himself forward and grabbed the microphone. "Sergeant Decker, NYPD, homicide. You will all disperse now. Come on, party's over, folks."

Nobody moved.

"Sergeant? Wouldn't it be easier if you just let me finish?" Saint Just asked, motioning for Maggie and Wendell to step closer. "I'm convinced it would. Now, Giancarlo? Stop me when I'm wrong, all right? Martha did not hit you. Liza did not hit you. You did not, as I once opined, hit yourself. *Rose* hit you."

"Rose Sherwood hit him? Why?" Decker asked. "I don't understand."

Saint Just favored the sergeant with a short, dispassionate stare. "Lord, man, why should you? You're dead as a house. More than that, you're dreadfully in the way. Please step back. And, to tell you the truth, I'd rather tie up another loose end before I continue with my deductions. Liza Lang? You planted the tainted caviar, didn't you? Felicity Boothe Simmons, a dear woman, but with a tongue that runs on wheels, told you we were investigating Rose's murder, and you decided to distract us with a rather painful intestinal ailment. Please, don't bother to deny it. *Left*-tenant Wendell—good man, the *left*-tenant—checked with Room Service, and you had three dishes of the stuff delivered to your suite, where you dosed it with, well, who knows. I do not believe anyone save the police will be asking for your recipe."

"My turn to throw something," Bernie said, coming up to stand beside Maggie. Felicity followed her, probably because there were several cameras now pointed in their direction. The woman was even *smiling*. It was sickening.

Liza began to cry.

Saint Just held up one hand. "Tut, tut, my dear. No affecting waterworks yet, if you please. We aren't done yet. Back to Giancarlo, and the quarters. Rose's assault was unexpected, but it seemed fortuitous, because it was taken as one more prank, and because it most effectively removed Giancarlo from any list of suspects. If there was ever a perfect time for an impromptu murder, this was it."

"Murder?" Decker parroted, obviously shocked. "You're accusing Giancarlo of murder?"

"I would, yes, if you'd cease interrupting," Saint Just said, lifting a hand to adjust his cravat.

Maggie narrowed her eyes. Which was it, Giancarlo or Liza? Then she shook her head in disgust. *Two, dummo, they did it together. Duh!*

"No," Decker protested. "Giancarlo didn't do anything. He's a great guy. He says he's going to make me a star. Says I'm a fresh face in the industry." Clearly the good sergeant was seeing his rosy future fading to a ghastly white (fading to a white over red, third-hand, 1994 Volvo with a *Lovers Do It Better In Niagara Falls* sticker on the dented back bumper, to be exact about the thing).

Wendell grunted. "Decker, you're a fucking idiot."

"Nice," Maggie said, wincing

"Sorry, it just slipped out. Blakely, I've had a long day. Mind if I take it from here?"

Saint Just stepped back, bowed as he waved Wendell to the microphone.

"Okay, people, here's what we've got," Wendell said, blinking in the glare from the television lights. "One, Giancarlo? Nice name. Except it isn't yours. Yours is Mel Harper."

Giancarlo paled beneath his artificial tan as Socks and Sterling stepped up behind him, blocking his exit if he should decide to make a run for it, then each of them taking hold of one musclar arm and holding on tight.

"Mel Harper, of Kentucky, Louisiana, and Virginia. Mel Harper, who made a fine living in those states, romancing old ladies. You're a good looking guy, Melvin, so that was easy, wasn't it? Romance them, and even marry them for their money. But not divorcing any of them," Wendell said with a small shake of his head. "That's not nice, Melvin. When things got too hot for you down south, you moved up here, to the Big Apple. And you met Rose Sherwood."

Maggie's mouth had dropped open several sentences ago. "Wait, don't say it. He *married* Rose Sherwood?"

"Give the lady a cigar," Wendell said, and Maggie narrowed her eyelids at him. The guy was getting just a little too much like Saint Just for her liking. "Yes, Melvin married Rose, and together, they begot *Rose Knows Romance.* Rose was the brains, and Mel here was the model. Rose pushed, Mel flexed and posed, and an empire was born. How am I doing so far, Mel?"

"Eeuuwww," Felicity said, "Rose and Giancarlo. That's just *gross."*

"You knew all this?" Maggie whispered to Saint Just. "And didn't tell me? Why?"

"Again, just keeping you safe, my dear. I may have come up with the list of suspects for Wendell to investigate, but he provided the rest. I saw no choice but to agree with him when he declared that you were to be kept out of it."

"Remind me to hate both of you. So Gian—Mel killed Rose? Not Liza? Damn, I was so sure. Wait a minute. You were sure, too. Didn't you agree with me about Liza a couple of minutes ago?"

"Shhh. Now for *le coup de grâce.*"

Wendell held up his hands for quiet, as the crowd was getting a bit loud, discussing the idea of Rose and Giancarlo, married. A few more *eeuuwww's* were heard.

"Okay, let's finish this now," Wendell said. "Melvin, you had a good thing going, you really did. And then you screwed it up. Literally. But let's start at the beginning of your troubles. You were cheating Rose. Taking gigs and not handing over half to Rose. Photo shoots, autographings, personal appearances. Rose was pissed—sorry, Maggie, slip of my cop tongue again—and getting ready to dump you, and planned to put Damien in your place. You could have divorced her, tried for half her money, but you weren't legally married, were you? You had to find another way. And you did. Ms. Lang? Would you care to tell us what happened next?"

"Wait a minute," Maggie whispered to Saint Just. "Screwed it up? Steve did say screwed, right? Oh . . . oh, no." She raised her hands shoulder high, as if to push away the thought. "Don't tell me, please. Blue condoms? While Rose was sharing the suite? *Eeuuww.*"

Wendell waited a few moments, but Liza wasn't talking. She was crying. It was easy to hear her, because there wasn't another sound in the ballroom.

Wendell shrugged. "All right, I'll do it. One, Giancarlo wanted Rose's money. Two, he couldn't get it, even if Rose kicked the bucket. Three, Liza could get it, right, Liza? Four, romance Liza, Rose eventually kicks the bucket, and you own everything—all in good time, you weren't in a hurry. *Rose Knows Romance,* her inheritance from her first husband, the whole nine yards, it would all be yours, right, Melvin?"

Liza was sobbing now.

"Nice, neat, and pretty sickening," Wendell went on. "Except Rose walked in on you two lovebirds, didn't she—because you were keeping both women happy—and she cold-cocked you with her bag of quarters. Bad timing, all the way around. Not only that, and we're guessing a little here, but we're pretty sure we're right, she told you both to get out and neither of you would ever see a dime of her money. She'd already been planning with Damien. Man, tough break. The jig was up—unless you two could get rid of Rose, permanently."

Maggie tugged on Saint Just's sleeve. "I'm lost. How does romancing Liza get Rose's money?"

"Simple, Maggie, and we should have thought of it, both of us. Wendell's research revealed everything. Liza is Rose's daughter, her legal heir."

Maggie shifted her eyes to the left, then to the right. Left was Liza being Rose's daughter, sticking around, taking abuse, because she stood to inherit everything some day—and being called a slut on an open mike. Right was Giancarlo, married to Rose, sleeping with her daughter.

Then she looked straight, at Saint Just. "They did it together. They *both* murdered Rose. Her own mother? Wait . . . I can almost relate to that," she ended weakly.

"You're afraid to speak to your mother on the phone, Maggie. I doubt you could plot anything this shameful."

Maggie watched as Wendell reached into his pocket and came out with two pair of handcuffs. "So Gian—

Mel stabbed Rose, then Liza let him cut her, too? To keep her from being a suspect?"

Wendell was slipping the cuffs on Liza, who was still sobbing, swearing she never knew Giancarlo was going to kill her mother.

Saint Just explained: "We're not sure, but we think Mel, probably not Liza, got a master key from somewhere—maintenance reported one missing—and used it to send the elevator wherever they wanted it to go. Technology. Isn't it wonderful? That explains how they had the privacy to kill Rose, and how Giancarlo got away, just getting off the elevator and then sending it off again. The only hitch was that the elevators all stopped on their own—or because he didn't know how to use the maintenance key correctly."

Sterling and Socks led Giancarlo forward and Wendell motioned for him to turn around, to be cuffed. Decker, doing his best to stay in camera range, was already reading the guy his rights.

"Excuse me," George Kolowsky said, tapping Saint Just on the shoulder. "He won't put cuffs on my Martha, will he?"

"I imagine someone would have to press charges first," Maggie said. "I mean, they were sort of practical jokes. Nobody got hurt."

Maggie hadn't noticed Felicity standing beside her. "Nobody got hurt? *Nobody got hurt!* I'll give you nobody got hurt!" she yelled, and launched herself past Maggie, her hands out and aiming for Martha's neck.

All the lights in the ballroom went out.

"Oh, gosh," George Kolowsky said, "I guess I forgot I set up that last one. Sorry. Don't worry, there's an emergency generator. They'll be back on real—see?"

Maggie certainly did see.

When the lights had gone out, Giancarlo had been

about to be cuffed and led away to the slammer, Saint Just had been polishing his quizzing glass, and Felicity had been about to get her hands around Martha's neck.

When the lights had come back on, Sterling was on the floor, Socks was rubbing his jaw, and Giancarlo had Felicity hard in his grip, Decker's gun to her throat.

"Nobody moves," Mel Harper yelled, backing toward the door as women screamed and damn near trampled each other, trying to get out of the way.

Maggie didn't think. Well, all right, she thought a little bit. She thought: *Leave me out of it, will they?* Followed by: *I must be nuts.* And then she threw herself at Giancarlo, hoping to surprise him into letting go of Felicity.

It almost worked. He did let go of Felicity . . . but he grabbed Maggie instead.

Her head was bent into an uncomfortable angle as the muzzle of the police issue pistol was pushed into the side of her neck. Talk about deja-vu all over again . . .

"Ohmigod, he's going to kill her!"

"Cripes, Faith," Maggie said, wincing, as talking was painful with a gun in your neck, "don't give him any ideas he doesn't get on his own."

Saint Just, his hands held out at his sides, probably to prove he was harmless—ha!—said, "You know, of course, that you are only delaying the inevitable. Now, be a good fellow, and release the woman."

"Fat chance of that, pretty boy," Giancarlo said, still backing toward the hallway. Maggie was having trouble keeping her feet under her, but the pressure against her windpipe drove any thoughts of pretending to faint from her, because Giancarlo would probably just choke her. Or snap her neck. The guy had *big* forearms.

And she had a hole in her head—what had she been thinking? She winced, and not from pain. She'd been thinking that she'd been kept out of the loop, and it was time *she* got to do something. That's what she'd been thinking. She sure hadn't been hiding behind a door when the gods were handing out Idiot Pills.

They were in the hallway now, backing toward the elevators as the WAR attendees shrieked and ran as far away as they could.

Where was Saint Just? Where was Steve? Did they have a plan? God, please let them have a plan.

She heard an elevator door opening, felt the ridge of the front of the car as she was dragged inside. The doors closed. "Where . . . where are we going?" she managed to ask Giancarlo, who just tightened his grip.

The elevator stopped and the doors opened. Giancarlo waved the gun at three women standing in the hallway, and the doors closed again. The elevator began to rise once more. . . .

"Come along, Mr. Kolowsky," Saint Just said, dragging the reluctant man with him into the elevator. "That elevator was going up, not that Harper planned it that way, he just hopped on the first elevator to arrive. However, it's going up, isn't it? Probably all the way to the roof now, as trapped animals always climb. You've been to the roof, when you put Bunny up there, you know the way."

"Yes, but . . . but he could get off anywhere. You don't need me."

"Get in the damn elevator," Wendell said, pushing him in hard enough to send the guy flying across and landing with his hands splayed on the glass. "How do we get to the roof?"

George babbled, Saint Just paced, and Wendell cursed, but eventually the elevator stopped at the topmost floor . . . just as the doors opened on the adjoining elevator and Giancarlo came out, dragging Maggie with him.

"Hold it right there, Harper," Wendell yelled, dropping into the standard policeman-with-a-gun stance, knees bent, both arms out straight, both hands holding onto the weapon. "Drop it. *Now.*"

Saint Just unsheathed his sword stick from his cane and pointed it at Harper. "Maggie?" he asked calmly. "How are you, my dear? You look rather flushed."

Another elevator arrived at the floor and Sterling was disgorged into the hallway. "Oh, my stars. Saint Just. Do something."

"Patience my dear Sterling, patience. Wendell, a question, if I might. I watched a television program the other week, very interesting. Set here in Manhattan. In it, the crime was a murder for profit, and the penalty was death. Lethal injection, if I recall correctly. Does Harper here qualify for that sentence? He did murder Rose for profit, yes?"

Maggie's voice was slightly hoarse. "What are you doing? Don't tell the guy with a gun that he's got nothing to lose."

"On the contrary, I'd say he has much to gain. A good word from you, perhaps, *left*-tenant? A life in jail, granted, but life. Life is almost always preferable to the alternative, isn't it, Harper?"

"Shut up, shut up. I'm thinking here. I . . . I want a helicopter on the roof in ten minutes. I . . . I want a million dollars, cash, in small bills. I—"

"Oh, just shoot her, Harper. A helicopter? Don't be asinine," Saint Just said, sheathing his sword stick and turning away from the man. "Come along, gentlemen. I believe there's still a bit of a tangle going on downstairs. If you'll recall, we seem to have left Sergeant

Decker in charge. Now there's a thought to chill your marrow."

"Wait! Wait a minute," Harper yelled, pointing the gun at Saint Just, then at Wendell, moving it from one man to the other while his strong forearm clamped Maggie close to him. "You can't leave me here. You can't! That's not how it works, damn it. I'll kill her, I swear it!"

Saint Just winked at Wendell, then turned on his heels, to look at Harper once more. He didn't look at Maggie, for that might unman him, or make him so angry that he'd do something stupid. He concentrated on Harper, and on looking as relaxed and unflustered as possible.

"I'll kill her!" Harper yelled again. The man was ridiculously redundant.

"Really? The prospect leaves me unmoved. As you may recall me saying to you just recently, other people's troubles are such a bore. I'm sorry, Maggie. Although, as your cousin, I will have to avenge you. Harper? Do you understand? Kill her, and I will be forced to kill you. Tedious, but there it is, matter of honor, you understand. Maggie? Remember? Very much the same as in the climax of that book? What was it called? Oh, yes, *The Case of the Absentminded Cardsharp,* written by one Miss Cleo Dooley. You do remember the scene?"

Maggie blinked at him, then smiled, and Saint Just's taut insides relaxed marginally. He went up onto the balls of his feet, not noticeably, but just enough to be ready to move at a moment's notice.

Harper was still waving the gun about, keeping it pointed at the two men rather than at Maggie. Really, a most cooperative fellow, when you got right down to it.

Saint Just silently counted to three before Maggie picked up her left foot and brought her fortunately pointed heel down hard on Harper's soft suede covered instep.

"Bitch!"

Saint Just moved at the same time, as did Wendell, who was pleasantly astute, Saint Just grabbing Maggie free even as the lieutenant made a rather impressive flying tackle of Mel "Giancarlo" Harper.

Saint Just put Maggie to one side as he watched Wendell pull Harper to his feet and give a very good impression of a man who wanted to throw his captive into the closest wall. But he restrained himself, obviously with great effort. He was a copper, and coppers had rules.

Saint Just didn't, and wouldn't have played by them even if he had.

"Very good, Wendell," Saint Just said, smiling. "It occurs to me that we work very well together."

"We do, don't we? Come on, Harper, let's go."

"A moment, if you please," Saint Just said, handing his cane to Maggie. "You know, it also occurs to me that Edmund Burke was right. Even for us civilized, sophisticated sorts, 'There is, however, a limit at which forbearance ceases to be a virtue.' Don't you agree, *left*-tenant?"

"Oh yeah," Wendell said, grinning.

"Good. I knew we were getting along famously."

"What do you have in mind?" Wendell asked.

"Just this," Saint Just said, and then he punched Mel Harper, square in the middle of his pretty face. The man fell back, hit the wall, and slid to the floor.

"You know what?" Wendell said. "I didn't see that. Must have been looking away, looking for my cuffs, or something. What happened? The bastard slipped, right?"

"Oh, famous, Saint Just!" Sterling said, punching his own fist in the air.

"Yes," Maggie said, both hands to her chest as she looked to Wendell, to Saint Just, as if deciding whom she should hug. "You were both wonderful."

And then she turned and hugged Sterling.

EPILOGUE

Hallo, again, Sterling Balder here.

Well, we've had a bit of a to-do, haven't we? One thing I must say, life with Maggie and Saint Just is never boring.

Cleaning up the odd bits can, however, be tedious. Unlocking the broom closet later that so-distressing last night at WAR, and untying Damien, for one. I must say the man was far from grateful, until Saint Just told him he was passing his crown as Cover Model of the Year to the man. Saint Just is like that, magnanimous to a fault, especially now that he and Mare will be posing and primping for *Fragrances By Pierre.*

Maggie is still slightly flummoxed from her second encounter at gunpoint, but she is bearing up bravely. If only she could dissuade Felicity Boothe Simmons from sending her flowers, candy, and even, just today, a potted plant, all to show her gratitude. Maggie doesn't do well with such attention. She also is still waging her fearful battle with Dame Nicotine, so that we often tread quite lightly when she is in one of her moods, poor dear.

My career as a songster is, happily, over now, as I

truly do not believe I was cut out to trod the boards, putting myself on display. I'd much rather ride my motorized scooter in the park. I've attached a small shelf to the handlebars, to hold Henry's cage, and I report happily that the dear creature quite enjoys taking the air with me.

What else? Mrs. Goldblum will be departing for Boca shortly, and Saint Just and I are shopping for a large flat screen television machine injected with plasma—which I find rather unnerving—along with something called "surround sound." It's all quite technical.

Saint Just remains a happy man, although I see the occasional shadow, and I believe our own dear Maggie to be the cause. He says, quite confidently, that she loves him, and when I point out that she ain't quite tumbling over herself to show that love, at least as far as I can see, Saint Just only smiles. An odd fish at times, Saint Just, but we're toddling along, the three of us—the four of us now, as Wendell continues to be underfoot quite often.

Tabby's husband is home again, and Bernie and Socks are now running a pool as to the day and time she next tosses him out on his ear.

Even with recent events, I retain high hopes for an unexceptional future here in Manhattan. But to be honest and forthright and all of that, with Saint Just, and his nose for trouble, I admit to a few qualms in that quarter. . . .

New York Times *bestselling author Kasey Michaels is back with another hilarious Maggie Kelly misadventure. This time, two of Maggie's friends are in big trouble—and Maggie may just be in over her head . . .*

I've got a successful writing career, a great apartment, two hot guys . . . and all I want to do is curl up on the sofa with my cats, a DVD, and a bag of Funyuns. What's wrong with this picture? I should be reveling in my freedom—and/or in the company of Alexander Blake, Viscount St. Just, the all-too-real hero of my historical mystery novels. Problem is, ever since Alex and his sidekick, Sterling, materialized in my living room, I've been dodging dead bodies. Of course, the random acts of violence *have* had the less dubious benefit of introducing me to thoroughly modern (and cute!) NYPD detective Steve Wendell, but still. Playing amateur sleuth and roomie to two Regency gents can get pretty exhausting. So how ecstatic was I when Alex and Sterling got a deal on a rent-controlled place across the hall? Ah, sweet solitude. Naturally, it couldn't last. My first morning alone, I get a hysterical call from my recently widowed friend and publisher, Bernie Toland-James. Recently widowed, as in, she just woke up next to the bloody corpse of her estranged husband . . .

See? This is what I'm talking about. I used to count my life adventures in successfully avoiding my mother's phone calls. Now I keep on my toes by getting my friends off murder raps. Things definitely don't look good for Bernie. She'd made no secret of the fact that she wasn't too broken up when Buddy "disappeared" seven years ago—but she's no killer, and I intend to help prove it. Meanwhile, Sterling's been on the receiving end of some weird threats. Threats none of us were taking particularly seriously until some thugs vandalized his and Alex's apartment, slashing up their beloved "plasma-flat-screened-television machine." As if that weren't enough to prompt some serious gauntlet-throwing, now someone's actually kidnapped dear, sweet Sterling, leaving a ransom note that's at best cryptic, and at worst, badly misspelled. Talk about rubbing a writer the wrong way . . .

OK, this case just got seriously personal. Messing with my friends? Bad move. Messing with my friends while I'm going through nicotine withdrawal? Watch out, mister. What with trying to help Bernie and Sterling, trying to quit smoking, trying to evade my therapist's more pointed questions, and trying to meet the deadline for my latest St. Just novel, I'm edgier than J-Lo's wedding planner. Then there's the new habit I've developed of kissing Alex. And kissing Steve. Repeatedly. Yeah. With the clock ticking on Bernie's freedom, Sterling's safety, and, very possibly, my own sanity, I'd better get down to business with both my detectives (no, not *that* kind of business . . . well, maybe a little) and get a clue—before my mother finds out what I've really been up to . . .

**Please turn the page for an exciting sneak peek of Kasey Michaels'
next Maggie Kelly and Saint Just novel
MAGGIE WITHOUT A CLUE
coming in hardcover in August 2004!**

CHAPTER 1

Maggie sat hunched at her computer desk in the living room, staring at the screen. She'd been staring at the screen for five minutes, wishing the words displayed on it to change, reassemble themselves in a more pleasing manner, but it wasn't working. They were still there, damning her.

"Amazon.com? *Again?* Really, Maggie, self-flagellation is so unbecoming," Saint Just said, leaning over her shoulder to press a Post-it note on the edge of the computer. "There. Does this help?"

Maggie took off her computer glasses, threw them to the desktop, and grabbed the note. "'The trade of critic, in literature, music, and the drama, is the most degraded of all trades.' Mark Twain."

"You seem to enjoy him," Saint Just said when she turned her chair to glare up at him. "I've become a bit of a devotee myself. A pity he wrote after the Regency. I would dearly love to quote the fellow in our books."

Maggie crumpled the note and threw it into the garbage can. "Mark Twain didn't have to put up with these damn reader reviews."

"Maggie. Dear Maggie. There are, at last count, seventy–three reviews posted there on our most recent opus. A starred review from *Publishers Weekly,* a quite flattering review from *Booklist*, and *Kirkus* was its usual damning-with-faint-praise self. Add to that sixty-seven unremittingly marvelous remarks from readers."

"And three one-star rips," Maggie said, reaching for her nicotine inhaler. "They drive me nuts. I can't answer them, I can't do a thing about them. Why in *hell* would a Web site that wants to sell books show reviews that say a book is the worst piece of drivel they've ever read? And this one," she said, turning her chair to the screen once more. "See this one? It gives away the murderer, for crying out loud."

"That would be the reader from Iowa? The reference was oblique at best. I wouldn't say she spilled all the gravy. Mostly, she complained that if you knew anything at all, you'd know that English gentlemen of the Regency era did not swear or take the Lord's name in vain."

"Yeah, right. We invented all that in the last fifty years or so. I can hear Wellington now." She dropped into a British accent. *" 'Please, my dear fellows, if the spirit so moves you and I'm not interrupting your tea break, might you redirect that lovely cannon over there, as I do believe the Frenchies are advancing up the hill at us in a rather sprightly manner.' "*

"God's teeth, woman, if I might further depress the hopes of our Iowa reader with some mild swearing, would you please *stop* obsessing? And your accent is atrocious."

Maggie wasn't listening. "And this one. This guy said he figured out the murderer halfway through the book. That's not good, Alex. That's really not good."

Saint Just leaned closer. "And does it also say that he most likely peeked at the ending before he began to read?"

"You can't know he did that."

"You can't know he did not do that. You can't know if he's just another frustrated—what are we not supposed to call such people? Oh, yes, another frustrated wannabe. That's it. Can't do, so he attempts to rip apart those that can. Anyone with a computer and a modem—and an axe to grind—can submit a review on these things. Now, are we quite done with this morning's descent into the pits of self-pity?"

"No, we're not. This last one's the worst. She says you and Leticia weren't together enough. You know what that means, don't you, Alex? It means there wasn't enough *sex* for her. The 'together' enough bit is a tip-off. So's 'I wish there had been more emotion.' And 'It was a little light on the romance.' There's a dozen ways they say it, but they all mean the same thing. Didn't feel the romantic tension, the characters didn't connect enough, on and on. They're all buzz words. What they mean is there wasn't enough nooky for them. Not enough hot, sweaty, jungle sex. Why don't they just say it? Why don't they just say, Hey, lady, put them in bed on page three and keep them there? Better yet, have them do it in public. On horseback."

"Well, my dear, speaking as the hero in question, may I say it's not—minus the horse—an entirely unpalatable idea."

"If I wrote soft porn, no. I'm writing mysteries, damn it. I'm writing about people, not positions. I'm writing characters, not fifty ways to screw your lover. Can't they just get subscriptions to *Playgirl* and stop pretending they're looking for anything more than a cheap thrill?"

Maggie sank against the back of the chair, inhaled deeply, and blew the air out on a sigh, her bravado gone, to be replaced by her usual insecurity. "Maybe they're right, Alex. Maybe the books need more sex."

"Do I get a vote?" Saint Just asked, waggling his eyebrows.

"No, you don't. And maybe you shouldn't say 'Christ on a crutch' anymore."

"I shouldn't?"

"No, maybe you shouldn't. Or 'God's teeth.' "

"Perhaps, just perhaps, I should be all things to all people. Has anyone ever succeeded in that sort of lofty endeavor?"

"Only until after they win on election day. Whoops, can't talk like that, either. Democrats and Republicans. Saint Just's Whigs and Tories. You name it. You saw the e-mails I got. There are people out there who'd like me lined up against a wall and shot for treason and heresy, just because I uttered one little opinion on free speech at the WAR conference and that reporter ran with it."

"Ah," Saint Just murmured. "We Are Romance. The mind still boggles over that unfortunate name."

"Yeah, yeah. Back to me, okay? I'm in pain here." Maggie clicked the mouse over the SIGN OFF menu. "I'm nuts, aren't I? Bernie says I'm nuts. Hell, Bernie said if I ever talk to another reporter *she's* having me shot."

"Never be afraid to speak your mind, Maggie. You simply tend to worry overmuch about everyone else's opinion," Saint Just said, holding out a hand to her as she rose from her chair. "It's a failing you mercifully did not pass along to me. Simply stop obsessing."

Maggie pushed a hand through her recently clipped and streaked hair. "I am not obsessing. I do not obsess. Really. I'm not obsessing." She flung herself inelegantly on one couch as Saint Just gracefully lowered himself onto the facing couch. "Okay, okay, stop grinning at me. I'm obsessing. Just a little. Why do I even *read* these reviews?

"Again, dear love, you're insecure. You are, in fact, the greatest mass of insecurities I have ever encountered, and I have resided with Sterling. Oh, wait, you know that. You created him."

Maggie looked at her nicotine inhaler, then at the pack of cigarettes on the coffee table. Would she really sell her soul to the Devil for a cigarette? Good thing that so far all her imagination had managed to dredge up was Alex and Sterling. If she could summon a guy with horns and hooves and a tail, she'd be in some serious trouble. "Poor Sterling. I think I gave him all my more vulnerable traits."

"Yes, and gifted me with everything you wish yourself to be, and could be if you'd only believe in your own considerable worth. Now, having said that, you might notice that I am holding a key in my hand."

Maggie felt her stomach do a small flip. Was this it? Was this really the big day? Was she ready for the big day? "Mrs. Goldblum's key?"

"Until recently, yes. But, as of this morning, all mine. Mrs. Goldblum wasn't to leave for another few weeks, but her sister took a tumble on the shuffleboard court or some such place and fractured her hip, as she informed me last evening. Mrs. Goldblum rushed off at first light, leaving us full access. In quite a dither to be gone, poor woman. We'll be transferring the remainder of our belongings as soon as Socks arrives. What will you do without us, Maggie?"

She tipped up her chin (the better not to see the pack of cigarettes on the coffee table). So this was it. Mrs. Goldblum had (verbally—she put nothing in writing) subleased her apartment to Alex and Sterling while she left for a lengthy, open-ended stay with her sister in Boca Raton. "You're moving across the hall. I think I can manage."

Saint Just crossed one long leg over the other. He was the picture of sophisticated elegance, even in modern-day clothing, although in her mind's eye, he was the perfect hero when dressed, by her, in Regency costume.

She'd made him perfect, at least her idea of perfect. The man every woman drools for, to be honest. Handsome, with Val Kilmer's sensuous lips. Physically long and lean and muscular, like Clint Eastwood in those old spaghetti westerns women still sighed over on cable. Eyes blue, Paul Newman in *Hud* blue. Tanned skin, smile lines, a tumble of ebony hair. The voice of a young Sean Connery as James Bond—that Scottish burr mixed with an English accent that had been melting feminine knees for decades. Peter O'Toole's aristocratic nose. To die for; that was the Viscount Saint Just.

She'd made him self-confident, which she was not. She'd made him witty, which she could only be on paper, and so seldom in public—having lived her life as one of those people who wake at two in the morning to say, *"That's* what I should have said when she made that crack about my hips!"

She'd made him brave, to cover her own fears, made him independent of his parents because she was still fighting to saw through a cast iron umbilical. She'd made him daring, witty, cuttingly sarcastic, deliciously sophisticated.

The perfect hero—perfect Regency hero, that is.

And then she'd given him a few flaws, because a totally perfect person would be nothing more than a stereotype; plastic, unbelievable. The sort of flaws that would make him more real, and yet weren't really flaws in Regency England, where the gentlemen ruled and the ladies poured tea. She'd made him arrogant. A tad selfish. A bit domineering.

A know-it-all.

Which had been all well and good, as long as he stayed between the pages of her books, solving crimes and bedding the ladies. Having the perfect hero live in her apartment? That had proved problematic.

Maggie knew she could leap into this man's arms and yell, "Take me, you gorgeous man, you!" If she were that sort of girl, which she wasn't. If she didn't worry that he might one day poof out of her life as unexpectedly as he'd poofed into it. If she was the chase 'em down and tackle 'em type, which she most definitely wasn't.

Although, right now, at this very moment, he was looking pretty damn good . . .

"Maggie? Maggie, please be so kind as to at least pretend you're paying attention?"

"What? Oh, sorry, Alex. What were you saying?"

"I was saying, I think Sterling and I should celebrate our first evening in our new home by escorting you to dinner. I've already taken the liberty of making reservations at Bellini's, as a matter of fact. For eight o'clock. Unless you'd rather remain here all day and night, punishing yourself with other people's opinions?"

"I'm not going to read any more reviews, all right? Ever. Because you're right. They don't help me, do they?"

"Not unless you can be convinced to allow me another romantic tryst per book, no, I would say they aid none of us."

"Okay, okay, give it a rest, you made your point. I really have to write today. What time is it now?"

Saint Just looked at the small clock on the table beside the couch. "It's already gone ten. Sterling was up and about early, for his daily constitutional in the park. He should return soon, with shining eyes and dreadfully blue lips. Why?"

"Because I want to call Bernie. Or hadn't you thought about inviting her?"

"The reservation is for four people, yes, allowing you a guest of your own choosing. Bernice would also have been my choice."

"Ten, huh? I'll wake her up if I call now. You know how she is on Friday nights."

"Drunk and disorderly, I believe was the charge last month. There's a lot to admire about our dearest Bernice. And one recent development in her life to lament. That would be her ever-increasing affection for the grape."

Maggie leaned over the arm of the couch and snagged the portable phone. She hit the speed dial button and punched 1, for Bernie. "She doesn't have it easy, Alex. Kirk left behind a mess when he was killed, and she's still reorganizing. Damn, I got her machine. She never checks her machine. I'll call again later. In the meantime, what can I help you carry across the hall?"

Saint Just blinked. "I beg your pardon?"

"Carry. Across the hall. Your things?"

"Me?" He pressed both hands to his chest in mock dismay.

"Oh, cut it out. Of course, you. What? You were going to hire movers for some clothes and a few boxes?"

There was a knock at the door, and Saint Just rose to answer it. "Ah, Snake, Killer. And you, the most estimable Socks. Just in time, in the nick of time, actually. The boxes are stacked in the bedroom on the left, directly down that hall. Yes, there you go. Have a care with the clothing in the closet, if you please."

Maggie watched as Snake (unfortunately christened Vernon), Killer (handsome in a downtrodden, Byronic sort of way), and Socks headed for the hallway. "You hired all three of them, didn't you? No, wait, scratch that. They *volunteered*."

"Absolutely. Vernon and George no longer labor on Saturdays now that they've been elevated to management in our small enterprise."

"Your street corner orators. I still can't believe you turn a profit."

"Minimal, I agree, but an opportunity is an opportunity, and it pleases me to have found a legitimate device for George and Vernon to pad their pockets. I should think you'd be proud of me. Now, if you'll excuse me, I do believe I will adjourn to my new apartment, to direct the placement of my belongings."

"Yeah, yeah, you do that," Maggie said, waving him away as the phone rang. "Hello?"

"Maggie? *Maggie!*"

"Bernie? I just called you to—"

"Maggie! Ohmigod, Maggie! I was sleeping! The phone rang! I had to pee, so I—he's dead, Maggie. Sweet Jesus, Buddy's dead!"

Maggie closed her eyes, hugging the phone close to her. Oh, yeah. Her friend had tied on a big one last night. "Bernie, calm down. Buddy's dead. Yes, he is. He's been dead for a long time, honey. What were you doing last night?"

"What? He's *dead,* Maggie! It's terrible!"

Maggie was already on her feet, heading across the hall to motion to Saint Just. "Bernie, I want you to calm down," she said, raising her eyebrows to Saint Just, who followed her back into her apartment and took the second portable phone she handed him.

"Keep her talking," Saint Just said, then lifted the phone to his ear.

Maggie did her best, even as her hands shook, because this one was bad, very bad. "Do you want to talk about Buddy, Bernie?"

Had Bernie gotten some bad drugs? She only snorted

a little cocaine a couple of times a year, for dietary purposes, Bernie promised, but the woman also drank like a fish. In these past weeks? Like a whale. Maggie felt tears stinging her eyes; why couldn't she do something to help Bernie?

Saint Just was moving his hand in a circular motion, urging her to keep talking.

"Bernie, honey, Buddy went out on his boat seven years ago and he never came back. He's dead. We know that. *You* know that. A couple more weeks and it's officially official. He's dead. What happened, honey? Did you have a bad night? Bernie? Stop crying, honey. Talk to me."

"I . . . I don't know. I don't know. I don't *remember.* I—damn it, Maggie, he's *dead!* I woke up, and there was this *blood.* All over. Blood. And . . . and there he was. God, look at all this blood! I'm blood all over! Help me, Maggie. What do I do?"

"Bernice," Saint Just said and Maggie looked to him in relief. He sounded so calm. "Bernice, darling, this is Alex. Now, you're at home?"

"Alex, thank God! He's in my bed. Alex! Buddy's dead in my bed!"

"Call nine-one-one," Maggie suggested, earning herself a frown from Saint Just. "No. Stupid idea. Scratch that, Bernie. Don't call nine-one-one. Alex?"

"Bernice," Saint Just said soothingly, even as he took the phone from Maggie and hit the Off button. "Maggie and I will be with you in ten minutes. In the meantime, exactly where are you?

"In . . . in the living room. The blood, Alex. It . . . please come! Maggie, I need Maggie."

"We're already on our way. I want you to sit down, take several deep, cleansing breaths, and await our arrival. Do nothing. Touch nothing. We'll be right there, and you will let us in, and then we will see all this blood. All right?"

"Blood? What blood? Who's seeing blood?"

"Not now, Socks," Maggie said as the doorman stood in the living room, half of Saint Just's wardrobe over his arm. She grabbed her purse, checked to make sure her cell phone was in it. Tossed in her cigarette pack; there was a time to abstain and a time to suck in that nicotine for all she was worth, damn it. "Just drop that junk and run down to hail us a cab, okay?"

"Correction. Place my clothing back where you found it, and then go downstairs and secure a hack for us. Oh, and I'll take the blue jacket, if you don't mind," Saint Just said, crossing the room to pick up his cane (the one with the sword in it—when Maggie wrote fiction, she wrote fiction she liked, and fiction she liked had her hero a whiz with weapons).

"Alex, we don't have time to—"

"Maggie, dearest, there is always time to be properly attired. That, in case you may be wondering, is offered in the form of a polite hint. Ah, thank you, Socks," he said, taking the jacket. "Now, please hold the elevator for us. We're right behind you. Maggie?" he asked, extending his arm.

"What do you think, Alex? Is she drunk? High on something? She sounded so *scared.* And Buddy? God, she hated him. Why would she dream about Buddy? Let's go. Damn it, let's just *go.*"

Saint Just motioned for Maggie to enter the elevator ahead of him. "There is such a thing as a nightmare, Maggie. Now, I'm afraid I'm woefully uninformed about this Buddy person. Please correct that lapse."

"Okay, okay," Maggie said, dashing out of the elevator, only to have Socks pass her as he jogged to the front doors and the street. "Buddy is—was—Buddy

James. Bernie's second husband, after Kirk. Bernice Toland-James, remember? I never met him."

"Interesting," Saint Just said, waving to Sterling, who was scootering toward them, his lips distressingly blue to anyone who didn't know his proclivities in confections, a large red-covered book tucked under his arm. "Come along, Sterling," he said. "Give the scooter to Socks and join us. It would appear Bernice is having a bit of a come-apart."

Maggie stood back so that Sterling could enter the taxi first, then crawled in after him, only then noticing that she was wearing her pajama top with her shorts. Had she combed her hair? No, she couldn't remember combing her hair. But she had brushed her teeth after drinking her morning orange juice. That had to count for something.

She looked at Saint Just as he issued calm commands to the driver, at his neatly creased slacks, his expensive sport coat, his pristine white shirt. "I could hate you."

"A gentleman is always prepared for any circumstance," he said, smoothing down his slacks. "Now, Buddy?"

"I don't know his real name. After Kirk dumped Bernie for ten or twelve younger versions, she went for the first guy who was as far from Kirk as she could find. Buddy James. They married, bought a house somewhere in Connecticut. Near the water. He wasn't in the business. Sold insurance, I think."

"Fascinating man, I'm sure, but perhaps we can move on? The marriage was a happy one?"

"Sure, until Bernie got sick of the commute, and being domestic. Bernie was born for high-rises and doormen and limousine service. Sailing made her hair frizz. Just being near the water in Connecticut made her hair frizz.

After a while, just looking at her gardens and her snazzy kitchen and weathered clapboard and anything that looked remotely like an Early American antique made her hair frizz. She was planning to divorce Buddy when he took his boat out one day. A storm came up, and they never found him. Not even the boat. Just some wreckage of some sort."

"A boating tragedy. I see."

Maggie nodded, then leaned forward and knocked on the glass. "Hey, you up there. Cut through the park, all right?"

Sterling was still attempting to fasten his seat belt, as well as trying to catch up. "I don't understand. Bernie married a buddy? A friend?"

"In good time, Sterling, in good time. Now, Maggie. How long ago was this boating mishap?"

"Seven years ago. Well, almost seven years ago. Buddy left behind a pile of debt, but Bernie had no proof he was dead, so she couldn't even get his life insurance money, and he had a bunch of that, because he was an agent, remember. She's been paying off his bills for years. I think she's planning to have a party next month, when he's officially dead. A Bury Buddy party, she calls it, or something like that."

"And yet, according to Bernice, he's dead now. In her apartment. In her bed."

"What?" Sterling abandoned his search for the end of the seat belt and grabbed at the hand strap.

"Obviously Bernice had a difficult evening last night, Sterling," Saint Just said, patting Maggie's hand.

"Don't pat my hand," Maggie said, drawing away, holding her spread fingers out in front of her. "I'm hanging on by a thread here. I never heard her sound like that before. You think she's hallucinating? God, Alex, what are we going to do? Should I call Doctor Bob?"

"For you? Never. For Bernice? It is a tantalizing prospect, as she'd eat him alive. But no, Maggie, we'll handle this. Hopefully. Ah, here we are, and I'm afraid I am not quite as prepared as I believed. Maggie? Pay the gentlemen, please?"

Maggie glared at him, then searched in her purse, coming up with a ten dollar bill. The fare was four dollars and eighty-five cents. And she knew she could wait for change until hell froze over.

"Perfect," Saint Just said, snatching the bill from her as the taxi pulled to the curb on Park Avenue.

"Yeah, yeah, I know. The last of the big tippers. Just get a receipt."

"Of course, as you are the last of the cheeseparers." Saint Just helped her out of the taxi and, with Sterling following behind, still looking bemused, they gave their names to the concierge. As they were all named on Bernie's list of allowed visitors, they then were imperiously directed to proceed to the elevator that would take them to the penthouse condominium.